STORMS OF ALLEGIANCE

A Mage's Apprentice Series

Winds of Courage

Storms of Allegiance

Tempests of Truth

And set in the same world:

A Mage's Influence Series

Seeds of Glory and Ruin

Vines of Promise and Deceit

Thorns of Hope and Betrayal

Forests of Grandeur and Malice

STORMS OF ALLEGIANCE

A MAGE'S APPRENTICE BOOK 2

MELANIE CELLIER

LUMINANT PUBLICATIONS

STORMS OF ALLEGIANCE

Copyright © 2023 by Melanie Cellier

A Mage's Apprentice Book 2
First edition published in 2023 (v1.3)
by Luminant Publications

ISBN 978-1-922636-97-3

Luminant Publications
PO Box 305
Greenacres, South Australia 5086

melanie@melaniecellier.com
http://www.melaniecellier.com

Cover Design by Karri Klawiter
Editing by Mary Novak
Proofreading by James Packer
Map Illustration by Rebecca E Paavo

For Jitske
the perfect companion on many fun adventures

HIDDEN CITY
NOMAD LANDS
KINGDOM of CALISTA
VIRIDIAN RIVER
CALINARA
CELADON RIVER
LAKE ATERRA
CADENCE'S HOUSE
HUNTING LODGE
NOMAD LANDS
CELADON RIVER
KINGDOM of TARTORA
TARONA
VIRIDIAN RIVER
N
W
E
S

CALINARA
LAKE ATERRA
CELADON RIVER
CEVPON RIVER
VIRIDIAN RIVER
ELDRIDA
CALTOR
TARONA
ROSTARIA
TARIN
Kingdom of Tartora

ONE

I ran up the shallow steps leading to the grand entrance of the law keepers' hall. I hadn't intended to be late, but the most recent group of guests at the inn had taken a liking to Ember. They had kept me over breakfast, admiring and patting the fox while they fed her choice scraps of their meal. Every attempt to escape to our room had been blocked until Ember had finally gorged herself so completely that she fell asleep in my arms.

I had been running ever since, depositing Ember in her box by our fire and hurrying straight to the hall. Even so, I was later than the time specified in Amara's note.

My tardiness looked even worse against her early morning activity—she had been up and gone from the inn before I even woke. Of course, based on the contents of her note, she had forgotten it was a special day. Perhaps she would take pity on me when she remembered.

With that thought in mind, I pushed through the double doors and rushed into the spacious entrance hall. My footsteps echoed on the white marble beneath my feet, but no one looked my way.

I focused on the small knot of people around the lone

counter and immediately wished I hadn't. If it wasn't for my distraction and hurry, my ability would have given some warning of the disaster waiting for me. But taken by surprise, my body reacted before my mind could.

One look at the unnatural angle of the man's leg was enough to send darkness rushing across my vision. My ears rang as my stomach heaved, an unpleasant reminder that I still hadn't completely conquered my squeamishness. Sinking onto my knees, my head lowered of its own volition, only stopping when it met the cool marble of the floor.

Excellent. I had embarrassed myself before even making it across the entrance hall. At least I hadn't actually lost consciousness.

Sucking in a deep breath, I sent my power spreading through me. Like a wave receding, my nausea settled and my eyes and ears cleared, my breathing slowing to a normal rhythm.

I remained in place for several more seconds, however. As I focused on my breathing, I tried to convince myself I hadn't just completely humiliated myself in the middle of the law keepers' hall. It wasn't working.

"Delphine?" The concerned voice of my influencer made me groan and lift my head.

Amara was reaching a hand down to me, her face concerned. I took the offered assistance and hauled myself to my feet.

"Are you all right?" she asked, her brow still creased. "I thought you'd moved past the squeamishness?"

I sighed. "It's still there. I have enough control now that I can suppress it, so it isn't usually a problem. But if I'm caught by surprise..."

I gestured toward the group by the counter, forcing myself to look at them without flinching. Now that I was prepared, it was a simple matter to keep a firm hold on my reactions, driving away both my mental and physical response to the sight of someone with a significant injury.

Amara grimaced. "An unpleasant business—and unfortunate timing. I should have met you at the door."

I shook my head. "You had no way of knowing I'd rush in here headlong, like a fool. If it had been the hospital, I would have been more circumspect." I looked at the injured person again, squinting to see them better across the remaining distance. "But what are they doing here? They seem strangely composed given..." I swallowed, feeling the faint brush of my mastered squeamishness.

There was something disconcertingly unnatural in the scene before me. The injured man was gesticulating wildly, his primary emotion anger, none of his attention on his horrific injury. His two companions seemed equally irritated, one of them constantly interjecting over the man's words, although from her manner, the woman seemed to be backing him up rather than disputing his words.

The fourth person stood apart from the other three, his position suggesting he was on the opposite side of whatever dispute was underway. He wasn't speaking, but not from any lack of engagement. Instead he appeared too enraged to speak, his face growing redder and redder whenever he looked at the injured man.

"He has already been attended to by a healer," said a new voice as a man almost two decades my senior strolled toward us. "He isn't feeling any pain, and he's in no danger, either."

"Not just any healer," Amara added. "Hayes did it himself, so I'm sure the injured man doesn't feel a thing."

"You did it?" I asked my master's close friend and my sometime instructor. Given Hayes's strength, I was surprised he hadn't completed the healing fully.

"Thankfully I happened to come across the patient within minutes of the injury occurring. In normal circumstances, I would have healed him fully on the spot, but he claimed it was a deliberate attack." Hayes threw the man a look that suggested he doubted the story. "So naturally I didn't dare cross Anka by doing anything other than alleviating the patient's discomfort and ensuring he was in no danger."

"But you're not a weak or inexperienced healer," I protested. "Surely you could have healed him and Anka could have questioned you about the injury later?"

"Thank you for your high praise," he said gravely, despite the twinkle in his eyes. "But I assure you Anka doesn't hold me in such high esteem. In her eyes, I'm as green as any apprentice when it comes to matters of law keeping. I wouldn't even know what it is they're looking for when they examine an injury, so how could I report on it later?"

Amara snorted at this assessment of her aunt, the head of the Caltor law keepers' hall. I gave Hayes a grin of solidarity, though. The older woman was a formidable presence, and I wouldn't want to get on her bad side either.

"So he's claiming it wasn't an accident." I looked at him thoughtfully. Would he have been so quick to insist on going to the law keepers' hall instead of the hospital if there hadn't happened to be a healer on hand to almost instantly relieve his pain?

Before either Amara or Hayes could respond, a new figure appeared in the entrance hall. The law keeper faltered slightly as she saw the injured leg. She quickly regained her stride and hurried over, however, remonstrating with the small group before she'd even reached them. All four of those in front of the desk turned on her immediately, their voices rising again.

"I should have left him a sliver of pain," Hayes muttered in obvious solidarity with the beleaguered law keeper.

When Amara turned a stern look on him, he gazed at her innocently.

"Just to ensure he doesn't forget and try to use the leg, of course."

"Of course," she said with another snort.

The female law keeper, who I recognized as a healing mage—soon had the matter in hand, however. The regular law keepers who had trailed in her wake lifted the injured man, and with a few choice words and a warning about not jostling the man's leg, she had them all out of the entrance hall. I knew enough about the law keepers' processes to know she would be taking them all to a smaller assessment room. Once there, she would complete the healing and any other investigation necessary.

I breathed a soft sigh of relief once they were gone, releasing my hold on my own body.

"I'm sorry for embarrassing you," I said to Amara. "And in the middle of the law keepers' hall, too. I'll be more careful next time."

"I hope you will be." She narrowed her eyes as she examined me. "But for your own sake, not mine. Your squeamishness isn't your fault."

"Maybe not, but I'm not newly activated anymore. I'm a healing apprentice, and I should have better control over myself."

"I didn't realize it still affected you so badly." Hayes sounded intrigued rather than censorious. "I would have expected it to have faded by now through exposure. You've certainly seen far worse injuries while training at the hospital with me—and connected with the injured bodies in those cases as well."

I shrugged, not sure what to say. My squeamishness had abated somewhat, but it definitely hadn't disappeared.

"Hmm..." Hayes rubbed the side of his jaw. "If it's still there at this point, I'm afraid you may be dealing with it permanently. It's unusual for a healer not to overcome it, but as you've already experienced, it won't stop you from completing your duties as a healer."

I groaned. "A squeamish healer. It's bad enough being a squeamish apprentice, but you're saying I'll still be like this after I graduate and become a proficient?"

"Sorry," Hayes said seriously, but I could see the amusement around his eyes.

"You're laughing at me," I grumbled, and he gave a full chuckle.

"You're powerful, Delphine, and a quick learner too. You have excellent control for someone only months into their apprenticeship. You can't blame us seniors for being grateful when we discover the young upstarts have some weaknesses."

I laughed. "You're not fooling me, *Master* Hayes. You're strong enough to hold your head up regardless of any new arrivals in the healing affinity."

"Ah, but that's what old Drake and the others thought until Airlie arrived," Hayes said, referring to the head of the Elements affinity and the young arrival who had shaken up not only the Guild but the whole kingdom with her unprecedented power. She was not only part of the royal family now, but also sister to the queen of neighboring Calista.

I shivered slightly at hearing myself compared to the princess, even in the most casual way. I wasn't like her. I didn't have unprecedented new levels of power. The only unusual thing about my healing ability was that I hadn't been born into a family with an established lineage of strength. And that was by no means unprecedented. The very Master Drake mentioned by Hayes had been born into a family of blacksmiths.

"So Master Anka wants that injured man healed by one of her own healers as part of their investigation of the crime," I said, getting the conversation back on track. "Is that why we're here?" I directed the question at Amara.

I'd been doing a lot of training at the hospital under Hayes's tutelage, since Amara's elements affinity meant she couldn't give me direct training in healing. But she'd mentioned recently that Anka wanted me to do some more training at the law keepers' hall. Apparently the experienced law keeper was always on the lookout for any healing apprentices who showed even the faintest interest in law keeping.

"Actually I didn't know anything about the case when I planned our day," Amara said, reminding me of her early departure.

"I'm so sorry I'm late," I hurried to say, trying to remember if I'd already apologized amid the distraction of my embarrassing collapse. "There was a group swarming Ember in the dining room, and…"

I let my voice trail off, suddenly worried that it sounded like I was making excuses. But Amara just rolled her eyes and smiled.

"That fox. She attracts attention wherever she goes."

The affection in her voice was obvious, despite her complaints. Over the weeks we'd spent in Caltor, Amara had grown almost as fond of Ember as I was. We'd both be sorry if she ever chose to go back to the wild.

"Is there another case going on, then?" I asked, looking around for any sign that something out of the ordinary was happening in the hall. There was no sign of anything, however, the open space now empty except for the usual clerk behind the counter.

A glaring absence suddenly caught my attention, and I looked to Hayes. "Wait, where's Luna?"

The second-year apprentice was usually glued to her master's side, her enthusiasm for learning making her tireless, despite the sometimes long hours of our shared training.

"She's already inside." Hayes gestured at a different corridor from the one taken by the earlier group.

I frowned in the direction he was indicating. I had to be

even later than I'd realized if Luna was already deep in the bowels of the hall. But why were we all gathered here? If we weren't assisting with the injured leg, was there a more substantial injury that needed investigation?

As I hurried down the corridor behind Hayes, I braced myself for the possibility of an even more shocking scene. I was determined not to embarrass myself again, regardless of what was about to confront me.

When he opened the door to one of the small rooms lining the corridor, I paused for a beat to steel myself. Preparing to act swiftly and suppress any reaction, I took a deep breath and stepped through after him.

I scanned the room quickly, looking for either a victim or perpetrator. I saw neither.

Instead, an explosion of noise and color made me rock back on my heels as Luna launched herself in my direction.

"Happy birthday!" she squealed as she thrust an enormous bouquet of vibrant flowers into my face.

"Happy birthday, Delphine!"

"Happy birthday!"

A chorus of voices rang out, making me peer around in bewilderment, my vision obscured by the mass of petals and leaves.

"Luna? What's going on?" I took the flowers from her, lowering them so I could see the room.

"You look so surprised!" My friend was grinning with joy at having caught me off guard. "Did you really think we'd all forget your eighteenth birthday?"

Warmth suffused my face as I finally realized what was happening. I twisted around to look at Amara who was watching from the doorway with an amused expression.

"You didn't have to do this," I said.

"I didn't," she replied. "It was all Luna's doing. I was just responsible for getting you here."

"I'm glad you're pleased," said a vaguely familiar voice. "I was afraid that rousing you from your bed at the crack of dawn might not be the friendliest birthday gesture."

While several people exclaimed that it was hardly dawn, I located the speaker and gasped.

"Master Clay?" I stared at the animal healing specialist, who lived in Ostaria. "What are you doing here?"

"How could I stay away when it's the birthday of my favorite healing apprentice with a pet fox?"

"She's not a pet," I said automatically before shaking my head. "You're as outrageous as ever, though! You can't possibly have come to Caltor just for my birthday!"

"I may have had one or two additional reasons," he acknowledged with a suppressed smile.

Hayes snorted. "I can see you haven't changed a bit, Clay."

Stepping forward, he greeted the other man with a firm handclasp and a slap on the shoulder. Clay grinned back at him, the two of them exchanging the greetings of old friends.

Even though Clay specialized in animal healing and Hayes in healing people, it wasn't surprising they knew each other. Not only were both master healers—a small group—but both knew Amara from their apprentice days. They must have all been at the Guild at the same time.

I looked past them, taking in the rest of the room. A small table against one wall had a cake with crisp white icing decorated with yet more flowers. But my eyes were immediately drawn to the girl standing next to the table. She looked uncertain, hanging back with a hesitant smile.

"Serena?" I gasped and hurried toward the older girl. "What are you doing here? I thought you returned to Tarin to finish your apprenticeship? You can't be done yet. It's only been a matter of weeks. Surely your old master didn't refuse to take you back?"

"No, no, thankfully he's been more than considerate about

the whole thing." She hesitated before giving me a bigger smile. "Happy birthday, Delphine."

"Thank you." I smiled back, my old animosity for the plants apprentice long gone.

After facing Grey together with me, Serena's previous resentment of me had completely disappeared. I had even been disappointed when she had to rush straight back to Tarin to resume her broken apprenticeship.

I had admired her bravery in facing the issue head on, however. She must have been nervous since her master hadn't been required to take her back. And even if he did accept her, a stigma would still have remained. Once her apprenticeship resumed, it lifted her status of reneger—and relieved the complete social ostracization that the whole of Tartoran society was required to show those who abandoned their apprenticeships. But that didn't mean people would welcome her back with open arms.

"When I heard your old friends were going to be in town, I knew we had to have a party." Luna slipped her arm around my waist and gave me a squeeze before throwing herself at Serena for an enthusiastic embrace.

Serena accepted the hug, blinking at me over Luna's shoulder.

I chuckled. "Sorry, she's just like that."

"Like what?" Luna disentangled herself, giving both of us a cheeky grin. "Kind, thoughtful, and friendly?"

"Yes, that." A smile tugged at my lips, the disastrous start to the day fading from my mind.

"Sorry, did I overstep?" Luna grimaced at Serena. "You feel like an old friend, and not just because of Delphine. It's a strange sort of bond, healing someone when they're close to death. I sometimes forget that the patient doesn't always feel the same way. Especially since you had to leave Caltor so soon afterward."

Serena's and my eyes met, and I knew we were both thinking the same thing, remembering the extensive injuries she'd suffered at Grey's hands.

Luna broke me out of the moment, bumping my shoulder with hers.

"Today is supposed to be a happy day! No thinking sad thoughts!"

I laughed and reached for the cake, digging one finger into the icing. As I tasted the sweet confection, I gave a hum of pleasure.

"Delicious."

"Delphine!" Luna tried to look reproving but failed when she broke into giggles. "I guess you are the birthday girl, so you can do whatever you want."

Serena smiled as well, the expression more hesitant as she glanced between Luna and me.

"I hope *you're* not going to try to claim you came all this way for my birthday," I said to Serena. "Did you come with Clay?"

I glanced across at the older man who was still deep in conversation with Hayes and Amara, the expressions on their faces suggesting the topic had turned more serious. Clay lived in Ostaria, which was the closest city to Tarin, but it wasn't close enough for me to think he and Serena would know each other—especially given Serena wasn't a healer.

Serena shook her head. "I met him five minutes ago while we were waiting for you to arrive."

I winced. "Sorry I was late."

"You don't have to be sorry on your birthday," Luna said. "I'm pretty sure it's a rule."

"I had no idea you were so into birthdays." I shook my head. "If I had, I would have been more prepared."

Luna grinned unapologetically. "We didn't have a lot of access to new things in my settlement growing up, but my mother always made an effort with our birthdays. I don't know how she managed it, but she always found enough ingredients for a feast, and she would make us presents herself."

Her words brought up thoughts of my own mother and the small celebrations we would have every year on my birthday. Tears pricked at my eyes as I realized it was my first birthday without her.

But I didn't wish myself back home. Despite the passing months, I still hadn't worked out my complicated feelings toward my father. He had always been a warm presence on my birthdays, and yet, the whole time, he had been secretly holding me back, letting his fear hold sway over my life.

I shook my head, forcing my thoughts back to Luna. She talked about her parents often since she clearly missed them both. She had supported their decision to move to Calista six months before, however. They had only stayed in Tarona for so long to support her, and she had grown comfortable enough in the Tartoran capital not to need them anymore.

She had assured me it was better for them to go on ahead so many times that I could tell she had mixed feelings about it. But since she would be joining them after her graduation, it wouldn't be a long separation. She had never wavered in her loyalty to Calista, so I knew we would be losing her to the newly created Calistan Mages' Guild once she became a proficient.

Luna was one of the members of the secret settlement who had remained across the border during Calista's years of devastation. They had survived in the wasteland by raiding Tartora, but all had now been forgiven. The Tartoran Mages' Guild had even agreed to train many of the settlement youngsters on behalf of the new Calistan Guild in exchange for the influx of new power the settlers brought to our Guild and Tartora in general.

I had heard people speak of the recent changes in the Guild, but getting to know Luna had made it seem possible those changes were real. If the Guild was now overflowing with young people like her, how could it possibly stay the same?

"Will your clinic be all right without you?" Hayes asked from across the room.

There was an odd tone to the otherwise friendly question that caught my attention, making me look across at the small huddle of master mages. Hayes was looking at Clay with an expression I couldn't interpret.

Clay responded with his usual smile, however, giving no sign he had picked up the underlying discordant note.

"I think Tara is relieved I won't be there to cause her any problems. She's convinced I'm the root of all the clinic's problems, and I'm sure my absence will only prove her right. I'll no doubt return to find everything in absolute order."

I grinned at the memory of the woman who ran Clay's clinic for him. I'd never met anyone who gave such an impression of competence and order.

Amara laughed, and after a moment, Hayes chuckled as well. Whatever I had picked up from him earlier seemed to disappear, his usual good humor returning. He looked our way, his eyes catching on Luna, who was trying to silently signal to him.

For a moment he looked confused, but then his brow cleared, and he gestured for the other two with him to join us by the table.

"I think my apprentice might burst if we don't sing now."

"Sing?" I cried, horrified, but it was too late.

Luna burst into enthusiastic notes, the rest of them following in a ragged chorus. I pressed my hands to my burning cheeks, laughing despite myself.

"Thank you," I said as soon as they'd finished. "But please don't ever do that again."

"Was it really that bad?" Clay pretended to look hurt. "I've previously been told I'm an excellent singer."

I stared at him until Amara's chuckles clued me into the joke. I let out a breath of relief which made him start chuckling as well.

Hayes cleared his throat. "I hate to hurry along your celebrations, Delphine, but Anka will be waiting if we take much longer."

"Anka?" I looked between them all. "So there is a reason we're in the law keepers' hall of all places?"

Luna grimaced. "Obviously it wasn't my first choice. But I really wanted Clay and Serena to be here, and we don't know how long the law keepers will keep them. The only safe option was to meet before they're all due to report to Master Anka." She gave me an apologetic look. "First thing in the morning wasn't my preference either. But you and I, at least, will be having a celebratory meal later, whether you like it or not."

I smiled back at her, but my attention was on the reason for Clay and Serena's presence.

"So Master Anka called you both here?" I looked between them. "Something's going on." It wasn't a question.

I turned to Amara. "Do you know what it is?"

She exchanged a look with Hayes which made me raise both eyebrows.

"You're both involved in these meetings, too?" I asked with a sudden sense of certainty.

Amara hesitated. "For now, she doesn't want apprentices included."

"Except Serena, who's still an apprentice," I said slowly. Meeting Amara's eyes, I gave her a disappointed look. "It has something to do with Grey, then."

"Sorry, Delphine," she said. "We can't say anything more for now. And I'm especially sorry it's happening on your birthday. But Luna has promised to spoil you in my absence."

I managed to dredge up a smile despite the burning curiosity that was now surging through me. After all these weeks of silence, what had Grey done to merit Anka calling in people from other parts of the kingdom?

"I'm grateful to Master Anka." Luna had a determined light in her eyes. "It might not have been her intention, but she summoned some of your new friends just in time for your birthday, and now she's providing you with a day off. It's perfect."

I couldn't help smiling at her spin on the situation. When she put it like that, I had no justification in being disappointed.

She didn't summon all my new friends.

The errant thought hit me from nowhere. I squashed it back down, careful to keep my face neutral. I had once thought Nik and I were becoming friends, and he had even kissed me, suggesting he was interested in something more. But he hadn't been honest with me, and he'd chosen to leave. I hadn't heard from him in all the weeks since he left to chase after Grey, and I had no business thinking of him now.

I summoned a smile, linking my arm with Luna's as she waved off the others. "Well then, what did you have in mind for the day?"

TWO

Despite it not being long since breakfast, Luna insisted we both eat a slice of cake before leaving the law keepers' hall.

"Master Anka will surely give the others a break at some point, and they can have some then," she said, leaving the rest of the cake behind on the table.

She scooped up the bouquet, however, and pressed it on me. "You can't leave this behind! I went to a lot of trouble to source those flowers for you."

"It's beautiful." I sniffed at it appreciatively. "It reminds me of all the window boxes they had in Ostaria. I miss those."

Luna led the way outside, nodding in easy agreement, although she'd never been to Ostaria herself. "It's such a pity window boxes are against regulations here. But people still have gardens behind their houses. I visited some of the patients you've healed while we've been training here and asked them to let me raid their gardens. They were all more than happy to help. So they're not just flowers—they're flowers grown and picked with love."

My spirits lifted in response to her beaming smile, my hand tightening around the bouquet. Learning how to control my squeamishness enough to actually help people had been the best part of our extended stay in Caltor.

Luna pulled me out into the flow of foot traffic on the street. I fell into step beside her, guessing we were on our way to the nearby marketplace.

"Do you have any idea what that's all about?" I asked, tipping my head back toward the law keepers' hall. "I don't suppose Hayes dropped any hints?"

"Sadly, no." She tugged me out of the way of an approaching cart, continuing once we were safely past the large wheels. "I'm not sure when he would have told me any secrets. You and I spend so much time together, I barely managed to organize your birthday surprise."

Her grin took any potential sting from her words. Luna had already told me many times that she liked having another girl her age to share her apprenticeship. It was fortunate we got along so well since she was right about how much time we spent together.

After Amara had agreed to Hayes and Anka's combined request that we stay in Caltor for the time being, we had made some adjustments to our accommodation arrangements. Amara had moved out of our shared room into a smaller room of her own, Luna taking her place. I had been surprised at the change but not unhappy. Amara and I got on well, but she was significantly older than me and was a master besides. Swapping Amara for Luna felt like receiving a sister in exchange for a mother as a roommate. I had never had any actual siblings, but if I'd had an older sister, I would have liked one like Luna.

My early fears that I would have nothing in common with an apprentice from the Guild had soon faded in the face of her friendliness and my growing understanding of her background. Luna had grown up isolated like me, even if it was in a different way, and she had known nothing about the ways of mages or the Guild before Hayes activated her.

"It's strange to have a complete day off," I said, trying to remember the last time I went a whole day without using my healing ability.

Luna groaned. "Right? They've been working us without mercy! At least at the Guild we had regular days off. I don't know how you cope with life on the road all the time!"

"We've hardly been on the road," I pointed out with amusement.

"You know what I mean. It's the same thing, just without the travel. And Amara is a hard taskmaster!"

I shook my head, a smile on my face. I was used to Luna's lighthearted complaints by now. She had been apprenticed to Hayes for more than a year when the Triumvirate sent them to Caltor, so she found it an adjustment to leave behind the more structured Guild schedule for the chaos of our ever-changing life.

"But she's kind," I pointed out, as I always did. "And I prefer a master who includes me and views us as a team over one who treats me like a schoolchild."

"Hayes is the kindest person I've ever met!" Luna exclaimed, following the predetermined script. She could never hear even the vaguest allusion to an insult to her influencer without leaping to his defense.

"I know, I know," I said hurriedly. "He saved your whole settlement and negotiated you a place in Tartora. He's a paragon of every possible virtue and an excellent healing teacher. Look! We've arrived."

I steered her off the street and into the large square which hosted the daily market. Despite my cavalier attitude, I meant my words. During our stay in Caltor, Hayes had included me in all the lessons he gave his own apprentice, leaving Amara free to work with Anka on matters they both kept close to their chest. And he had never once made me feel like a burden.

Of course, Amara was still involved in my training—the law

required her to be. She visited our sessions daily and took charge of our training on general matters such as mental discipline and control. She had also taken both of us for several sessions on the elements affinity. Although Luna wasn't cross-influenced, all mage apprentices spent at least some time familiarizing themselves with the capabilities of the other affinities. And in my case, it was extra fascinating since I had healing cross elements, thanks to Amara's elements ability.

Watching her use her power was like feeling an itch somewhere just out of reach. I couldn't actually connect with the elements like she could, but they felt achingly familiar, as if touching them might be possible if I just stretched out a bit further.

"Look!" Luna tugged me over to a stall selling ribbons, buttons, and lengths of material. "Have you ever seen anything so beautiful?" She lovingly stroked a length of shimmering blue silk which looked remarkably like a living stream.

The stall keeper glared at her, and I shook my head, tugging her away.

"What would I do with something like that? Do you think I have time to sew myself gowns? The hospital is happy to provide basic clothing, and that's more than sufficient for me."

"Delphine!" Luna groaned despairingly. "It's your birthday! You have to buy *something* that's beautiful, not just practical. Don't pretend Amara didn't give you a pouch because I know she did."

My hand went to my pocket where the small pouch sat concealed. Amara had slipped it into my hand with a warm smile and murmured birthday wishes. I'd wanted to protest, but she'd been gone out the door before I could, and once on the street myself, I'd remembered that gifts of coin were common from masters to apprentices on their birthdays.

Relieved of my momentary discomfort, I agreed with Luna

on the matter of a birthday purchase. But I wasn't going to buy material that would just sit in our inn room untouched.

"There!" This time I was the one tugging Luna through the crowd.

She smiled, pleased by the stall full of beautifully worked leather. But when she saw what I picked up, the smile fell from her face.

"Really, Delphine?" She groaned again. "You're hopeless! Won't you even look at that bag? The leatherwork is gorgeous, and it would be perfect for carrying your healing supplies. You heard the conversation between Amara and Hayes yesterday. You might be strong enough to heal almost anything completely, but she still wants you to be fully versed in the ways of weaker healers, including carrying bandages and tinctures and other supplies."

"I know." I glanced absentmindedly at the bag she was holding out. "She and I have talked about it a lot. When we're on the road, we travel through a lot of smaller villages and towns, and she wants me to be able to train the locals who have a healing affinity, like she does with those with an elements affinity. So I need to be able to demonstrate the techniques." I ran a hand over the detailing along the strap of the bag. "Plus, if we ever encounter a large scale disaster, I might need to spread my ability out, saving it for the more serious cases."

Luna shook her head. "You really are embracing life on the road." She held the bag out toward me and shook it slightly. "So wouldn't you like this beautiful bag?"

I laughed, returning my gaze to the thin, elegant collar in my hands. The polished green stones that dotted its length winked up at me. They weren't expensive gemstones, but they would still serve my purpose.

"An excellent choice," the stall keeper said hopefully. "It would look very fine on a large cat or small dog."

"How about a fox?" Luna grumbled under her breath, earning a confused look from the man.

I ignored her, beginning to haggle with him over the price.

"This doesn't count, you know," Luna said. "Buying something for Ember isn't the same as buying something for yourself."

I gave the bag she was still holding a closer look.

"What price could you give if I bought the bag as well?" I asked the stall keeper, causing Luna to instantly brighten.

After several more minutes of haggling, we left the stall, my new bag slung over my shoulder with the collar tucked safely inside and several coins still left in my pouch. Amara had been generous.

"Are you really going to put a collar on Ember?" Luna wrinkled her nose.

"I don't have any interest in collaring her in the traditional sense," I replied, busy looking around for the source of a particularly appealing, sweet aroma. "I won't be attaching a lead or anything like that. But she likes to wander the streets at night, and I worry that someone is going to mistake her for a wild animal and a pest and attack her. I want anyone who encounters her to know she isn't a wild fox."

"I suppose that makes sense." Luna sounded disgruntled at having to acknowledge the value of my purchase.

"Ooh, it's those hot cakes making that smell." I pointed to the line in front of a small stall, instantly distracting Luna.

"You've still got coin left, don't you?" She gave me a cheeky smile. "Feel like buying us a birthday treat?"

"Of course," I said promptly. "As many as we can eat."

We joined the end of the line, Luna rising onto her toes to try to peer ahead at the stall.

"I hope they don't run out before we get to the front," she said. "I don't have the patience to wait for them to bake a second batch."

"I'm sure they've prepared plenty," I said absentmindedly.

My mind was going rogue again, reminding me of the early days in my travels with Amara when my heart would leap every time I caught a glimpse of any tall, broad-shouldered, and dark-haired figure. Over the weeks, I had grown used to Nik's permanent absence, but apparently my morning's wayward thoughts had brought my old bad habits back to the surface.

In a large marketplace, there were plenty of tall men, so I hoped I would get on top of the instinct quickly. I was going to develop a twitch otherwise. I forced myself to focus on Luna, who also seemed to be having trouble standing still.

"You've been so focused on me, but is there anything you need to buy?" I asked.

"Only some practical things." She quickly added, "But I can get those later."

"No, why should you? We're here now, so we should get everything done while we have the chance. Why don't you go now while I wait in line for our cakes?"

Luna hesitated, her eyes flicking toward the far end of the market and back.

"Are you sure?"

"Of course I'm sure! Go, go." I pushed her lightly, propelling her out of the line toward the direction of her gaze.

"Thanks, Delphine. I won't take long." She flashed me a quick smile and disappeared into the crowd.

I readjusted the bag on my shoulder and shuffled forward as the line moved. The baker served more quickly than I expected, and I soon had a bundle of hot cakes wrapped in a length of clean material and tucked into my new satchel.

Congratulating myself on the usefulness of my recent purchase, I tucked myself out of the way of the crowds, between the baker's stall and the neighboring one selling metalwork. From this vantage point, I would see Luna as soon as she returned—an unexciting option but one much less fraught than plunging into the crowd in an attempt to find her.

I watched the people lining up for the cakes, idly guessing at their stories and trying to tune out the overwhelming awareness of so many beating hearts and pumping lungs. Hayes had said I would always have to live with some level of squeamishness—an unwelcome prospect. But at least the mere presence of other people no longer made me feel ill. I didn't even have to suppress symptoms unless I touched someone who was actually injured or ill—or else was taken by surprise like I was at the law keepers' hall.

I eyed a man in line whose breathing was slightly labored, trying to guess at the cause, when a hand grasped my upper arm and pulled me backward. Caught completely off guard, I stumbled into the side alley behind me, defenseless. I would have fallen if I wasn't supported by strong, steady hands that deposited me against a wall.

As soon as I caught my balance, I thrust out one hand, seeking any inch of my attacker's skin. It didn't matter how large he was, the moment I touched him, I would have the upper hand.

But a second before I made contact, my eyes flashed up to his and my hand froze, just short of touching him. It wasn't a stranger or thief attacking me, but a familiar figure who had haunted more of my thoughts than I wanted to admit.

Nik. Also known as Prince Nikolas.

CHAPTER

THREE

"Nik?" I gasped, too shocked to use the proper form of address. "How are you here?"

But a moment later my body stiffened as I remembered myself.

"I mean, Your Highness." I bowed, but it was hard to manage more than a slight incline when he was standing so close, trapping me between his body and the alley wall.

He watched me with an unfamiliar look—a dangerous mixture of amusement and affection. But at the sound of his title, he drew back, his face darkening.

I sighed. Everything about this scene was familiar. His unexpected proximity rolled back time, forcibly reminding me of the nighttime adventures that had marked the beginning of my apprenticeship. Those days had been lost in the sea of endless training since, but suddenly they seemed so close I could touch them. It felt like only yesterday when I had stood like this—too close and yet also too distant from the searing blue eyes that seemed to see straight through me.

"Don't call me that," he said, his voice rough.

I arched one eyebrow. "Why not? It's your title." I left the statement hanging between us like a challenge, and he was the first to look away, running a hand through his hair, the lines of his body taut.

The silence between us grew heavy.

My mind spun through the various questions I wanted to ask him. I should start with Grey and whether Nik had located him. I should ask about where he'd been all these weeks.

I did neither.

"Why didn't you tell me?" The words came out more angrily than I'd intended, bearing a load of emotion I hadn't intended to reveal. "Why did you hide your real identity?"

"That's not my identity anymore." The tone was harsh, and he wouldn't meet my eyes.

I laughed darkly. "You mean because you're a reneger?"

He pulled back as if I'd hit him, but I couldn't tamp down my rising anger.

"You might not be wielding the authority of a prince right now, but that doesn't change your birthright. You grew up in a palace, Nik! Your father is *King Marius*. How could you not tell me something like that?" The next words hung unspoken on my tongue. *You saved me. You kissed me. But you didn't tell me who you were.*

"I..." He ran his hand through his hair again, and I realized I'd never seen him so hesitant, so unsure.

Some of my anger deflated. It felt pointless being angry at someone who was clearly lost and alone. Whatever choices Nik had made that had led him here, he had left himself nothing but his ability and the strange determination that drove him.

He had chosen to cut himself off from everyone and everything, so who was I to think I should be an exception? He had made me no promises.

"Never mind," I said. "The important thing is Grey. Did you find him? What about Miranda?"

I rose onto my toes as the questions poured out of me, my eyes fixed urgently on his face. A hot wave of worry and guilt was rising inside me. Grey had fled with Miranda as a captive, and we had all abandoned her.

We might have had our reasons, but for Miranda, at least, those reasons meant little. Nik had gone after her, though, and I hadn't realized how much of my peace had been built on that knowledge. But now he was back here in Caltor, apparently alone. Had something happened to Miranda?

Nik gazed at me for a moment, absorbing the change of topic. Emotions raced across his face too fast for me to read before he shut them all behind a wall, returning to his old closed-off expression.

"Miranda is fine—physically, at least. Or she was when I left to come here."

When I flinched at his final words, his voice softened.

"I saw no indication that situation will change. Grey wants to use her, not harm her."

I sank back, both relieved and disappointed by his words. I was glad to know she was safe for now, but my earlier sense that I had betrayed her was growing. Until now, I had been able to cling to the hope that Nik would find a way to free her. Now I could no longer deceive myself.

"Why are you here?" I asked, my voice dull and my eyes trained on the ground.

A gentle finger under my chin lifted my face until my eyes met his.

"Happy birthday, Delphine," he said in the gentlest voice I'd yet heard.

Something pressed into my palm, and I looked down to see an object wrapped in a length of plain material.

"A present? For me?"

He didn't bother to answer the obvious question.

I looked back up at him, but he was looking away, one hand rubbing the back of his neck.

I unwrapped the object, exposing a thin, elegant dagger,

possibly the smallest one I'd ever seen. I looked at him again, and this time he was watching me.

He cleared his throat. "If you're going to worry about everyone else all the time, you need a way to protect yourself."

I quirked one eyebrow, lifting one of my hands and waggling my fingers.

He shrugged. "I don't care how powerful you are, there are some situations and people that should be approached with a sharp blade, not bare fingers."

I looked down at my hand and frowned, thinking of Grey. He was a healer like me, and Nik was right. When it came to a fellow healer, making physical contact gave them the same access to me as I had to them. Not to mention Nik's own trick of covering all patches of exposed skin.

I shivered, trying not to think about the kind of situation that might require the use of the blade. I hoped I was never going to find myself in such a position again.

"Thank you," I said softly, strapping the dagger and sheath to my belt. "I'll keep it close."

Nik nodded, looking satisfied, and I considered his choice of gift. It was a good reflection of him—dangerous and unhelpful on the surface but surprisingly thoughtful underneath.

"How did you know it was my birthday?" I asked.

He shifted uncomfortably, and my eyes narrowed.

"Have you been following me?"

"I needed to speak to you—alone."

I flushed. He couldn't possibly have been inside the law keepers' hall, could he? Surely there was no way he could have seen my embarrassing start to the morning.

A moment's reflection reminded me of the more important point. Nik had been off searching for Grey and had apparently found him—and now he had something to tell me. That was far more important than my foolish embarrassment.

"How have you been?"

His question caught me off guard, and I just stared at him. There was no way Nik wanted to speak to me alone just to ask about our time apart. He did seem different, but not that different.

The memory of our last encounter made my heart speed up, my awareness of his current nearness heightening. We had been standing very similarly before he had kissed me, and my eyes were drawn irresistibly to his lips.

He cleared his throat and took a step back, giving me room. My rebellious heart sank at his movement. Surely I wasn't foolish enough to hope for a repeat of that particular encounter? Nik was a prince and a reneger—a combination that was still hard to process—not to mention arrogant, condescending, and dangerous. As the enemy of Grey, I could appreciate him as a formidable ally, but I couldn't let myself see him in any other light.

But all my sensible lectures did nothing to change the way the air turned cold around me or to still the fluttering in my stomach that was uncomfortably similar to my squeamish reaction to blood. My mind could pretend I didn't react to Nik's presence, but my body wasn't as easily deceived.

I had never been immune to the prince, and his lengthy absence had apparently changed nothing.

"You've been training hard," he said to fill the silence when I didn't respond to his earlier question.

I started, staring at him again. Exactly how long had he been watching me?

"I see Hayes really did take on that Calistan girl." Now he sounded like he was talking just to cover my awkward silence. "I can't remember her name. Something to do with the sky..."

"Luna," I said, finally finding my voice again.

"Oh yes." He sounded entirely uninterested. "That was it."

"You've met her before?" I couldn't help feeling intense

interest in his past. What had led him to reject his life of privilege in favor of becoming an outcast?

He shrugged. "Briefly."

I fell silent when my mental calculations told me Luna's apprenticeship must have started at a similar time to Nik's disappearance. After our confrontation with Grey and Nik's departure, Amara had told me what little she knew about Nik's situation, but it hadn't been much. Because Amara was the most senior traveling mage in the kingdom, the king and queen had taken her into their confidence, hoping she might encounter their son. But even so, they had been short on detail, which was hardly a surprise. The last thing they must have wanted was for the kingdom at large to discover their son had chosen to exile himself from both them and society.

I examined his face, and Nik met my eyes steadily. Ever since he'd pulled me aside, he'd been behaving more gently and considerately than in any of our previous interactions. But I could still see traces of defiance behind his expression, and it made me uneasy.

Whatever had caused the changes in Nik, plenty of his old attitude still remained.

As if reading the mistrust in my eyes, Nik stepped closer again, capturing one of my hands in his.

"I'm sorry about last time," he said in a low, husky voice that was nearly my undoing. "I never should have asked you to become a reneger. I wouldn't choose that life for anyone, let alone you."

My mouth dropped open.

"Careful, Nik," I said playfully. "It almost sounds like you care about me."

He flushed and looked away, making the joking smile fall from my face. I had been half teasing, half probing, hoping to expose the simmering emotions I could see beneath his surface. I hadn't expected him to take my words so seriously.

Awkwardly I cleared my throat. A heedless part of me wanted to believe that Nik had thought as often of me in the weeks of our separation as I had thought of him. I wanted to believe he had truly softened when faced with my absence.

But the more realistic part of me fixated on the reasons for his return. Nik had been unable to convince us to join him and had been forced to follow Grey alone—just as he had always done. His brief experience of allies had ended in a betrayal of sorts—at least from his perspective—and now he was back for reasons I still didn't know. My instincts told me he needed something from me, and I would be wise not to read anything more into this interaction than that.

"Why are you here?" I repeated the question in a firm voice, trying to let him know that I wanted the truth this time instead of distracting comments that made it sound like he'd come back for me.

Nik leaned forward, putting one hand on the wall beside my head, his eyes trained on mine.

"I need you." His low voice sent a thrill through me, sending my thoughts into free fall.

What had he just said? And what could he possibly mean by it? My mind struggled to form coherent thoughts as my pulse spiked dangerously high and my eyes once again dropped to his lips.

But his face remained maddeningly still, just too far away for me to be sure of his intentions, although he was close enough for me to feel his breath against my skin. Whatever Nik had meant, it wasn't what the treacherous part of me wanted it to be.

"What..." My dry mouth failed me, and I licked my lips and tried again. "What do you mean?"

"I think I know a way to rescue Miranda and to take Grey down for good. But my plan requires you." He swayed closer, speaking against the curls beside my ear, his breath making them move and sending goosebumps down my arms. "It involves danger."

His words reached the faltering parts of my brain like a jolt of lightning. I reared back and hit my head against the wall behind me.

Wincing, I reached up to rub the sore spot, but his hand was faster, cupping the back of my head and massaging it gently while his eyes sent me an apology. I gulped and tried to pull back, but his free arm had somehow found its way to my waist, holding me firmly in place.

I tried to ignore the searing effect of his touch and forced my tongue to resume function.

"Why would you need me? There are plenty of healers as powerful as me, and most of them must be better trained."

"I need you precisely because you're young and new to training," he said. "You fit the profile of Grey's targets. He wants people young and malleable—ones who can be bent to his will. And, in particular, he's already intrigued by you. He's tested your strength, and he's curious about your ability. Not many people would be capable of fending him off like you did. He wants you, Delphine, and that's why it has to be you."

For a long moment I stared at him, my eyes trapped by his, something unspoken and charged hanging between us.

But the longer Nik looked into my eyes, the darker his became. "I've spent weeks trying to think of a different plan. I would never suggest this if I could think of any other way. But I believe in you, Delphine. You're strong enough for this."

"You've changed your tune," I said weakly, remembering how often he had rejected me as useless after we first met.

He released me so suddenly, I almost staggered. As he stepped back to put space between us, his eyes dropped away from mine.

"I've already acknowledged your usefulness—I was the one

who suggested we work together to capture Grey, remember? And I'm the one who asked you to chase after him with me."

I slowly nodded, confused by his seesawing manner.

"I'm not running away with you, Nik," I warned. After everything she'd done for me, I couldn't abandon Amara like that—not even for Miranda. "If you really have a workable plan, you'll need to convince Amara of that, not just me."

He nodded once, the movement abrupt and the shadow in his eyes at odds with his apparent agreement.

"Delphine!" A distant call from inside the market reached my ears, bringing the rest of the world rushing back to my awareness.

"Luna." I looked toward the end of the alley where I could see a glimpse of the back of two stalls and the crowd beyond.

When I turned back, Nik was staring in the same direction.

"Tonight," he said abruptly. "At the inn. After your birthday meal. I'll be there to convince Amara."

"Wait, what?"

I heard my name called again and glanced back toward the market, frustrated. I needed longer to question him. He couldn't say all that and then just...

Disappear. I sighed as I surveyed the place he had been standing. I couldn't see his exit route, but somehow Nik was already gone.

FOUR

I emerged into the market feeling dazed. Luna immediately pounced on me, her face creased with concern.

"There you are! What happened? Where did you go?" She clutched my arm as if she was afraid I'd disappear again if she wasn't holding onto me.

I leaned a bit closer so I could lower my voice in the noise of the crowd.

"Nik."

She reared back, her eyes wide. "Here? In the market?" She looked wildly from side to side.

I shook my head. "I think he's gone now."

But even as I said it, I snuck a glance around myself, remembering my unanswered question about how long he had been tailing me. Was it possible he was still here, just keeping out of sight? I couldn't imagine a reason why he would hang around, but I felt certain I wouldn't see him if he wanted to stay hidden.

We continued to wander around the market, pretending to look at the stalls, but it was hard to muster any interest in shopping after the shock of Nik's return. And even the celebratory evening meal Amara had organized at the inn struggled to hold my attention.

The others had returned from their day at the law keepers' hall early enough to join us for the meal, but there had been no time for me to pull Amara aside before it began. As we ate, I caught Amara sending me a series of concerned glances. I couldn't explain my mood to her, though, not with Serena and Clay present.

Clay didn't know anything about Nik's involvement in our fight with Grey, and while Serena knew the prince had helped rescue her, I didn't think I should tell her he was back. But although I kept quiet, I couldn't stop myself constantly glancing at the door and even the windows. I knew logically that Nik wasn't going to come bursting through one of them into the inn dining room, but I couldn't seem to keep still.

When Amara caught me looking for the twentieth time, she leaned closer, her brow lined.

"Delphine?" she murmured. "Is something wrong?"

I shook my head slightly, keeping a smile pasted on my face. "Later," I breathed back. "I'll tell you after."

Amara sat back, accepting my words, although she still watched me with a curious gaze. At least Serena seemed oblivious, too impressed with the feast to notice my odd behavior.

"The inn in Tarin doesn't cook anything this fancy." She poked at an elaborate roast duck with a serving fork.

"Will you have to head straight back?" I asked, unable to think of a more interesting conversation topic when half my mind was on what would happen after the meal.

Serena nodded, something in her face catching my attention. "After going reneger, I don't have a lot of leeway. Of course my master agreed to this trip given Master Anka had sent for me specifically, but I have to return in the morning."

I glanced from her to Amara, real curiosity flaring. Did that mean the issue that had occupied them all day was resolved? Or just that Serena's part in it was done? From the somber faces of the three older mages, I was afraid it was the latter.

"Do you not want to return?" I asked, wondering about the reluctance I had seen in her face.

She sighed. "Tarin isn't the most comfortable place for me right now. But I know it's my own fault. I just have to win back people's trust. And to do that, I have to return as quickly as possible." She brightened. "I don't know how I'll move a step after stuffing myself so full, though."

I smiled back and put an extra honeyed carrot on her plate. I had been right to label her brave, although I'd never thought of her that way during our shared youth in Tarin.

Eating herself into somnolence, Serena was the first to finish and head for her room. We exchanged goodbyes before she left since she would have an early start in the morning, and then I took my seat again. I waited for Clay to also take his leave, my impatience growing when he made no move.

Instead he sat back in his chair, looking relaxed as he chatted with Amara, a wine glass in his hand and his long legs stretched out beneath the table. Even when Hayes began to make murmurs about wrapping up for the night, he remained in place, merely raising his glass at the other man in a casual way, as if bidding him goodnight without any intention of following suit.

I frowned between the two of them, wondering if there was any way for me to send Clay on his way while hinting at Hayes not to leave. I would prefer him to be present for the meeting since I felt sure Amara wouldn't agree to anything involving Nik without consulting Hayes first.

My worry regarding Hayes was unfounded, however. As soon as he saw Clay intended to stay, he also remained in place. Apparently he didn't want to leave before the party broke up for the night.

He didn't seem to be in a celebratory mood, though, sitting straight in his chair on the other side of the table and making no move to eat or drink. My attention was distracted, wondering where and when Nik was going to show up, so it took a while to realize Luna was trying to signal me, her movements somehow both frantic and subtle.

My first instinct was to look around the room for some hint of Nik, but when I saw nothing, I looked back at her, frowning a silent question. Her eyes were gleaming as if she was bursting with news she couldn't verbalize.

Once she saw she had my attention, she inclined her head sideways at her master. I glanced at Hayes beside her, but he looked just as he had a minute ago. I frowned back at her, and her eyes widened. She gestured at Hayes again before tilting her head across the table and raising her eyebrows.

I blinked, looking from Hayes's stiff posture and watchful eyes across to the object of his attention. Clay still leaned back, relaxed, laughing at something Amara had just said. His body was angled slightly toward her, giving her all his focus.

My mouth fell open as I looked back at Luna. It was easy to read her delight that I was finally receiving her message.

Had I been too distracted all evening to notice the dynamics between the older members of the group? It seemed likely.

But now that I was paying attention, it was hard to dispute Luna's obvious interpretation of the situation. Hayes seemed uncomfortable at Clay's presence—even...territorial.

But weren't they all old friends? I remembered his strange manner in the morning, and my curiosity grew.

I could see Luna was bursting with interest, but after a moment she glanced once at the door and then at me, tilting her head toward Clay with a question in her eyes. She was obviously fascinated by whatever dynamic was going on between our two masters and the new arrival, but she was also the only other one at the table who knew Nik was coming.

"Enough conspiratorial glances, you two," Amara said suddenly.

Hayes's eyes snapped to hers, a hint of guilt showing in his expression, and Clay straightened, his hand tightening around his wine glass. But Amara's attention was on me and Luna.

I winced, but Luna didn't look in the least abashed at being called out. She seemed more curious at where the conversation was going to go, looking from Amara to Clay and finally to Hayes.

But Amara's eyes had landed on me and stayed there, her expression commanding. It took me a moment to realize that while she had been speaking to me and Luna, she hadn't been referring to our silent conversation about the three of them.

"I don't know what happened in our absence and what you have to tell me, but you don't need to be so jumpy. Anything you can say to Hayes and me, you can say in front of Clay. I promise he knows far more state secrets than either of you."

Clay chuckled lightly at this endorsement and even Hayes nodded, whatever earlier antagonism he had been feeling swallowed. It seemed that if Hayes had an issue with Clay, it was definitely personal and didn't cause him to doubt the reliability of the other healer.

I cleared my throat, unsure what to say now I had everyone's attention. After a moment, I glanced around the dining room, which still held a couple of other groups of diners.

"Let's go up to our room," Luna said. "Since it's the biggest."

Amara looked once more between us, her eyes narrowing, but she ended by nodding agreement. Rising to her feet, she signaled to the rest of us to follow, leading the way to the stairs.

At the top of them, she glanced at me, a smile in her eyes.

"Why do I have a terrible feeling about this?"

I grimaced. "It wasn't my idea."

Both her eyebrows shot up. "You know that only makes everything seem worse, right?"

I chuckled reluctantly, unlocking my door and ushering the small group inside. The room had always felt spacious, but so many bodies inside made it shrink. I cast a quick glance around, hoping not to see any mess I might have left out, and instead encountered a dark shadow in one of the corners—a hulking figure that couldn't entirely blend with his surroundings.

Hissing, I slammed the door shut behind us, making the rest of the group start and look toward me. When they saw me staring into the corner of the room, they all followed my gaze.

Amara immediately stepped forward, one arm raised in a protective gesture, holding me and Luna back. But the figure stepped forward into the light, a provocative gleam in his eyes.

"Prince Nikolas!" Hayes exclaimed as Amara sucked in a breath and slowly lowered her arm.

Clay whistled slowly, raising his eyebrows as he looked first at Amara and Hayes and then at me, his gaze both curious and calculating.

Ember trotted out of the same corner where she had clearly been sitting at Nik's feet, her new collar winking in the light. I stooped to pick her up, murmuring "traitor" against her fur.

"I didn't expect such a crowd," Nik said, still with that superior look that made me want to smack him.

He focused on me. "You didn't warn them?"

Now it wasn't just Clay and Nik looking at me. Feeling the weight of five sets of eyes, I stepped past the others, facing Nik.

"I didn't get the chance. We weren't alone until just now."

"I wouldn't call this *alone* exactly." His eyes gleamed at me, suggesting he wouldn't have minded the two of us being alone.

Amara cleared her throat, giving him a quelling look as she stepped to my side and pulled me back. Whatever else Amara thought of the renegade prince, she did not approve of her apprentice having any involvement with him.

Involvement. My lips burned as I remembered the kiss Amara had nearly witnessed after we fought Grey. She hadn't seen enough to be sure, but she'd clearly been suspicious.

She didn't need to worry now, though. Nothing like that

was going on. How could it when I knew the full truth of who he was?

I glanced behind me and saw Luna's excitement and Clay's bright curiosity. I sighed. "Why don't we all sit down? Somehow I don't think this is going to be quick."

Amara raised an eyebrow but helped everyone find somewhere to perch. I deposited Ember back into her basket, with a firm command to stay there. I didn't want her injured underfoot with so many people in the room.

Amara gestured for me to sit beside her, conspicuously far away from Nik. And he seemed to have noticed based on the less-than-friendly look he was giving her.

I glared at him. He was here to convince Amara, Hayes— and now Clay—of a plan they would probably all violently disapprove of. So the least he could do was try to play nice. I didn't think Nik knew how to be subservient, though—even before three master mages. And now that I knew his title, I knew why.

I ran a hand over my face. He hadn't even started talking, and I was already tired.

When I opened my eyes again, he was watching me. Was that concern in his eyes? I shook my head at my own fancy. It wasn't likely.

Amara cleared her throat, giving Nik a disapproving look. "I suppose I should start by asking why you broke into the bedroom of my apprentice."

Nik gave her a cool glance. "We needed a private place. This isn't a conversation we want overheard, and I'd rather not be seen by anyone outside this room." He glanced briefly at Clay, as if he would have preferred not to be seen by him either.

"That's Master Clay," I said quickly. "He's a friend of Amara and Hayes and a master healer. And he's also a trusted advisor—"

"I know who he is," Nik's cool voice cut me off. He gave a

curt nod in Clay's direction, and the man responded with a half bow from his sitting position.

"This is a great surprise, Your Highness," he said in a level voice that revealed nothing.

I sighed and sank back. I should have known Nik would be familiar with Clay, given he knew Amara and Hayes. Nik might have been a young child when the three of them were apprentices at the Guild, but that didn't mean they hadn't been back since. And as a prince it was probably part of Nik's role to know all the master mages in the kingdom.

I would do well to remember that I was the outsider in this room, not Clay.

Amara had ignored the attempted introduction, her attention never wavering from Nik. "So you're telling me you expected me to enter this room with Delphine?"

He shrugged. "That was the point of the meeting."

"Meeting?" Amara turned to me with a raised eyebrow. "So you really were expecting him to be here?"

"Not exactly here." I glared at him. "Nik didn't bother telling me *where* we were all going to meet after the meal."

"It seemed the most logical place, since it's the largest room," Nik said, unflustered.

Amara sighed and rubbed her eyes. "I'm not going to ask how you know that. I don't want to know. Let's focus on the more important points. What have you discovered about Grey in all these weeks, and why are you here now?"

"I've learned Grey is a bigger threat than we realized and where his base is," Nik replied promptly. "And I'm here because I need Delphine."

Everyone in the room responded to his final words, their reactions covering the full spectrum. Luna looked delighted, as if we were enacting a play purely for her entertainment. Hayes looked pained. Clay looked shocked, his eyes traveling back to me and staying focused on my face in a way that made me squirm with embarrassment and glare at Nik, who looked entirely unmoved by the reactions he'd just unleashed.

Amara, however, straightened, and spoke. "No. Absolutely not. You cannot have my apprentice."

"Obviously you would come, too." Nik met her eyes, his face utterly serious, and her demeanor changed slightly, her expression becoming less determined and more inquisitive. Whatever else she was feeling, Nik had successfully captured her curiosity.

"I mean it, Master Amara," Nik said quietly, and neither Amara nor I missed his use of her title. "Delphine cannot become a reneger."

Amara nodded once, her movement slow. A single crease appeared between her eyes, and when she finally broke gaze with Nik, it was to glance at Hayes.

I couldn't read everything that passed between them, but I could tell they were both surprised. Something had changed in the weeks Nik had been away, and I wasn't the only one to recognize it.

"I think someone had better fill me in," Clay said in his usual good-natured tone. "It's becoming clear that your report on your encounter with Grey was missing some key facts." He sounded amused rather than resentful.

Amara grimaced. "Apologies, Clay. Naturally we gave the full report to Anka, but the instructions from court were to keep the prince's involvement quiet." She glanced at Nik. "I have to confess that after all this time, I wasn't expecting to see His Highness back again."

Nik narrowed his eyes. "I'm not going to ask what you mean by that statement."

His tone sounded vaguely threatening, and both Hayes and Clay bristled, a fact Luna noticed with yet more delight. I rolled my eyes at her, but at least someone was enjoying this painfully awkward interaction.

Amara was entirely unfazed by the animosity in Nik's words, continuing her explanation to Clay.

"Apparently Prince Nikolas had been tracking Grey for some time before Delphine and I crossed paths with him in her hometown. We unknowingly trailed him all the way here, and along the way I discovered my apprentice and the prince had been spending their nights hunting Grey."

She threw me a disapproving look. "I still don't know the full extent of every interaction, but it culminated in the fight you've heard about. Delphine rescued the young people while His Highness dealt with Grey's people."

"Ah!" Clay smiled, apparently pleased. "I did think that story didn't quite add up."

The healing master might run a clinic for pets, but he clearly had his share of experience with court. He'd known something was missing from the report, but he had also known not to question the official story.

"As you know, Grey managed to escape," Amara continued, "and His Highness was...displeased with our response. He wanted us to chase after Grey instead of taking the freed captives to Anka. In the end, he chose to go after Grey alone."

There was the slightest emphasis on the final word, making me squirm a little. At least she hadn't told everyone how Nik had tried to convince me to go with him.

"That was some time ago." Clay leaned forward, his eyes alight as he watched Nik. "But you're saying you succeeded in tracking him to his base? He's there now?"

Nik nodded. "I have reason to believe he's still there, yes."

"That's excellent news." Hayes straightened. "We should lose no time in riding for the capital. King Marius can assign us enough troops to confront Grey head on and end this whole thing."

He met Amara's eyes, another unspoken message passing between them.

Nik smiled slightly, as if he'd expected that reaction.

"I assume from your response that you've finally caught on that there's something suspicious about this blight," he said calmly. "But bringing in troops is exactly what we can't do."

If his earlier pronouncement had caused shock waves, this statement was more of an explosion. My own confusion and curiosity was nothing compared to the reaction from the others.

Hayes surged to his feet, his eyes wide, while Amara sucked in her breath loudly. Clay also rose, striding over to the door and wrenching it open to peer up and down the corridor. When he had satisfied himself that there was no one outside in hearing distance, he closed it again, turning the key that sat inside the lock and exchanging glances with Amara.

Even Ember had responded to the sudden shift in the room, scrambling to her feet in her basket and letting out a terse yip. I hurried over to reassure her, keeping a hand on her soft fur as I exchanged confused glances with Luna. At least I wasn't the only one who had no idea what was going on.

But one glance at the burning expression in Amara's eyes made the confusion sour in my stomach. Whatever was going on, it wasn't good.

"What blight?" I asked slowly. "What is he talking about?"

CHAPTER

FIVE

"How do you know about that?" Clay asked in a hard voice, his eyes boring into Nik.

I expected Nik to make some half-mocking response, but when he remained deadly serious, my stomach sank even further. Was there really a large-scale blight I hadn't heard about it? And if there was, what could it possibly have to do with Grey?

I sucked in a breath as I realized it had to be related to the meeting that had brought Clay and Serena to Caltor.

Hayes held up a hand to prevent any further words, looking uneasily at Luna and me. I tried to look as harmless as possible, desperate not to be kicked out of the meeting at this juncture.

Amara came to our rescue, however. "I don't think there's any point trying to hide things from Delphine and Luna any longer. Given His Highness is in possession of relevant information—and clearly intends to involve Delphine in the matter—our participation is no longer purely advisory. Involving our apprentices is only natural."

Hayes hesitated a moment longer before nodding and sinking back into his seat.

"I hope you haven't been speaking of this to others," Clay said sternly, his focus still on the prince.

Nik actually laughed, his expression wry. "Who would I be telling?" My heart contracted as I thought of his lonely life, but his eyes hardened as he continued. "You don't need to be afraid. I may be a reneger, but I'm still loyal to this kingdom. I know how to keep state secrets."

To my surprise, it was Clay who backed down, looking away and nodding. It was a strange thing seeing these older, powerful mages navigate their interaction with a prince who was now an outcast. No one seemed quite sure where Nik should be ranked within the group.

"This blight was what you were meeting with Anka about all day," I said, no doubt in my mind. "And you had Serena there, so you already knew there was a connection with Grey."

Amara's expression tightened slightly. "It would more accurately be called a suspicion than knowledge. We have no proof." She looked at Nik. "Perhaps that is about to change?"

"How far has the blight spread?" I leaned forward, my past as the daughter of farmers rising to the fore. "How many different crops can it infect? Is it a new one?" I couldn't quite keep the panic from my voice.

Blight was rarely an issue for farmers—not when the kingdom was full of people with a plants affinity. But every now and then a new blight arose, one resistant to plants power. Guild mages were always called in for such cases, and thankfully they had always been able to get it under control in the past. Once they had properly studied and defeated the new blight, they would train the less powerful members of their affinity in techniques that would keep it away. Acts of service such as these were among the many reasons the Guild was able to adopt such a high and mighty attitude. I might resent them, but I couldn't deny that the kingdom needed their power.

But Clay, Hayes, and Amara weren't plants mages. And

neither was Master Anka. If they were being called in for consultations with her on the topic, then this wasn't just a simple blight. How many farmers had already been affected? And what did Grey have to do with it?

If there really was a blight beyond the control of the plants mages, then the whole kingdom could be in dire trouble. An untamed blight could sweep through vast stretches of crops.

I caught Nik watching me, a hint of concern in his eyes. I took a deep breath and forced myself to relax, loosening my shoulders and unclenching my hands. Whatever was going on, there were clearly far more powerful mages than me worrying about it. I had to trust they would find a solution.

"So far it's contained to the north," Amara said. "But it isn't acting like a usual blight. It's been appearing on unconnected farms, and no one can identify a link. The plants mages can't see any obvious signs of tampering, but they also haven't been able to drive it out."

I put my hand to my mouth, my eyes wide. "What do you mean they haven't been able to drive it out?"

It was one thing for the Guild to still be working on a method of suppression that could be implemented by someone with a weak ability, but it was another thing not to be able to do it themselves.

"Enough fields have had to be burned that the king and Triumvirate are getting worried," Hayes said. "We're too close to harvest for there to be time for replanting, and the kingdom could find itself short on food over winter if we have to burn any more."

"It's that bad?" Luna whispered, her face pale.

"Normally the plants affinity would handle blights on its own, and we wouldn't be involved," Amara said. "But ever since Grey left Caltor, Anka has been gathering any hint of his movements, however small or unreliable. And one of her law keepers noticed a correlation between sightings of Grey and the locations where the blight has been appearing."

I gasped. "Grey is somehow causing the blight? But he's a healer! How is that possible? And shouldn't the plants mages be able to tell if it's an unnatural phenomenon?"

"It does seem impossible." Clay steepled his hands and used them to prop up his chin. "We discussed it in extensive detail yesterday, and Hayes, Anka, and I are all in agreement. A healer couldn't possibly use their power to spread a blight among crops. They could possibly unleash a disease in an animal population, but even that is by no means certain. And with plants, it's simply impossible."

I nodded slowly, processing his words. At least now I knew why Clay of all people had been called in. He might have chosen to set up a pet clinic in a small city, but he was clearly powerful and well-respected in our affinity. And from the way he spoke of Anka, I suspected he knew her well—and might even have trained in law keeping beside her at some point.

"So it's not Grey," I said, strangely disappointed. I preferred an enemy we could fight to a natural blight that was beyond our control.

"Not directly, it would seem," Amara said. "And unfortunately Serena never heard Grey or his people make even the smallest allusion to a blight. But that doesn't mean there isn't a connection." Her shrewd eyes dwelt on Nik. "We weren't willing to discount it earlier today, and now it seems we were right."

"I believe you are," Nik said. "On both counts. Grey hasn't been spreading the blight. He couldn't possibly be. But I'm convinced he knows something about it."

"You have a plants seed," Clay said. "Have you examined the blight for yourself? Did you notice anything odd about it? I know some of the most powerful mages of your affinity have been sent out from the capital, but..."

Nik shook his head. "I haven't had the chance to see it for myself. I was following Grey, and he always arrived after the fields had been burned and the capital mages had departed."

Amara and Hayes exchanged a frustrated glance.

"Then it's possible there isn't a connection after all," Amara said. "Grey may have merely been tracking reports of the blight for his own purposes. Perhaps he thought anyone touched by the blight would be more susceptible to his message?"

Nik frowned. "I don't think that could be the case. When I say we arrived after the fields were burned, they were usually still smoldering. And I heard astonishingly few rumors about the situation on my travels. The crown might not be succeeding in defeating this blight, but they've been successful at keeping tight control of the news about it."

That made sense. With a blight this concerning, I should have already heard about it on the streets of Caltor. But if the winter food supplies were in danger, it was no surprise the crown wanted to keep the news quiet until they had a solution. A scared and angry populace wouldn't help matters.

"What are you saying?" Amara asked.

Nik frowned. "I can't be sure, but it felt like we weren't following the blight itself but something else. Something that arrived at each location just before the blight broke out."

Amara sucked in a breath. "You think Grey wasn't causing it, but he knows what—or who—is, and he was following the cause? How is that possible?"

Nik shrugged. "I have no idea. I'm just reporting what I saw."

"It sounds like you followed him across half the kingdom." Hayes's voice was hard to read.

"I did." Nik glanced at me and then away. "It seemed more important to finally find the location of his base than attempt a lone rescue."

I now knew why he suddenly wasn't meeting my eyes. He

knew I cared about Miranda and wanted to see her rescued. He thought I would be angry he hadn't charged in alone and liberated her while Grey was separated from his remaining followers.

But my concern for Miranda didn't mean I was heedless about the rest of the kingdom. This matter was too big to ignore.

"So you did find the location?" Amara asked. "Where is it?"

"It's in the desert."

"The desert?" Everyone in the room exchanged surprised looks.

"Over the border, then?" I asked, trying to imagine how anyone could survive for long in the low dunes of the Calistan desert.

"Yes, which is why we never found any sign of him here in Tartora. But since the desert is on the coast, it barely counts as part of Calista. It's too barren to support any population, and the coast along that stretch is too treacherous for boats. The Calistans use the rivers to get north to the nomad lands and south to Tartora, so the desert is untouched. It would be a perfect place to hide if it wasn't so dry and barren."

"So how is he living there?" Amara asked. "I know he spends much of his time in Tartora, but still..."

"The Calistan shoreline is rocky and steep," Nik said, "but at one point a crevasse juts into the desert. And given how green it is, it must contain a freshwater oasis. The crevasse isn't big enough to support a proper settlement, and it's surrounded by desert on three sides and treacherous rocks and reefs on the fourth, so it doesn't appear on any maps. I don't even know if anyone has found it before."

"So how in the kingdoms did Grey stumble on it?" Luna asked.

"He didn't happen to mention the matter to me." Nik's response made her roll her eyes.

"So that's where Miranda is now?" My hand tightened around Ember until she squirmed and I forced myself to relax it.

"This news only makes it more imperative that we ride for the capital immediately," Hayes said. "There can be no question King Marius will support us now. Once we capture Grey, we can find out exactly what is causing this danger to our crops."

"Perhaps we would find out, and perhaps we wouldn't," Nik said. "It would be a chancy business."

"You don't think he'd talk?" Clay asked, his expression thoughtful.

"I think he most definitely wouldn't," Nik replied promptly. "I might hate the man, but I can recognize his strengths. He has a rare determination and focus. We might be able to tell when he's lying, but we can't force him to tell the truth. I'm not convinced anything could."

"Then what do you suggest? We just leave him be?" Amara gave Nik a disparaging look.

"If we can't force him to talk, we need to trick him into it. That's where Delphine comes in."

"Me?" I gasped. "How could I trick Grey into telling us anything?"

"I overheard him talking about you more than once." Nik's voice remained calm, but his hands balled into fists at his sides. "He's fascinated by you, just like I predicted." He met my eyes, his gaze steady, clearly concealing some deeper emotion. "He didn't choose Miranda to take with him by accident. He clearly has an interest in healers, and she'll be a reasonably strong one once she's ready to be activated. But you're on another level. You don't just have mage level power, but master level."

"I'm no master mage!" I exclaimed.

"Not yet," Amara said softly. "Mastery requires more than just raw strength. It requires great skill and control as well. But you have the necessary power to take the mastery exams one day if you wish."

I gaped at her, trying to process her words. I had always known I had strength, but somehow I had never considered a future where I actually became a master.

"You've spent too much time with Amara," Hayes said with a hidden laugh in his voice. "It gives a person a skewed perspective on strength."

Amara gave him an exasperated look, but he continued. "Neither you nor Luna were raised at the Guild, so you're probably not aware of the significance of Amara's very early ascension to mastery."

"Back in Ostaria, someone mentioned she was one of the youngest masters in generations," I said slowly.

Hayes nodded. "Only an exceptional combination of both strength and skill allows someone to take the exam so early. I, myself, only took it recently."

"And what Hayes isn't adding," Clay said with a smile, "is that there's every likelihood he will end up as the next head of our affinity after Master Colton. So it's a significant comparison."

"Are you saying Amara could be Master of the Elements one day?" I stared at my master with new eyes.

She scoffed and shook her head. "Of course not. I have no interest in such a position. And, Hayes, I am well aware you could have taken the mastery exam sooner if you hadn't chosen the route of being a second first." She turned to me. "All three affinity heads and the Royal Mage have seconds. They're always proficients, but only the strongest are chosen for the role. It's considered training ground for future masters. Those who dream of one day becoming head of their affinity almost always choose the path of being a second before they take the exam."

Clay chuckled. "Yes, while Amara has the skill and strength to head her affinity, she lacks the necessary interest in politics."

Hayes drew a breath only to slowly expel it, his eyes narrowing as he looked from Clay to Amara and then away. But it was Amara's expression that caught my attention. She seemed to be showing something akin to guilt and sorrow as she averted her eyes from Hayes.

I had now spent many weeks in close companionship with both of them, and I knew they were old friends. But whatever was going on between them—exacerbated and stirred up by Clay's arrival—was obviously more complicated than I'd realized.

When I glanced at Nik, I found him watching the two of them thoughtfully. Did he know more about their history than I did? When he turned to look at me, I drew back, however, all thought of asking him forgotten. A discomfort blazed in his eyes, and I couldn't shake the feeling that if I touched it, I would be burned.

"The relevant point here is Delphine's strength." Nik stressed my name slightly. "Or, more accurately, that Grey is aware of her strength. He hasn't been able to access anyone as strong as her. And it's more than that, too. He's also intrigued by her wall."

"He knows about that?" Amara looked at me with concern.

I winced. I had freed myself from the fears that had kept me hiding behind the wall before confronting Grey, but when he tried to attack me, I had still reached for it instinctively. And it had successfully driven his power out of me.

"I had to use it to protect myself in our fight."

"This is the wall you had in Ostaria?" Clay asked. "You were able to use it to protect yourself against Grey's power?"

I bit my lip as I nodded, realizing that was a point I probably should have shared before now.

"I guess that's significant. Sorry I didn't say anything earlier. There was so much going on, and I just didn't think of it."

"And of course I didn't ask," Hayes said ruefully.

He threw Amara a glance. "Yes, yes, I know this is the

problem with how we train. There isn't a lot of room for innovation."

Clay sat back, rubbing his chin as he thought. "If the effect could be replicated, it would be significant. I was curious after meeting you in Ostaria and tried to do it myself, but I couldn't manage it. I was thinking it might be helpful for other apprentices in your situation, but healer assassins are a much greater threat. While rare, thankfully, they're extremely dangerous. Having a way to block them..."

I shifted uncomfortably, making Ember whine. Murmuring an apology to the fox, I slipped back to my original seat.

"Sorry," I said again, not sure what else to say to the shocking news that Clay had failed to do something I could do with ease.

Not that I'd used my wall in weeks.

"It's not your fault," Hayes said. "I should have asked more questions about your encounter with Grey. I'm the teacher, so it's my responsibility."

"No." Amara sighed. "Delphine is my apprentice, so it's my responsibility."

"Regardless of who has failed whom," Nik said coldly, "the important point remains. Grey knows she's strong, and for some reason he's been trying to gather strong healers. And he knows she has an ability he hasn't encountered before as well. To put it simply, Grey wants Delphine. Badly. And that's where our opportunity lies. We use his greed against him."

Amara stared at him with narrowed eyes. "You can't possibly be suggesting we hand Delphine over?"

"That is precisely what I'm suggesting." Nik said it calmly, not breaking gaze, but I could see the subtle shift as his jaw tightened, and the muscles across his shoulders flexed. He was pretending coldness and indifference, but something else lay underneath.

Amara stood in one fluid motion. "This meeting is over."

SIX

"Amara." Hayes spoke softly, his eyes pleading with her. "We should at least hear the prince out. I'm certain he doesn't want any harm to come to Delphine."

"I've spent a great deal of time considering the matter," Nik said. "If I could go in there myself, I would, in a heartbeat. I would have already gone. But Grey is cautious now in a way he wasn't before. Delphine is the only one he wants badly enough to take the risk."

"Even if he does want her," Clay said slowly, "why would he ever trust her? Didn't he stab her during their last encounter? Surely he's not such a fool as to think she would want to join him after that?"

"Not willingly, no." Nik looked to me. "That's where Miranda comes in."

"Ooh." Understanding slowly bloomed. "You want me to offer myself in her place. Like a prisoner exchange."

For the first time I could see the appeal of his plan.

Nik nodded. "It's the only believable reason you would go to him. And once you're inside his camp, you can find out the information we need—even better if you can get him to trust you."

"Even with an exchange..." Clay shook his head. "He'll be on guard around her all the time, surely? Will she really be able to learn anything of value?"

Nik leaned forward, his manner indicating he had thoroughly thought through every aspect of this plan. "Grey is a very confident man. I would write it off as foolish arrogance except that he really does manage to win people and situations over—even when it seems like they should be beyond his reach. Take Miranda as an example. She tried to escape him here in Caltor, and yet she now seems to have accepted her lot completely. She didn't make a single attempt to fight him or escape in their whole journey north. Grey believes in his ability to convince people, and that will work to our advantage. He might be suspicious of Delphine at first, but I don't believe he'll stay that way. If she makes it look like he's won her over, he'll believe it."

"How long is she supposed to stay there?" Luna asked, sounding horrified.

Nik's eyes lingered on me again. "As short a time as possible."

"And we're just supposed to let an eighteen-year-old face that kind of danger alone?" Amara asked.

"Of course not. We'll be there, too, as close as possible without being discovered." He hesitated, his jaw tensing again. "But there will be some risk. I can't deny that. And if I could think of any other way, I would never suggest this."

Something in Nik's expression made my stomach flip over. How long had it been since he'd found Grey's base? How long had Nik been resisting bringing this idea to us?

"And you think your father will agree to this strategy?" Hayes asked.

Nik was silent in response, and I snorted. "Telling the king wasn't part of your plan, was it?"

His eyes flicked between the three master mages. "If you

all insist on involving him, then yes, I think he'll agree. After all, we're only risking one apprentice mage in exchange for saving the whole kingdom." The derision in his voice made me flinch.

"That's not fair," Amara said in a softer voice than I'd yet heard her use with Nik. "Your father cares about his people."

"But he cares about his kingdom more." Nik's eyes were like stones, cold and unreadable.

A question flashed through my mind. Did Nik have experience with what—or who—his father was willing to discard for the good of the kingdom?

"That's his job," Hayes said. "He couldn't be a good king without that quality."

Nik stood, every line of his body taut, his eyes alight. "If you have something to say, just say it," he ground out.

Hayes continued to regard him with compassion on his face. "All I'm saying is that consulting the king is a necessity. We can't go racing off to attempt something like this on our own."

My brow furrowed. Where were the royal family in all this? Why were they only being consulted now?

"If this problem is so big," I asked the room at large, "why aren't the royal family coming themselves? Where's the king? Aren't they the most powerful mages we have? Maybe one of them could stop the blight without needing to involve Grey."

Hayes hesitated for a moment, casting a glance at Nik that was so quick I wasn't sure I'd really seen it.

"It's true they have great personal strength," Hayes said. "But the royal family are traditionally elements mages. And what is needed in this crisis is plants mages. I'm sure if one of them was a plants mage, they would send him."

The silence after his words vibrated with something unspoken and weighty, something I didn't understand. I looked at Nik and found him completely still, his eyes riveted on Hayes.

"Is that true?" he finally asked, in a voice I didn't recognize.

"Do you really believe they would have trusted me with this if...?"

Hayes held his gaze. "You would have graduated by now if you'd never left. You'd be a proficient—a powerful one, on your way toward mastery. I have no doubt they would have sent you. Although naturally, you wouldn't have been alone."

For a second Nik looked so tense I feared he might physically lash out. But instead he swung around, turning his back to us and striding toward the door. Once he had it open, he paused, speaking without looking back over his shoulder.

"Talk in your endless circles if you must. You'll see my plan is the only way that makes sense. When you're ready to take action, I'll be waiting. The rest of you can go to the capital if you insist on groveling before the throne. But Master Amara and Delphine must continue on in their usual way. We don't know what spies Grey may yet have, and we can't tip him off to our plan."

He finally glanced back, his eyes somehow both cold and alight. "Consult whoever you must, but don't put Delphine in danger by doing so."

Without waiting for a response, he stepped out of the room, shutting the door firmly behind him.

Hayes watched him go sadly. "So much potential wasted," he murmured under his breath.

"What happened?" I asked, finally mustering the courage to voice the question that had been burning inside me ever since I found out the truth about Nik. The question I knew I didn't really have a right to ask. "Why did a royal prince become a reneger?"

Hayes opened his mouth only to close it again and shake his head. When his eyes met mine, they were tired and sad.

"I think that's information he should tell you himself. When he's ready. If he wants to."

I flushed, looking away. Spending time in the company of

master mages and royalty made it surprisingly easy to forget who I really was—nobody of any particular importance. There was no reason for a farm girl from a remote part of the kingdom to be given information on the private matters of the royal family. It was only by chance I had even been included this much.

"Are we really considering it?" Luna asked. "Will we send Delphine to Grey?"

"His plan does have some merit," Clay said softly.

"Clay!" Amara glared at him.

He held up both hands placatingly. "Just think about it, Amara. We don't know why Grey wants powerful youngsters, but it's clear he has no interest in causing them any immediate harm. And Delphine is a healer—one who knows how to protect herself from other healers. I wouldn't consider it if she was defenseless, but she can both protect herself and heal herself if needed. Grey wants to use her, not hurt her."

"I can't believe we're considering this." Amara threw up her hands, but I could see she was starting to think about it.

But could I do it? Could I voluntarily walk into Grey's hands and turn myself over? I shuddered at the idea, remembering the feeling of his blade plunging into my middle.

More powerful still, however, was the image of Miranda's face as Grey dragged her away. I had rescued everyone else, but I had failed her.

And then I thought of my parents. The usual conflicting emotions surged immediately to the surface. But as soon as I pictured our fields covered in blight, the roiling confusion settled. I might not know how to feel about my father, but I couldn't bear the idea of our farm ruined in such a way. If I was the only one who could help the farmers of Tartora—and my friend along with them—I had to try.

"I don't know if I can do it," I said. "I don't know if I can convince him to tell me his secrets. But I'm willing to try."

"Delphine…" Amara put a gentle hand on my knee. "It isn't something you need to decide right now."

I smiled at her. "I'm not going to change my mind. Not unless the situation changes. We have to do something, and this seems like the best option."

I didn't add the rest of my thoughts. Nik didn't wish me harm. He was another person I had conflicting emotions about, but I was certain of that. If he truly believed this was the only viable option, then I believed it had at least a chance of working.

"Amara's right," Hayes said briskly. "There's no need to make any final decisions right now. Prince Nikolas himself said it's essential that Amara and Delphine head northeast in their usual way. That gives us time. Clay, Luna, and I can go to the capital and consult with King Marius and the Triumvirate. If they endorse the plan, they'll assign us guards. We can meet in Eldrida and make our final decisions there. If the situation has changed, or if you don't want to take the risk, Delphine, you can say so then. No one will force you to do this. If necessary, we can take Grey by force and find a way to make him talk afterward."

I knew my mind wasn't going to change, but I nodded. It was obvious the adults weren't going to accept my certainty until they'd had a chance to put it to the test.

"That means we have to split up." Luna gripped my hand, her face drooping. "I thought we were going to stay together for several more months."

"We'll see each other again in Eldrida," I said, patting her hand.

She scrunched up her nose. "Where even is that?"

I stared at her for a moment before remembering she hadn't been raised in Tartora. It was understandable she didn't know our kingdom's geography in great detail.

"It's our north-easternmost city," Hayes said absently. "On the coast, close to the border with Calista. North of Eldrida, the coastline is unnavigable, but south is safe to sail. There are limited safe harbors, though, and Eldrida is the largest of those. It serves as both a fishing center and a trading hub for the towns of the eastern hills. The eastern section of Tartora is good grazing land, but it's isolated from the rest of the kingdom by both the Viridian River and the dense forest that runs along its eastern bank."

Luna nodded, but I could tell from the glazed look in her eyes that she hadn't absorbed the impromptu lesson. No wonder she still didn't know Tartora's cities.

"The important point is that it's as close to Grey's base as we're going to get this side of the border," I said. "At least in terms of a large enough population that we won't draw attention."

Amara sighed. "I suppose I'll have to accept that plan. But make sure the king and the Guild know I won't be pressuring my apprentice into anything. And even if she's willing, I may still choose to withhold my permission."

I clenched my teeth, trying to read her expression. Would she really do that? I wanted to go, but if she refused me permission to leave, then going anyway would make me a reneger, like Nik.

I slowly relaxed my jaw. Nothing was happening immediately. I had time to convince her.

"In that case, Luna and I will leave for the capital in the morning." Hayes gestured for the door. "The rest of us should leave so our apprentices can get some sleep."

Clay nodded. "I'll head to the capital with you, of course." He followed Hayes out of the room, the two of them making travel plans as they walked.

Amara stood as if to follow them but stopped to give me a stern look. "No lying awake all night stressing, Delphine! We'll leave tomorrow as well, after I've consulted with Anka. So get as much rest as you can. You know what it's like when we're traveling. It might be a while until you find a bed as comfortable as this one."

I stood. "We're leaving just like that? But what about Nik? Don't we need to talk with him further? He's the one who knows where Grey's base is located."

Amara gave me an exasperated look. "Don't worry. If there's one thing Nikolas is good at, it's taking action. You heard him—he'll be ready. And there's no way he'll be going to the capital with the others, so I have no doubt that—like it or not—we'll be seeing him on the road."

She gave me a look that was too knowing—as if she was well aware which of those two categories I fit into—and then departed. Ember slipped through the closing gap in her wake, escaping for her nightly hunt before Amara closed the door.

"I know he's a reneger, but he's devastatingly handsome, isn't he," Luna whispered, punctuating her words with a giggle.

I hurried into my nightclothes to hide the flush in my cheeks.

"I don't know what you mean," I said, voice muffled by my clothes.

Luna laughed again. "You're not fooling anyone, Delphine! I saw all those loaded glances between you. The two of you were just as bad as those other three."

I emerged from my battle with my garments and sat on my bed, my eyes fixed on her.

"Do you know about the history between Hayes and Amara? There's something there, right? It's not just my imagination?"

Luna slid into her bed but lay on her side, her head propped up on her elbow and her eyes conspiratorially bright.

"Hayes has never spoken about her as anything more than an old friend, but I know there's more to it than that. I have eyes, after all."

I slipped between my sheets, also turning onto my side so I

could look across at Luna with wide eyes. "Are you saying he feels more for her than friendship?"

She dropped her voice to a whisper although we were the only ones in the room. "No one has told me directly, but I heard rumors at the Guild. Apparently they were apprentices at the same time, and Hayes was wildly in love with her!"

"What?" I gasped, clutching my blankets. But even as I felt the thrill of it, my more sensible self questioned Luna's excited interpretation.

It seemed hard to imagine anyone whispering such things about Hayes. But even if it wasn't quite the dramatic love story she was imagining, it seemed possible Hayes could have cared for Amara when they were young.

"Apparently lots of them were in love with her," Luna said, "since Amara was so outstanding. But she didn't have any patience for most of them, or for the Guild itself even. She was always speaking up against the way things were done. She only had time for two of her peers—" She paused in what was clearly meant to be dramatic tension before announcing, "Hayes and Clay!"

"Are you saying Clay was in love with her as well?" My mouth fell open.

"Apparently he wasn't as obvious about it, but most people think he must have been."

"So what about Amara? Did she have feelings for either of them?"

"She was good friends with Clay, but apparently she was closer to Hayes. According to the reports, they spent most of their time outside of class together. Some people even say that's why Clay left the capital and settled in Ostaria."

I gasped. "Because he was so heartbroken?"

"Maybe?" Luna looked delighted at the idea that our masters had such a thrilling history. "Or maybe he moved there because Amara never goes to the capital. At least in Ostaria, he gets to see her whenever she passes through."

I shook my head, not quite able to believe this flight of fancy. "But what about Amara and Hayes? What happened with them?"

"Everyone thought they would get married after they graduated, but instead Amara left her old master and the Guild behind and took up a traveling life."

"She just left Hayes?" I asked. "Why didn't he go with her?"

Luna grimaced. "That's the bit that everyone has a different theory about. I don't think anyone really knows what happened for sure. Amara just left, and Hayes was *devastated*."

She looked at the door which remained firmly closed before continuing. "Apparently, at the time, everyone thought it was such a pity and a waste—the general consensus was that her potential would be lost away from the Guild. They thought that on her own she'd never develop her skills much further. But then she reappeared in the capital only two years later, asking to sit the mastery exam. Everyone thought it was a joke until she actually passed."

My eyes widened and my lips curved upward as I imagined Amara's triumph. I wished I could have seen it myself.

"Hayes was the only one who believed she could pass from the beginning. So then everyone was convinced this time they would get married." Luna's shoulders slumped. "But she just left again. And all these years have passed, and Hayes has never been romantically linked to anyone else."

She flopped over to lie on her back. "At least that's what the people at the Guild say."

"He still loves her," I breathed, also lying down and staring at the ceiling.

Luna turned onto her side again, her grin back in place. "He must, right? Isn't it thrilling? And don't you think Clay still likes her, too? Why wouldn't he?" Her voice grew wistful. "I wish I could grow up to be half as amazing as she is."

"You will," I said firmly. "I know it. You'll be the Amara of the Calistan Mages' Guild."

"Do you think so?" Luna covered her face and giggled. But when she looked back at me, she wore a more thoughtful expression. "It feels surreal sometimes. All those years in my home settlement, I never dreamed I could have a life like this."

I nodded, knowing what she meant. "It feels surreal to me too—all the time. I was convinced the rest of my life would be spent on my parents' farm. And now I don't know if I'll ever live there again."

Even as I said the words, I knew they weren't true. I did know the answer to that question. Even without my issues with my father, my life had grown past the farm and there was no going back—not to live anyway. I had seen the way Amara and Hayes helped people, and I wanted to do the same thing. I had been given power when others had almost none, and I owed it to them to make use of my gift.

Luna sighed wistfully. "I just hope one day someone loves me enough that they would wait for me for fifteen years."

I sighed, imagining the love Amara had apparently given up all those years ago. She had told me once that she was alone on her travels but not lonely. I only hoped that was true and she didn't regret what she had given up when she chose the traveling life.

CHAPTER

SEVEN

As we prepared to leave the city, I kept a close watch for any sign of Nik, but I didn't catch so much as a glimpse of him. Unsettled and disappointed, I had no choice but to leave without speaking to him, trusting that Amara was right and he would also be making his way northeast.

Much of our travel thus far had been following the Celadon River. But when Amara and I left Caltor, we struck out northeast, moving away from the water. Our intention was to pass north of the capital and through the kingdom's northern farmlands. This was the part of the kingdom marred by the blight, and I was already steeling myself for the sight of burned-out fields.

We didn't encounter any until our second day of travel, however, and by then, I had almost forgotten to look for them. The stretch of black hit me hard, a stark difference compared to the waving green stalks on the other side of the road. Even the air had a faint acrid stench, although I wasn't sure if that was just my imagination, since the burning looked old.

The more I gazed at the ashy, blackened fields, the more my stomach churned, until I had to reach for my power to settle it.

Beside me on the front bench of our cart, Amara sat still—unnaturally so. I glanced at her face and caught the sorrow and concern in her eyes.

She met my gaze and managed a small, sad smile.

"I bet it hits you even harder," she said. "Since you grew up on a farm. So much effort wasted, and so much food lost."

I nodded, not ready to put my feelings into words.

"I've never lived on a farm," she continued, "but I've traveled among them for long enough that it's horribly jarring to see burned fields."

I kept my attention on her face, trying to ignore the glimpses of black in my peripheral vision. For the first time, it occurred to me to wonder where Amara had grown up. Somehow I'd never thought of her as a child. I knew a little of her apprentice days, but I hadn't thought further back than that, as if she had sprung into existence already experienced and powerful.

"Were you born in Tarona?" I asked, suddenly curious.

Her eyebrows quirked slightly, as if taken off guard by the question.

"I just realized I don't know anything about your childhood or family," I said. "Except that Anka is your aunt. Given both of you are strong mages, I'm assuming your family is a mage family based in the capital?"

She took a moment to answer, my curiosity rising further with each second of silence. Was I wrong? Was it possible that two powerful mages had come by chance from the same weak family?

"Yes," she said at last. "I come from Tarona."

I nodded, examining her face for any hint as to why that history gave her pause. It was the most common story for mages, especially master mages.

"Do you have any brothers and sisters?" I asked. It was the one part of her childhood I would envy her, if so.

She shook her head. "My mother wasn't the maternal sort."

I frowned, trying to parse out the layers of meaning in the statement. Did she have a bad relationship with her mother?

"She was an elements mage, like me, but not a master. She resented that."

"Did she resent your passing the exam, then?" I asked in a small voice.

"Resent it?" Amara laughed. "Quite the opposite. I only took it so early at her endless insistence. She was convinced I could achieve everything she had failed to achieve herself."

From her expression of distaste, it was obvious a young Amara hadn't appreciated the pressure.

"You keep saying *was*," I said tentatively. "Has she changed, or is she...?"

"She passed away many years ago," Amara said, matter-of-factly.

I blinked, trying to process that information. It was rare for a mage to die so young given their access to powerful healers. Even the regular populace rarely passed away so young unless they had a sudden accident or a chronic condition that required constant healing.

"I'm sorry," I ventured at last.

She closed her eyes for a moment, but when she opened them, there was no sign of moisture.

"It was a tragic waste of both a life and a gift that could have helped so many." She sighed. "But my mother was never interested in helping others. Her whole life was consumed by bitterness at the status and power she wasn't able to achieve. She married my father, a healing mage—despite looking down on healers—because he was a master. Something he didn't realize until after they were married."

She shook her head, whether at her mother's coldness or her father's foolishness in falling for it, I wasn't sure.

She gazed ahead, her eyes fixed on Acorn's ears as she

continued her story. "When he first tested me and discovered I had her affinity and his strength, she was triumphant—she'd achieved her aim, and she was determined I would be her pass to power and influence."

"That's awful," I whispered.

I knew what it was like to have a parent who twisted themselves with bitterness, but at least my father had always treated me with affection. Even his betrayal had been because he wanted to keep me with him.

Almost against my will, I felt a crack in the wall of my own bitterness and resentment. My father had done something terrible, but did that mean I had to poison all my memories of the good moments?

Amara looked sideways at me, a wry smile twisting her mouth. "You can see why I don't talk about my parents much. My father, at least, is warm and loving, but he never knew how to stand up to her. I've been telling him for years that he should marry again, but I think he's lost trust in himself after making such a terrible first choice."

I nodded, not sure what to say. Everything she was describing was entirely outside my experience.

"Since you're too polite to ask, I'll just tell you how she died," Amara said after a protracted silence. "It was after I'd left Tarona, so I only heard about it afterward. I wasn't surprised, though. She was always pushing her ability, convinced she was capable of more than she really was. She knew she couldn't win renown by being the strongest, so she was always attempting experiments, trying to discover something new."

She paused to shake her head, and I thought uncomfortably of the strange way I used my healing ability. It had never been my intention to win any sort of renown by being different.

"She was out on the Viridian River, apparently," Amara continued. "I don't know exactly what she was attempting, but she pushed herself too far and lost consciousness. When she toppled into the water, some fishermen saw her, but by the time they fished out her body and got it to a healer, it was too late for resuscitation."

"I'm sorry," I repeated again, and she merely nodded in reply.

Amara had clearly had a complicated and acrimonious relationship with her mother, but that didn't mean she'd wanted her to die. How had she felt when she got the news? I didn't dare ask.

"So now you know why I've never had any interest in politics," Amara said in a lighter voice after the silence had lengthened and softened. "Being hungry for power doesn't serve anyone—not even yourself in the long run."

"Do you think everyone interested in a position of authority is hungry for power?" I asked, thinking of Hayes.

She hesitated for a moment before sighing. "Perhaps not. I hope not. But it was what was modeled for me growing up, and I swore to myself early on that I would never be like my mother."

"So did you grow up living at the Guild?" I asked, hoping to steer into a less fraught conversation.

Amara nodded. "As a master healer, Father had a suite at the Guild big enough for my mother and me as well as his endless stream of apprentices. I'm glad for it since it means he's not alone now."

"He doesn't work in one of the capital hospitals?" I asked.

"No, although he'll assist on occasion if there's a special case. In general, he much prefers teaching, though. Now that my mother and I are gone, he has more apprentices than ever."

She gave a more natural-looking smile, and I tentatively smiled back. Her story had taken us past the edge of the burned fields, and despite the heaviness of what she had shared, it felt easier to breathe now.

"I can't imagine having apprentices of my own one day," I

said, twisting to pat Ember's fur where she lay curled just behind us in the bed of the cart. "One fox seems to be more than I can look after."

Amara laughed. "Don't worry. I used to find it equally hard to imagine and look at me now."

I smiled back, but it was impossible to see myself ever having the same poise and confidence as Amara.

"Will we be making camp by the road again tonight?" I asked, glancing at the lowering sun.

"I'm hoping for a proper bed, but no promises." She signaled for Acorn to increase her pace, but the mare merely flicked her tail and continued plodding on at her usual pace.

I stifled a giggle as Amara frowned affectionately at the horse.

"There's a village close by, then?" I asked.

She nodded. "It's a small one, though, so they don't have a proper inn. With so much of the kingdom's traffic using the rivers, the roads through this section aren't heavily enough traveled for regular, large inns."

"It's the same if you head east from Tarin." I glanced at the sun again, and then reached forward with my power, trying to sense if there were people ahead of us. "Will we reach the village before nightfall at this pace?"

Amara smiled ruefully. "I'm afraid there's not much we can do about it if not. Unless you think you can convince Acorn to speed up?"

"I wouldn't dare!" I grinned at the unbothered horse. "She might like me because of my healing affinity, but I don't think she likes me that much."

Ember stirred enough to let out a soft bark.

"See. Ember agrees."

Amara chuckled. "I'd almost believe that fox understands us at this point. She seems unnaturally canny."

I smiled affectionately at the curled ball of orange, black, and white in the back of the cart. "I couldn't ask for a better companion."

We lapsed into silence as the miles fell away. On our previous travels, Amara had pushed me to use the travel time to work with my ability. I had much better control now, and I was no longer a danger to myself, but I still fell into the old habit.

I could feel the upcoming village, a distant cluster of beating hearts and pumping lungs, and I monitored the distance, matching it against the setting sun.

"We're going to make it," I eventually announced with satisfaction.

Amara smiled, pleased. "You can feel the villagers? Are we getting close?"

"I think we'll be there in less than an hour."

Satisfied with the location of the village, I turned my attention away from the villagers and monitored the surrounding wildlife instead. There was an unexpected exhilaration in the ease of using my ability compared to those first few days and weeks of my apprenticeship. I really was gaining skill and control.

I breathed deeply, enjoying the endless stretch of sky around us which was showcasing the beginnings of sunset. Even the air felt clearer out here without buildings hemming us in. I had enjoyed the novelty of the bustling city, but these wide-open spaces carried the familiarity of home.

The whole atmosphere seemed designed to lull me into a state of calm and peace. Even the late summer air was pleasantly warm without being stifling. But I couldn't quite relax into the moment. Overlaid over everything was a sense of urgency that I couldn't shake. Miranda was out there right now with Grey, and we actually knew where she was at last.

My mind knew the reasons we had to move at our usual pace and understood she wasn't in any immediate danger, but I couldn't shake the desire to mount a swift horse and ride at full pace. How could we meander through the fields when the kingdom was in danger? How many more fields would end up burned before we got answers from Grey?

I forced myself to focus on a nearby flock of sparrows. Their darting bodies were always hard to track, and the concentration required distracted me from the sense of helplessness.

"Delphine." Amara's voice was quiet, but it carried an edge that broke through my focus.

After a brief glance at her tense face, I darted a look around but could see nothing out of place.

"Do you hear that?" she asked.

Now that I was paying attention, I caught what she was referring to—the distant sound of hoof beats pounding along the road at a gallop.

Amara was clearly waiting for something, so I reached out with my ability, trying to pick up as much information about the approaching person or persons as possible.

"It's a lone rider," I said after a pause. "Their heart is beating hard—even for riding at a gallop—but they don't seem to have any injury or illness."

"They're close, then?" Amara tightened her hold on the reins and guided Acorn away from the middle of the road.

"They must have come from the village."

While I had been distracted with the surrounding wildlife, we had nearly reached it. Beyond the approaching rider, I could sense a dense clump of people, although most of my attention was on the rider.

A slight bend in the road revealed a man racing toward us. He was bent low over his horse's neck, as if he hoped to marginally increase their pace by reducing his wind resistance.

Amara's eyes narrowed as she took him in, and she pulled Acorn to a gentle halt. The horse slowed agreeably, always happier to stop than to increase her pace.

The man was slower to see us, but as soon as he did, he shot bolt upright, also pulling on his horse's reins. The animal reduced his pace, dropping to a walk by the time he approached within easy speaking distance of the cart.

The man was dressed in a typical fashion for a farmer, but the quality of his horse told me he was a prosperous one. His eyes swept straight over me, discounting me because of my age, I assumed, and latched onto Amara.

"I don't suppose you're a healer?" he called in a rough voice.

Her shake of the head made him slump in the saddle, his expression that of a man who had been holding onto hope, however unlikely, and was starting to lose it.

He moved to spur his horse back to speed again, but Amara held up a hand to stop him.

"You're in need of a healer?"

The man pulled his horse to a complete stop, now nearly level with our cart. The hope had sprung back into his eyes at her question.

"Do you know where one can be found? Are they nearby? If I have to go all the way to Caltor..." He didn't have to finish that sentence for us to read on his face what a journey of that distance would mean.

"I'm an elements mage, but my apprentice is a healer." Amara gestured at me, and I tried to look less terrified than I felt.

If someone needed me, I would try to help—I had to. But the man's question reminded me there was no backup within reach, no more experienced healer to guide me.

For a moment the man looked taken aback and unsure, looking me up and down and no doubt noting my age. But it was a sign of his desperation that the hope had returned to his eyes.

"You're a mage, you say? So she is, too?"

He started suddenly and bowed awkwardly from the back of his horse as if he had only just remembered the formalities.

When Amara confirmed our status, he bowed again, the hopeful look in his eyes growing as he clutched at whatever straws he could. Clearly he hoped my strength would make up for my lack of experience.

"Are you in need of a healer yourself?" Amara asked, giving no indication she already knew the answer to the question from my earlier information.

"No, not me. It's my daughter. Back in the village."

"Your village doesn't have its own healer?" Amara asked with a frown.

"She doesn't have the strength," the man said as he slid from his horse's back.

I frowned at him, wondering why he was dismounting until he circled around to my side of the cart and held up his hands as if he intended to help me down. I turned wide eyes on Amara.

He gestured for me to hurry. "You take my horse. He's a strong one, and he can gallop a bit longer, but he'll go faster with only one of us."

"You want me to go on alone?" I asked, my fear rising even higher.

"Follow the road into the village," he said. "You can't miss it." He swallowed. "Or her."

I looked at Amara again, and she indicated for me to climb down.

"Amara," I whispered.

She held my eyes in her gaze, which was strong and calm. "You can do this, Delphine. And if you can't, that's not your fault. From the sound of it, you're this girl's only hope, so you certainly can't do any harm. You have to at least try."

I swallowed hard. "I have to try." Parroting her words let me pretend I could also mimic her strength.

Accepting the help of the villager, I scrambled inelegantly down from the cart and raced around to the saddled horse, who was breathing heavily and tossing his mane.

The stranger followed me and before I could ask for help mounting, he put both hands around my waist and threw me up into the saddle. I gathered the reins and paused for a moment to look at Amara.

She nodded. "Go, Delphine. We'll follow as fast as we can."

I took a deep breath, leaned low over the horse's neck and kicked my heels into his flank.

CHAPTER

EIGHT

The horse shot off faster than I expected, and I had to grab handfuls of his mane to keep my seat. I wasn't an elegant rider, but my childhood around farm horses had made me a functional one, and since my activation my skills had improved. I was more in tune with the animal beneath me now, able to sense the shifts in his muscles and adjust my own position accordingly.

Even so, we flew down the road at a breathless pace, and I wondered if the horse had picked up that I was scared. He was responding by racing home, unaware he was carrying me closer to the source of my fear.

My heart pounded in my ears, and it took all my self-restraint not to use my ability to slow it down. I knew better than to try that, though. Amara hadn't known the safety lectures usually given to new healers, but Hayes had been quick to fill in where she had lacked.

Within an impossibly short time, the outlying buildings of the village came into view. As promised, the main road ran straight through the center of the village, and at this hour it was clear enough that I barely had to check my pace.

But as we neared what looked like a central square, the

edges of a small crowd came into view. I frantically pulled back on the reins, and the horse responded instantly.

The sound of our arrival caught the attention of those nearest us, and their curious gazes fixed on me. Someone recognized the horse and set up a shout, and within moments everyone had deduced the meaning of an unfamiliar person riding a horse that had just left town in search of a healer.

By the time I slid down from the saddle, hands were reaching for me, propelling me through the press of people. I barely had time to ready myself for an unknown situation before I was thrust into the small space at the center of the crowd.

For a second, all I could see was blood. The red seemed to be everywhere, coating everything, and my vision swam, a roaring sound filling my head. But I was prepared for it. Pushing my power through my own body, I ruthlessly suppressed the reaction, washing it away.

Fear was still left in its wake, however. There was so much blood. Too much blood.

I forced myself to push the fear away as well, using my own determination instead of my power this time. Focusing on what mattered, I tried to assess the situation.

A young girl—not more than twelve—lay on the paved street near a small fountain. Mercifully, she had passed out because I had never seen a leg mangled as badly as her left one. I could only imagine how bad the pain had been while she was conscious. Had she had a run in with her father's farm equipment? If so, he must have carried her all the way into town. No wonder she had lost consciousness.

It took me another second to take in the older woman kneeling beside the girl. For a moment, I thought it might be the mother, but she was too old.

The woman looked up at me with wild eyes. "I can't get it to stop," she gasped out. "It won't stop."

Her hands and clothes were coated in the red, her face almost as ashen as the girl's. She kept her eyes trained on me, and I saw the moisture in them.

"All I could do was help her sleep." The tears welled enough to fall from her eyes.

I drew a shuddering breath, trying to make sense of the situation. That this older, experienced healer was looking to an eighteen-year-old with such desperation, her face pleading for help, told me more about the situation than I wanted to know.

It didn't make sense, though. A small village wouldn't have anyone with mage level power, but no one would qualify for the title of village healer unless they could at least staunch blood loss. She might not be able to heal the leg, but she should at least be able to keep the girl alive until she could be taken to a more powerful healer.

I dropped to my knees on the other side of the girl. Gripping her wrist, I thrust my power into her. My studies hadn't progressed as far as the level of reconstruction needed for her leg, but I had brute-forced my way through healings before. I would just have to do the same thing here, trusting in the instincts of my power to heal her.

But as soon as my senses reached her leg, the fire of my power quenched, slowing and dimming. I frowned and pushed more power into her, but where my ability should have blazed through her, it instead moved sluggishly, like a fire dimming and flickering from lack of air.

I rocked back on my heels, looking up at the other healer while keeping my hand on the girl's wrist. Now I understood the healer's desperation, even though I didn't understand how a young girl's body could fight me in such a way. I could barely make headway with all my strength; a regular healer wouldn't have been able to do anything at all.

All I could do was help her sleep, echoed in my head with the same tinges of horror as when it was first said.

I gritted my teeth. I refused to give up.

Leaning forward, I grabbed her wrist with both hands, pouring power into her. My fire burned and flared, pushing back against the resistance, making slow headway into her leg.

Beads of sweat popped up along my hairline and behind my ears. Gasping for breath, I kept pushing. I could feel the scope of the injury now, and I could already tell that even with the best will in the world, I couldn't pour enough raw power into her to fix her leg. I was fighting the tide.

I loosened my grip, thinking quickly. I wasn't a weak local healer, but the same principle applied. I only needed to stem the blood loss and keep her alive until she could reach a stronger healer—or in this case, a team of strong healers. I didn't have to heal her leg immediately, I just had to stop the bleeding.

Changing focus, I sent my power searching for broken veins, sealing each one as I found it until, at last, I sensed that no more was flowing out of her. With a final burst of effort, I helped her body produce new blood—just enough to stabilize her. As soon as I'd finished, I groaned, letting go of her and collapsing backward.

I lifted a hand to rub my face but stopped when I saw the red coating it. Lowering it again, I looked across at the healer.

Before either of us could speak, a higher, weaker groan sounded. We both turned to see the girl's eyes fluttering open. Lunging in unison, we reached for her arms, gripping a wrist each. But when the local healer saw I had taken hold of the girl, she released her, leaving the job to me.

Within seconds, the girl was returned to a deep sleep.

"Easier, in the circumstances, than blocking the pain and keeping her calm," I said in a breathless voice.

The woman nodded, and another woman stepped forward from the crowd. Sinking down to take the girl's head in gentle hands, she sat and rested it in her lap, heedless of her gown.

This woman looked a similar age to the man who had fetched me, and I suspected I had now found the girl's mother.

I looked from her to the healer, gesturing at the motionless child.

"Why...why is she like that?"

"You haven't felt it before?" The older healer understood immediately that I wasn't talking about the injury, but she looked surprised, peering at me in concern. "How old are you?"

"Eighteen. But I started my apprenticeship late. I was only activated a few months ago." I tried not to look self-conscious at the words.

The woman let out a huff of air. "A new apprentice? Then you have a master nearby? What brought you riding in here alone?" She looked up hopefully, trying to peer through the crowd, although she was still sitting on the ground.

"My master is coming in our cart with the girl's father." I glanced at the mother and then away. "But she's an elements mage. That's why they sent me on. I wouldn't usually try a healing like this on my own, but..."

The healer deflated, her shoulders slumping in defeat. After a moment, she took a fortifying breath, her manner turning brisk.

"If you're a new apprentice, you did well to manage as much as you did. You obviously have strength—which makes sense if your master is a mage. But cross-influenced..." She sighed and shook her head. "Still, we can be grateful for what we have because it's more than we looked for. This is Marla, Josie's mother, and I'm Esme. I'm the local healer here. I have rooms nearby, so I'll put some of this crowd to use and have Josie carried there."

"I...I'm Delphine," I said, still reeling from the strangeness of everything.

"We're mighty glad to meet you, child," Esme said. "You came along in perfect timing. I just hope you have strength left for what's next. At least we can do the next part less hurriedly. I have the tools we'll need in my rooms, and once I've caught my breath, I'll be able to guide you through the process. You won't have any experience with this, but you'll only have to provide the strength. I'll provide the skill. I assume you've worked in tandem before?"

I nodded, since that was the way Luna and I worked with Hayes when we learned techniques we hadn't tried before. But even as I was nodding, I held out my hands to stop her.

"Wait. What are you talking about?" I was still struggling to make sense of the situation.

"How can we?" The mother sobbed. "Oh, how can we?"

"Steady there, Marla." The healer clapped a hand on her shoulder, her voice at once bracing and gentle. "We thought we were going to lose her altogether. This is better than that."

"What exactly is better than death?" I projected my voice more forcefully, determined to get an answer.

The healer frowned at me and gestured at the injured leg. "We have to take it off, of course. Healing it is out of the question. You saw that for yourself. But I'm hopeful you have the strength to heal an amputation site, at least."

"Take off the leg?" I stared at her, appalled. "But she's only a child!"

I had heard of the phenomenon before but had never actually seen someone without a limb. It was only those whose limbs were crushed in the remotest locations who needed such drastic treatment. Usually healers could keep the person and the limb alive long enough to reach a hospital.

"It's true I've never done it before," the healer admitted, "but those of us without the strength to heal wounds outright learn wound management you mages don't need. Many of the same principles will apply."

"Wise mages learn all aspects of their ability," said a familiar voice, and my shoulders slumped with relief.

Amara had arrived, and I no longer had to bear the burden of this situation alone. I turned to her with a look that felt as wild as the other healer's expression when she couldn't stem the blood loss.

"They want to remove her leg!" I exclaimed.

"So I deduced." Amara frowned, taking in the situation more fully. "You weren't able to heal the leg?"

There was no judgment in her voice, but I felt guilt all the same.

"I don't understand why not. It was like her body was... resisting me."

I modified my language, avoiding mention of my power burning through the girl like fire. I had learned in Caltor that other healers didn't sense their power in the same way, and some were unnerved by such language. Amara would understand, since it was the influence of her elements power that had likely made me this way, but I didn't want to confuse Esme, who was listening intently.

"I didn't realize Delphine was such a new apprentice, or I would have warned her when she arrived," Esme said, interjecting into the conversation. "If she had started training on elderly patients, she'd have recognized it easily enough. But that's usually left until second year."

Amara's face crumpled, compassion filling her eyes. "She's been sick?"

The mother gave a soft, hiccupping sob. "From when she was three until she was eight. A blood disease. We had to travel to Caltor so many times because it kept coming back. But she's been clear for four years, and the doctor said it was finally defeated. It took three of them working together the last time, though. When she gets ill with all the normal childhood ailments, we have to keep her home instead of sending her to the healer like the other parents do. She can't do anything for her..." Her words dissolved into further sobbing.

I swallowed, finally understanding what I had been so slow to grasp. Although Luna had done some work with the elderly in Tarona, Hayes had planned those lessons for when I was occupied with Amara. New apprentices didn't work on the elderly because over time the body developed resistance to healing power. It was that resistance that meant even the most powerful healers eventually died. And the same effect could be caused by excessive healings.

The more a person had been healed—and the more extreme the healings—the harder it became to heal them. It was usually only a problem for soldiers who had experienced many years of training injuries and battle wounds, and for those who suffered from a small number of deadly illnesses that couldn't be cured by a single healing—the type that kept recurring as had happened to this girl.

Still...I shuddered to think how many healings she must have had to develop such intense resistance at such a young age.

"Is amputation really the only option?" Amara directed the question at Esme.

She pulled herself to her feet, groaning slightly as if she was too old to be kneeling on a hard road.

"When Delphine arrived, I briefly hoped...But it can't be helped. Better to lose her leg than her life."

I expected Amara to argue, to come up with some solution none of us had thought of. But instead she merely nodded, her lips thinning as she cast a sorrowful glance at the girl lying in her mother's lap.

"No!" I said stubbornly. "We can't! There has to be a way."

Amara sighed. "Perhaps there is. But I'm no healer. If there's an answer, I don't know what it is." She moved closer, her voice dropping lower. "I'm sorry, Delphine. I truly am. But this girl still needs saving, and the local healer clearly can't do it on her own."

Her eyes were sympathetic and understanding, but there was no give in her gaze. I had to be part of this whether I liked it or not.

I looked to the mother, thinking I'd have an ally in her, at least. If she protested, refused to give her permission, insisted someone ride for Caltor...

The father pushed through the crowd, his eyes leaping from his daughter's face to his wife's. She looked up at him with a tremulous smile, tears still streaking down her face.

"She's alive. This girl saved her."

The father almost collapsed in relief, the healer catching him under one arm and steadying him.

"We'll need to organize some of the men to carry her to my rooms. I believe this apprentice has sufficient strength to keep her alive once I remove the leg."

I expected the father to exclaim and reject the idea, and his face did flicker, his features sagging. But a moment later, he forced a smile, giving his wife what was clearly meant to be a look of strength.

"Josie will be all right. We'll help her adjust to it. She'll be alive, that's the important thing."

"No!" I shouted, unable to contain myself. "How can you say that? How can you restrict her life like that? How can you accept anything less than her full potential?"

Hands gripped my shoulders, shaking me until I fell silent, the whole crowd hushed in the wake of my outburst.

I was shaking all over, unable to calm my emotions. Defiant, I gazed at Amara's face.

"Delphine, control yourself!" she snapped. "This isn't about you!"

I refused to back down, though, glaring at her with all my overflowing outrage. How could they all agree to this so calmly?

Amara sighed, her grip on me softening.

"We can take her to Caltor," I said, reaching desperately for any option. "I can keep her alive long enough to get her there. They can heal the leg. She doesn't have to lose it."

Amara glanced at Esme, who slowly shook her head.

She didn't quite meet my eyes when she spoke. "You had to stop all the blood flow to her leg to prevent her bleeding out. Maybe you're too new to have learned yet, but a leg without blood can't last more than a few hours before it dies. Caltor is two day's ride. Even if you don't stop overnight and get there in one day and one night, the leg will be past salvaging."

I flushed, finally looking down. I did know that. I had read it in one of the anatomy books Amara bought me. I was talking wildly, from emotion and not reason, and everyone here must know it. I was reflecting badly on both myself and my master, but I couldn't seem to rein myself in.

Esme moved closer to Amara, giving me a sideways look as she lowered her voice.

"If she can't do it...If she's not in a fit state, or if she doesn't have the strength..." She grimaced. "I can't do it on my own, not with the patient's level of resistance."

"Don't worry," Amara said in crisp tones. "Delphine can do it. She just needs a moment."

I wanted to be grateful for her belief in me and proud of the strength she thought I possessed, but anger still raged through me, my embarrassment only adding further force to the tossing waves of my emotions. Everyone was so calm and rational— didn't they care? Did no one care that this young girl's life was going to be made small?

"Is there time?" Amara asked the healer. "Can you keep her sleeping for a while?"

The healer scratched at the side of her face, her eyes distant as she considered. "I can at least keep her asleep. That much I can manage. And it will take us time to get her moved and for me to get everything set up. You can have an hour, even two, if you must. There won't be any lasting damage in that time."

She glanced at the two parents, and even through the fog of my fury, I could read her expression. She and Amara believed that a longer wait would only be delaying the inevitable—a cruelty to the parents who were in great distress.

I tore out of Amara's hold and dove into the crowd. I thought I would have to push through them, but people parted before me, melting away to give me a clear path. When I looked at the wide-eyed stares and then down at my gown, now streaked with blood, I could see why. I seemed like a madwoman, beyond reason or sense.

I ignored them, breaking into a run as I dashed toward the edge of the crowd and the open fields beyond. I needed to get away, I needed to feel my legs pounding and my breath rasping harshly in my lungs. I needed to stop thinking, stop feeling, stop—

A hand grabbed at my arm, pulling me back so abruptly that my momentum carried me around in a half circle. I almost collided with Amara who had firmly planted her feet, a solid presence in the middle of my storming sea.

"Go," she said once I had steadied. "Run it out of your system if that's what you need. You have an hour." She took my chin firmly in her hand and forced me to look her in the eyes. "But you have to be back in an hour. I know this isn't easy for you. I know you haven't properly processed your own pain yet. But this girl's future has nothing to do with the choices your father made for you. No one is reducing this girl—they are saving her life. And they need you to do it. Delphine, do you hear me? You cannot leave this girl to die."

I stared at her, and she continued, unbending. "Promise me. One hour and you'll be back at that square."

I jerked a nod. "I'll be back."

As soon as I spoke the words, she released me, and I fled from the village as if wolves were chasing me.

NINE

For a short time I could see nothing but the field beneath my feet and hear nothing but my rough breath grating in my ears. Everything else had disappeared.

But as my legs began to burn and my breathing became more labored, the world slowly returned. My first awareness was of the animals around me. The wild ones had scattered at my frantic approach, but I could feel one familiar presence behind me, her heart pumping as she matched my speed. Ember.

Without conscious intention, my feet slowed. I wasn't alone. Faithful as always, the fox had followed me, expending the effort she would usually reserve for short dashes after prey. She knew nothing of the situation, she only recognized my distress. Just her presence brought a small measure of calm to my fevered mind.

But as soon as I slowed and started paying attention, I realized Ember wasn't the only one following me. A human was behind me as well, carefully keeping pace so as not to overtake me.

I kept my jogging steps steady, resisting the urge to look

around as I reached out with my power. Out here in the fields, running through the crops, there could be no mistake. Someone was following me.

My heart rate, which had finally started to slow, instantly spiked again, my already ragged breathing becoming frantic. Who had followed me out here and what was their purpose? I knew it was a man, which meant it wasn't Amara, but who else would have any reason to follow me?

If it was related to the injured girl, did they intend to force me back immediately, not trusting me to return on my own? Surely no one would want to block Josie's healing, so they couldn't wish to prevent my returning.

Or could my pursuer be unrelated to the incident? Had someone seen me running alone and thought I was weak prey?

Determination filled me. My hands clenched into fists and then stretched out again, my fingers extending to their fullest reach. As soon as my pursuer felt my touch, he would realize his mistake.

Steeling myself, I prepared to make a move. Better to take him by surprise than allow him to dictate the interaction. Readying my muscles, I jerked to a sudden stop, whirling in the middle of the field to face my pursuer.

It took the man several strides to process my abrupt halt, and by the time he slowed his forward momentum, he was close enough for me to grab his wrist. But at the same instant I made contact, I recognized his features.

"Nik!"

I let him go, my legs collapsing underneath me at the sudden release from tension. Cramping pain shot through my calves as they protested my recent intense and unusual activity.

"Whoa there!" Nik caught me under the arms, supporting my weight. "Are you all right?"

The pain in my legs made me wince and shake my head, even as my power reached for the seizing muscles. Within seconds, the pain had stopped completely, but I couldn't bring myself to take my own weight again. The reality of the situation was crashing over me, and the strength I'd feigned only moments ago was already being sucked away.

Nik stared into my face, his brow creased. When I didn't respond, he grunted and swept me into his arms, carrying me like a baby.

For a second, I considered protesting, but I didn't have the will. Instead, I wrapped my arms around his neck, burrowed my face into his chest, and shamelessly let him carry me. For a short while there was only the soothing warmth of his body and the rhythmic fall of his steps.

But all too soon he was lowering me into a sitting position on a large, sawn-off tree trunk. I blinked and looked around.

He had taken me to the edge of the field, aiming for a small cluster of trees that provided an area of shade. Someone had cut down this tree, but for some reason, the others had so far been spared.

I glanced from the grain in the nearest field to the low-lying crop in the next one over. Did they belong to different farms? I knew I was letting my mind wander to avoid the real issue, but I couldn't seem to muster the energy to stop myself.

An orange blur leaped from the ground into my lap, curling up and pressing her head against me. Tears immediately pricked my eyes as I wrapped my hands gently around the fox's body. Her soft fur was familiar and comforting in a way beyond words.

Nik knelt on one knee in front of me, his eyes worried as he examined my face.

"I saw Ember running, which is how I found you," he said after the silence grew too long. "I thought you might be in danger at first, but..." He trailed off, tactfully not mentioning that there had been no pursuer to fuel my desperate sprint. "What happened? What's wrong?"

"I…There was an accident…" It was all I could manage.

"An accident?" He went taut, his face tightening as his fingers slid up and down my arms, looking for an injury not visible to his eyes.

I shook my head. "Not me. A girl. In the town…" Again I struggled to go on, and he waited silently with a patience I hadn't realized he possessed. The same patience he must have used all those times when he watched Grey.

Taking a deep breath, I forced myself to speak, quickly relating what had happened as we approached the village and what I had found when I tried to heal the girl.

He listened silently, showing neither sympathy nor judgment, simply allowing me to get it all out. When I finished, he sighed, maneuvering himself onto the stump beside me and running a hand over his face. Instinctively I knew it was the sort of situation he hated—a life was hanging in the balance, but there was nothing he could do and no one he could fight.

It was the sort of situation that was supposed to provide a moment of glory for a healer, not a warrior. Except when it didn't.

"So there's nothing you can do to save her leg," he said at last.

"How can you say that?" The words exploded out of me. "How can they all just accept that such a young girl should lose a leg? She won't be able to walk or run or dance or…" My words broke off in a choking sob.

He took one of my hands in both of his, seeming to understand that my anger wasn't really directed at him. I looked up at him, my tears making his image watery.

"How can her parents do that to her? They should be fighting for her! It's their responsibility to save her!"

"Her parents…" He repeated the words softly, the look in his eyes impossible to read. For a moment there was silence, and then he squeezed my hand. "Your parents didn't protect you." He didn't say it as a question.

I heaved a shuddering sigh, my whole body trembling. There it was—the thing I had been trying to flee from. The quivering heart at the center of my raging emotions. And just like Amara, Nik had seen straight to it.

I looked up at him, struggling to comprehend this Nik who was both like and unlike the one I knew before. It was like him to see straight to the heart of the issue and to name it without prevarication or softening. But the sympathy in his voice and eyes was entirely new.

The two aspects combined defeated me completely. I deflated, my whole body collapsing inward, my shoulders sagging.

"It's not that they..." I tried again. "No one ever hurt..." I groaned. Trying to dance around the truth was hopeless. "My mother never did anything wrong, but my Father..."

Nik's hold remained gentle, but I could feel his body tense as he waited for me to continue.

"He tried to keep me small so that I would never leave our farm," I said. "He had his reasons for being afraid, but those reasons don't change what he did. He convinced me I should never be activated—telling me my squeamishness would cripple my ability to use my power. I thought it was a horrible joke that I, of all people, had been given a strong healing seed but no way to ever use it."

Nik's mouth fell open slightly, but he quickly recovered himself.

"You're squeamish?"

I blinked. "I never mentioned that?"

"I'm fairly sure I would remember," he said dryly.

"Oh, sorry." I considered. "I guess even after I discovered the truth in Ostaria, it was hard to shake the old habit of finding it shameful."

"I've heard it mentioned occasionally at the Guild. It didn't seem like something to be ashamed about."

"No, I realize that now. Once I had control of my power, it became easy to manage. And before that I had my—"

"Wall!" His eyes lit up. "So that's why you had one. I've wondered about that."

"Really?" I frowned at him. Did he really think about me when we weren't together?

He shrugged. "It's an unusual use of your ability. I don't think I've ever heard of healing power being used that way—and it seems like the kind of thing I would have heard of."

"What?" I asked, managing a light tone I didn't feel. "Did you think you were the only one who could come up with new uses of your ability?"

He looked uncomfortable enough that a real laugh escaped me. "Oh, don't tell me I'm right? You really did think that!"

He shifted slightly on the tree stump. "Of course I didn't think I was the *only* one. But you were a fresh apprentice, then. It didn't make any sense."

I shoved him lightly with my shoulder. "So you're relieved now that you realize I did it by accident because I'm weak, not because I had some kind of unparalleled strength?"

He met my eyes, his own serious. "I don't think you're weak, Delphine."

My stomach contracted, the momentary amusement dissipating.

"Well, that's a new tune," I managed, my fingers twisting in Ember's fur. "I thought you only valued me for my fox."

Nik looked away, and I suddenly, desperately wanted to know what he was trying to keep me from seeing in his eyes. For several silent seconds, I thought he would remain silent, but he finally spoke.

"I've been alone for well over a year now—first roaming the kingdom at will, and then pursuing Grey. For most of that time,

I didn't mind the solitude—in fact, I preferred it. I was convinced that my own strength was the only safe thing to be relied on."

He turned to look at me at last, but his eyes were veiled and hard to read. "I was even arrogant enough to think I could keep you safe as well as myself."

"Me?"

I frowned. Did he think he'd failed me somehow?

"I used to be furious that my family wouldn't acknowledge my strength," he said quietly. "But when I looked at you with Grey's knife coming out of your middle, I knew there was absolutely nothing I could do to save you. All my plants strength meant nothing."

"But it didn't matter," I said. "I could heal myself."

He sighed. "And I'm grateful for that. But what if you weren't a healer? I took you in there, and you could have died. Sometimes, our strength just isn't enough. You have a strong seed, but even the strongest healers have limits. Real ones—not the false ones your father tried to impose on you. You've thrown off his limitations, but that doesn't mean you don't have any."

I blinked, considering his words. I wanted to protest, but was it possible he was right? Did I think that by breaking free of my father, I could now do anything and save anyone?

If I truly accepted that nothing could save Josie's leg, it changed everything. Esme's face appeared in my mind, filled with desperation and grief as she knelt beside Josie. Unlike me, she knew this girl and her family. She clearly wanted to save her, and she had far more investment than I did. She also had far more experience as a healer—especially a healer far from a hospital. If she said this was the only option in the circumstances, I was sure she was right. No one was trying to manipulate or limit this girl. All they wanted was to save her life.

Guilt flooded me, followed by shame at my ridiculous behavior back in the village. I was a healer, and healers were supposed to help, not make an already tragic situation more difficult.

I jumped to my feet. "I have to go."

Esme had been right—the sooner we completed the healing, the better it would be for everyone. I couldn't dally out here in the fields. I had to get back quickly and help save that girl's life. And then I would have to apologize to Esme, to Amara, and to Josie's parents. At least Josie herself had been unconscious and oblivious to my outrageous response.

Nik stood as well, grabbing my arm.

"Delphine, I'm sorry. I didn't mean to offend you. I—"

I let him pull me toward him, smiling up at him. His words faded as he took in my expression.

"I'm not upset with you," I said. "I'm upset with myself because you're completely right. And that means I have to go back and face the mess I made."

I swayed toward him, wanting to lean against his chest and soak in his strength and warmth. I was just pulling myself together and straightening when his arms swept around me and clasped me against him.

I melted into him. His chest and arms tightened, squeezing me closer, and my name escaped his mouth on a breath, as if he hadn't meant to utter it. For one second, my eyes fluttered closed, and I allowed myself to relax and imagine staying here forever.

But then I forced my eyes back open and pushed against him. For a brief moment, he held on tightly, not letting me go. But with a quiet groan he released me.

"You have to go." His eyes sparked in the gloom of dusk, and my heart quickened.

"I have to go," I repeated, as much to myself as to him. But I hesitated for one last question. "How are you here, turning up just when I need you most?"

"I told you back at the inn that I would be waiting and ready to act. I've been with you since before you left Caltor."

"You have?" I shook my head. "Amara said something like that. She was expecting to meet you somewhere on the road. You should have joined us instead of lurking behind."

But even as I said it, I remembered why he couldn't. We didn't know what eyes Grey had watching us or what tales he might be receiving. Amara and my travels had to look natural.

I looked around, suddenly alert in the way I should have been all along. But I could see no one else in the rapidly gathering darkness.

"Go," Nik said softly, giving me a light push in the right direction. "And don't worry. I'll be watching over you until you're safely back in the village."

I nodded, wanting to say too many things but not having time for any of them. Glancing at the setting sun, my feet took off of their own volition. Anything I had to say would have to wait. I was needed to save a life.

CHAPTER

TEN

"You need to rest." Amara's firm but gentle voice reached through the haze of my exhaustion.

"But I need to—" I looked at Josie, still unconscious in the bed, and realized there was nothing left to do.

Had I been working for hours, or did it only seem like hours? A glance at the window told me it was dark outside, but I didn't know how late.

They had all been waiting for me when I returned, the anxious look on Esme's face bringing back the uncomfortable feelings of shame. After my behavior, she hadn't been sure I would return. But Amara's expression told me she, at least, had never doubted me. And her confidence filled me with determination. I wouldn't let her down again.

Her clasp on my shoulder told me she understood the remorse in my face, but I wasn't selfish enough to start my apologies immediately. I had an important task to do, and seeking forgiveness would have to wait until no one's life was in danger.

Josie's parents had wanted to be present, but thankfully the healer had convinced them to leave with several of the villagers. Since Josie was still safely ensconced in assisted sleep, she had no need of their comfort, and once Esme removed the cloth covering her tools, I was grateful no family members were present.

If I hadn't been fully prepared to squash my squeamish reaction, I would likely have collapsed myself just at the sight of them. And I had further reason to be grateful to Esme as she took me through the operation with a calm professionalism that grounded me. She talked me through everything she was doing as she removed the damaged limb, at the same time using her power to demonstrate what she needed me to do inside Josie's body.

She didn't have the strength to change anything inside Josie —not with the level of Josie's resistance—but she went through the motions, her power guiding mine. Following her direction, I provided the strength to actually complete each step of the healing.

We sealed her leg just above the knee, regrowing the skin and burning out the infection that had already crept its way into her blood. As we worked, I sank so deeply into the healing that I didn't realize how tired I was until I finally pulled free. I had been so determined to redeem myself that I had freely poured in my strength, fighting against Josie's natural resistance. Only once I felt Amara's hand on my shoulder did I realize I was swaying, barely left with the energy to stand.

"It's time to rest," she said again. "Josie is healed."

I gazed down at the girl, who looked so painfully small beneath the light blanket covering her. Her face was peaceful in sleep, but how would it look when she awoke and discovered what we'd done? I had helped save her life, but I wouldn't be the one to guide her through all the grief and adjustments to come. It felt like I was walking out on the hardest part of the journey.

"Do you ever feel bad?" I asked Amara. "Changing someone's life and then just walking away? Adjusting to change isn't easy."

Amara put her arm fully around my shoulders, helping to support my weight.

"Sometimes I do," she admitted. "Sometimes I feel a pull to stay somewhere just a little longer and a little longer again. But if I did that, those would be the only people I ever helped. There are certain things I can do that most others can't, so I have to use those skills in a strategic way. I can't do everything for everyone."

I shivered, hearing the echo of Nik's words in hers. I couldn't deny their truth, but they still hurt. I didn't want to face the reality of situations my healing power couldn't fix.

"You did well," Amara said softly. "I'm sorry I couldn't go with you earlier to help you process your emotions. I should have been there for you, but if we'd both left...But you obviously did well on your own."

I shook my head. "I had the help I needed." She looked at me oddly, but I pushed on. "I'm sorry, Amara. My reaction was childish and inappropriate, and my accusations were untrue. I let my response to Josie's situation become tangled up in my feelings about my father when it was never the same issue. Please forgive me."

"Of course." She pressed her cheek against the top of my head, the uncharacteristic motherly gesture making tears leak from my eyes and down my cheeks. "You were already forgiven. In the first few months of your apprenticeship, you've been put into far more stressful situations than most Guild apprentices see in their whole two years. And you're still dealing with deep hurt from what happened with your father. The wounds we received from our parents are hard enough to process at thirty-five, let alone eighteen. I don't expect you to be perfect, Delphine." She shifted me slightly so she could look me in the face, her eyes grave. "But you will need to apologize to more than me."

"Of course!" I looked around, but Esme had already disappeared. "Did Esme go to get the parents? I could talk to them all now..."

Amara shook her head. "First you need to sleep. Everyone will be here in the morning."

I wanted to protest, but one look at the dark night sky told me she was right. I let her lead me to one of the nearby houses, too exhausted to take note of its features. Someone had prepared beds for us, and I sank into the clean sheets, merely grateful for a soft pillow and proper mattress.

When I finally woke again, I was more aware of my surroundings, but there was nothing to distinguish the neat home from any other village dwelling. Neither was there anyone else present. Food had been left out on the table, however, and I wolfed it down ravenously. Only once I'd filled my belly did I grow alert enough to realize why I was alone—I'd slept away half the day.

I washed my face even more quickly than I'd eaten and hurried outside. I expected to have to search the village for Amara, but the house sat only one street from the central square. Like the day before, it was filled with people, although the atmosphere was very different.

I hurried into the crowd, noting that all evidence of the previous day had disappeared. Even the cobblestones had been cleaned by some compassionate hand, and the mood was one of good cheer.

In the center of the group, sitting on the edge of the fountain, was Josie. She was perched on a cushion, a plate full of fruit beside her, and a smile on her face.

I stopped, staring at her in confusion, and Amara appeared at my side.

"The whole village is feting her today," she murmured

quietly. "So there's little room for grief or sadness. Although that will come, I'm sure. But clearly she has people to support her, and that will make a difference. She'll have sorrow, but she can still have moments of happiness as well—just as we all do."

"Today the village wants to remind her that her loss doesn't have to define her or steal her future," Esme said from my other side, having approached close enough to hear Amara's words. "The hardest part will come once the attention and sympathy dies down. But Josie's a strong lass, and I have no doubt she'll find her way through it."

I nodded, wondering uncomfortably if I had that same strength. I hadn't shown it the day before, but I wanted to in the future.

"Thank you, Apprentice Delphine," Esme said suddenly, filling me with fresh embarrassment. "I'm well aware I couldn't have managed yesterday without your fortunate arrival."

I shook my head rapidly. "Please don't thank me! I'm more than aware I owe you an apology instead. I acted as if you wanted to do something terrible when you were only doing your duty as a healer. I let my own history and issues overcome me. Please don't count my disgraceful behavior against my master. She's trained me better. I was the one to fail."

Unsure what else to do, I gave a respectful bow.

"Goodness, all of this isn't necessary, child." She placed a comforting hand on my shoulder. "You don't spend a lifetime as a healer without learning that some wounds can't be seen by the eye or felt by our power. What matters is that you came back, and you did what needed to be done. You were an excellent student, in fact. I didn't expect it to be so easy to guide you, given how new you are." She hesitated, as if she'd intended to say something more but thought better of it.

"And given how strong she is?" Amara asked in an amused tone.

The healer gave a reluctant chuckle. "Aye, that's right."

"What do you mean?" I looked back and forth between them. "Surely my strength made it easier. And as for following healing instructions, Master Hayes has me well trained by now." I grinned at the woman, confident that even a country healer would know Hayes's name.

"Ah, that explains it!" The woman smiled. "He was never one to stand for any nonsense."

"I am not one to favor nonsense either," Amara said, clearly still amused. "Plus Delphine has never even been to the Guild."

"Never been to the Guild?" The healer stared at me in astonishment.

"She was born to southern farmers and signed up for a traveling apprenticeship with me directly from her home," Amara said.

"Well, well, well." The woman clucked her tongue. "I know apprenticeships outside the Guild aren't much in favor, but clearly they should be if they produce students like Delphine. I'm due for one of my annual visits to the Caltor hospital soon, and you can be sure I'll put in a good word on the matter to the healing mages there."

"I'd appreciate it," Amara said with a genuine smile. "The more voices, the better. Change is slow to come, but I'm hopeful we're in a season of it at the moment."

"I'm still not sure why my strength would be a detriment," I said, not entirely following their conversation.

The healer chuckled and clapped me on the shoulder again. "You're one of the good ones, Delphine."

She wandered back into the crowd, leaving Amara to give me actual answers.

"Unfortunately, strength often comes with arrogance," she said. "And arrogance doesn't pair well with learning."

"Oooh!" I felt dense for needing it pointed out. As soon as she said it, I could picture exactly the sort of mage student I'd always imagined the Guild filled with. My old expectations had been so different from the actual mages I'd met that I'd started to forget them—especially since so much of my thinking had been shaped by my father. But clearly my preconceptions hadn't been entirely wrong.

"Of course not all the Guild students are like that," Amara said, "even the strong ones. Just look at Hayes. It's easy to see he was never that kind of student."

"Not to mention you," I said, shaking my head at her humble focus on Hayes. "You're the very opposite of everything I imagined powerful Guild mages to be."

"We can't express how grateful we are that a Guild mage was on hand," a new voice said, making me start.

I whirled around to find both of Josie's parents standing hesitantly to one side.

"Thank you so much for saving our daughter," Marla said. "I don't know what your fee might be, and I'm afraid we might not be able to..." She trailed off before rallying quickly. "But of course we'll find a way to pay it, whatever it might be."

"Oh no, no!" I held up both hands. "I'm only an apprentice, and I couldn't possibly..." I stopped as I suddenly remembered that as an apprentice, it was my master who set the fee for my services. It was how they paid for the expenses of housing, feeding, and training us.

I glanced at Amara to find her watching me with amusement.

"Given the circumstances, I don't think there's any need to talk of a fee," she said. "It was a valuable learning experience for my apprentice."

"Oh yes!" I agreed gratefully. "And please allow me to apologize to you for my behavior yesterday in the square. I allowed myself to become emotional and to unfairly accuse you. I want you to know it was never about Josie or her leg. It was my own issues, and it was terrible of me to allow those to intrude on such a difficult moment. Please accept my heartfelt apology."

"Did you behave terribly?" The mother turned her blank expression on her husband who looked equally clueless. "To be honest, it was all so traumatic, I remember almost nothing. From the moment of the accident through until I had my baby healthy in my arms again, I can only remember snatches. I was certain that..." She stifled a sob, and her husband put an arm around her shoulders.

"From what we've been told, she would have died without you," the father said. "You saved her life, and that's all that matters to us."

"Thank you." I gave them the same half-bow I'd given the healer. "I'm most grateful for your understanding."

After a few more protestations on both sides, someone appeared to take their attention, and I turned to Amara.

"Everyone here seems to be excessively understanding."

She smiled. "I've noticed that happens after you save someone's life. Especially a child."

"I'm sure you've had plenty of experience with that, even if you aren't a healer," I said, remembering the way she had held back the flood that nearly swept us both away.

"You'll soon have grateful friends of your own across the kingdom." She grinned at me. "Maybe you'll even decide you like a roving life yourself. I hope you do. Tartora could do with more traveling masters."

I shook my head. I wasn't ready to think about a future as a master.

"I'm just glad everything worked out this time. If the poor girl is ever injured again..." I winced.

Amara looked across the square at where an older lad was doing a jig, making the girl laugh.

"I spoke to the parents earlier. This was the final straw for them. They did everything they could to hold onto their farm, but they're going to sell it now and move to Caltor. If their daughter is injured again, she'll be able to be rushed to the hospital there where a team of healers can work on her."

I nodded, relieved at the news. After yet another major healing, I suspected Josie would be beyond the efforts of any single healer, no matter how powerful. Moving to the city would be a difficult adjustment for the family, no doubt, but it was the only safe course.

"Will we stay here long?" I asked, hesitant but trying to keep it from my voice. I had already made enough of an emotional fuss.

Amara smiled at me knowingly. "Of course we've had several offers of accommodation for as long as we want it, but I think this village is in enough uproar. I thought we would move on as soon as I've finished some consultations with the village leadership over the pathway of a nearby stream. And once you've recovered your energy, of course."

"Oh really?" I brightened. "I already feel fine after that enormous sleep. We can leave as soon as you like."

Amara grinned at my hopeful expression, and I tried to school myself into neutrality. It was probably cowardly of me to run away, but it was painful to be so conscious of my bad behavior while everyone kept plying me with gratitude and praises.

"I should be done within an hour or so," she said.

I gazed toward the edge of town. "Would you mind if I went out walking while you finish your business? I feel out of place here."

Amara gave me a piercing look, but after a moment she sighed and nodded. "Try not to get into trouble while you're out there."

I frowned at her. She didn't usually worry about me being a troublemaker. Had her view of me changed after my foolishness the day before? But she threw me a knowing smile that didn't seem to match that thought.

I was still trying to work out what she meant as she moved away toward a small clump of village elders. I turned my own feet toward the edge of town, nearly making it to the edge of the first field before I remembered what I had let slip the night before. I had told her that someone else helped me process my emotions. Given her smile, she must have had a good idea who that person was.

My cheeks heated although there was no one left near me to see it. I didn't stop walking, though. My last conversation with Nik had been cut short by the urgency of the moment, and I would far rather continue it than linger awkwardly with the villagers.

CHAPTER

ELEVEN

This time I didn't run, but I did hurry straight to the clump of trees we had sheltered under previously. The sawn-off tree stump stood waiting, but I skirted around it. Casting a lingering glance at the apparently empty fields around me, I pushed into the middle of the trees. There were just enough of them to provide screening from watching eyes, something I had foolishly not thought about the day before.

I just had to hope Nik was on the lookout again today and had seen me arrive.

The minutes ticked by, and I tried to restrain my growing impatience. What if he hadn't seen me? I could spend hours waiting fruitlessly among the trees. Should I go somewhere more visible?

"No Ember today?" a deep voice asked, making me jump.

"Nik! You startled me!" I put a hand on my chest, tracking my racing heartbeat.

"Sorry." His expression didn't match the apology. Was he amused by my fright?

"Ember sleeps at this time of day usually." I paused. "I wasn't sure if you were coming."

"Of course." He said it simply, as if it was the sort of fact that required no further explanation.

Something warm grew inside me, wiping away the irritation at his earlier amusement. I had come trusting Nik was watching for me, and I had been right.

"What happened?" he asked. "With the injured girl."

I rubbed my eyes with remembered exhaustion. "It was a long operation—I'm sure my inexperience didn't help with that. But it was successful. Her health is stabilized now, and she's not in any more danger—at least not from this injury. Her resistance will have grown even further though, unfortunately."

He nodded, but something in the way he looked at me gave me the impression he was more interested in how the healing had affected me than in the future of a girl he didn't know.

"My great-great grandfather did a good thing building the hospitals," he said after a moment. "But there's a shortage of healers in the towns and villages."

I raised my eyebrows. "I didn't realize you noticed that sort of thing."

"What's that supposed to mean?" He sounded stung. "Just because I operate alone doesn't mean I want everyone else to die."

"No, of course not." How had I managed to get off to such a bad start? "I didn't mean that. It just seems like the kind of detail that..."

"Those with a plants affinity are most drawn to farming," he said, not meeting my eyes. "They suffer disproportionately."

I considered his words, slowly nodding. It was true the affinities weren't evenly spread across the kingdom. There were always people of all three affinities in any village, but villages located in farmlands always had more with a plants seed.

"Someone has to think of the people the crown has forgotten," Nik muttered, and my eyes snapped back to his.

What was lurking behind that comment? Gathering my

courage, I blurted out the question Hayes had refused to answer in Caltor.

"Obviously you don't travel alone because you hate all people, but I have no idea of the real reason. I can't make any sense of why a royal prince is roaming the kingdom alone."

Nik's eyes tightened, and I stood in silence, wondering if I'd gone too far.

"I've had my share of traveling with others," he said finally. "And I prefer it this way. There's no one to let you down if you're alone."

My heart sank at his words, and it took all my willpower not to reach my hand up to cup his cheek. He looked so strong, but his words told me how much pain was hiding behind his appearance.

Stepping forward, I took one of his hands in mine. "I know people can let you down." I only had to think of my own recent behavior to remember that. "But is it really better to always be alone?"

Nik hesitated, looking down at our clasped hands with an expression I couldn't read. "I used to think so," he said quietly.

"But not anymore?" I struggled to keep my voice even.

He looked up at me. "I found an ally. And then I went off without her, and it was different from how it was before. I used to be satisfied with protecting people from the shadows—I preferred it even. But this time..." His hand shifted, twisting so that now he was the one holding onto me. "I missed having her beside me."

"Your ally..." I murmured. The word felt cutting—someone useful for his mission and nothing more—and I needed that reminder given the way my heart leaped at his other words.

I looked away, afraid of what he would see in my eyes. If I was honest, I had felt an attraction to Nik almost from the beginning, but this new sympathetic, almost vulnerable side of him was appealing in a whole different way—dangerously appealing, considering he was a prince who viewed me only as an ally.

"Sometimes allies don't let you down," he murmured. "Sometimes they make you stronger."

"I want to be that kind of person." I tried not to relive my recent lesson in humility. "But you've known from the beginning how weak I am."

"I don't think you're weak, Delphine." His words pulled my gaze back to his. "When I said you were strong yesterday, I didn't just mean your seed. Everyone has weaknesses, but that doesn't have to mean you're weak. Sometimes weaknesses can turn into strengths. Like with your squeamishness causing you to create the wall. You achieved something amazing, and you only did it because of your weakness."

"So what about you?" I asked, hoping to distract him from the rising heat in my cheeks. "Have you accepted your own weakness?"

His eyes stayed steady on mine, his expression piercing. "Didn't I already say that? I long ago realized that what I thought was my weakness was the most valuable thing to me."

The warmth in my cheeks heated to burning, and no words came. He couldn't possibly be talking about me, could he?

"Your father was fighting the tide trying to suppress you, Delphine," he murmured. "He was never going to succeed. After all, you even managed to win me over."

He flashed me a smile that hit my heart like a thunderbolt. I drew in a gasping breath of air, and his eyes dropped to my lips.

A feeling of panic engulfed me, and I stumbled into speech.

"You now know what my father did to me, but what about yours? How did he fail to protect you?"

He managed to keep his face still, but his whole body stiffened, his muscles snapping tight, as if ready for combat.

"What are you talking about?" he asked stiffly.

I gulped. I hadn't meant to say anything, but I was committed now.

"Last night you saw straight through the nonsense I was spouting to the heart of my real issue. I guess it seemed like you understood me so quickly because you knew how it felt. And since you chose to leave your title and family in favor of roaming the countryside alone, I thought...If I'm wrong, I'm sorr—"

"My parents might be king and queen," he said abruptly, "and they might have power most other families don't, but in some things their hands are tied. They never lied to me. I don't claim my situation is the same as yours."

"But they still hurt you." I examined his face, trying to read the emotions hidden in his eyes.

He shrugged and looked away. "Everyone gets hurt sometimes."

His words were clearly a dismissal of the topic, and it stung after his earlier moment of vulnerability. I looked down, wondering if I should pull my hand free. I shouldn't have pushed so hard.

When I looked back up, Nik was watching me. He had clearly caught my reaction to his words, and his face had softened in response.

"Sorry," he said quietly. "Like I said earlier, I've gotten out of the habit of accommodating other people. You're right that my family let me down, but it's a complicated situation. They weren't the ones to act against me." He paused, pulling his hand free and turning completely away from me. "But perhaps if they'd ever believed in me..." He sighed in frustration, running a hand through his hair.

I watched him from behind, taking in the lines of his straight back and broad shoulders. It was hard to imagine Nik ever feeling weak and helpless, but something in his manner told me he knew how those emotions felt. And I didn't need him to tell me to know he'd hated them.

His shoulders straightened, and he turned back to me. Seeing my expression, his lips curved upward. "I can read all your emotions on your face, you know." He said it humorously, but the tender note beneath nearly undid me.

I needed to extract myself from this situation before I did something even more outrageous.

"I need to get back," I said hurriedly. "Amara and I are planning to continue traveling this afternoon, and she's probably finished her meeting by now."

Nik took a step back, nodding. His face closed off, the moment of openness between us over.

"I guess I'll...I'll see you on the road. Maybe. If we can—" I gestured vaguely at the trees around us before finally cutting off my stumbling words.

"Goodbye, Delphine." There was a shadow in his eyes I didn't want to interpret.

I fled back across the fields, telling myself I wasn't running away. But even I didn't believe it.

And as I went through the motions of saying our farewells to the villagers, the feeling of having disgraced myself grew. Why had I panicked and rushed off? What was Nik thinking of me? It was hard to contain my roiling thoughts while accepting a second round of thanks and polite niceties.

When our cart rolled past the last of the houses, I let out a long breath of relief.

"Are you that happy to be gone?" Amara asked.

I gave an embarrassed grimace. "I know I shouldn't be. And if we'd been needed, I would have stayed. But being there with the villagers, it was hard not to think about the scene I made yesterday evening."

A dreamy, reminiscent look came into Amara's eyes. "I remember a southeastern village where I thoroughly disgraced myself in the early days of my travel. I still haven't been back there."

"You disgraced yourself, too?" I asked.

Amara laughed at the enthusiasm in my voice. "Don't worry. We're all fools in our youth, one way or another. There have to be some advantages to aging. I just hope your experience will leave less of an enduring stain than it did for me. I wouldn't want to have to avoid this village in future, given its position on this road. I suspect we'll be back within your apprenticeship, let alone after."

I smiled, my mood rising now we were on the road. "I'm sure time will help. My mistakes won't sit so heavily on our next visit."

"Ah, optimism—another characteristic of youth." Amara's eyes danced as she surveyed the road ahead.

"You're not actually that old, you know." I narrowed my eyes, considering adding a comment about what Hayes and Clay would have to say about the matter but decided to refrain. I felt comfortable with Amara, but I wasn't sure I felt that comfortable.

We fell into a companionable silence, and my attention moved to our surroundings. Once the village fell from view behind us, I looked for any sign of another traveler shadowing our progress, but I could see no sign of Nik. When I reached out with my power, I could sense no one behind us on the road. An occasional person was located in the surrounding fields, but I couldn't distinguish between the local farmers and Nik, so I couldn't identify which one was him.

I refused to consider the idea that none of them were. He had to be out there. He had promised. And I needed to show him that I could behave normally again.

When we set up camp for the night, well short of the next village, I half expected him to appear. But again there was no sign of him. I could sense another traveler out of sight, but I couldn't be sure it was Nik. Especially given he gave no sign of stopping for the night. If it was him, he should be resting and not roaming around in the dark.

I would tell him so the next time I saw him.

"You seem unusually jumpy." Amara looked at me with suspicious eyes. "Are you expecting someone?"

I quickly refuted the suggestion and decided to stop reaching out to the countryside around us. Ember had already disappeared into the darkness, but Amara wasn't going to let me follow her, and there was nothing I could do to make Nik appear. He would show up when he was ready.

CHAPTER

TWELVE

I slept fitfully, but my dreams were about accidents and mangled limbs rather than the absent prince, so I couldn't blame him for my poor rest. Amara took one look at my face when we woke and thankfully refrained from any questions.

We packed up quickly and got back on the road. As the sun rose higher in the clear blue sky, my lingering exhaustion fell away, and my mood lifted.

I took a deep breath, stretching my arms high. "There's something about clear skies and broad, open spaces that's freeing."

Amara looked sideways at me and smiled. "Whenever I leave a town and get back on the road, it's always such a relief. But strangely, whenever I ride into a town, heading for a proper bed and a hot bath, I feel the exact same relief."

She chuckled, and I joined her. I had been on the road for a much shorter time than Amara, but I already knew the phenomenon she described.

"I used to think I was happy at home on our farm, but now I wonder how I endured the monotony."

Amara launched into some lighthearted stories about her

own childhood adventures in the capital, and before I knew it, we were stopping for a midday meal. We decided to take the time to prepare a warm meal since we had several nights on the road ahead of us, meaning we had no particular destination that needed to be reached that night.

While Amara established the fire and heated the food, I wandered away in search of the brook I could hear burbling nearby. Amara's elements ability could probably have told me exactly where to find the water, but I preferred to stretch my legs and find it myself.

We had stopped on the edge of a small stretch of trees in order to make use of the shade, but the trunks grew densely enough to conceal the water from my view. Following my ears proved successful, however, and the narrow stream had just come into view when a different sound caught my attention.

Although the cry wasn't especially loud, the series of sharp, rapid notes clearly indicated distress, the intensity of the sound rising as I stopped to listen. Reaching out with my power was instinctual, but it took me a moment to identify the source of the strident call: a bird—and a big one from its feel.

I changed course, moving as quickly through the trees as the undergrowth allowed. Ember, who had roused from her usual daily sleep when we stopped, stayed near my heels, her ears pricked and her nose raised to the wind.

When I finally reached the location of the distressed creature, I realized I had struggled directly through the heart of the thicket and come out the other side. It would have been faster to skirt the grove and avoid the undergrowth altogether.

All such thoughts fell away when I spotted the bird trapped in a dense section of bush. Interlocking branches and long thorns had entangled the wings and feet of the enormous creature, holding it captive.

My early studies, under Hayes's guidance, had focused on human anatomy, so I had yet to learn all the different species of animal found in Tartora. However, I knew enough to recognize the bird as some kind of eagle. I had rarely seen one with such a large wingspan, however.

At the sight of me, the eagle let out another series of harsh notes and flapped its wings. I fell back a step, awed at the bird's size. At full stretch, it would be wider than I was tall.

But the movement only caused thorns to tear into its wings, and the bird fell still again, letting out another, more desperate call. I hesitated, but my compassion soon drove me forward. There had to be a way to free the bird.

Ember hung back, letting out a low whimper.

"Don't worry, girl," I said softly. "I won't let that beak near me."

Even as I said it, I eyed the sharp, curved beak warily. The claws were even more worrying, but with the bird's legs caught in the undergrowth, it would have little chance to use them.

Streaks of red marred the luxurious feathers, but there was no use healing the bird if I couldn't free it. I bit my lip as I examined the tangle of greenery. How had a high-flying creature like an eagle gotten caught in the first place? It wasn't likely to have come zipping beneath the canopy like a smaller bird.

I put the matter from my mind as I focused on the more immediate issue.

"How am I going to free you, good sir?" I asked aloud, tapping my fingers against my belt.

They brushed against the leather of my dagger's sheath, making me pause. Drawing the thin blade Nik had gifted me for my birthday, I smiled at the sight of its sharp edge. I had worried about the sort of circumstance that might require me to use the weapon, but this was a use that made me glad to have it—even if Nik scolded me later for dulling the blade against branches and vines.

"Now just hold still, good sir," I murmured, trying to reinforce my calming tone with overlays of my power.

I had no idea what I was doing in that regard, however. I had heard of healers who managed to attract animals to them with their power, but I didn't know how to do it. Without physical contact, I could identify the bird's presence, but I didn't know how to affect its mood.

I pushed my power outward, attaching to the sense of the bird and hoping that somehow it would sense me back. All I needed was for him to recognize me as a friendly presence and stop fighting.

At first, I thought it had worked. The eagle stilled, regarding me through one beady eye. But as I stepped closer, he resumed his thrashing motion, letting out a cry that was louder than the reedy calls I'd heard so far.

I held out both hands, letting loose a flood of pleading words in my most gentle voice. But it made no difference. The bird, too dazed with pain to recognize my intent, only thrashed harder.

Tears ran down my cheeks as fresh red appeared along his feathers, and I fell back several steps. The bird instantly calmed again, and I took a deep breath. I needed to think of another way, but my mind was coming up blank.

I grunted in frustration, kicking my foot against the ground. What use was all my power if I needed physical contact to use any of it? I was sure if I could just get a hand on the bird, I could calm him.

I continued to push out my power, blanketing the whole area in it, as if that would make a difference. After a while, the eagle seemed to calm further, so I risked moving forward again.

As before, he waited until I was close before launching into frenzied movement, this time swiping his head forward and nearly catching me with his sharp beak.

I leaped back with a quiet shriek that slipped out without my intending it. Ember whined her protest, pressing herself against my leg. I sighed and crouched down, resting a hand against her back.

"What are we going to do, girl?" I asked. "We can't just leave that fine fellow there, trapped like that. He'll die for sure if we can't rescue him."

Ember growled quietly, and I scolded her.

"I'm sure he's never eaten any of your relatives, so you needn't talk like that."

With a sigh, I straightened again. I had to find a way to get close to the bird.

A sudden shrill, chattering call pierced the air as a blur fell from the sky. On instinct, I threw my hands up to protect my head. We didn't get many eagles down south, but we had plenty of merlin falcons, and I recognized the cry, although I had no idea why one would be attacking.

As my mind caught up with my body, I pulled my arms down, my eyes flying to the trapped eagle. Had the falcon perceived his cries as some kind of threat? They were remarkably agile and aggressive birds, and even in the air they wouldn't be discouraged by the larger size of an eagle, let alone now, when its opponent was trapped and helpless.

"Wait! Stop!" I cried, jumping forward and throwing out my arms, as if to shoo the newcomer away.

Even as I moved, I recognized the futility of my actions. But to my surprise, the falcon had already pulled up, flying out of reach of the eagle's snapping beak without having touched the other bird.

My mouth fell open as the falcon swooped in a second time, flying fast and low as it sped toward the eagle, only to pull up at the last moment and fly away, once again with the same chattering call. I tried to remember when I had last heard such a noisy falcon and failed. Something about this bird's behavior was extremely strange.

As I watched, still frozen in shock, the falcon swooped a

third time. The eagle waited until the smaller hunter was close, snapping its head forward at the last moment and nearly catching it. The falcon swerved out of reach, however, pulling back out from under the trees.

Staring at the eagle, I realized all of his attention was now focused on the falcon as it dived in and swooped back out, constantly threatening attack, although it never actually touched the eagle. For a startling moment, an impossible thought ran through my mind. Was the merlin doing it on purpose to distract the eagle for me?

Surely that couldn't be the case, but the opportunity was there, all the same. I hurried forward, making sure I approached on the opposite side to the merlin, who was in the process of diving back toward the eagle.

The trapped bird was still, waiting for the right moment to strike, and I lunged forward, grabbing the largest vine trapping it and sawing at it with my dagger. As soon as it gave way, I seized another, sending a silent apology to Nik as I continued to misuse his blade.

When the second vine gave way, only a small branch remained. As the falcon chattered and dove, I gripped the branch in both hands and snapped it cleanly in half.

The moment the wing was free, the eagle swept it forward, nearly knocking the merlin from the sky. Dodging at the last second, the falcon escaped.

The eagle flapped, off balance now that it was partially free. He couldn't go far, however, since his legs were still held in place. I scrambled forward, trying to crawl beneath the freed wing. Red dripped on me as I did so, and my breath caught. How injured had the eagle become in his time in the bush?

I considered stopping and grabbing his wing, taking the time to heal the scratches and tears, but he was further damaging himself with each flap as he tried to pull free of the undergrowth. And the merlin might disappear at any moment, taking away my opportunity.

Gripping the dagger more tightly, I reached for the tangle of thin, thorny branches that trapped the eagle's legs. The seconds stretched out as my sweaty hand slipped on the dagger's hilt. It wasn't designed for a sawing motion, but I eventually managed to cut through the last of them.

As the final whip-like branch gave way, the eagle lurched free, tearing his other wing out of the ensnaring vines. His sudden movement knocked me over, sending me sprawling across the ground. I barely managed to fling the dagger free before I landed on top of it, the breath momentarily knocked out of me.

As soon as I could move, I rolled over and scrambled backward across the ground, gazing at the eagle in consternation. I had intended to grab hold of the final wing and heal the bird before freeing him completely. I hadn't realized the second wing was less ensnared than the other limbs.

He turned on me, his eyes unnaturally bright as he made a flying hop in my direction. I scrambled further back, trying to work out why he wasn't taking off now he was free.

He gave the same alarm call I'd heard previously, but it was even quieter and more reedy than before. And the flow of red had become heavier instead of tapering off as I'd expected in the absence of the thorns.

Staring at his body in horror, I realized I'd misunderstood the situation. His bleeding hadn't been caused by the minor scratches from his captivity. He had clearly sustained major wounds—most likely in a fight with another eagle—and his struggles had merely been exacerbating those wounds.

My hand flew to my mouth as I realized I'd made a grave error. When the falcon distracted the eagle, I should have used the opportunity to heal the trapped bird instead of focusing on freeing him. But since I hadn't made direct contact with him, I'd failed to realize the extent of his injuries.

I instinctively tried to move toward him, but he beat his wings powerfully, driving me back again. Tears sprang to my eyes as more blood flowed from his body. No wonder a majestic eagle had ended up trapped in the underbrush. He must have been driven down during the fight, perhaps even unable to fly. It also explained why he was still on the ground now.

He hopped toward me again, and I scrambled back even further only to collide with a tree trunk hard enough to make my head spin. I gasped and rubbed at the back of my head, staring into one of the bird's bright eyes. It wasn't a natural expression, and with a sick feeling I realized his behavior from the beginning had been the fevered madness of a dying animal. If he'd been merely trapped, my power would likely have calmed him. But he certainly wasn't going to let me near him now.

Tears dripped down my face, but before I could give way to the grief, he stumbled even closer, and a more primal fear swept over me at the sight of his sharp beak and claws.

He lurched forward, swiping at me with his beak, but a blur raced through the air, spearing straight for the eagle's head. Rearing back, the larger bird swept his wing around and finally caught the falcon. Knocked from his path, the bird was flung against a nearby tree, falling like a stone to lie at its base.

"No!" I screamed, trying to scramble toward the collapsed falcon.

But the eagle moved to block me, managing to lift itself off the ground so it could reach for me with its talons.

I flung up my hands to protect my face, but a growl from the ground beside me made me scream.

"Ember, no!" I flung myself sideways, landing protectively over the small body of the fox.

She tried to slither out from under me, but I clasped her in both hands, curling over her and leaving my back exposed to the eagle. I braced myself to feel slicing pain across it, but instead I heard running feet, a thud, and then unsettling silence.

Pushing off the ground, I peered back at the eagle. It was no longer standing or hovering but lay still on the ground, one wing spread out and the other trapped beneath it. It wasn't moving.

I scrambled up and raced over to it, pressing my hands against the closest feathers. But my power didn't respond when I tried to push it into the bird. There was no life left for me to connect with.

"No, no," I sobbed, trying again. But I was too late.

I looked up at Nik, the source of the running feet. He stood beside us, sadness in his eyes as he looked at the broken bird.

I scrambled up and threw myself at his chest, beating it with my fists.

"What did you do? How could you? You killed him!" Tears streamed down my face.

He captured my hands, stilling me. "It was a mercy."

I shook my head stubbornly. "I could have healed him."

"You had to be touching him for that. Were you going to let him kill you while you worked on him? He was too far gone to see you as anything but a threat."

I pressed my face against his shirt and sobbed again. A gentle hand stroked my hair, and somewhere in the back of my mind I remembered our first few meetings and wondered how we'd ended up here.

"Even if it hadn't been a mercy for the animal, I would have acted to protect you, Delphine," he murmured against my hair, and a shiver ran through me.

A moment later, a sudden thought made me push against him, staggering backward and staring around. Before Nik's arrival, someone else had protected me first.

My eyes found the falcon, and I raced toward him, Nik only half a step behind. As I dropped to my knees beside him, I held my breath, desperate for him to still be alive.

"Please, please, please," I murmured to myself as I laid a gentle hand against his feathers.

My power connected with him, and I nearly collapsed with relief. But the relief didn't last long.

I had never healed a bird before. I'd never even connected with one, and his system was unfamiliar and strange. Too much of him seemed to be lungs, his hollow bones structured around air sacs that seemed to fill most of his body. Vaguely I remembered a comment Clay had once made about birds. They didn't breathe like a human or a fox, with their lungs inflating and deflating. They should maintain constant volume, not lie still like an empty balloon.

Grasping the thought, I let my instincts take over, pushing air through the falcon. As it moved through his body, my power followed, healing the crushed airways and sacs.

He twitched beneath my hands, the movement growing until he shook his head and hopped to his feet, regarding first me and then Nik with one beady eye. I pulled back and gazed at him in return.

"Is he healed?" Nik asked, sounding equal parts fascinated and wary.

"I think so," I said cautiously. "I don't know much about birds."

For several seconds of silence, the three of us continued to regard each other.

"But I do know there's something strange about this one," I added.

Quickly I explained his behavior to Nik, detailing how he had helped me, first by distracting the eagle and then by launching a true attack to protect me.

"I've never seen a falcon act like that," I finished.

Nik rubbed at his jaw. "It's unusual, certainly, but not completely beyond the scope of what I've seen before."

"You have?" I stared at him.

He leaned forward, and I expected the healed falcon to dodge back, but the animal held his ground, one of his eyes glued to Nik.

"Aha! I'm right!" Nik sounded smug as he pointed at the merlin's legs. "Do you see how one is darker than the other?"

I examined the yellow coloring, quickly seeing what he meant. One leg was definitely darker than the other.

"That's strange." I frowned. "I've never seen a marking like that before. Does it mean something?"

Nik nodded. "There are a couple of healing mages at the palace who raise and train falcons. I don't know how they do it, but they somehow change the color of one leg so that anyone who comes across one in the wild knows it's a trained bird."

"They change the color of its leg! How is that possible?"

Nik shrugged. "You're the healing mage."

"Apprentice," I grumbled, once again feeling my ignorance acutely. "And I've barely learned anything about animals."

"They're intelligent birds, and the ones raised by healing mages are even more so." Nik gave the falcon in front of us an even closer examination. "Did you send your power out seeking animals to help you?"

"Not intentionally." I grimaced. "I don't really know how to do that."

"If he was raised by a mage, he probably responded to your power, regardless of your intentions. You probably feel familiar to him."

"But does that mean he belongs to someone?" I asked tentatively, reaching beyond the trees for any indication there was another human nearby.

"Not if he's all the way out here." Nik held out his arm, bent slightly and parallel to the ground. The falcon responded immediately, hopping onto it and preening. "I'd guess his trainer died while this bird was still young, and he's been on his own for a while. You can see he has a different look from a kept bird."

"I'll have to take your word for it since I've never seen a trained falcon before." I slowly climbed to my feet, shaking myself off.

Looking down at my traveling gown and bedraggled hair, I grimaced. I looked a complete mess.

Ember trotted over to us, growling quietly as she watched the falcon on Nik's arm.

"Stop that," I told her sternly, accompanying the words with a glare. "Phoenix is one of us now." I glanced at the bird. "If he wants to stay that is."

"Phoenix?" Nik raised his eyebrows.

"You know, rising from the ashes and all of that. It seems fitting." I ran a hand along the soft feathers of the bird's back. "He will want to stay, won't he? If he was raised by a person and lost them?"

"Given you just did a major healing on him, it seems likely." Nik glanced down at Ember. "At least if she's anything to go by."

Ember gave a small whine and trotted off around the edge of the grove, heading back toward our makeshift camp.

"I think she has the right idea," I said wearily. "I'm sure we could all do with some food, and Amara must be wondering where I got to. But we can't just leave..." I looked at the motionless eagle, fresh tears welling in my eyes.

I gave Nik a pleading look, and he nodded gravely. He didn't say anything, but a moment later the earth beside the eagle began to move. Within seconds, the remains of the magnificent bird had disappeared, swallowed by the ground. Only a patch of disturbed dirt showed the location of his grave.

"I couldn't just leave him to be..." I faltered. "It's my fault, you know. If I'd just paid more attention, I could have healed him while he was still trapped. I'm supposed to be a healer, and I didn't even realize how badly he was injured."

Nik placed a hand on my shoulder. "Don't do that to yourself, Delphine. What happened wasn't your fault. You put yourself in danger to try to save him which is more than anyone could ask of you."

He held my gaze, his expression compelling me not to look away. "Do you think the limitations of circumstance are any less real than the limitations of your strength? No healer has ever lived who could heal everyone of everything. And we would know," he added sardonically, "since they would still be alive, healing themselves into immortality."

I drew a deep breath, holding onto his words as I pulled myself together. He was right. Animals died all the time in the wild, and there was nothing I could do to change that. It was a fact I'd always known, but even as a child I'd struggled to reconcile myself to it. Clearly, I was going to have to learn, however.

Phoenix ruffled his feathers, eyeing me from his place on Nik's arm. I managed a smile for the proud-looking bird. At least I could take comfort in having managed to save him.

Once I was sure I had myself under control, I followed in the direction Ember had taken, planning to circle the trees this time. But I halted when I realized Nik wasn't keeping pace.

I looked back at him. "You are coming, aren't you?"

He hesitated, and I walked back to grab his free arm and pull him along.

"We haven't passed anyone on the road all morning. There's no one to see you with us. You can at least have some hot food."

"I'm fine. I can—" A rumble from his stomach made him fall silent.

"See, your belly knows what's best for it," I said in my best imitation of Amara's firm manner. "You can go skulking off on your own once you've eaten."

"Skulking?" Nik murmured under his breath in disbelieving tones, but his feet followed me, so I let it go without comment.

As we rounded the trees, he picked up his speed until we were walking side by side, Phoenix between us. He looked from the bird to me and sighed.

"What would have happened to you if this gentleman hadn't been on hand? Why do you insist on throwing yourself into danger whenever you see the opportunity?"

"I couldn't just leave that poor creature. He would have died —" A shudder passed through me. But even knowing the eagle's end, I couldn't have just walked away and left him there.

"Didn't you even think about your own safety?" Nik asked sourly.

I looked at him, warmth filling me.

"No," I said simply. "I didn't need to think about it because I knew you would."

"Me?" He looked sideways at me, a guarded expression in his eyes.

I nodded. I hadn't thought about it in so many words, but ever since Nik had appeared in the fields near the village, I had been conscious of his watchful presence, just out of sight.

"It might have seemed like I was walking alone in the woods, but I felt safe because I knew you were watching over me."

"I nearly didn't get there in time." Nik's words came out low and gravely, as if he was judging himself.

"But you did arrive in time," I replied with a smile. "You always do." I patted the sheath at my waist, my smile brightening. "And I found a good use for this."

"That's not why I gave it to you," he grumbled, but a small smile played around the corners of his lips.

"Delphine! There you are!" Amara's exclamation made us both stop. "I was about to ask Ember to lead me to you. What took you so..." Her mouth fell open as she saw the state of my dress and hair. "What in the kingdoms have you been—" She cut herself off for a second time when she finally noticed Nik, Phoenix still perched on his arm.

"It's a bit of a long story," I said. "But we have two extras for the meal."

"A prince and a merlin falcon." Amara shook her head. "I should be surprised, but somehow I'm not. Sit down and tell me from the beginning."

THIRTEEN

Amara had prepared a simple stew, but she made me scrub my hands and face before she let me taste any of it. I could see the concern in her eyes, so I told the story as simply as I could, pausing only to shovel in mouthfuls of bread and stew.

"And so you've been following us," she said to Nik at the end of my tale. "I wondered."

He gave her a closed look. "I told you I would."

"Not in so many words!" I protested, nudging his shoulder with mine.

He didn't respond at all to my attempt at playfulness, eating with quick efficient movements.

"His Highness clearly didn't see any value in going to the capital," Amara said dryly. "I surmised the rest."

Nik met her eyes, his expression hard. "I don't have patience with wasting time."

"But you do want to see Delphine protected."

He continued to meet her gaze without flinching. "I will ensure it."

For a moment, the crackle of the fire was the only sound.

"Because she's essential for your plan," Amara eventually

said lightly. But her eyes remained serious, as if she were probing him.

"I will always make sure Delphine is protected," Nik's voice sounded like granite, certainty in every line of his face, but I still struggled to make sense of his words.

They hadn't exactly been a denial of Amara's statement. But there was something so sure in the way he spoke about me.

I shoved another spoonful into my mouth, glad of an excuse to look down at my bowl. Since his return, Nik seemed like a different person—but only when we were alone. Around others, the old hardness and arrogance were still there.

I didn't know what to make of it. Why was he so different with me? He had told me he thought about me during his absence, had even suggested he missed me. And I couldn't ignore the new softness in his manner toward me. But neither could I be sure what it meant.

"So you intend to join us now?" Amara raised an eyebrow, her manner still challenging.

Nik shook his head. "As I said in Caltor, you need to make your travels toward the border look natural. Having me with you would destroy that impression."

"And yet, here you are."

"That was me," I said quickly. "I insisted he come for a meal. We haven't passed anyone on the road this morning, so there isn't likely to be anyone overtaking us while we eat."

"I'll be leaving as soon as I've finished," he said.

"Not straight away!" I protested.

When both of them gave me a surprised look—Amara's with a hint of censure and Nik's a spark of amused pleasure—I hurried on. "You clearly know something about caring for falcons. You need to instruct me before you disappear!"

"So this one is staying permanently?" Amara reached out a cautious finger to stroke along Phoenix's back. "I suppose I'm going to have to resign myself to accumulating a menagerie by the time your apprenticeship is finished."

I gave her a guilty smile. "I'll try not to adopt any more wild animals into our ranks, but Phoenix is different. According to Nik, he was bred and raised by a healing mage, so I couldn't just abandon him in the wild for a second time. Not if he wants to stay with me."

"A trained falcon?" Amara looked at Nik who nodded confirmation.

In short tones, he outlined the reasons for his assumption, including his guess that Phoenix had lost his master during the bird's adolescence.

"Oh yes! I'd totally forgotten about the legs." Amara leaned closer to peer at the different tones of yellow between Phoenix's two legs. "I used to see the falcons around the Guild sometimes when I was a child and apprentice. It seems like a long time ago now."

"So he can stay with us?" I asked eagerly.

She smiled indulgently. "How could I turn away such an aristocratic fellow?"

Phoenix chose that moment to preen, as if he'd understood her words, and we both laughed.

"Welcome to our makeshift family, Phoenix." I pointed first to Amara and then to Ember. I didn't know what I was doing, but I tried to put the weight of my power behind my words when I added, "The fox is not for eating. And that goes for you, too, Ember. No bothering your new brother."

Phoenix blinked, training one eye on Ember. After an extended tense moment, he ruffled his feathers and placed his head along his back as if he meant to sleep.

"I think that's agreement," I said with a laugh.

"He reminds me of someone," Amara muttered, glancing at Nik, who pretended not to hear her.

We each had seconds, no one seeming to want to hurry the

end of the meal, and Nik waited while I changed my gown and tidied myself up before he told me the little he knew of caring for a falcon.

"Since we'll mostly be traveling through open countryside, he shouldn't need much care," Amara said. "He can hunt for himself and otherwise engage in activities normal for a wild falcon."

"Like Ember." I placed a hand on the fox, who was still regarding our newest arrival with displeasure.

"It's fascinating how they bond with you," Amara said. "I'm only now realizing how little I know about a healing mage's connection with animals. Since most mages live in the capital, or at least one of the larger cities, I'm not used to seeing them interact with wild animals. I regret not finding the time to ask Clay more questions about it."

"I'm not sure Phoenix truly counts as wild," I said. "And both of them were near death when I healed them. I don't think I could just bond with any wild animal I came across."

Tears pricked my eyes as I thought of the eagle. If I could only have formed even a loose connection with him, I could have calmed him enough to save him.

"It's not your fault." Amara put a hand around my shoulders and squeezed. "You can't save every animal any more than you can save every person."

I glanced at Nik. They both kept saying it, and I knew they were right, but I was still dreading the day I experienced losing a person. Every healer eventually had to deal with patients they couldn't save, but thankfully they didn't put new apprentices in those situations.

"If you start accepting it now, it'll make it easier later," Amara said softly, as if reading my thoughts.

"Can something like that ever be easy?" I asked.

"Not easy." Nik reappeared from where he'd been making Phoenix a makeshift perch in the back of the cart. "Death is never easy. But healers and warriors both have to find ways not to be crippled by it."

I looked at the ground. I didn't want to think about what experience Nik had with death, or about the deaths to come in my own future. Today's had been hard enough.

"You're still young," Amara said softly. "You'll learn." She turned to Nik. "I suppose you'll be close by, Your Highness, even if you're out of sight?"

My head snapped up. "You should join us at night."

Amara gave me a quizzical look, but I kept my attention on Nik, remembering the person I had sensed roaming through the darkness the night before.

"Once we set up camp for the evening, if there's no one else around, it would be safe for you to join us, wouldn't it? I know you can't in the villages, but when we're camped by the road..."

Nik glanced at Phoenix, perched in the cart bed, and then back at me. I noticed he didn't look at Amara.

"I suppose that would be safe enough."

I turned a pleading look on Amara. "It makes more sense than setting up two camps and preparing two meals, don't you think?"

"I think...His Highness is welcome anytime we're alone."

I breathed a sigh of relief, but she took a step closer to Nik and continued in a stern tone. "As long as I'm around, that is. I overlooked the other evening because Delphine was in crisis, and it's obvious you helped her, but I think the two of you have done quite enough meeting up alone at night."

I gulped. "So you did know I saw Nik then?"

She gave me an exasperated look. "I'm neither inexperienced nor foolish. I didn't say anything because whatever he said seemed to help you. But I haven't forgotten the damage done back in Ostaria and Caltor. I'm responsible for you during your apprenticeship, Delphine."

"I understand," I said quickly. "I didn't mean to do anything behind your back. I had no idea Nik was watching us so closely, so I didn't even think of it, but he saw me sprinting through the fields and thought I was in trouble."

"If it's safe, I'll reappear tonight." Nik gave me a half smile, the warmth in his eyes sparking an answering warmth in me. But his fire cooled to ice as he turned to Amara and gave a barely respectful half-bow. "Tonight, then."

Before either of us could respond, he strode away, disappearing into the trees.

"I can't work him out," I said quietly, staring after him. "Sometimes he seems to have changed completely, and then other times..."

"His manner masks it, but he's still young," Amara murmured back. "You've shaken him, Delphine, and he's not used to that."

"Me?" I turned to her. "What do you mean?"

She gathered the last of our things, checking the fire had been fully extinguished.

"Prince Nikolas has always been overly confident. From what I've heard, his twin sister is the only one of his peers he ever liked or respected. And his relationship with her has always been...complicated."

"Complicated how?" I climbed onto the bench seat of the cart beside her.

She flicked the reins, sending Acorn into lurching motion. "It's always complicated between older and younger siblings when a title is involved, let alone a crown. But it's more complicated with twins when it's only a matter of minutes between them."

"Princess Morgiana is the older sibling," I said, remembering my lessons. "But she isn't the crown princess anymore. And Nik isn't heir either." I frowned. "I'll admit when the news of the change in succession reached Tarin, I didn't quite understand what had happened. I don't think my parents did either, but we didn't pay it a lot of attention. My father insisted it didn't matter who wanted to sit in a fancy chair and lord it over the capital."

Amara raised an eyebrow. "Who sits on the throne has an enormous impact on all Tartorans—which is why we can be thankful there are mechanisms in place to try to ensure the best successor."

"And that isn't Nik?" I asked, offended on his behalf.

Amara hesitated. "I think only the royal family and the Triumvirate know the truth of how and why the change in succession happened as it did. If you want that story, I think you'll have to hear it from your new protector."

I flushed. "I can hardly ask him why he isn't the heir!"

"Why not?"

"What...But..." I spluttered, trying to put into words what seemed obvious. "He's a royal prince. And he's Nik!" I rolled my eyes. "He's not exactly what you would call open."

"You said he seems changed at times—I can only assume you mean when he's alone with you. So next time you have the chance, ask him about his history. I don't think you'll be able to make sense of him until you know it. And if he's not willing to share it with you...Well, that will tell you something important about him and your relationship as well."

"Relationship..." I muttered under my breath. "What relationship?" But I couldn't get her words out of my head. Could I really just come out and ask Nik about his history as a prince? Usually when it was just us I tried to forget about his royal status, and the one time I'd asked, his answer hadn't exactly been forthcoming. But Amara was right. It was better to be direct and know the truth of where I stood with him.

"All right," I said at last. "I will."

True to his word, after we stopped to make camp in the dusk of evening, Nik appeared from out of the shadows. He silently greeted Phoenix and helped gather water and firewood, keeping his distance from the road until true darkness fell.

"Tomorrow we'll look for a more secluded spot a little further back from the road," Amara said, and Nik nodded his thanks.

My earlier conversation with Amara was ringing in my ears, but Nik was obedient to her instructions and made no attempt to separate me from her. I wanted to respect my master's instructions, but I couldn't help a pang of disappointment. If I was going to bring myself to ask Nik questions, it would only be if I could talk to him without an audience.

When I woke in the morning, sometime after dawn, Nik had already disappeared. But after that, he joined us every night we were on the road, sometimes even appearing for the midday meal if we'd stopped in an out-of-the-way location.

We continued northeast across the kingdom, and I began to look forward to our makeshift camps more than the proper beds we were sometimes offered in the small villages we passed. And as my preference for days on the road grew, so did my impatience at our meandering route through every nearby village.

It was one thing to respond to any immediate need we encountered, but it seemed unnecessary to go out of our way, detouring to villages just so Amara could conduct training sessions for those with an elements affinity. It galled me not to move more quickly when Miranda needed us.

Eventually Amara lost patience and remonstrated with me. "I realize it's disconcerting that Miranda seems to have fallen for Grey's charm. But that's exactly what will keep her safe until we can extricate her."

"And what about the blight?" I asked. "If Grey knows something about that…"

"The blight is a matter of serious concern," she said with her usual unflappable and slightly infuriating calm. "But harvest is underway now. If we haven't discovered the root of the problem by the next planting season, then Tartora will have a significant issue. But for right now, these particular villagers will be without clean water soon if I don't show them how to keep contamination out of their dam."

When she put it like that, I couldn't protest further. I might have preferred to be sleeping by the fire with Nik in the next bedroll, Ember patrolling outside the firelight, and Phoenix only a foot away, but I couldn't deny that these people were isolated and in need of assistance.

And once I began to pay attention, I found the variety of problems we encountered fascinating. It was a pity Nik couldn't travel openly at our side since many of the farmers we encountered would have benefited more from a plants mage than an elements or healing one. And I especially wished for his assistance when we came upon the blackened stretches of burned fields.

One night on the road, I finally asked him if he had examined any of the blighted fields. He shrugged and said there was nothing left to examine.

"The fire completely destroys the blight—that's the point of it. What I need is to find a contaminated field before it's burned. But I always arrive too late."

The topic put him in a silent mood all evening, so I didn't bring it up again. I could only imagine his feeling of helplessness in the face of the growing crisis. For a plants mage, it had to be similar to my emotions when I failed to heal the eagle.

As both the days and the miles passed, Nik seemed to relax around Amara, losing some of his stiff coldness in her presence.

"You truly care about all these people," he said to her one

night as we sat together around the fire after our evening meal. "I could see it out in the field today. How do you do it?"

"You were there?" I stared at him, wondering where he'd been concealed. I hadn't seen any sign of him.

He gave me a single, piercing look, his expression reminding me that he'd promised to always watch over me. I flushed and looked away, falling silent.

Amara replied, seeming oblivious to the short moment between us.

"It isn't something I have to consciously do. Caring is easy for me."

Nik snorted. "Criticism duly noted."

I gave him a light shove, but he didn't take back the words.

"I didn't mean it as a criticism of you," Amara said, sounding sincere. "But it's interesting you take it that way. Do you consider yourself uncaring of your kingdom's people?"

He was silent for a moment, considering her question, and I noticed he didn't refute the sense of responsibility her phrasing had implied.

"I don't care like you do," he said at last. "You seem to be genuinely interested in each individual and care about their state and their emotions."

Amara nodded. "I do. But that's because connecting with people comes naturally to me. It isn't the only way of caring, though." She paused. "Tell me, Prince, after choosing to leave the capital, why have you spent a year and a half roaming the most remote regions of the kingdom?"

Nik looked away, either unable or unwilling to answer the question. But whether or not he realized it, he had already told me the answer. He thought the people of regional Tartora were forgotten by the crown. He might not think about it the same way Amara did, but he clearly cared—for some people, at least.

"How about this question, then," Amara said. "Why have you tracked Grey so single-mindedly?"

"He's abducting children and creating a threat to the entire kingdom. And now he might be involved in poisoning our food supplies. How could I not work against him?"

"Exactly." Amara nodded in satisfaction. "You do care. You're just motivated in a different way from me. We don't all have to approach situations and people from the same perspective—different motivations can lead to the same outcome. What matters, at the end of the day, is that you're helping people, not hurting them. Not everyone loves in the same way."

"Love?" Nik scoffed, looking away into the darkness.

"There are different kinds of love," Amara said, her words a rebuke. "For example, the love a king has for his people."

Nik's head whipped around, and he stared silently at her for an extended period. I held my breath, wondering if one or both of them was going to bring up the mysterious reason for his current status. But neither spoke, the popping of the fire the only accompaniment to the more distant sounds of the night.

Eventually Amara suggested sleep, and we all spread apart, banking the fire and preparing the camp and animals for the night. I stepped out of the firelight to check on Acorn's tether and arms encircled me, pulling me close.

My squeak of surprise was muffled by Nik's chest, and I fell silent, letting him hold me tight. My arms were trapped at my sides, but I didn't try to free them, merely resting my head against him.

His body was tense, and I could tell without needing to see his face or hear him speak that he needed comfort in this moment. The longer we stood there, however, the faster my heart began to race. When I heard his heartbeat meet mine, he abruptly let me go and stepped back.

"I'm sorry." His voice was low and gruff.

"No." I put a hand on his arm, stopping him from escaping. "I can't promise to watch over you or protect you from any danger, but I can do this much, at least. If you need someone, I'm here for you, Nik."

He hesitated for a long moment before speaking again, even lower than before. "Thank you."

He swept me abruptly into a second embrace, this one even tighter, but far shorter, than the last. When he released me, it was with a low growl, thrusting me away before striding off into the darkness.

I peered after him, my eyes finally adjusting after the brightness of the fire, but he was already lost to the shadows. And he didn't return that night.

CHAPTER

FOURTEEN

Most of our journey had been through farmlands, with farmers busying themselves with the harvest. Their industry only highlighted the tragedy of the empty, still sections of blackened earth.

And although talk of the blight had been severely contained by the efforts of the crown and Guild, the issue couldn't be concealed from the villages at its center. As we moved further from the capital, the villages became more and more unsettled. All conversations circled back to the blight, and endless debates raged on what the response from Tarona should be. Some blamed the king, some blamed the Guild, and others declared that a disaster had struck the kingdom beyond the ability of either to fix.

The worst were the empty houses, where families had packed up and gone north into Calista, with no one new arriving to take their place. Since Calista had so far been spared from the blight, those who remained talked of it in suspicious tones that matched the way the southerners had viewed Grey's influence.

Nik's mood grew grimmer by the night, and Amara wasn't far behind him.

"It's worse than I realized," she finally admitted as we camped on the western bank of the Viridian River. We had passed the last of the farmlands, entering the hilly grazing lands of the northern border region.

"Why do you think I proposed such a desperate plan?" Nik's eyes lingered on me, discomfort in their depths.

As the weeks had passed, he had grown more and more reluctant to speak of the plan he'd suggested or of what might await me in Grey's camp. No amount of reassurance seemed to convince him that I wasn't going to change my mind, or that I was perfectly capable of healing myself if something unpleasant befell me.

"I'm sure Amara will agree to my going," I said. "Now that she's seen the state of things up here. You will, won't you, Amara?"

Amara grimaced. "I find myself growing anxious to meet up with Hayes and Clay and hear their report from the capital."

"How much longer will it take us to reach Eldrida?" I asked, trying to picture the coastal city and failing.

"We'll cross the river in the morning," she said. "We've chosen to cross far enough north that we'll be able to head directly east for the coast, skirting just above the northern tip of the forest. The crossing itself will take some effort, so I would normally say we should take our time and do the journey to Eldrida in three days. In the past I've even taken a week, veering south to pass through one of the hill villages. But given the situation, I think we'll take the direct route, and push ourselves. We should be able to make it in two days."

I nodded a quick agreement, glad to finally be moving with some urgency.

"Don't expect to see me tomorrow night," Nik said. "You won't need my protection on the open land between the river and the city. The direct road is well traveled."

I tried not to let my dismay show on my face. I had become

accustomed to his constant presence—either seen or unseen. But while I might like knowing he was nearby, I didn't actually need him. Amara and I had enough strength between us to keep ourselves safe.

"You're planning to head straight for Eldrida, then?" Amara asked shrewdly. "You'll travel through the night?"

Nik grunted confirmation.

"Careful," she said lightly. "Traveling in the dark can be dangerous."

"Not for a plants mage," he said with a smirk. "And besides, I'm used to it."

She fell silent, unable to argue the point. A plants mage didn't need light to know the ground beneath his feet.

I slept fitfully after his words, though, and when he slipped out of bed in the morning, I woke as well, sitting upright in my bedroll. For a moment our eyes met, and we both stayed frozen in the early dawn light. Then he looked away and resumed his movement, gathering his things and slipping from the campsite.

I scrambled up and hurried after him, stopping him with a hand on his arm, just far enough away that we wouldn't wake Amara or the animals.

"You're really going ahead?" I asked.

He looked down at my hand, which was still resting on his arm, and nodded. "I want to get a feel for the state of things in Eldrida and see if I can find any word of Grey. Even when he's not gathering more followers, he and his people sometimes travel there for supplies."

I let my hand slip away, slowly nodding my understanding. I had no real reason to ask him to stay near us, and I wasn't ready to confess that it was just because I appreciated his presence.

He didn't immediately leave, however, instead stepping closer and erasing the small distance that lay between us.

"Amara is an experienced traveler and a strong mage," he said. "She'll keep you safe."

"I know," I said quickly. "It's not—" I stopped, dangerously close to the confession I didn't want to make.

Nik slung his pack over his shoulder and gripped my elbow, somehow maneuvering himself even closer.

"Delphine..." he breathed.

His eyes dropped to my lips, and I stiffened, my breath catching as I swallowed.

"I'll miss you," I said in a rush, and his grip tightened, his eyes darkening.

"Delphine, I—" He swayed toward me, his head tilting toward mine.

But a dark rush of movement through the air made us jerk back, springing apart to avoid Phoenix's hunting flight.

"Traitor," Nik muttered after the bird.

For a moment it looked like he was going to step toward me again, but a sleepy groan and the sound of movement back by the campfire made us both peer toward Amara.

"I'll see you in Eldrida," Nik murmured and was gone.

I wandered back toward the fire, feeling disgruntled and out of sorts. Amara greeted me with suspicious eyes, but she mercifully refrained from questioning my uncharacteristic early morning rising.

We packed up more quickly than usual, both driven by the previous night's decision. At last we were free to move at speed, and I could sense us both transitioning from the forced meanderings of the previous weeks into the more natural urgency that now drove us.

"I'm coming, Miranda," I whispered as we led Acorn the short way to the edge of the river.

Most westbound travelers and traders took the direct road from Eldrida to the river. There they either crossed it and took the river road southwest to the capital, or they boarded a boat and floated downriver to the capital. To aid those wishing to cross the river, a barge operated, run exclusively by those with an elements affinity.

Amara had brought us to the river slightly south of this popular crossing point, however, which was the only reason Nik had been able to join us the night before. There was often more than one group camping by the crossing, waiting for the barge to begin daylight operations. Now that we were alone again, I had expected us to move northward to meet the road and the barge, but apparently Amara was happy to facilitate our crossing herself.

When I saw the breadth of the river, however, I had second thoughts. Glancing back at Acorn, who was hitched to the cart, I looked doubtfully at the swiftly moving water.

"It won't take us long to go north to the barge," I said hesitantly.

Amara chuckled. "Have some faith, my apprentice."

"Oh no, no, it's not..." I let my clearly insincere protestations die out.

"The forest on the other side will force us to head north to the main road anyway," she said. "But Nik was right that it's a well-traveled road, and the barge berths on the eastern side of the river. It will load up on that side first, so there can sometimes be an extended wait for the barge on this side. We're in a rush and are able to cross with our own power. But I would prefer to complete this spectacle without an audience."

I raised my eyebrows. Spectacle? Exactly how was Amara intending to get us across?

"Climb up," she said, hopping up onto her usual seat on the cart.

I opened my mouth to ask if she was sure but clamped it shut again before I could say something so foolish. Clearly she was sure.

I perched on the edge of the bench, trying not to look like I was on high alert. Ember picked up on my mood, slinking over the back of the cart to curl up on my lap. Phoenix responded to the fox's movements by taking off, ringing upward and then flapping his way directly across the river.

"It's easy for some," I muttered, watching him go.

"Don't worry," Amara said in amusement. "It will be easy for us, too. At least as far as the rest of you are concerned."

She flicked the reins, and Acorn started forward, walking calmly toward the river. She had clearly been with Amara for a long time because she didn't halt when she reached the shallow stretch of bank, clopping into the water, the cart dragging behind her.

"What is she—?" I cut myself off, biting my tongue to keep myself from speaking. I needed to have faith in Amara.

My hands were white where they gripped the edge of the seat, however, as Acorn made it all the way into the water. She set off swimming, moving unconcernedly forward as if there was no current and she wasn't harnessed to a fully loaded cart.

"How...?" I gasped, but the answer was obvious the second our cartwheels left the riverbed, the whole cart floating in the water as if it were a barge itself.

I whirled around to peer into the back of the cart, expecting to see water flooding our bags and crates, but it was just as dry as before. There was only one way such a thing was possible, and remembering the unnatural wall of flood water, I knew the source of our impossible passage.

Amara was using her power to float both Acorn and our cart through the water, keeping us cocooned in some sort of bubble, so that the water didn't flood in.

I gazed at her in awe, once again shocked at the easy way she used power most people couldn't dream of.

"You needn't look at me like that, Delphine," she said with a small smile. "I assure you that any elements mage from the Guild could manage such an easy feat as this."

"Perhaps so," I said in a slightly strangled voice. "But I don't come from the Guild. No one I know with an elements affinity could possibly do this."

Acorn's feet hit the ground on the other side, her movement making the cart sway as she clambered out of the river, dragging us behind her. As soon as the cart had been dragged fully clear, water streamed off the outside of the wood and the horse until everything was completely dry, including Acorn's coat.

"Now that is a handy skill," I said, nodding my approval.

Amara grinned. "One of the first I perfected. The air is getting too cold at this time of year for Acorn to be wandering around wet."

On this side of the river there was only a dirt track following the curve of the river north, but it was wide enough for our cart. We moved off at a brisk pace by Acorn's standards, the horse apparently invigorated by her unlikely swim across the river.

Further south, the forest pressed close to the river, but here we had a bit of room to breathe as the forest tapered off to its northern tip. I could see the trees in the distance, however, and I reached for them, encountering a wealth of animal life beneath their sheltering boughs.

"Here comes the main road," Amara murmured, pulling my attention back to my immediate surroundings.

Phoenix dove from above us, spreading his wings to land in the back of the cart. Ember, startled awake, barked in protest, leaping forward to join me on the front seat once again.

I gave Phoenix a disapproving look but didn't have the heart to actually scold him for his dramatic entrance. Instead I petted Ember back to sleep as I watched the approaching road grow closer.

As warned, a slow but steady trickle of travelers moved along it, ranging from single walkers and riders to chains of several wagons, clearly bearing goods toward Eldrida.

"It looks like a barge has just disembarked," Amara

observed, directing Acorn to swerve right and join the road, heading east.

We fell in behind a small group of riders, but without the encumbrance of a cart or carriage they drew ahead, eventually disappearing from view. I thought the carriage behind us might overtake us as well, but Amara somehow inspired Acorn to a faster than usual pace, managing to stay just ahead of the travelers to our rear.

Our stop for lunch was also shorter than theirs, but several individual riders overtook us over the course of the afternoon, and one carriage pulled by a team of four went thundering past, causing Amara to draw our cart off the road entirely.

"Is that how Hayes, Clay, and Luna will be traveling to Eldrida?" I asked, watching the carriage disappear into the distance in a cloud of dust.

"Not if they're trying to avoid attracting attention," Amara said dryly. "And there's not much point in their hurrying if they're only going to arrive in the city and then sit around waiting for us."

I remembered our meandering path through the mid-north of the kingdom, our road taking us through all the villages.

"I suppose they'll be in Eldrida already."

"Perhaps." Amara gazed ahead, although the carriage was almost gone from sight. "That depends on exactly what happened in the capital and how many soldiers King Marius decided to send with them."

"You don't think he'll have forbidden them from leaving at all?" I asked, dismayed at the sudden thought.

"No, I can't imagine he'll do that," she said thoughtfully. "Even if he wishes to block our plan, he'll let one of them, at least, come to inform us of it."

"He must want Grey stopped, though."

"Of course. But he may prefer to take his chances with a

more direct route." Amara glanced at me but said nothing further.

"He might not trust me, you mean," I said slowly, catching on.

"That is one possibility."

I drew a deep breath, glad she hadn't denied it. I preferred that she was honest with me, even if it wasn't the most pleasant thing to hear. But the king didn't know me, so I couldn't blame him if he didn't want to commit to a plan that relied solely on me.

And then there was Nik. I had no idea if his son's involvement would turn the king toward or against the plan. Was it possible he'd send Hayes and the soldiers to Eldrida only so they could collect the prince and take him forcibly home to the capital?

Once the thought had entered my mind, it was hard to dislodge. Was that why Nik had left early, planning to slip surreptitiously into the city to gauge what was going on there? Did he worry that he would be more easily apprehended if he stayed near us?

I shook my head. King Marius had the whole Guild at his command. If he'd wanted to find Nik and force him home, he could have done so before now. The fact that he hadn't suggested he wanted to deal with the matter quietly—even if that meant allowing his son a time of freedom.

Unless this new crisis had changed his mind.

I shook my head, pushing away the circular thoughts. There was nothing I could do about it either way except wait and see what we found in Eldrida.

We camped at a place with a large wooden shelter, open on one side but providing protection from the wind and rain on the other three. Several other groups had also gathered there, arriving before or after us, and we ended up gathering around one large bonfire, the atmosphere bright and cheerful. At the halfway point, it was a stopping spot for those making the journey in two days, and everyone was anticipating a warm bed and proper meal the next night.

Ember slipped out early on, and Phoenix remained outside the shelter in the bed of the cart, with Acorn tethered nearby. That left only Amara and me from our usual small group, and it felt lonely, despite the crowd of people around us.

It took me a long time to fall asleep, thoughts of Nik circling in my mind. Was he still hurrying on through the darkness? Surely he would need to snatch some sleep at some point.

I awoke the next morning with a jerk to the sound of one of the groups pulling away onto the road, calling a cheerful farewell as they made an early start. I couldn't remember when I had fallen into sleep, but from the aches of my body, I had slept in a strange position, my muscles tense.

Amara and I ate a cold breakfast, hurrying out not too far behind the first group. Ember had returned sometime during the early hours, curling up beside me in my bedroll, and she happily settled into the back of the cart. But Phoenix, preferring to hunt at dusk and dawn, was off chasing smaller birds as soon as we hit the road.

We spent most of the morning in silence, and I suspected Amara's thoughts were in the same place as mine—what awaited us in Eldrida and, beyond that, in the desert.

When we stopped for a midday meal, Amara assured me we were making good time and should arrive in Eldrida well before dark. We continued on our way, again mostly in silence, until sometime in the middle of the afternoon.

Amara, who had been sitting with a distant expression, the reins slack in her hands, suddenly straightened, her eyes going wide. I began to ask a question, but she whipped up a hand, indicating I should be quiet. It was such an uncharacteristic gesture that I fell instantly silent.

When she turned to look north, I mimicked the movement,

but nothing looked out of place, the green hills stretching away toward distant clouds. Whatever had alarmed her, I didn't think she had sensed it with her eyes.

I threw out my own power, searching for an unusual group of people, but I could feel nothing beyond the normal wild animals, the travelers ahead and behind us, and a distant shepherd with his flock.

The cart jolted, making me let go of my power and grip the seat instead. Amara flicked the reins again, calling for Acorn to pick up her pace, and I added my own voice of encouragement, trying to reinforce it with my power.

I didn't know if I succeeded, but Acorn's speed increased. I remained silent, afraid to disturb Amara in case she was concentrating. Instead, I focused on the group who had left the shelter ahead of us.

We had remained close behind them, just out of sight, for most of the day, but we quickly gained on them at the faster pace. When we reached their rear, Amara guided Acorn to one side of the road where a flat patch of ground gave us the opportunity to overtake them.

As we drew level, she leaned over me, calling to the closest driver.

"Do you have anyone with an elements affinity among you?"

The man looked surprised, distracted by our unexpected appearance, and she called the question a second time. This time he blinked and nodded slowly.

"A couple, but not of any particular strength. Just the usual weather trackers. Why?" He glanced uneasily at the sky, and I did the same.

With a start, I realized the distant clouds in the northern sky were much closer than they had been before, their color an ominous dark gray.

"Get off the road, now," Amara shouted. "And form a storm huddle."

"Storm?" The man called, but we were already passing him.

The next driver had heard the shouts, though, and took up the conversation.

"Our weather trackers didn't say anything about a storm coming." He looked at us both with suspicion.

"Ask them again," Amara yelled with uncharacteristic irritation.

"She's a master elements mage from the Guild," I bellowed at the man. "If she says get in a storm huddle, I'd listen if I was you."

"Master mage?" The man's eyes widened, and he immediately turned to call something to someone on his other side.

Amara nodded once, returning her focus to the front, satisfied her message had been received. Within a short time, we had passed the entire group and pulled back onto the road.

Twisting, I looked behind us and saw the wagons were rapidly falling away into the distance as they slowed to a stop and pulled off the road.

"They're doing it." I turned back around. "But what's a storm huddle?"

Amara replied without looking my way, her focus flicking between the road ahead and the storm clouds to our left.

"There's no proper shelter nearby, so they'll have to do the best they can on their own. They'll turn the wagons with their backs to the wind and get the animals calmed and protected as much as possible." She sighed. "If they'd had any warning, they would have stayed at the overnight shelter. Everyone will have left there by now, and most of the others are still behind us."

A single rider, approaching from the direction of Eldrida, caught her attention and she fell silent, waving a hand to flag him over. He slowed, both of us coming to a halt so they could exchange words.

"Good afternoon," he began, but Amara jumped straight in, ignoring the usual pleasantries.

"There's a bad storm coming."

The man's eyes immediately flicked to the clouds, indicating he'd been aware of them already.

"It's a severe one, then?" He frowned. "I'm a plants mage, so I wasn't sure…"

"There's a group of wagons who've just pulled over not too much further along," she said. "You should wait it out with them. The next proper shelter is too far."

The man's hand went to his horse's neck, and I wondered if the gelding was especially jumpy in storms.

"Are you certain?"

"She's a master elements mage from the Guild." I jumped in, hoping to save us some time.

"Oh, well in that case…" The man bowed from his saddle. "I appreciate the warning, Master."

Amara nodded distractedly. "Hurry on, then. If we encounter anyone else, we'll send them to join you."

The man kicked his horse's flank, and Amara flicked the reins, each of us starting off in opposite directions.

"If the storm is so bad," I began hesitantly, "should we be…?"

I trailed off when Amara began to shake her head.

"I can protect us. We need to get to Eldrida."

"We do?" I asked, still confused about what was happening.

"It's not just a bad storm, it's really bad," she said in clipped tones. "And more importantly, it's come on with almost no warning. Anyone with an elements affinity—from medium non-mage strength upward—should have been able to track a weather phenomenon that big from hours ago."

"What does that mean?" I asked, but even as I spoke, I remembered the preparations we would make on the farm if we got word from Tarin that there was a big storm due the next day. "No one's going to be prepared."

"That's right," Amara said grimly. "The fishing fleet will have left this morning as usual, and trading ships will be out at sea as well. Not to mention any damage the actual city may sustain."

I gasped. I hadn't even thought of ships at sea.

"And once the initial chaos dies down," she continued, her voice dark, "people are going to start asking questions."

"Questions? Will they blame the elements mages?"

"Not ours."

"What do you mean, not our—oh." My eyes widened as I caught on to her meaning. A large and dangerous storm had come in too quickly, and it had come from the north.

"Do you think it's possible some Calistan mages drove the storm south?" I asked in a small voice.

"I would like to think no one with the strength and control to do so would be so reckless," she said savagely. "But I can't absolutely guarantee it."

Her shoulders sagged. "Everyone knows Calista is still in the process of rebuilding, and that includes their Mages' Guild. They lack the structure and experience that governs our own mages. Even if they didn't do it, people will suspect they did. And when the whole countryside is already on edge..."

"Plus, if they didn't do it, and this storm isn't natural..." I didn't need to complete the question because we were both already thinking it. If the Calistans hadn't sent this storm, who had?

FIFTEEN

The winds reached us first, followed quickly by a sheet of driving rain. The wind alone might have been enough to knock us from our seat, but it never had the chance to touch us.

An invisible bubble sprang up around us, an unnatural circle with neither wind nor rain. And when lightning began to arc down from the sky, none of the branches came near us.

The storm spooked Acorn, however, and she picked up her pace again, speeding us toward the shelter of the city walls. Ember was equally unhappy, huddling in my lap and shivering almost constantly while Phoenix sat unusually still on my shoulder.

"How long can you keep this up?" I asked Amara, lifting my voice above the storm. "How long can Acorn?"

"For me, as long as we need." She peered at the horse. "As for Acorn—shouldn't I be asking you that?"

I grimaced. "She's in good health, but this is a fast trot for her given she's pulling the cart. I'd have to touch her to know how her energy levels are going, though."

"For now she should be fine. She and I have been together for a long time, so I think I have some idea of her limits."

We both lapsed into silence, which was easier than trying to be heard above the beating rain, roaring wind, and unpredictable cracks of thunder. It didn't scare me, though, which surprised me until I remembered I was healing cross elements now. Storms would probably never scare me again.

Thoughts of the people in Eldrida did worry me, though, so it was an uncomfortable ride. After some time, Amara eased Acorn to a stop, directing me to climb down and check on her. I did so quickly, almost collapsing when I landed on my stiff legs. But it only took a moment to recover and rush forward to place a hand against Acorn's flank.

She was tired, that much was easy to tell. I sent my power into her, easing her aching muscles and refreshing her fatigue. I'd never done it to a horse before, but Luna and I used to secretly practice on each other when Hayes's lessons went long. We knew if we told him we were doing it, he would lecture us on the difference between a healer easing our fatigue and true rest. But this wasn't a time to worry about the difference.

When I climbed back into the cart, I nodded at Amara. "She's ready to go again."

Amara smiled tightly. "I knew it would be handy to have a healer along."

We pushed on, the sky unnaturally dark for the hour, and the rain blocking visibility for more than a few feet. It felt as if we were alone in our small cocoon, the rest of the world a raging storm of wet and cold and noise.

Given the visibility issues, we were nearly at the gates of Eldrida before the walls loomed out of the storm in front of us.

"We're here," I gasped, rubbing warmth and life into my cold fingers. "We made it."

"Now the real work begins," Amara said, immediately dousing my momentary joy.

Silently, we continued through the open gate, exchanging

looks as we noticed the absence of the normal gate guards. We hadn't made it far into the city when I realized why.

Out on the open plains, the winds had been terrifying and fierce, and at first I had been relieved by the shelter of the city walls. But once we moved past their immediate vicinity, the wind picked up its tempo again, even scarier than before. The streets only served as wind tunnels, channeling and strengthening the trapped wind.

Everyone must have sought shelter inside because the cobblestones were deserted. Amara seemed to know where she was going, though, directing Acorn with confidence.

"The harbor," she said when I gave her a questioning look. "That's where the elements mages will be, trying to keep the ocean from flooding the city and bringing in any ships close enough to reach land."

I shivered, picturing the terror of being out on the open sea in winds and rain like this. If ships did make it to harbor, they might be in need of a healer. It was the most logical place for us to be.

Before we made it there, however, we turned a corner and came to a stop, our passage barred by absolute chaos. Large buildings lined what appeared to be the city's central square, standing firm against the weather. But the square itself was a litter of broken wood, scattered wares, and terrified animals. And between the cracks of thunder, I caught screams. My eyes found the evidence of trapped people who must have attempted to shelter beneath the market stalls when the rain started.

Amara's face paled as she looked from left to right, struggling to know where to settle her gaze. We couldn't drive through the square, but how could we turn our backs on this disaster to take a different route?

While we lingered on the street, shocked and uncertain, the creaking of wood sounded, and an enormous wooden gate swung open. It appeared to be the entrance to a small stables—whether of an inn or private property, I wasn't sure—located just down from the square.

"In here!" a voice yelled. "You'll have to leave the cart, but there's room for you and your horse."

Startled, I peered inside to see a mass of huddled, frightened faces gazing back.

A grizzled, elderly man stumbled out, passing through the rain briefly before entering the bubble that surrounded us and starting to unhitch Acorn. Amara slid down and hurried to join him, me at her heels.

"I thought I heard hoof beats just before that last thunder," the man said. "Couldn't think who would be out riding in this, though. But mighty handy that is." He pointed upward at the invisible barrier holding back the rain. "You'll be a mage, then, which explains it. But mage or not, you'll want somewhere safe for this lady." He patted Acorn's neck.

"Have you seen what's happened in the square?" Amara asked in a stern tone.

The man nodded, his expression serious. "That's where all them came from." He gestured over his shoulder with his thumb. "It came on so quick there wasn't much warning, so I opened the doors for anyone fleeing this way. Best not to be out traveling in this."

Amara nodded, her expression softening. Meeting my eyes, she gestured at the cart, and I hurried back to it. Scooping up Ember, I pointed at my shoulder, waiting for Phoenix to give a flying hop into position there. When I had realized he preferred that spot to my arm, I had added leather padding to the shoulder of several of my dresses, and we had become practiced at the movement.

Looking at the remaining bags, I scooped up two of the most precious—all I had room to carry in my remaining arm. Amara appeared at my side and took several more before we followed the elderly stable master and Acorn into the dark building.

The man led Acorn toward the only empty stall, the crowd squeezing together to allow enough room for them to pass. Amara watched them go, but as soon as she was satisfied that Acorn had a place to go, she turned back to the crowd.

"I don't suppose there are any mages among you?"

A sea of shaking heads confirmed her guess. "What about those with medium or high strength?"

This time, a number of hands were hesitantly raised.

"Any healers?" Amara asked, but all of the hands went down.

"The healers stayed in the square," the woman nearest to us volunteered. "There were a lot of injured."

"You're right," Amara said coldly. "There are many in need. Are you telling me only the healers went to help? I didn't expect to be ashamed of my own affinity."

Silence spread through the group, people shifting uncomfortably and exchanging glances.

"What would you have us do?" the woman asked, half defiantly, half curiously.

"Since you didn't put your hand up, you must have a weak seed," Amara said. "That means you're exactly where you should be. We don't want to create more victims. But those with sufficient strength and an elements affinity should come with me to the harbor."

"The harbor?" several voices called, followed by someone exclaiming loudly, "The ships!"

Amara nodded. "I'm an elements mage, and that's where I'm going. I'm sure that's where I'll find others with an elements affinity. Who will join me?"

After a brief hesitation, several people stepped forward, about half of the group who had raised their hands. The rest were probably plants affinity, and it only took me a moment to realize what Amara wanted them doing.

I raised myself as tall as I could go and tried to project my voice. "As for those with a plants affinity of reasonable strength, you'll be with me. I'm a healing mage, so I'll be staying here at the square. But people are trapped, so I'll need help with all that fallen wood and stone."

Amara took my arm, pulling me slightly aside. "Are you sure?" she whispered. "These are all adults, but officially you're still underage. By rights, I shouldn't be abandoning my apprentice in a dangerous situation like this, but I'll be needed at the harbor, and your strength could make a real difference out there."

"Don't worry about me," I said with more confidence than I felt. "I'll have these people to help me." I gestured at the remaining people who had stepped forward. From the look of it, Amara had successfully roused all of those with high enough strength to be useful.

A girl who looked about twelve watched me with sorrowful eyes. "I have a high strength seed," she said. "If only I was older, I could help."

"You can help now." I cradled Ember, whose body trembled in response to another peal of thunder, and held her out to the girl. "Could you look after my fox for me?"

"Your fox?" The girl took her, sheltering her against her body and stroking her fur with an amazed expression.

"Her name is Ember, and she doesn't like the storm."

I glanced upward to where Phoenix perched on one of the stable rafters. He had taken off from my shoulder almost as soon as we stepped inside and would be fine up there until I returned.

"I'll take care of her," the girl promised, still focused on Ember rather than me.

Managing a small smile, I murmured thanks and turned for

the door, bracing myself for what was to come. We all stepped outside together, Amara's bubble still keeping the rain off. But we were about to part ways, which meant I would soon be wet.

Amara hesitated for a final second, looking at me with concerned eyes. But I shooed her away, calling for the plants people to follow me. Taking a deep breath, I jogged out of the protective bubble, gasping as the freezing rain hit my face.

Almost immediately I was soaked, the enormous drops quickly permeating my layers of clothing. But within a few steps we were inside the square and the chaos around us drove out thoughts of my own discomfort.

Other people scurried around, pulling at fallen structures or kneeling over injured people, but with the rain affecting visibility, it was hard to see how many or how organized they were.

Don't look at everything, I told myself. *Just focus on one thing you can fix.*

I looked at the closest collapsed stall and then the next one down. No one was at the nearer one, but at the further one, a man knelt beside a trapped woman. From the way he held her wrist, I guessed him to be a healer.

"Two of you go help him." I pointed at the healer. "The other two, help me lift this."

I hoped they didn't need more detailed instructions because I had no idea how to direct someone to use their plants power. Nik would be helpful in the situation, but he could be anywhere in the city. I didn't doubt that wherever he was, he was helping, though. And with his strength, he would be making a difference.

Thankfully, the young lad and older woman who had stayed with me got to work on their own, calling out words to each other that I couldn't clearly hear over the sound of the storm. Their coordination worked, however, and the jagged planks of wood slithered to the side, as if moving of their own accord.

The man beneath was soon uncovered, but as they were

about to move the last piece of wood, I screamed for them to stop. Both of them froze, staring at me wide-eyed.

"Wait a moment," I shouted and dropped to both knees beside the man.

I had nearly missed that the wood, shorn in half and turned into a spear, had impaled the man in the side. I'd never dealt with an injury like that, but I knew you needed a healer ready before you removed any object still piercing a person. The blood loss when the wood came out could be immense.

"It's all right," I yelled at the man, trying to sound reassuring despite my volume. "I'm a healer."

The man instantly relaxed, although his eyes remained wide and wild.

I pushed my power into him, masking his pain as I tried to ignore the discomfort of feeling something foreign that didn't belong. He had several broken bones as well, but I bypassed those, focusing on the severed veins and seeping blood.

My two assistants approached, kneeling beside me and staring at the man in horror.

"It will be all right," I said when the wind quieted slightly for a moment. "Just be ready to pull the wood out when I say so."

The older woman nodded and gripped it with both hands, watching me closely.

I sent my power to wrap around the organs closest to the wood, nodding my head as soon as I was ready.

"Now!" The woman pulled and the wood slid out, the patient screaming in response, although his pain was only a shadow of what it had been before.

I let my power guide me, instinct taking over as I restitched veins and sealed organs, sending a tendril to calm the pain that still darkened his brain. He immediately quieted beneath my hands, his breathing steadying as I knit the wound in his side, sending my power blazing along his bones, reforming those that had cracked under the weight of the stall.

As soon as I was finished, I let go and sat back, taking deep, gasping breaths. If I had been Hayes, I could have done that with much less energy. And for the first time I fully understood the value of that. How many more people in this square still needed my help?

"Come on," I told my two assistants as I lurched to my feet. "There will be others."

The man called out his thanks, and I stopped to look at him. "What's your affinity?"

"Elements, but I had no idea...I didn't see this coming when I can normally sense—"

"What's your strength?"

"Weak," the man admitted reluctantly.

I pointed out of the square. "There's a stable just down that road. If you knock on the door, they'll let you shelter inside."

Without waiting for a reply, I hurried further into the debris field, picking my way over fallen wood, torn material and what seemed to be several spilled baskets of potatoes.

The group at the next stall had already freed the trapped woman, although the healer was still working on her. I left them to it, continuing on in search of more victims. A piercing scream pulled my attention to the right, and I hurried in that direction, trying to peer through the heavy rain. I kept wiping the drops from my eyes, but they were coming down so hard it did little good.

A woman staggered toward me, blood streaking her already soaked gown. Before she could reach me, though, someone else responded to her yell, catching her as she collapsed. For a moment, I didn't recognize the sodden figure assisting her, but something in the way he laid her down and knelt beside her was familiar.

"Hayes!" I cried, and he glanced up briefly, meeting my eyes with a shock of recognition.

I waved his attention back to the woman, though, turning to look back into the square. If Hayes had charge of her, then she was in good hands and didn't need me.

Several steps brought me to another collapsed stall, this one surrounded by scattered items, all made from leather. Two people seemed to be beneath the pile of broken wood, but a man and a girl were already pulling planks aside, working to free them.

These two were also familiar. Clay and Luna.

I nearly called a greeting before thinking better of it. They didn't need a distraction, and there were more people in need. I continued deeper into the square, passing several more injured people who sat or lay on the ground. Those with significant injuries had someone kneeling beside them wearing the focused, slightly absent, expression of a healer at work.

A hysterical woman who grabbed at my arm turned out to be fine, but her young daughter had been struck in the head by a flying piece of stone. I paused to heal her, sealing her gash and pushing out the pressure threatening her brain.

The girl brightened as soon as I'd finished, putting a hand to her head.

"My headache is gone!" she exclaimed. "Thank you!"

I could barely hear her high voice over the wind, as much reading the words on her lips as hearing them.

I nodded, hurrying on to where my two assistants were already pulling the wood off another trapped stall keeper. This one had escaped with a single broken bone and a deep gash, so it didn't take me long to burn through his injuries.

Both my assistants were now shivering uncontrollably, so I took a moment to give them a burst of warmth and energy. They smiled their thanks, the woman grasping my arm and leaning close to talk into my ear.

"Don't forget yourself, child!"

I nodded and sent a spark of power through my own body, just enough to drive away the uncontrollable shaking. I didn't want to waste too much, though. I already felt worryingly weak and tired, and people still needed me.

The next few stalls were already deserted, the people around them having fled before the wind hit or else having been rescued already. I almost began to hope the square was nearly cleared when we reached the west side and found an entire building had collapsed.

Stone and wood lay everywhere, and from the moans and cries, there were still people trapped beneath.

An arm appeared from the rain, and I grabbed it. "What happened here?" I shouted.

"A building was still under construction," the man yelled back. "It wasn't sturdy enough to withstand the—" He broke off. "Delphine?"

"Nik?" I stared up at him, blinking against the hard drops of rain and sputtering slightly.

I swayed, and he grabbed both my arms. "How many people have you already healed?"

"Never mind that! How many are still trapped?"

"I'm not sure. I just arrived. I was working on the other side of the square."

I glanced in the direction he was pointing and saw a far more orderly stretch of ground, the various collapsed stalls swept out of the way, as if by a giant's hand. Nik at work, no doubt.

"Don't worry about me, then," I said. "Tell these two how they can help you." I gestured for my assistants to come forward. "They both have plants seeds, like you."

Reluctantly, Nik let go of my arms, turning to the woman and the boy. He began issuing rapid fire instructions that I tuned out, glad not to have to take responsibility for something outside of my field.

Within a minute, the three of them were at work, several other people appearing out of the rain to help them. Under Nik's guidance, the fallen stones and broken planks of wood lifted into the air, flying in neat formations to form piles against the base of the closest sturdy building.

Nik seemed to be the one actually lifting the stones, but from the expressions of concentration on the faces of the others, they were using their power to assist in some way. Working as a team, they soon had the first person exposed, and I dropped to my knees, feeling the jarring thud all the way through me.

It was a young boy, looking terrified and in pain, so I sent my power into him, blocking off the pain before I even examined his injuries. He drew an immediate, gasping breath, stuttering out a thank you.

"Just lie still," I called, closing my eyes against the water that streamed down my face.

One of the boy's feet was twisted at an unnatural angle, and I sent my power racing through his ankle, popping it back into place and fusing the bones back together.

When I opened my eyes, he was watching his foot with curiosity, apparently undaunted by the process now that he was no longer in pain. As soon as I checked the rest of him and let him go, however, he pointed back at the still shifting mound of debris.

"I'm Coby," he said inconsequentially, his face twisted in an expression of worry that was out of place on a young child. "Have you seen my mother? I think she might be under there still."

"We'll get to her," I yelled as the wind picked back up. "But you should move out of the way." I looked around until I saw a small group huddled against a stretch of wall some way from where Nik was piling the rubble. "Over there. I'll send her there to find you as soon as she's free."

He hesitated, but when a stone came floating past our heads, he nodded agreement and hurried off. I turned back to the building, hoping desperately that his mother was still alive under there.

The next stone to lift revealed a leg, followed by a second one. Something about the look of them made my stomach turn, although I wasn't sure why. The urgency and chaos of the crisis had so far suppressed my nausea almost as effectively as my power could.

The sight of the person had an effect on Nik as well because all the remaining stones covering them began to lift at once. I didn't wait to see who the legs belonged to, however, wrapping my fingers around one ankle.

I tried to push my power into the person, but it wouldn't move. I had experienced the effect only once before, but I refused to accept it, trying again and then again.

"No, no, no, no, no, no," I muttered over and over until a loud moan broke through my daze.

For a heady moment, I thought the groan was evidence I'd been mistaken, but it wasn't coming from the body in front of me but from someone deeper in the rubble. I hadn't been wrong. The owner of the leg was beyond my help.

The last of the rubble lifted off the body, and I steeled myself to look at their face. It was an elderly man, lying still, his eyes closed.

It wasn't the boy's mother, then. Guilt washed over me at the spear of relief I felt. This man had just lost his life, and someone, somewhere would soon be crying over it.

Nik's voice echoed in my memory. *Death is never easy. But healers have to find ways not to be crippled by it.*

It had seemed unthinkable and almost cruel at the time, but I understood what he'd meant now. I couldn't let myself think about this man or his family. Someone nearby was still moaning, which meant that person wasn't beyond my help. I couldn't fall apart now.

I crawled around the man, not bothering to push myself back up against the wind and rain. Gradually it filtered through to my awareness that the storm seemed to be lessening, the wind no longer so strong and the rain starting to ease. I couldn't think about the weather, however.

More rocks lifted into the air, and I crawled along in their wake, seeking the owner of the moans. When the floating rubble finally revealed a woman a similar age to Amara, it was clear she was in bad shape.

But when I crouched beside her, I realized she wasn't giving wordless groans of pain but was saying two garbled words over and over again.

"My son. My son. My son."

I grabbed her hand, squeezing it as gently as possible. Sending my power into her, I first eased her pain. "Is your son young? Maybe eight?"

"Coby! He's nine!" The words came out clearer now that her pain had lifted, although from the sound of her breathing at least one of her lungs was in trouble. "Have you seen him?"

"I healed him just earlier," I said in my most soothing tones. "He told me his name was Coby, and I sent him somewhere safe. I also told him I'd send you after him, so I need you to work with me and stay strong."

The woman collapsed, her tense muscles loosening now that she was freed from both pain and fear. But as my power raced through her body, I sucked in a breath. Her internal damage was severe, far worse than any of the others I'd so far healed.

My head spun, and I shook it, trying to get a hold of myself. I was already so drained from the previous healings, but I couldn't lose focus now. This woman didn't have much time, and her son was waiting for her.

I sent my power into her, wishing I knew more about the parts I needed to fix. Pages from my anatomy books swam before my eyes, and when I touched her collapsed lung, I tried to remember everything Hayes had ever told me about the organ.

But I was too tired for finesse. I would have to do what I'd done too often before and rely on strength and instinct to force a healing. The fire that spread out from me seemed to flicker instead of burn, though, nearly exhausted. I coaxed it brighter, pushing it onward through her body. From her lungs, it traveled to her ribs, her kidneys, her liver, her stomach, mending and repairing and regrowing as it went.

The woman gasped. "The sensation! It's so strange!"

I frowned. Patients didn't usually feel our healings. They found it distressing, so we blocked the sensations. I knew how to do that. Didn't I? Wasn't I doing it right now? I thought I was. My thoughts flew out of my grasp, fuzzy and indistinct. I tried to grab hold of them, tried to remember what I was doing. Blocking the sensation! That was it. I told my power to do it, but nothing happened. I reached deeper and finally it responded.

The woman calmed, and I pushed on. How it felt wasn't important anyway, as long as she was healthy at the end of it.

Her bones came after the organs, then the veins and finally the single patch of torn skin. I knew I should do a final sweep to be sure I'd fixed everything, but my power didn't seem to be responding to me anymore.

"Make sure you see a healer soon," I gasped out. "To check..."

The woman pushed tentatively to her feet, looking down at herself in wonder.

"I thought I was dying. Absolutely everything hurt, and I

couldn't breathe. But now I feel fully healed." She peered into my face. "You're so young!"

"Promise you'll check," I whispered and realized the wind had nearly stopped completely because she could hear me.

"I will, I will!" She reached down a hand to help me to my feet. "Thank you! Thank you so much."

As she hauled me upward, I noticed the rain had also stopped. I knew I should be relieved by that, but I felt too numb to care.

I couldn't seem to feel my feet either, which must have been why I was swaying, but the woman didn't seem to notice, distracted by her visual search of our surroundings.

"Over there." I somehow managed to raise my arm and point. "Coby is waiting for you."

"Thank you!" the woman cried again, spinning and dashing off across the wet ground.

"Careful," I tried to call, but the word wouldn't fully form, my voice strangely quiet.

What was wrong with me? I tried to lift a hand to my head, but my limbs weren't responding now, like my power hadn't earlier.

A roaring filled my ears, although the wind didn't seem to have picked back up. My legs gave out completely, and I collapsed.

Strong arms broke my fall, and I thought I heard a familiar voice frantically calling my name. But my eyes were closing against my will, and all sounds faded away, replaced with deep, refreshing, nothingness.

CHAPTER

SIXTEEN

The first thing to reach me was noise. But it wasn't the wordless roaring of the wind or the pounding of heavy rain. A babble of voices overlapped each other, mingling with footsteps and the various bumps and bangs of industrious activity.

The next thing was the soft fur of a familiar, sleeping animal, her warm body tucked under the blankets by my side.

I tried to open my eyes, but they resisted. I reached a hand up to my face and found a cloth lying across my eyes. From its stiff feel, it had once been wet, although it had long since dried.

I pulled it off, opening my eyes, only to quickly close them again. Without the protection of the material, the bright daylight speared at me even through my eyelids. Taking several deep breaths, I waited for my eyes to adjust to the daylight filtering through my closed lids. Only once it reached a comfortable level did I try cracking my eyes open again.

For a second time I had to wait while they adjusted to the new level of light. How was it already full day? How long had I been sleeping?

"She's awake!" A jovial but unfamiliar voice called out the news, and a renewed flurry of footsteps sounded.

I barely had time to take in my surroundings—a row of beds in a suspiciously familiar looking room that had a bright, airy feel—before a small crowd of people surrounded me. They all beamed down at where I lay flat in bed.

"Our sleeping beauty awakens!" the original speaker cried, in the same beaming tones. "Which means we can officially discharge our last storm patient."

A resounding cheer went up from those gathered around my bed, although I couldn't spot any familiar faces among them. The speaker seemed to be the one in charge as well as the oldest, a round-faced, matronly woman who regarded me with the affectionate indulgence of a grandmother. I wanted to ask who she was, but that seemed rude. My second thought was to ask where I was, but I was fairly sure I already knew the answer to that.

"Where's Master Amara?" I asked instead, hoping she would have answers for me.

"Ah yes, someone must inform the girl's master!" The woman turned to the group around her, and the youngest of them jumped to attention, hurrying out of the room, presumably to search for Amara.

In the wake of his departure, the older woman shooed most of the others away as well, directing them to return to their regular tasks or seek rest of their own. From the way she addressed them, it appeared they had been working hard for an extended time and were now reaching the end of their labor.

"Don't worry," the woman said to me in comfortable tones when she turned her attention back to me.

I felt more confused than concerned, but I remained silent, hoping she would continue.

"Master Amara is perfectly well." She folded her hands across her belly and beamed at me. "She would have liked to be here at your bedside, I'm sure, but she's a woman much in demand." She chuckled to herself before continuing. "She visited briefly, of course, and confirmed your identity and condition, but she barely had the chance to leave the harbor until this morning, and the city's leaders and mages have all been clamoring to consult with her."

I tried to sort through this flood of words for the important points.

"Confirm my identity? How did I get here?"

I didn't bother to ask where *here* was. Now that I'd had a more complete look at the room and its occupants, I was utterly certain I was in the Eldridan hospital. My training with Hayes in the Caltoran hospital made it a familiar space since all the hospitals in Tartora had been built with the same design.

"You arrived just after the end of the storm, unconscious," the healer said. "It was true chaos here, then, so I didn't get the name of the person who carried you in. But he was the whole package." She leaned forward and winked broadly. "Tall, dark, and handsome, so you're a fortunate young lady."

From the matron's satisfied beam, it seemed she thought a mid-storm rescue was the immediate precursor to a betrothal announcement. I groaned and rubbed my head, but I didn't ask any more questions about my rescuer. The healer's description gave me a good idea who it had been, and hazy memories were starting to return of a familiar voice calling my name and strong arms scooping me up and holding me close.

Gingerly, I sent my power around my body, searching for any sign of illness or injury or even of recent healing. I found nothing. Every part of my body seemed perfectly normal.

I looked again at the broad daylight outside the closest window and frowned.

"How long have I been here? How many hours has it been since the storm finished?"

"Hours?" The healer rubbed her chin. "I'm not sure I could tell you that. I've been on my feet for too long to be worrying around with numbers and sums."

"Sums?" I pushed myself up to sitting, making Ember stir in protest. "How long has it been?"

A younger man, maybe a decade older than me, joined us. "It's late afternoon, the second day after the storm."

"Two days!" I shrieked, swinging my legs out of the bed.

The man immediately put his hands on my shoulders to stop me. "Slowly now, Apprentice. You've been lying down for a long time. No need to rush things. I'd rather not have you collapse for a second time."

I didn't fight him, sitting on the side of the bed, my mouth hanging open. "It's really been two days? And I've just been lying here the whole time? What in the kingdoms was wrong with me that it took that long for you to heal me?"

I could imagine many of the injured and ill had been forced to wait in the immediate aftermath of the storm, but I was the only one left in the room now, and the older healer had declared me the final storm patient.

"We didn't heal you at all," the matron said in the same hearty tones as always. "Didn't use a lick of power on you, in fact. All we did was provide a bed and keep an eye on you."

A nose appeared from under the crumpled blankets, followed by a lithe body moving sleepily. I put a hand around Ember's middle, guiding her as she curled back up at my side, this time on top of the blankets.

"We don't normally allow pets in the hospital," the male healer said. "But every time someone shooed her out, we would turn around to find she'd snuck back in again. I've never seen such devotion from a wild animal—even to a healer. We gave up in the end, since everyone was too busy to keep watch for one small fox."

"I'm sorry. I seem to have caused you a lot of unnecessary trouble." My fingers brushed over the stiff cloth that had been covering my eyes.

"Ah, now, that wasn't one of us," the matron said, her smile hinting at an intriguing secret.

"No one will swear they saw anything for sure, given the crowds that were coming and going," the man said with an amused smile of his own. "But given the legends already springing up about you and your master, the younger ones have been talking. They all swear they haven't had time to come near your bed in the busyness, but at least half of them claim to have seen glimpses of a tall young man slipping in and out among the crowd."

The matron chuckled, and I realized her earlier comment had been based on more than just Nik's supposed rescue of me. Warmth rose up my cheeks, and I cleared my throat uncomfortably.

"Nothing like a bit of mystery to add to a legend in the making," the matron said. "It's good for the youngsters to have something to focus on other than where that storm came from."

She exchanged a weighted glance with the man, and I remembered Amara's words on the road as well as the matron's assertion that Amara had been in demand among the city's leaders. What had been happening in Eldrida while I slept?

"But why was I here?" I asked, trying again for a straight answer. "Why did I sleep so long? And what do you mean by legend?" My head was starting to spin almost as much as it had in the square at the end of the storm.

The man, who had a much brisker air than the matron in charge, answered my questions in order.

"You're here because you overextended yourself in the square and collapsed. That's what happens when you push your power too far." He gave me a censorious look. "And you weren't just sleeping but unconscious, regaining your energy. For two days. That's also what happens when you overuse your ability. There's a reason people try to avoid doing it."

My flush deepened as I realized I hadn't been injured at all. I had just humiliated myself by making the rookie mistake all apprentices were sternly warned against. I hadn't known my own limits.

Looking back, all the signs had been there: the flickering fire of my power, the fuzzy thoughts and confusion, forgetting to include basic elements of a healing. I had ignored it all and pushed my way onward without thought.

And once again, Nik had saved me. It had been a dangerous risk, though. Given my location, I could easily have fallen and hit my head—even killed myself, as had happened to Amara's mother. And I had certainly rendered myself unable to help anyone else—a patient taking up the hospital's resources instead of another healer to help finish off the less severe cases the following day.

I could still feel the lingering sensation of Nik's arms around me, carrying me, but I could also hear his voice in my mind. *Even the strongest healers have limits.*

I had once again tried to ignore that truth, attempting to heal based on the need before me, without considering what was possible.

I tried to look at the matter objectively. The last woman I healed had been badly injured. Should I have left her to die, saving my power to heal multiple other people with dangerous, but less complex, injuries? Could I have done so?

Remembering Coby's face, I didn't think I could have. It was only natural to respond to the known need in front of me. But that didn't mean I had to burn myself out until I sputtered and died. I could have done enough to save her life and then stopped, saving my energy for other patients. And I should definitely have stopped once I felt myself reaching my limits. If I had fallen and died, unnoticed in the middle of the storm, how many future Cobys would have lost their mothers as a consequence?

I never wanted to become a person who refused to give

what they had to give, but neither could I act foolishly and rashly, as if I was invincible. That was the action of a child. Part of the gift I had been given involved using my resources wisely.

I looked up, meeting the matron's eyes. She smiled at me kindly.

"Don't worry, Apprentice." Her voice was gentle. "You're not the first, and you won't be the last. Some things have to be learned through experience. You'll know better next time."

I managed a smile, grateful for her words. Tentatively I glanced at the younger healer to find his face had also softened.

"To tell the truth, you weren't even the only one in the storm. Although you did need to sleep the longest. The other apprentices seem to think it means you won some sort of contest." He exchanged a long-suffering look with the matron. "And of course that only adds to the mystique."

"Mystique?" I asked uneasily, remembering his earlier talk of legends.

"Well, as to that..." He hesitated. "A boy and his mother came looking for you and had to be turned away. They were very insistent about needing to thank you."

I smiled, tears pricking my eyes. So Coby's mother had found him. That was a relief.

"They say you're only an apprentice like us," a young man of seventeen or eighteen said from the end of the bed. Three others of a similar age clustered around him, eight eager eyes trained on me.

"Even newer than us, I heard," one of the girls added. "But that mother said she was on death's door when you got to her."

"I heard you'd already healed half the injured in the square before her," a third said. "They say you rode into the city in the middle of the storm, mustered a rescue party, and healed everyone."

"You pulled them out from under the stalls, and then moved on to the next one like it was nothing," the fourth added.

"Me?" I gaped at them. "People are saying *I* did that?"

"Not alone, of course," the first one said, and I relaxed for a second before he continued. "You had your master with you, naturally. And while you were fixing the square, she was at the harbor."

A new layer of awe settled over the group at the mention of Amara.

"They say she single-handedly stopped the waves breaching the harbor."

"And she saved five ships as well as countless sailors who'd gone overboard."

"My cousin was there, and she saw a ship sailing into harbor like they were in a bubble—the sea at their prow and stern as calm as if there wasn't any storm raging at all."

"It wasn't just the ships everyone could see either," the first boy assured the second. "She saved ships too far out for the other mages to even sense."

"I heard the winds quieted, and those who'd gone overboard flew through the air until they reached the dock, like a bird coming in to land," said one of the girls.

I clapped both my hands to my head. Now I understood what the older healers had meant about a legend. In the chaos of the unexpected storm, many people had helped rescue the trapped and injured—most of the helpers being local Eldridans. But in the wake of the tragedy, people wanted heroes, and powerful and mysterious strangers made much better fodder for legends than the person next door. Especially when Amara was such a compelling figure. I had no doubt she really had achieved impressive feats at the harbor—even if not quite to the level of the stories circulating among the apprentices.

Hayes and Clay must have done more than me in the square —just to name two—but they hadn't come in the company of a mage who could make sailors fly.

"What I want to know," one of the girls said, "is who's the

man who carried you in? Because I heard some things about him, too."

My eyes snapped open, but I stayed in position, my face lowered and hidden from their view. Apparently Nik was another reason for my so-called mystique.

The other girl giggled. "I heard he's terribly handsome." She sighed. "And powerful, too. They say he cleared half the rubble in the square single-handedly, but he disappears whenever someone starts asking questions."

Even without seeing it, I could feel her eyes boring into me.

"Do you know who he is? Why doesn't he want anyone to know his identity?"

"I heard," the first girl said, her voice dropping to a whisper, "that he's a *prince*."

My head whipped up, my hands falling away. They couldn't possibly know the truth of Nik's identity. Their imaginations were simply taking them to the furthest reaches of romanticism. But whereas the other rumors led them to painful exaggeration, in this case, their flights of fancy had brought them dangerously close to the truth.

"This is all ridiculous!" I snapped. "Of course I did my part and healed as many as I could, but I didn't do anything outstanding. And while Master Amara is strong, she's still just one mage. I'm sure she had a whole team of people helping her bring in the boats."

The two girls exchanged disappointed looks.

"Are you sure you don't know who he is?" one of them whispered. "Because I got a glimpse of him putting that cloth on your eyes, and the way he looked at you—"

"That's enough," the male healer said sternly. He gave the girl an exasperated look. "You saw him, did you? Because when I asked, you all said that none of you got a good look at anyone who didn't belong in the hospital."

"Well, of course, I didn't get a *good* look," the girl muttered, flushing. "But I'm sure I saw *someone*."

"Someone!" The man threw his hands up in the air and gave the apprentices a look of such exasperation that they all scattered, mumbling about urgent tasks that needed their attention.

The healer shook his head as he watched them flee. "A prince? Really?" he murmured. "Anyone would think we hadn't just run our apprentices off their feet."

The matron, who had watched the whole thing in silence, chuckled. "Leave them be. They're young, and the young need something to talk about."

"Not just the young." The man eyed two older healers who were murmuring together on the far side of the room, casting frequent glances our way.

The matron shook her head, her smile dropping from her face. "With so much lost and so much to grieve, they need something thrilling to provide moments of relief."

"But why me?" I asked. "I'm sure you both healed more people injured by the storm than I did."

"Aye, that we both did." The woman's belly swayed with her laughter. "But we did it from within the walls of this hospital, which is much less romantic."

"I saw lots of healers in the square," I continued stubbornly. "Most of them must have been yours."

"They were, of course," the man said. "We sent everyone we could possibly spare when we heard of the disaster. But we didn't send out our apprentices, so you were probably the youngest there—and you held your own despite your age and lack of training."

"Luna isn't that much older than me," I muttered rebelliously. "Why don't they make legends about her and Master Hayes, instead?"

"Oh, you know Master Hayes, do you?" the matron asked.

"We were most grateful for his assistance, along with his apprentice and Master Clay, as well, of course. And I'm sure people would be talking about them if they'd ridden into town with someone who spent the storm flying ships through the air. Don't go getting a big head, child. It's your master who caught the crowd's attention. It merely made the story even better for her apprentice to be a prodigy as well, saving the city in a different way."

"Now the *ships* are flying, I see," the man said caustically. "You're as bad as the apprentices."

The matron winked at him. "We were all apprentices once. And I've received enough laurels in my time not to be hungering after recognition at my age. By the time you're weary from running this hospital for two decades, you'll be more tolerant as well."

"Delphine!" The shout from the doorway was half-enthusiastic greeting, half wail.

Luna shot across the room and threw her arms around me, nearly knocking me back onto the bed. Ember stood and shook herself, growling slightly until I reassured her with a quick hand on her head.

"You're awake!" Luna cried in my ear, making me wince.

"You're here?" I asked, in unenthusiastic tones. "Come to laugh at me for making a fool of myself?"

Luna pulled back and grinned. "Don't worry about that. I would probably have been in the bed next to you if Master Hayes hadn't stopped me in time."

"A salutary reminder to the person who actually deserves the scolding." Amara entered the room much more calmly, Hayes a step behind.

She stopped at my bed and looked down at me with a guilty expression.

"I'm sorry, Delphine. I failed in my duty to you, and I wasn't even here when you woke up."

I struggled to my feet, fighting against Luna's weight. I could see the shadow in her eyes, and I wondered if she was thinking of her mother. Amara, of all people, knew the dangers of pushing yourself to the point of losing consciousness.

"You don't need to worry about that. Of course you needed to be at the harbor saving lives during the storm, and I can understand them wanting your help in the aftermath as well. I'm the one who made the foolish mistake."

"I'm sorry as well, Delphine," Hayes said. "Unlike Amara, I was in the square, and I even saw you'd arrived. I should have kept an eye out for you, like I did for Luna. You might not be my apprentice, but you are my student."

"Don't worry," I repeated. "I've finally learned my lesson. No more attempting to do the impossible for me. Next time I feel like I'm getting close to the end, I'll pull back. And sit down. That would have been a helpful move in the circumstances."

Amara laughed. "The lesson you learned is that next time you should sit down?"

I scrunched my nose. "When you put it like that..."

Amara stepped closer, and Luna and the local healers moved back to give her room. She put a hand on my shoulder and smiled at me.

"In all seriousness," she murmured, "I'm proud of you. It isn't an easy lesson to learn. And you shouldn't expect yourself to suddenly be perfect at it. But it does you credit that your desire to help others is so strong. I hear you saved a lot of lives."

I grimaced. "Unless you actually did single-handedly bring five ships flying in from the depths of the ocean with a singing chorus of mermaids to accompany them, I wouldn't believe everything you hear about my supposed feats."

She laughed. "Well, there weren't any mermaids..."

"Amara!" I stared at her, and she chuckled again. "The rest might be a little exaggerated as well."

She leaned closer, her voice dropping to a whisper. "I may

be proud of you, but I would prefer not to repeat this particular scenario for more reasons than one. A certain someone has already reminded me of how I failed in my responsibilities where you're concerned. And since he's not the most responsible person himself, I'd prefer never to find myself on the receiving end of that particular lecture again, please. Especially when I don't have a word in my own defense."

I pulled away, flushing. But a moment later, a horrible thought occurred to me.

"Wait, does that mean you're going to refuse my going—?"

She put up a hand to silence me, her eyes sending a warning. "Not here," she mouthed, and I quickly stopped talking, my flush deepening.

"Does she have your official permission for discharge?" Amara asked the matron who was still standing nearby, an expression of interest on her face.

"Of course, of course," the matron assured her.

"Properly speaking, you didn't need to be here at all," Hayes said, "since healers can't do anything to speed recovery from ability overuse. But since you were brought here in the first place, and we've all been run off our feet without break, it seemed sensible to just leave you here. No one wanted you lying alone in our accommodation without anyone to watch over you."

"It certainly relieved my guilt to have you here," Amara said with another apologetic smile at me.

"I'm grateful for your care," I told the healer. "Please pass on my thanks to all the other healers as well."

"We should be thanking you for being by far our easiest patient," she replied with a laugh at her own joke. "You can never tell with healers. They're either the best or the worst patients."

"Do I want to know which you are, Hayes?" Amara murmured, and Luna broke into giggles.

"I can tell you all about that if you want to know," Luna said.

Amara stepped closer to her with a broad grin, but Hayes cleared his throat loudly.

"There's no time for such things now. There are people waiting for us."

All three of us laughed at that blatant attempt at distraction, but his words still caught my attention. I glanced at Amara, and she nodded confirmation of the question in my eyes.

Whisking Ember off the bed, I declared myself ready to depart, ignoring the knowing look in Amara's eye.

As we left the hospital—which really was eerily similar to the ones in Caltor and Ostaria—I directed a question at Hayes.

"What about Master Clay? I saw him at the square as well. Is he one of the ones waiting for us?"

"He should be, although he's been busier than the rest of us in the aftermath of the storm."

I directed a questioning look at Amara, who explained.

"Given the scale of the disaster, the injured humans got all the initial attention from the healers, regardless of their specialization. But now that the hospital is cleared, the animal healers have been in great demand. Sadly, many animals were also injured during the storm."

Her words made me look up into the clear sky. Surely Phoenix had been safe in the stables where I'd left him and wasn't one of the casualties?

Before I had time to ask, a speck appeared in the now cloudless blue, growing larger rapidly. A blur descended toward us, pulling up at the last minute to reveal a bird twice the length of my hand with a blue-gray back and an underside speckled orange and black. Phoenix.

I flicked my hair off my shoulder just in time for him to execute a neat landing.

"Other than hunting flights, he's been waiting near the hospital," Amara said. "I think he was keeping watch for you to emerge."

"Thank you, kind sir." I ran a finger along the feathers of his underside.

"Even I wasn't able to lure him back to our lodgings," a cheerful voice said from the other side of the street.

We all smiled at Clay's arrival, although I noticed the expression was more strained on Hayes than the rest of us.

"You're finished for now?" Amara asked Clay, her expression concerned. "Have you eaten anything today?"

"Yes, far too much, in fact," he assured her with a wide smile. "Everyone I visited plied me with food. I've been treated like a king."

"I should hope so, given you've been working for free for days," Luna said. "At least we ran out of patients yesterday when the local healers kicked us out of the hospital, saying they could handle the remaining injured themselves."

"How could I deny my help, given how the injuries came about?" Clay gestured for me to mount four shallow steps to the front door of an elegant, narrow home.

I blinked at it in surprise, pausing long enough that the rest of the group stopped as well.

"This is an inn?" I asked doubtfully.

"We have proper lodgings this time," Luna exclaimed in glee. "Apparently no one wanted to see the heroes of the disaster forced into ordinary inn rooms."

I groaned. "Please tell me you're talking about yourselves."

"Of course not," she said, her grin turning wicked. "I only healed a very average number of people in the square."

I groaned again but let her push me up the stairs and through the door. She guided me immediately left, through an internal doorway and into a large, bright sitting room furnished in light wood and elegant brocade.

A tall figure turned from the mantelpiece at our entrance, his eyes fixing on me. I stilled, and Nik and I regarded each other in silence for several seconds before he moved, striding across the room to meet me in the middle.

"You're fully healed?"

I covered my eyes with my hand. "I didn't need healing, just a long sleep—like a total novice. Please don't remind me."

He pulled my hand away with gentle fingers.

"Next time, please spare a single thought for yourself."

"I'll do my best," I murmured. "No more overreaching for me. But thankfully on this occasion I had you there. I only remember it vaguely, but you were the one who carried me to the hospital, weren't you? Thank you."

He shook his head, looking frustrated. "I hope you really mean that about the future. It was only chance I even knew you'd arrived in Eldrida. And there I was, foolishly thinking you couldn't run into any trouble in your two days on the road." He shot an accusatory glance at Amara, reminding me of my earlier fear about her withdrawing her permission for the plan against Grey.

"Never mind that." I put a hand on his arm and turned to my master. "The important thing is what happens next. If the storm wasn't natural, could it have been sent by Grey?"

"I've been wanting to ask the prince's opinion on that question myself," Hayes said. "He's our expert on Grey."

Nik's face twisted at the unwanted title, but he didn't deny it.

"Grey himself is strong," he said, "but he has a healing affinity. He couldn't direct a storm. And while he does have elements followers, he's been forced to take untrained youngsters from the fringes of society, so none of them are mage strength. And it would take several skilled mages working together to drive a storm that large."

"So it wasn't Grey," Clay muttered. "I wish that was better

news. But that storm came from someone, and if it wasn't Grey —who?"

"There's no way it was Calista," Hayes said with confidence. "Not unless it was a group of mages gone rogue. And honestly, I don't think they have the capacity for that to be an option yet. They still have so few strong mages that they're all gathered in the capital where most of the rebuilding work has been done."

"You have that much confidence in the integrity of their new Mage's Guild?" Amara asked. "They wouldn't consider it worth the consequences to push their problems south to us?"

"My confidence is in their king and queen," Hayes said. "As the strongest two mages in the kingdom, they work very closely with their fledgling new Guild, and they would never sanction such a thing."

"No, I suppose not," she murmured. "Not given Queen Cadence's sister's position in Tartora."

"They're not that sort of people regardless," Hayes said firmly. "I would stake my life on it."

Amara raised her eyebrows at that, shooting a glance at Nik. When he slowly nodded his agreement, she let the matter drop.

I spoke into the silence. "In that case, we have two mysteries on our hands. What is causing the blight, and where did that storm come from? Would anyone wager they're unconnected?"

All three of the mages exchanged worried glances.

"Which means we need answers more urgently than ever," I continued, fixing my eyes on Amara. "And we know Grey has at least some of those answers. So when do I leave for the desert?"

CHAPTER

SEVENTEEN

It didn't end there, of course. Amara protested about the danger to me, and we all talked in endless circles for over an hour. But we'd all been in the middle of the storm, and no one could deny the new urgency to discover Grey's secrets.

Adding weight to my position was Hayes's report from the capital. After extensive consultation with the king and Triumvirate, they had agreed to back Nik's plan with only a few modifications.

As well as the squad of guards they had brought from the palace, Hayes and Clay had already recruited more from the local barracks—focusing on those with experience of both the local area and the desert. They had even hired an expert desert tracker—a rare breed since no one lived in the desert region.

"I have a friend among the local mages who's helped us with the selections," Hayes said. "I'm confident the ones we've recruited can be trusted, and we've told no one else the purpose of our visit. Officially, I'm here to give my apprentice broader experience."

Luna beamed. "Happy to be of assistance."

"And I'm here consulting with some of the local clinics on

new techniques," Clay said. "The clinics in Eldrida have the most experience healing sea creatures."

"You get a lot of those in Ostaria do you?" I asked with a snort.

"I'm sometimes called south to the coast for consultations with local healers," Clay said with dignity before cracking a smile. "It was the best I could come up with, but I have old friends here, so no one has asked too many questions."

"We have no need of the tracker," Nik said caustically, having been mostly silent through the conversation, his eyes narrowed and steely as he watched the mages talk. "Or don't you trust that I can get you there?"

"I think it's getting back that's the primary concern," Hayes said when no one else immediately answered.

"Getting back?" I asked, not quite keeping the note of uncertainty out of my voice at this unsettling comment. I glanced at Nik who had straightened, giving Hayes his full attention.

"If we've really decided to do this," Hayes said, "then there's one other condition from the capital."

He glanced at Amara, but she didn't protest, apparently having been worn down either by their arguments or my deter-mination.

"The condition?" Nik asked when Hayes didn't immediately speak.

"We are all to accompany Delphine part of the way into the desert and set up our own camp in a suitable location, to be determined by you and the tracker. But Your Highness is to accompany Delphine the rest of the way and to stay close enough to Grey's camp to monitor her conversations."

Nik went utterly still.

"Only me?" he asked stiffly.

Hayes cleared his throat. "I believe it was felt that only one person could safely conceal themselves so close to the camp.

And since you're the one with both experience of the location and the necessary skills…"

"Necessary skills?" I looked between them. "What do you mean? How can Nik possibly listen to my conversations if he's not even inside the camp?"

"It seems Father has great belief in my ability." Nik's tone was impossible to read.

"Is he wrong?" Hayes asked quietly, not flinching in response to Nik's closed expression.

I threw Amara a desperate look, hoping she might rescue me with actual answers.

"Plants mages with sufficient skill and power can use root systems to listen to conversations happening at some distance." She looked at Nik curiously. "Can you really do it? You'll have to create and maintain the root networks yourself, since they won't exist in the desert."

Nik hesitated for a moment before nodding once. "I can do it."

Hayes smiled slightly, and I wondered if he had been the one to assure the king about his son's growth in skill during his time away.

But my initial uncertainty still hadn't been answered. "What does any of that have to do with needing a tracker to return?" I asked.

Nik's eyes turned dark, although his mouth curved upward in a humorless smile. "I believe there's another reason for sending only one to accompany you. It seems *His Majesty* considers me expendable." He looked at Hayes. "Or is that coming from my dear friends among the Triumvirate?"

I frowned. If I wanted to understand Nik, I really needed to find out what troubled history lay between him and the three most powerful mages in the kingdom.

"Expendable?" I asked instead, knowing it wasn't the time or place for the other conversation.

Hayes didn't seem daunted by Nik's observation, keeping his focus on the prince when he answered.

"That's one way to consider it. I prefer to think that they're giving you a chance."

"A chance?" Nik raised an eyebrow.

"To prove yourself...Among other things." For some reason Hayes's eyes flicked to me, and Nik's followed them, a strange look coming over his face.

What did Nik's proving himself have to do with me? A sudden horrible thought occurred to me. Had Hayes picked up on Nik's protective attitude toward me and reported on it to the *king*? Was King Marius attempting to win his son back by giving the order he thought his son would want—allowing Nik to stay close to me while also demonstrating that King Marius trusted in Nik's abilities?

I shook my head at my foolish thoughts. Surely not. The king would be interested in protecting his son, not pandering to Nik's strange insistence on shadowing me.

"Very well, then," Nik said suddenly. "We'll leave before dawn."

"Wait, what?" I asked, startled out of my thoughts.

"Why?" Nik looked at me with a shade of amusement. "Are you feeling short on sleep?"

"Quiet, you." I narrowed my eyes at him, but he just chuckled at my glare, his whole manner changed from the stoic, icy warrior who had observed most of the conversation. Whatever meaning he'd taken from Hayes's words, it seemed to have shaken him out of his earlier mood.

"That makes me feel better, actually," Amara said. "You should have mentioned it earlier."

"It does?" Nik looked at her in surprise.

"I'm not saying I approve of you, reneger," she said, and his remaining smile disappeared at the word. "But you've proven yourself when it comes to protecting Delphine." She held up a finger. "Which is all I'm giving permission for, mind you."

"Amara!" I cried while Luna cackled into her hands.

Nik ignored them both, turning back to Hayes. "Meet at the north gate just before dawn. With or without your guards and tracker. It makes no difference to me."

Hayes agreed to the meeting place, looking like he would have liked to say more but was refraining. But when Nik strode out of the room, heading for the front door, something else flashed into my mind.

I dashed after him, stopping him with a hand on his arm just as he reached for the door handle. He turned quickly, surprise and something else flashing across his face when he saw it was me.

"Is there a problem?" he asked, but the way his eyes lingered on my face made me think he wanted to ask something else.

I forgot my original purpose, a different question distracting me.

"You barely said a word back there. The plan was your idea in the first place—I thought you'd be the one working hard to convince Amara."

"Does that worry you?" He examined my eyes.

I considered the matter. "More curiosity than worry, I suppose."

"Seeing you in that hospital bed for so long..." His eyes tightened. "Let's just say I've been starting to agree with Amara's opinion on this."

"But it was your plan!"

"Exactly. What was I thinking to suggest such a thing? You might be strong, but even you have your limits."

"Don't worry," I said with a cheeky grin. "Out in the desert there will only be one of me to heal. I won't go collapsing on you again."

He cast his eyes toward the ceiling. "Yourself plus Miranda and about twenty animals, if I know you."

Phoenix, still perched on my shoulder, gave a chattering call, ruffling his feathers.

"Your objection has been noted," I said on a laugh. "I'll try to refrain from attracting too many more animal companions."

"Was that what you wanted to ask me?" Nik's eyes lingered on the hand that still rested on his arm. I pulled it back.

"Actually, it was something else. It might not be a problem, but..."

His brow instantly tightened, his expression turning serious.

"When I woke up, the apprentices at the hospital were full of talk. There seem to be all kinds of outlandish rumors flying around."

His face relaxed, and he laughed. "Oh, that. Don't worry, healer. I don't suddenly think you can heal multitudes or fell armies with a single touch. I won't relax my vigilance out there."

I shook my head. "I'm not worried about me," I said, exasperated. "It's you I'm concerned about."

"Me?" His amusement lingered, sparking with an added hint of warmth. "You don't need to concern yourself about my safety. I learned to look after myself long ago."

I rolled my eyes and pushed on. "They seemed to be competing with each other for the most dramatic exaggeration on the stories, but unfortunately in your case..."

"Goodness," he said lightly when I fell silent. "Whatever did they say about me?"

"A few people got glimpses of you coming in and out of the hospital." I gave him a reproving look, and he glanced away, apparently uncomfortable at being found out.

"Since you carried me in from the square, someone connected you with the unknown plants mage who was helping there. And from there they kept exaggerating the situation until they accidentally stumbled onto the truth. They were talking about a prince with the power to move stones. One with a connection to me."

I trained my eyes on him, hoping he would understand my concern.

He raised an eyebrow. "Which of those facts concerns you, exactly?"

"Nik!" I whacked his arm lightly. "Be serious! Unless you want the whole city to work out who you are, you'd better stay out of sight until tomorrow morning."

"Thank you for your concern, but didn't you hear Hayes? My father has graciously extended his permission for me to risk my life for the kingdom, so I no longer need to fear finding myself carted off to the capital with a sack over my head."

"Nik!" I cried again.

"Or are you worried the Eldridans will realize my identity, thus discovering I'm a reneger, and form a mob to punish me for trying to mingle in regular society?"

He raised an eyebrow, and I sighed.

"Never mind, then. Go and proclaim your identity from the steps of the law keepers' hall for all I care."

"Delphine." Both his face and voice softened. "Thank you for your concern—truly. But I wish you wouldn't waste any worry on me."

I glared at him. "Isn't it for me to decide if it's wasted?"

"Delphine," he said again, a different note in his voice.

One of his arms snaked around my waist, and my breath rushed out of me, my eyes jumping to his. The expression in them made my middle seize, and I held my breath, keeping still as I waited to see what he was going to do.

But a slight rise in the voice of the speaker in the sitting room made him glance over my shoulder at the closed door behind me. Sighing, he pressed a fast kiss to my forehead.

"Stay safe, Delphine," he said. "I'll see you tomorrow."

I tried to protest, but by the time I'd worked out what to say, he was already out the door and onto the street. I watched the front door swing closed with a sigh of my own.

Nik had now been back for weeks, and it was obvious something significant had changed in his feelings toward me since our unexpected kiss in Caltor. But in other aspects, it sometimes seemed like he hadn't changed at all.

Whenever his family came up in conversation, I didn't know what I hated more—his icy, bitter reaction or the reminder that regardless of Nik's feelings, his complicated status still stood between us. If his family ever did reclaim him, it wouldn't be with a bag over his head, and they wouldn't have any interest in an ordinary farmer's daughter clinging to his side. But if they didn't accept him back, then he would forever remain a reneger, never able to properly interact in normal society and shunned by anyone who discovered his identity. Whether as royal prince or outcast reneger, Nik wasn't someone I should be thinking about. And yet, every time he got close, I forgot all about those concerns. And when he left, I couldn't stop my thoughts from filling with him.

"Are you really going to do this?" a small voice asked from behind me.

I turned and managed to dredge up a smile for Luna. "Of course I am. You were out there in the storm, too. We have to do something."

"Someone has to do something," she agreed, "but does it really have to be you?"

I opened my mouth to answer glibly but stopped myself just before I spoke. She was asking earnestly, and it was a question worth proper consideration.

"I'm just an apprentice from Tarin," I said after a moment. "So, no, I don't think it's my responsibility to work out what's happening with the blight, or even the storm. But Miranda is my friend. I've known her since we were small children, and I promised her father I would look for her. I know where she is right now, and I can't turn away from that. I have to try to reach her."

Luna sighed, reaching out to squeeze me tightly. "Just make sure you come back."

I hugged her back. "I promise I'll do my absolute best."

She stepped away and gave a chuckle. "I'm being foolish, aren't I? Miranda's been safe all this time, and you'll be all right too."

"Exactly!" I said brightly, putting in more confidence than I felt. "We're healers, remember? We don't kill easily."

Amara appeared in the doorway, looking at me steadily. "If you feel in real danger at any point, I want you to just walk out of there. We'll be waiting for you in the desert, and no one is going to blame you if you don't succeed." Her fierce expression told me if anyone wanted to blame me, they would have to go through her.

"Thank you," I said softly. "I want to help if I can, but I don't have any plans for grand self-sacrifice. My first priority is getting Miranda out, and if that means leaving without discovering Grey's secrets, then I'll do that and leave the matter to the Guild mages."

She nodded decisively. "Then we'll depart in the morning as planned. I know you've just slept for two days but try to get a bit of rest before then, please."

EIGHTEEN

I tried not to be intimidated by the number of guards waiting for us just outside the north gate of the city. But it was hard to ignore them when most of them were throwing covert glances my way, clearly curious about the girl at the center of our plot.

How many of them had heard the rumors from the storm? It made me uncomfortable to think they might be giving me far more credit than I deserved.

Eldrida soon faded behind us in the pre-dawn gloom, and I was surprised that my mind lingered on the disappearing city instead of the task ahead of me. I had roamed the streets until it grew pitch black, hoping the activity would make me tired enough to sleep again, and I couldn't forget my breath-taking first glimpse of the ocean.

I had known it would be large, but the vastness of it still struck me somewhere deep inside. The seas were shockingly still after the furor of the storm, the blue growing darker as it approached the horizon.

The smell of salt on the air, the call of the seabirds, and the white spray thrown up by the breeze permeated all my senses, immersing me in the moment in a way I'd rarely experienced.

And when I returned to our lodgings, the sound of the waves chased me into a light doze.

Even the slate gray of the buildings—those near the harbor specked white with dried salt—seemed different from the buildings I knew from the rest of the kingdom. And the people were different as well, speaking with a lilt to their words that was refreshing and new to my ear.

"This is my first time east of the forest too," Luna had told me after leading me to the harbor and watching my reaction with satisfaction. "But I've heard talk about the people in this eastern stretch of the kingdom. Those in the capital say the easterners have their own ways. They're so isolated from the rest of Tartora that I suppose it makes sense."

I had hoped to find the two locals who had helped me during the storm, but I had no way to discover their names or locations. Even the grizzled stable master—who recognized Ember and Phoenix before he recognized me—had no idea who they were.

I had spent only a short time in the city—and for much of it I was unconscious—but fighting the storm shoulder to shoulder with the locals had given me a sense of kinship with Eldrida that I hadn't managed in months of living in Caltor. I just hoped I would have the chance to come back one day and spend more time here.

At first, we traveled north through the same sort of hilly grazing country as we had traversed from the river to the city. I didn't have much chance to observe it, however, since we traveled in closed trading wagons. Our mode of travel was one of the decisions made before Amara's and my arrival in Eldrida. The decision makers had decided that merchants traveling by an unusual route would draw less attention than a collection of royal guards and mages heading north.

Each wagon was pulled by a team of horses, and we made good time on the little used road that headed north and slightly west, heading for the northeast tip of Lake Aterra, where travelers could skirt the southern tip of the desert and join the fertile land that covered the middle of Calista.

We didn't camp for the night until after dark, when Nik appeared from the front wagon and told me we had crossed the border.

"You mean we're in Calista right now?" I asked.

He nodded. "My father will probably have sent word to Zeke and Cadence since the desert is officially part of their territory, but they have little true ownership over it since it's infertile and uninhabitable."

It took me a moment to realize he was talking about the Calistan king and queen. I nodded silently, reminded that Nik was the kind of person to casually refer to foreign monarchs by their first name.

An old memory suddenly surfaced of him claiming to have helped Queen Cadence restore Calista from its fallen state. I had scoffed at the suggestion at the time, but now I felt foolish for having done so.

Amara appeared, handing out bowls of stew, and our moment of private conversation ended. His words stuck with me, though, as we continued traveling the next day.

Even traveling at speed, starting before dawn and continuing until after dark each day, it took us two more days to reach the tip of the lake. A few settlers had moved into the rundown village there, but they had only restored three of the houses so far.

Our group slept under the stars before parting ways with the wagons and their drivers. They would return home at a more leisurely pace as the rest of us continued into the desert on foot.

I expected it to be burning hot on the desolate stretch of sand, but the pre-dawn cold of harvest season left me shivering as we stepped past the last scrubby patches of grass. As the sun rose, it grew hotter, but never to the blistering heat I had expected.

A comment from Nik told me it had been less pleasant during the summer, and I was glad for the timing that brought us here on the verge of winter. My legs soon grew weary of trudging over lightly packed sand, however, and they would eventually have been burning more than the noonday sun if I hadn't used my power to soothe the ache.

When I saw Hayes and Clay circulating among the soldiers —a soft word and brief handclasp enough to provide the same service for them—I offered my assistance. Hayes agreed, having Luna and me join him in providing relief for several of the guards. Like with our studies in Caltor, he used his own power to complete the task, having us join with him and shadow his activity with our power, amplifying his efforts. His demonstration, combined with a few words of explanation, showed me a more efficient way to target the relevant muscles, a method that required less power than I'd been using on myself to achieve the same end.

It was an interesting process—the only proper stimulation in the whole day—but he warned me that he had only permitted it as a training exercise.

"I don't want you using unnecessary energy from tomorrow onward. Keep it for whatever you encounter in Grey's camp."

I nodded, trying not to show how unsettled I felt at his words. The closer we got to Grey, the more real this whole situation became, and I was dreading the moment when I left the rest of the group behind.

Nik had spent the journey in the lead, accompanied by the desert tracker who consulted with him in low tones. I could only assume Nik was teaching him the route he was taking and the two of them were choosing the best place for the rest of the group to wait.

In the end, they led us to the coast, the sight of the sea

catching me by surprise. It had been huge and overwhelming from Eldrida's harbor, but from the desert it seemed vast and wild in a wholly different way.

We all traipsed down a short but steep cliff, finding a tiny hidden cove at the bottom. Gazing out to sea, the water looked tempestuous, roiling over unseen obstacles that occasionally reached above the water level, the jagged points of rock deadly and unwelcoming.

Turning, however, I saw that the small strip of damp sand led to a deep cave that stretched back into the cliff side.

"Even if Grey sends a team south from his camp, they won't see you in here," Nik said with satisfaction.

"How did you find this place?" I asked, gazing back up the invisible path that had led us down the steep incline.

He grinned. "Plants affinity, remember? I made that path. And I felt the cave under my feet when I first passed by. I used it to hide from Grey's people myself last time, so I know high tide doesn't even come close to filling it."

One of the guards gazed uneasily at the turbulent ocean beyond the cove. "That was a different season, though, wasn't it?"

"Don't worry." Amara's smile showed her teeth. "I'll take care of any water troubles we might encounter."

The guard immediately nodded and disappeared back into the crowd of his comrades, eyes wide. I hid a smile. Whether or not they'd heard of my supposed feats, our companions had certainly heard the rumors about Amara.

We all slept in the cave that night, the strange echoing space unfamiliar after the open skies of our nights on the road. Ember was fascinated by it, trotting away to sniff at dark corners until Amara warned her sternly not to wander.

"If you go far enough in, we might never find you," she said, making me clasp the fox tightly.

Phoenix was less impressed, however, opting to leave us for

the night in favor of sleeping in the desert above. I tried not to be offended by his desertion, but I would have appreciated his presence in the restless night that followed.

But when I reached the top of the cliff the next morning, he was already flapping his way toward me, landing on his usual perch on my shoulder. He stayed in position as Amara, Hayes, Clay, and Luna gave their final farewells, each giving various pieces of advice that I promptly forgot in the tension of the moment.

Now that the moment had come, I wanted to cling to Amara like I would have to my mother if she was there, but I restrained the impulse. I had told them all that I could do this, and I needed to prove that was true.

But I was incredibly grateful to have Nik at my side as I walked away. The comfort didn't last long, however. We'd barely lost sight of the others when Nik stopped, turning to me with a serious expression.

"You'll need to go the rest of the way on your own. If Grey is going to believe you came looking for him alone, he needs to see you coming."

I swallowed. "How am I going to convince him I came all this way alone, exactly?" All the plans we'd discussed seemed to have disappeared from my mind.

"You heard rumors in Eldrida," he said patiently. "So you came north. You've left your master and followed the coast to his camp. You made a promise to Miranda's father, and you're there to get her out by taking her place."

"I did make a promise to her father," I said.

He nodded. "Exactly. He's a healer so you can't lie outright to him. But he saw you in the warehouse—he knows you want to rescue Miranda. I think there's at least a chance he's been keeping her close in the hope you'll come."

"But surely he'll be suspicious," I said, knowing I was

echoing words from our very first conversation on the topic but not able to help myself.

"Probably." Nik shrugged unconcernedly. "But I've never seen anything to match Grey's confidence. He'll trust in his ability to win you over."

I straightened my shoulders. "Well, he's about to meet his match, then. I have no interest in whatever bright future he's claiming to offer."

Nik nodded approvingly. "All that matters is that he believes in his own persuasiveness. Just don't make the mistake of mentioning any of us. He has to believe you came on your own."

I nodded. "I'll tell him Amara thought it was too dangerous for me to seek him out. That's true, even if we did eventually manage to convince her."

"Just remember," Nik said. "You won't see me, but I'll be there. If you need help, shout for me, and I'll hear you."

I managed a tremulous smile. He might hear me, but that didn't mean he'd be close by.

I forced my back to straighten. Nik hadn't helped in my last confrontation with Grey, and I didn't need him now. I could face this.

And I wouldn't be completely alone anyway. I put a reassuring hand on Phoenix, who was heavy on my shoulder. No one had even suggested trying to keep the animals behind, and I had never been so grateful for such loyal companions.

Nik looked like he wanted to say something more, but he must have seen from my face that I was only just holding on to my composure. With a single clasp of my arm, he slipped away, disappearing down another steep incline just as the first rays of the sun slid above the ocean.

I watched the place where he'd been for a moment before turning north. The desert ended at the coast, but there were no gentle, sloping sandy beaches like on the southern coast.

Instead the desert ended abruptly, my vantage point allowing me to look down at the crashing waves below.

I had no idea how Nik would keep pace with me down there on the narrow, rocky coastline, but his plants affinity made him far more equipped to do so than I would ever be. I needed to trust he could look after himself and focus on my own task.

I carried a pack, but it wasn't heavy. Someone had carefully crafted it to look like I was near the end of a long journey, my supplies running low, so I was confident I could easily carry it for a day's walk.

As I traipsed along, the desert stretching to my left and the sea extending out to my right, I rehearsed what I would say to Grey. I would need to choose my words carefully, implying any untruths instead of stating them outright.

I had thought the day would last forever, but instead I seemed to blink and something green was breaking the monotony of my view ahead. I stared at it, trying to make sense of what I was seeing when shouted voices made me jump.

After the hours alone with Ember and Phoenix, the sound of human voices sounded strange and jarring. By the time I found their owners, two men had nearly reached me, running heavily across the rocky desert ground.

I stopped, waiting calmly for their approach. They were carrying drawn blades, but as they neared and saw that I was one girl, traveling alone, their posture changed, their weapons dipping.

As soon as they were close enough to hear me without having to shout, I spoke.

"I'm Delphine, and I'm here to see Grey."

"Here to see Grey?" One of them repeated, looking incredulously at the other. "Just come for a social call, have you?"

I tried to keep my tension from my face. "I'll discuss my purposes with Grey, and Grey alone."

"Will you now?" The second man stepped forward with a threatening air, but Ember's growl from near my ankles made him pause, his eyes jumping from her teeth to Phoenix's curved beak. The bird was regarding him with a steady eye, and the man quickly halted his approach.

"I'm not here to fight." I stretched my arms wide. "I carry no concealed weapons. All I want is to speak to Grey."

I had no idea if either of them were healers, but it seemed better to assume they were and watch my words, no matter who I was speaking to.

Once again the two exchanged looks, and this time they shrugged.

"Go on, then." One of them indicated with his sword that I should proceed, walking toward the green patch ahead.

I did so, forcing my head to stay high and my pace steady. The two men fell into place on either side of me, their swords still drawn. Given the careful distance they kept from me, they were either concerned I might be a healer or worried about my animals. Either option worked for me.

As we approached closer, the green ahead took further shape. The cliff side here stabbed inward into the desert, creating a sharp 'v' shape that must have a clean water source based on all the green that grew inside the sheltered area. The green I had glimpsed from afar was the tops of trees, but when I peered over the edge, I saw plants of various types below.

The men directed me to lead the way down an established path that snaked down into the crevasse. It was much easier to follow than Nik's temporary creation, and Ember was even able to walk at my feet.

Our height made us stand out, and by the time we reached the bottom, a small crowd was converging on the path. Many of them were of a similar age to me, but a few stood out from the others, their faces bearing the marks of greater age and their hands resting on sword hilts at their waists. Before I had time to be intimidated by the number of people, however, someone thrust through the middle of the crowd, pushing the others out of the way.

"Delphine!" Miranda screamed my name before throwing herself into my arms.

I clung to her, murmuring her name as I squeezed her tight. So many of the memories of my childhood had been marred since leaving Tarin, but Miranda remained as a bright spot.

I pulled back so I could look at her properly, holding her by the arms and examining her from head to toe.

"Are you all right?" I asked.

"Of course!" She beamed at me, her expression slowly growing confused. "Why wouldn't I be?"

"Well...I..." My words trailed off as I remembered the last time I had seen her.

Had she forgotten being threatened by Grey and carried off over his shoulder? Had she forgotten his casual attacks on first Serena and then me? It occurred to me that Miranda had been half out the window at the time and might not have seen him take out Serena. But she must have seen him stab me.

Her head cocked to the side, and her brow creased, as if she was wrestling with a large and confusing thought.

"I'm so happy to see you, Delphine. But what are you doing here?"

"I came to get you."

"Me?" She gaped at me, as if the thought were unimaginable. "But that can't be right. No one wants me back."

I frowned. "Why would you say that? Of course we do! Your father was devastated when you left."

"He...he was?" She slowly shook her head. "He must be very angry then. I heard he disowned me because of it."

"Don't be silly!" I said bracingly, remembering the lies Grey had told before Serena's departure. "He's waiting for you to come home."

"No..." She frowned, looking lost and confused. "That can't be right. My father never wants to see me again."

I moved my hands to her shoulders, angling her body so her eyes met mine.

"Your father loves you and wants you back at home. That's why I'm here. I promised Halmir that I'd find you and send you back."

She still hesitated, and I shook her lightly. "You have a healing seed, Miranda. I know it's not activated yet, but you must be able to sense that I'm telling the truth. Your father is waiting in Tarin for you."

Her eyes lit up, all her confusion falling away. "He is? And he sent you to bring me home?" She threw her arms around me again, nearly knocking me over.

"Well, well, well," a silky voice said, as Grey strode toward us, the crowd parting before him. "This is an unexpected visit."

"Is it?" I asked, putting my arm around Miranda's shoulders and pulling her close to my side.

His smile widened. "Maybe not entirely."

All the way here I had worried, but now that I was here, confidence settled over my shoulders like a cloak. I had forgotten that the healing power worked both ways. I could sense sincerity or deception on Grey as easily as he could on me. I had felt the lie behind his opening words, and it lent credibility to Nik's certainty. Grey wasn't surprised by my arrival. He had been hoping I would come.

"We've never had a recruit travel so far on their own," he said lightly, his eyes dwelling on me.

My arm tightened around Miranda, drawing his eyes to her, and for the first time I saw a hint of displeasure creep onto his face.

"I'm not a recruit," I said, not wanting to overplay the situation. "But I'm willing to stay on one condition."

"Oh?" He raised an eyebrow. "And what is that?"

"You let Miranda go free."

"Let her go?" He spread his arms wide. "No one is held here against their will."

A murmur of agreement ran through the crowd. I frowned as I examined his face. His words felt like the truth, but I couldn't shake an air of deception that I sensed hanging around him like a shroud.

"Is that true, Miranda?" I asked, turning to the younger girl for confirmation.

"There didn't seem any point leaving when I had nowhere to go." Her eyes shone as she looked up at me. "But now that I know Father is waiting for me, of course I want to go home with you."

"With me," I repeated the words softly.

It had never occurred to me that Grey might let me collect Miranda and walk straight out again. If he really did intend to let her go, should I accept? Miranda was my personal focus for this mission, but I still wanted to help the rest of the kingdom if I could. But if he was going to let us both go, what reason could I give for staying? I had already said I wasn't here to join him.

I looked straight at him, taking a gamble.

"Excellent. In that case we can leave immediately."

Grey tensed slightly at the words, his movement reassuring me. He spread his arms wide, however, keeping a friendly expression on his face.

"Come, come, there's no need to hurry away. You must have had a long journey here, and you'll be needing more supplies, surely?"

I hiked my pack higher on my shoulder, pretending to feel its light weight, as I acted out the process of wavering.

"You'd just give us supplies freely?" I asked.

"Well, everything in life is a negotiation, isn't it?" He grinned. "But I think you'll find I can be reasonable."

My hand moved to my middle, pressing against the place he had plunged his dagger. It was an intentional movement, but I hoped he would take it as an instinctive response.

"Ah yes, you must accept my most sincere apologies for that," he said. "I was under attack and acting out of a most foolish anger. I can assure you that I'm not usually so impulsive."

I raised an eyebrow, but I couldn't deny the challenge in his eyes. They were calling on me to acknowledge the truth of his words, and this time I could sense nothing but sincerity from him. He truly did regret stabbing me.

I remembered my words to Nik at the time. Grey had always known I could heal myself—it had been a petty moment of revenge. Now he was claiming the impulsive moment was uncharacteristic, and I could well believe he usually behaved in a much more calculated manner.

If it was true that Grey wanted me among his followers, he must have realized in retrospect that stabbing me hadn't been a good opening move.

"We'll soon be sitting down for our evening meal," Grey said. "Why don't you join us? That way we can talk comfortably, and any further travel can happen in the daylight tomorrow."

I glanced at Miranda, but she seemed perfectly content with this plan. She even volunteered to show me around the camp, chattering most of the way about the daily business of life in the desert.

I had imagined it as a harsh, sweltering place, full of dirt and heat. But the hidden crevasse teemed with life, an oasis in the desolate land around it. There were even a few proper wooden buildings, although most of the houses were made of heavy canvas hung over wooden frames.

Down here among the greenery, the heat of the day had already faded, the temperature pleasant and cool. A long wooden table sat in the open space between the two rows of dwellings, people already starting to lay out plates and trays of food.

It was simple fare, but plentiful, and I wondered how much they provided for themselves and how much they traded for. While I doubted Grey would have a moral issue with stealing, he knew better than to draw attention to himself with that sort of behavior.

"As you can see, we're an amicable community," Grey said, taking a seat at the head of the long table and gesturing for Miranda and me to sit beside him at the long bench that ran down the right side.

Miranda seemed pleased at the placement. She appeared to harbor no resentment toward Grey for his lies, seeming almost normal as long as the topic of her father didn't come up. When it did, confusion took prominence, and I noticed Grey steered the conversation away from any such discussion.

"So what do you want in exchange for supplies?" I asked as soon as my plate was full.

"Straight to business, then?" Grey gave me an amused smile and a tilt of his eyebrow.

I held my ground, silently waiting for an answer.

He chuckled. "Very well. In all honesty, I was rather hoping I might convince you to stay."

Miranda frowned. "If Father is waiting for me, I can't stay here. He must be terribly worried after all this time."

"Naturally, you need to go. I can see that," Grey said smoothly, his words oozing truth. He understood what I was demanding from this bargain. "But perhaps your friend might like to stay."

Miranda turned wide eyes on me. "But your parents must

be worried about you too! I saw you in Caltor, which means you've been gone nearly as long as I have!"

I looked away from her, real pain pinching my chest. "I have no interest in returning to my farm."

"What?" Miranda grabbed my arm, twisting me back around toward her. "What do you mean? Surely you didn't fight with your parents? You always seemed so devoted to them."

"I was." I looked down at my plate. "And then I left Tarin and found out exactly what my father had been keeping from me. I've seen a bigger world than one farm now, and I have no interest in that life anymore."

Despite my continued anger at my father, it hurt to reveal so much painful truth in front of Grey. But that truth was also the best tool I had against him.

Out of the corner of my eye I could see the sharp interest in his eyes, and the small upward curve of his lips. He was trying to look detached and disinterested, but he was delighted to read this particular truth on me.

"I've left everyone behind," I continued, "and I walked across the desert because I heard you might be out here. Unlike my own father, yours always fought for me, Miranda. I promised him, and I couldn't let him down."

"Oh, Delphine." Miranda took my hand, tears in her eyes. "I'm sorry. You'll always have a place with my father and me. You know that, right?"

I forced a smile, nodding my thanks. "And I appreciate it more than I can say. But I'm not ready to go back to Tarin yet." I tore a piece off the chunk of bread on my plate. "But the same doesn't apply to you. You need to get back to your father."

"How could I go without you, though?" she asked.

"It's easy. All you have to do is follow the coast south until you reach Eldrida. From there, you can buy a place with merchants heading west." I glanced at Grey, and he chimed in as I had hoped he might.

"Naturally, I will provide provisions and gold for the journey, since I was the one to drag you all the way out here."

Miranda laughed, as if she hadn't been carted away as a hostage. "I don't know if I should accept, but I will. I can't leave my father waiting."

"I just hope there are no more big storms while you're traveling," I said, watching Grey closely out of the corner of my eye.

"I hope not!" Miranda's eyes widened. "We were lucky to be so sheltered down here, but even so we sustained some damage."

Grey's eyes also darkened at my words, but not with the emotions I'd expected. Instead he seemed genuinely angry, as if the storm had been an attack on him as much as us.

I chewed on the inside of my cheek, trying to decipher what that could mean. Did Grey know who had sent the storm as we suspected?

"The worst storms won't be until the turn of the season," Grey said. "Your journey should be a safe one, Miranda."

"Will you really stay here, though, Delphine?" Miranda asked. "Do you want to go with Grey to the new land?"

I shook my head. "I don't intend to stay here that long. But I'm curious enough to hear more about it. If Grey is going to leave soon, I can always return the way I came."

I turned to him. "Isn't that right?" I challenged, wanting to see his reaction.

A small smile turned his expression smug. "Certainly. If you still wish it."

Truth. I couldn't stop the twitch of my brows as I read it on him. Everything was so smooth, so easy. I hadn't even had to outright bargain with him for Miranda's freedom.

Instead of bolstering me, my success sent a thrill of uncertainty through me. Nik had talked endlessly of Grey's confidence, but this seemed beyond excessive. He couldn't possibly mean to let me wander freely around his camp only to leave again whenever I wanted.

Grey lifted his glass to me in a silent toast, his expression suggesting he could read the wheels turning in confusion behind my eyes. He had to suspect something, but it wasn't giving him a moment's discomfort.

And that made me very uncomfortable indeed.

CHAPTER
NINETEEN

My half-formed fear that Grey would change his mind at Miranda's actual departure proved unfounded. At least half the camp turned out to see her off, the younger members hugging her in what seemed like genuine affection.

Watching them sent a spear of discomfort through me. Did they have families at home waiting for them like she did? Was it wrong of me to care only about freeing my friend?

But I reminded myself that our end plan was to dismantle the camp completely. At that point, everyone would be returning to their normal life in Tartora, so I wasn't abandoning these others.

Miranda appeared uncertain when it came to actually setting off alone, but the determination that had entered her when she realized her father still loved and wanted her hadn't waned. With an uptilt of her chin, she climbed out of the canyon and disappeared into the desert overhead.

"Will she really be all right on her own?" I murmured to myself, although I knew she would only have to travel for a day before being picked up by Amara and the others.

"You made it alone, didn't you?" Grey asked with a smile.

I nodded, glad for the first time that I'd had to walk alone for the last day.

"Well, not entirely alone," I corrected, making him stiffen slightly. But when I gestured at my two ever-present shadows, he relaxed.

"Ah yes, I never expected to be making recruits among the animal world."

I turned to face him, ready for a more direct conversation now that Miranda was safely gone.

"I already told you, I'm not a new recruit."

"You were here to rescue your friend," he said, speaking more openly than he had since my arrival.

"Can you blame me?" I asked.

"Not in the least. I behaved without circumspection in Caltor, and I hope you will accept my apology." Again his words rang true.

"I don't know what you're planning," Grey said. "But I have no doubt you came here with a plan."

I raised both eyebrows. I hadn't expected him to be that direct.

"And if I did? What do you intend to do about it?" I challenged.

"I intend to change your mind," he said. "After what you've seen of me, your suspicion is perfectly understandable. But I'm hoping that once you've heard more of the story, you'll see things in a different light."

A girl about my own age strolled past, a bundle of chopped wood in her arms. She smiled at us both, her eyes lingering hopefully on me, as if she saw a potential friend.

I smiled back uncertainly. So far Grey's camp had been nothing like I expected. Instead of a military barracks crossed with a prison, it felt more like a village or even an extended family, everyone working together cheerfully to keep the community functioning.

"It's not like you expected, is it?" Grey's ability to guess my thoughts unnerved me, but I smiled back as sweetly as I could manage, keeping silent.

"Other things aren't like what you think either. Like that storm."

"The storm?" I looked quickly at him, not bothering to hide my curiosity this time.

"You might have missed us if not for that storm, actually," he said, making my shoulders tense in retrospective anxiety.

What did he mean by that? We had thought there was no hurry to find Miranda, but had we been wrong?

"You're leaving for the island already?" I asked without thinking.

Both his eyebrows shot up. "You know about the island?"

I managed a weak smile. "I spoke to Serena. She told me she wanted to leave you because your promised new land turned out to be across the ocean."

"You saved her?" He regarded me with fascinated, hungry eyes.

I almost corrected him—it had been the combined efforts of Hayes and Luna that had saved Serena—but I bit my tongue just in time. I was supposed to be making myself an appealing recruit, and apparently Grey wanted strong healers.

"So you spoke to Serena," Grey murmured. "That's how you found me, then."

I looked away. My slip had turned out in my favor, giving him an explanation for my sudden appearance here. Serena had never made it as far as the camp, but she'd known it was on the coast of the desert.

"You've shown remarkable loyalty to your friend," he said. "But then I've always found that those disenchanted with their homes are most interested in talk of a new home."

I nodded slowly, easily able to acknowledge the truth of those words, even if they didn't apply to me. My truth the night before had served me as well as my slip just now. Grey wanted to be convinced, and I had given him just enough ammunition to do it. Was this a glimpse of how he worked on others when the roles were reversed?

"Let me show you our main work here," Grey said, gesturing toward the ocean.

I hesitated, but the whole point of my presence was to get him talking, so I followed obediently in his wake. Overnight I had been comforted by Miranda's presence, the two of us sharing her bed before she solemnly handed possession of it over to me.

But now she was gone, and I was alone. I surreptitiously ran my hand over the closest bush, wishing I could send my power along its roots as Nik could apparently do. Was he listening even now?

I clung to the sense of his presence, however false it was, taking what courage I could muster from it.

"Here you are." A note of pride entered Grey's voice. "Isn't she beautiful?"

I blinked at the size of the sleek wooden ship that had appeared past the screening line of trees. It was as large as the largest I had seen in Eldrida's harbor.

"Did you build that?" I asked in astonishment, even as I watched the girl from earlier walk back down the gangplank, her arms now empty of branches.

She waved when she caught sight of me, smiling brightly as she headed back into the depths of the crevasse. Grey watched her go with an indulgent expression before looking at the ship again.

He had a warmth in his eyes when he regarded the wooden vessel that I had never seen when he looked at a human.

"We had to build her here," he said. "That's why preparing for this trip has taken so long, even with a team of people using their plants power to speed the work. It was the only way since the waters are too treacherous to sail up the coast from Eldrida. We can reach the island from here, but only by charting a very particular course, and only from this exact spot."

"So there really is an island." I gazed out at the ocean, which appeared smooth and unmarred by any other landmass. "And you're saying it's some sort of paradise that will provide us all with a better life?"

Grey started to nod only to stop, giving me a calculated look that I pretended not to see.

"That is part of the truth, certainly," he said after a moment.

I turned to him. "And what's the rest of the truth?" I asked boldly.

For a second, I was sure he meant to fob me off, but instead he looked at the people moving industriously around the ship and gestured for me to follow him. I did so cautiously, but he only led me toward the oldest of the wooden buildings, making no comment when Ember and Phoenix followed me inside.

From the outside it appeared to be an ordinary shack, and the inside confirmed that impression. A square room served as sitting room, dining room, and kitchen, with a stove under a chimney along one wall. A door on the opposite side of the room gave a glimpse of a single bedroom beyond, and from the look of the bed, Grey had slept in it the night before.

It was a step above the canvas tent that Miranda had shared with three other girls, but it wasn't significantly more luxurious. And it had a worn, lived-in feel that made it seem as if it had been inhabited for decades, passed down from previous generations.

I looked around openly, trying to work out what this house told me about Grey. But the more I saw of Grey and his camp, the more confusing it became. The ruthless, violent man I had previously encountered had disappeared entirely, and if I had just met him, I would have believed him to be a kindly village head, beloved by his harmonious community.

It was impossible to reconcile the two pictures.

Nik's words echoed in my head, reminding me of Grey's slippery charm, and I put a hand to my middle, the gesture unconscious this time. If I wanted to avoid falling for Grey's story, I needed to remember the feel of his dagger plunging into me.

"Please, sit down." Grey pointed at a simple wooden chair at the worn table in the middle of the room.

I sat obediently, watching as he lowered himself into the chair opposite, stretching out his long legs in a comfortable gesture and smiling across at me. I tried to keep my gaze open and unsuspicious, but the hint of amusement in his eyes made me suspect I had failed.

"To most of my followers, I focus on the new life awaiting us," he said. "But I can see you know more than most." He leaned forward, his voice turning earnest. "Given our protected location here, most of my people don't realize the extent of that storm. But I can imagine what it did in Eldrida, coming on without warning like that."

I nodded, allowing some of the horror of those hours to show on my face.

"I don't know the final count of the dead," I said, "but there must have been many given how many boats were out at sea."

"A true tragedy," he said.

I frowned, trying to make sense of him. I didn't get the impression he particularly cared about the people of Eldrida, but I also didn't read any outright lie in his words.

"Are you saying it wasn't a natural phenomenon?" I asked. "You're saying someone created this tragedy?"

He nodded. "That's exactly what I'm saying. I can see that you're someone with a high sense of responsibility, and I applaud that. You came here to save your friend, but what if I told you that you can help save all of Tartora?"

I blinked. Whatever I'd been expecting, it hadn't been that.

He sat back with a satisfied expression.

"The people on that island live a comfortable life," he said. "And it's a life we can also experience. That much is true. But I have another reason for going."

"Wait." I sat up straight, my sudden movement making Ember growl, lifting up her head from where she lay curled on the floor.

I ignored her, too distracted by Grey's words. "You're saying there's already a community of people on the island—people no one here knows exist—and they're the ones who sent the storm?"

"That," said Grey, "is exactly what I'm saying."

"And the blight, too?" I asked, forgetting to be cautious. "They somehow caused that as well?"

Grey whistled quietly. "You know about that, too? You really have connected the dots."

I shrugged. "Never mind that. Tell me." I trained my eyes on him, determined not to misread the truth of his words.

"Yes," he said simply. "I have reason to believe they have been causing the destruction of Tartora's crops, as well as sending the storm."

There wasn't the slightest shade of deception around his words.

"What are your reasons?" I asked. "Do you have certain proof?"

Grey's expression closed off. "You're a healer. You can read the truth of my statements for yourself."

His manner made it clear I had pushed too hard. I sat back, forcing myself to relax.

"Of course," I murmured. "Sorry. I'm just shocked."

He relaxed slightly. "I can hardly blame you for that. I was shocked myself."

"But why?" I cried. "Why would they want to move against Tartora after all this time?"

Grey shrugged. "They have the power to rule over anyone. They seem to have decided it's time to wield that power."

"Rule?" I glanced down at the wooden planks under my feet. Could Nik hear through the dead wood of a house, or did it have to be a living network of roots? Was he hearing this? "Are you saying they intend to overthrow the king and take Tartora for themselves?"

"It's a supposition on my part, but I believe it to be a real possibility."

"Who are these people?" I asked, horror in my voice.

"They're mages," he said. "Powerful ones who don't answer to any Guild or tribe."

I swallowed. Amara was frustrated with the way the Guild ruled over all the mages in Tartora. But this was the reason Tartora maintained the Guild—the reason Calista was recreating theirs. The nomad tribes, located in the mountains north of Calista and the grazing lands west of Tartora, lacked a guild, but their tribal system had its own ways of keeping their mages under control.

"But where did they come from?" I asked.

"Calista," he replied.

"When it fell?" I asked slowly, trying to work out how they could have split off without anyone knowing.

He nodded. "A century ago, after the attack, most of the ordinary people fled to Tartora or the nomad lands, and some of the mages managed to find sanctuary among the tribes. Others were killed, of course, but not as many as everyone believed. Because of the chaos and destruction, no one ever even knew some were missing."

"So some of them escaped east while the others fled west," I said slowly. "And that was a hundred years ago, so they must have grown in number since."

"I see you appreciate the danger," he said. "They've been living peacefully on their island until now, attracting no attention. But they have never forgotten the route back to the mainland, and the time has come when they've decided to use that knowledge."

I jumped to my feet. "We have to warn the rest of Tartora! We have to warn the king!"

I raced toward the cottage's door, but Grey sprang to his feet, catching my wrist and pulling me to a halt.

"Do you want to see a mage war lay waste to Tartora like it once did to Calista? As you said, it's been a century, and Calista is only starting to be rebuilt now."

I stared up at him, my brain whirling in confusion. Of course I didn't want a war, but we couldn't just let the islanders take over unopposed.

"We have to—"

"We have to stop them, I agree," Grey said. "But we have to do it with as little disruption and bloodshed as possible. Which means I have to do it."

"You?" I stared at him, my brows lowering. "What do you have to do with the islanders?"

"Everything," he said simply, the single word ringing with truth. "On the island, a single family rules over the others. The Constantines. If the islanders are seeking war now, it's at the instigation of this family."

"And what does that have to do with you?" I asked.

"I'm part of that family."

"What?" I ripped my arm free of his hold, but I didn't try to flee again, instead waiting for his answer.

"My father was the oldest son of the family and should have been their next leader. But he wanted to run things differently—to give the people of the island more say in their own governance. He intended to change things, so his younger brothers turned on him. They murdered him while I was still an infant, but my mother escaped with me. She made it to a small boat and set out for the mainland. But she didn't have time to gather proper supplies, and by the time she arrived…"

He lowered his head in grief, and unwilling sympathy squeezed me.

"She was weakened to the point of death by the time the boat washed ashore," he said. "Since I was only an infant, I would have died as well if there hadn't been an old couple here who cared for me and raised me."

"Here? In the middle of the desert?"

"When the group of mages set sail for the island, a small handful chose to stay behind. These two were the last remaining of that group. My mother lived just long enough to tell them what had happened to my father and to sketch out the route to the island. She hoped I would have the chance to return one day."

"And you believe they'll accept you as their true leader if you do?" I asked.

He smiled wolfishly. "I'll make them."

"And that's how you're going to stop their attack?"

He stopped closer, his eyes earnest. "Do you see, Delphine? I need to get to that island—and for that I need people with both plants and elements abilities. We've been working on our ship for so long, but it's nearly finished now. Within a few days we'll have fixed the storm damage and be ready to sail."

I frowned, trying to work out why his words confused me. I finally realized the flaw.

"But I have a healing ability and so does Miranda. Why do you want healers?"

He smiled, placing a friendly hand on my shoulder. "I would never discount the importance of our own affinity! Since I've recruited all these people, I need to keep them safe. And that's the job of healers, isn't it?"

I nodded, pleased with his answer. The niggling feeling

remained, but I brushed it aside. I had thought I would never be convinced by Grey, but that was because I could never have guessed the truth. He had never been the one undermining Tartora—he was trying to save it.

"Do you really need my help?" I asked, gripped by a new sense of certainty.

"Of course." He held my gaze. "You and I are the most powerful here, Delphine. I may be the only one who can save Tartora, but I need you by my side. I need you to help me lead these people. Your family may have betrayed you, but I can lead you to a new people and a new home—a home you can reign over like a queen."

His words filled me, warming and lifting me. There was nothing romantic in the way he was looking at me—he didn't want me, he wanted my ability—but there was undeniable truth behind his words. People needed me—both the people of Tartora and this smaller community—and I could provide for them. I could keep them all safe.

"I don't care about ruling," I said. "But I'll do my part to keep everyone safe. You can rely on me."

His smile grew slowly, eventually covering his whole face. "I knew I was right to trust you with the whole story. Recruiting your friend was a mistake—she's too far from activation—but I was right to hope she might bring you to me."

He hesitated. "I'm hoping you can help me in other ways, too. I've never seen someone with your skills before. I'm hoping you can—" He cut himself off with a shake of his head. "No, never mind that. I don't want to overwhelm you. For now, it's enough that you want to help. The whole camp is busy preparing the supplies we'll need for the voyage, and as leader, I'm constantly busy. Could you circulate among my people and give each of them a physical check? I wouldn't want our busyness to mean I miss any illness or injury in any of them."

He shook his head with an affectionate smile. "They're all so devoted to the cause that they're prone to ignoring their own ailments."

I nodded. "I'm only an apprentice, but I'll do what I can."

He smiled at me. "I'm sure I can trust in your strength to make up for any lack in experience."

I nodded. That had usually been my experience so far.

I let myself out of the cottage, my mind whirling. The answers I was seeking had turned out to be far easier to uncover than I expected. But now that I had them, I couldn't follow the plan and leave.

I had seen the devastation in Eldrida from one storm, and I had witnessed the destruction left in the wake of the blight. What would be left of Tartora if it came to all-out war with the islanders? I might not like the way Grey had been luring young people away, but he was the only one who could save Tartora, which meant I had to work with him, regardless of my personal feelings.

I wandered across the camp toward my new bed in Miranda's old tent. How much had I misunderstood of what was going on here, anyway? Miranda hadn't been a prisoner like I expected—no one here was. And Grey really did mean to lead them to a new life in a new land like he'd promised. Maybe we had gotten the wrong idea about him, blaming him for undermining the king when it had actually been the islanders doing that all along?

I wished I could explain my intentions to Amara before I left, but I couldn't risk making the trip back to find her. It was a full day's trek each way, and Grey would sail soon. I couldn't risk missing the boat, not when I was needed onboard.

Phoenix nipped gently at my ear, and I scolded him lightly. The pain of the pinch shook something loose in my mind, reminding me of the earlier niggle at the back of my thoughts.

But the more I tried to work out what my concern had been, the less I could grab hold of it. Eventually, I gave up with a shrug. Whether or not I personally approved of Grey was irrelevant. We had a common enemy, and that was enough for now.

CHAPTER

TWENTY

It took me the rest of that day and all of the next to examine every one of Grey's followers. No one had any significant health concerns, although there were plenty of niggling issues for me to heal.

I had thought the issues were only natural, given the weak strength of their healers, and it wasn't until the second day that it occurred to me Grey himself was a powerful healer. I stopped halfway through my healing of an older woman named Ida, who had greeted me with a smile despite her pain. Her ailment wasn't a threat to her overall health, but it brought her significant pain, so I was glad to be able to heal it for her.

When I realized I'd stopped, I gave myself a shake and quickly finished. But as Ida thanked me profusely, relief shining from her eyes, I couldn't stop frowning. Why had Grey allowed her to suffer when he could have fixed it more easily than me?

"Why didn't you go to Grey before now?" I blurted out, cutting across Ida's thanks.

"Grey?" She stared at me, her brow creased and her eyes blank as if the idea had never occurred to her. "Why would I go to him?"

"He's a healer, isn't he?" I asked. "He could have healed this for you back when it first started."

"Go to Grey for healing?" Ida's eyebrows rose, and she gave me a curious look before shrugging. "I guess you're new here, so you don't know. Grey doesn't use his power for things like that."

"Things like...what?" I asked. "Healing?" I laughed as I said it, but Ida didn't smile back. My own smile fell away. "You're joking. Grey doesn't heal people?"

She considered my question. "I suppose he probably heals himself. And perhaps there are others, though I've never seen it." She shrugged.

I stared at her, appalled. "But why? He's a strong mage! He could easily heal something like this without straining himself. How could you just live with it when he had the means to offer relief?"

"The healers on the island would have fixed me soon enough." She patted my knee. "Don't worry. I've endured far worse in my past, and I could endure far more to make it to our new life. You'll see. It will all be worth it."

She excused herself with further thanks, and I watched her go, unsettled. Was Grey truly so uncaring about his followers, or were they the ones putting him on a pedestal, not telling him about their needs?

I sat alone for some time, wrestling with the thought, but eventually forced myself to move on in search of the next person. Grey had asked me to check everyone which meant he must have some care for them. Worrying about how far that care extended was purposeless when he was the only chance we had of defeating the islanders. My support for him stemmed from need, not from any admiration of his character.

I had to remind myself of that fact again when I sought Grey out to report my completion of my task. I found him berating one of his younger followers for accidentally smashing a barrel and spoiling the provisions it had contained. The poor boy was cowering before him, although Grey hadn't actually lifted a hand against him.

I could understand the boy's reaction, however. I was only a bystander, and even I felt shaken by the look in Grey's eyes. When he saw me, he calmed, however, his expression changing into a rueful smile.

After drawing a deep breath, he apologized to the boy for losing his temper and gave me a remorseful look.

"With our departure approaching, I fear we're all on edge, and I'm worst of all. But have you had a chance to check on everyone's health?"

Hearing the question calmed my agitation somewhat, reminding me that for all his flaws, Grey did have some consideration for his people. I might wish he had more restraint, but I could accept worse flaws if it meant saving an entire kingdom.

"Everyone is in good health," I reported. "I've just completed my final examination."

"Excellent!" Grey rubbed his hands together, his smile becoming broad and genuine. "In that case, we are clear to sail with the dawn tide."

"Really?" I cried, relieved I hadn't attempted to leave the camp. "Already?"

Even the boy smiled at the news. "May I tell the others?" he asked, and Grey nodded graciously.

The boy hurried away, and a buzz of excitement soon filled the camp as the news spread.

Phoenix, however, seemed unsettled by the commotion, fixing one of his eyes balefully on Grey, his small body tensed, as if ready to launch into flight.

I angled my shoulder away from Grey, hoping he hadn't noticed the bird's attitude. I had been carefully staying quiet about both Ember and Phoenix, hoping Grey wouldn't attempt to bar them passage aboard his ship.

"Can't you try to be a little friendlier?" I asked the bird after Grey hurried off for a final check of the restored ship. "I know he isn't our favorite person, but he's in control of who gets to go to the island."

To my dismay, Phoenix responded by launching himself off my shoulder and disappearing into the sky above the crevasse. I watched him go with a sinking heart. It wasn't a normal time of day for him to hunt, but perhaps he'd spotted some appealing prey.

I only hoped he hadn't decided he was ready to be a wild bird again. I had grown used to his weight on my shoulder and his company during the day while Ember slept—not to mention the way people treated me with increased respect now I came with a sharp beak and claws attached.

As the evening bore down and he didn't reappear, my worry grew. But there was nothing I could do about it. The people around me were all rushing hither and thither, packing their personal belongings now that the ship was finally readied.

I had so little to pack that I was soon at a loose end, my wandering feet taking me deeper into the crevasse, following it all the way to its tip. The greenery grew thicker as I went until I felt entirely ensconced in plant life, separate from the bustling camp that lay behind me.

Once I was sure I wouldn't be overheard, I crouched down and murmured into a particularly lush bush.

"Nik." Just speaking his name sent a pang through me, but I was glad he could hear everything and would be able to take a message to the others. He could explain my disappearance and the danger hanging over us all.

"I'm assuming you already heard about the islanders and the threat to Tartora. Obviously I have to go, but I'll return as soon as I can. Please tell Amara that I'm not abandoning her or my apprenticeship—I'm just completing the task she assigned me." I hesitated again. "I'll miss you," I finally added on a whisper.

The last three words might have been too quiet for him to hear, but I couldn't bring myself to repeat them. I was talking to a group of leaves right now, and I already felt foolish enough. I intended to be back sooner rather than later, and the rest of the conversation could be done in person—if I hadn't remembered by then exactly why it was a bad idea to have this conversation with Nik.

I hurried toward the ocean much faster than I'd meandered away from it, my cheeks burning. But by the time I reached the communal table, I had calmed enough to appreciate the feast being laid out on it. Every scrap of food that hadn't been packed was ready to be consumed by the excited camp of travelers.

Grey signaled for me to sit beside him yet again, patting my hand in an avuncular way when I took the place he'd indicated. He seemed in good spirits now that our departure had arrived, and the rest of the faces at the table matched his. Ida was on my other side, news of the dawn sail having brought a glow to her face and eyes. She had always been friendly, but she had carried a reserved air along with it. That reserve was gone now, and she seemed positively animated.

I expected her to talk about the island, but as one of those with an elements affinity, her immediate focus seemed to be on the voyage. I tried to nod in the right places, not really following her complicated talk of tides and rips and currents, and the other threats lurking beneath the surface of the ocean. I did gather enough to understand it was a dangerous voyage, and we would be relying heavily on the route charted for us by Grey's mother.

A team of powerful elements mages might have been able to keep the ship safe without the detailed instructions, but the underwater obstructions in this region created a series of narrow passages that became a maze without the correct map.

Stumbling on the path to the island would require either great luck or endless perseverance.

"Do we really have to sail at dawn?" I asked, leaning back at the end of dessert with a groan. I had overindulged and was considering asking someone to roll me toward my tent.

"Sorry." Ida's excited smile suggested she didn't really regret our early departure. "It's a matter of tides."

I held up my hand, forestalling any further spiels about our upcoming journey.

"Very well, very well, I believe you." I groaned again. "I shouldn't have eaten so much."

Everyone was starting to rise and drift away from the table, still talking animatedly in pairs or small clumps as they started toward the tents. I also rose, wishing I could enter into everyone else's excitement, and wishing I hadn't eaten so much in an attempt to placate the strange, unsettled feeling at the pit of my stomach.

I was doing the right thing. I knew I was doing the right thing because Grey was the only chance we had of defeating the islanders. He was the only one who could stop them, and he could do it without bloodshed. So why wasn't I more excited about setting sail?

I concluded it was because I was the only one not sailing toward a new and better life. Or possibly it was merely Phoenix's absence. If the falcon hadn't returned by the end of the night, I would be forced to go without him, a thought that set tears pricking behind my eyes.

I sighed as I pushed the tent flap open and prepared for sleep. Given the early start, I wanted everything ready so I could just roll out of bed and go. Ember got an especially stern speech about being back well before dawn—all while I wished she really could understand me as Amara always joked she could. If I was going to have to sail without Phoenix, I couldn't bear to be without Ember as well.

Finally there was nothing to do but climb onto the pallet. I lay on my back, staring at the canvas overhead and thinking about the people I could still hear moving about the camp. The unsettled feeling still continued to niggle at me—hinting at some truth lurking just beyond my reach—but in spite of it, I fell asleep quickly and slept deeply, undisturbed by dreams.

When I woke, I woke abruptly, sitting up and blinking in the near darkness. It took me several heart-pounding seconds to remember where I was and what the day ahead held.

I calmed only slowly, and my heart rate picked up again when I realized Ember had not yet returned. From the way the black around me was starting to creep toward gray, it was nearly time for the camp to stir. She should have been back by now.

I slipped out of bed, glad I had everything prepared. I had known she couldn't understand me, so I shouldn't have expected anything else. All I had to do was find her before full dawn arrived. It shouldn't be an impossible task given the limits of the crevasse that housed the camp.

Out of the tent, there was more gray than black, and my tension rose again. But I forced myself to breathe deeply and remain calm. I would find Ember, and everything would be all right.

I knew my anxiety over her absence was getting away from me, rolling into the queasy feeling from the night before and building to unnecessary heights. But even my power could do nothing to settle my stomach this time, the feeling clearly mental rather than physical.

My mind was convinced something was wrong, and it

didn't mean to let me forget it. Which meant I had to find a way to calm it and remind it that nothing disastrous was in the middle of happening after all.

"Ember," I called softly, not wanting to wake anyone from any of the nearby tents. "Ember!"

There was no answer or sound of movement. I moved further into the dense greenery at the back of the crevasse since I didn't think she would be likely to lurk near the ocean.

"Ember." I called again as I got further in.

A rustle of movement among the leaves ahead made me freeze. I peered forward, the increased light allowing me a glimpse of orange fur.

"Ember!" I rushed forward, pushing between overhanging leaves.

Strong hands grabbed me. Before I could protest, I was pulled further into the branches, out of sight of not only the camp but also the path leading to the back of the crevasse.

TWENTY-ONE

I stifled a squeal as I was wrenched through the leaves. I could see little against the blur of green rushing past my eyes, but something about the hands felt familiar, keeping me quiet.

When I came to a stop, my arms were being gripped in a rough hold, but the face looking at me held no animosity.

I sucked in a breath at the sight of Nik's familiar features, so welcome in this strange place. Tears welled up and spilled over my lids.

He let go of one of my arms to run a thumb across my cheek, wiping away the moisture.

"Delphine," he said in a rough voice that was half angry, half pained. "What's wrong? Did he hurt you?"

I gurgled a laugh, shaking my head. "I'm just happy to see you." I threw my arms around his waist and buried my face in his chest, making him rock back.

He froze for a moment and then his arms came up cautiously around me, gently rubbing my back.

"He didn't touch you?" His voice was low and gravelly in my ear.

"Everyone has been extremely nice, actually." I managed to

pry myself away from him, wishing I could hold on forever but already embarrassed at my display.

"*Nice?*"

I nodded. "It's not at all like we were thinking. Grey isn't like we were thinking. I guess you won't have talked to Miranda yet, but hopefully she's met up with Amara by now, so the rest of them will know—"

"Grey isn't like we were thinking." The repeated words sounded different in Nik's hard voice, like an accusation instead of a reassurance.

He grabbed my arms again, his eyes running over my face, as if searching for answers there. I tried not to think about how I probably looked, managing a weak chuckle.

"You're not going to find any hidden bruises, Nik. No one has offered me a harsh word, let alone a raised hand."

The thought of Grey berating the youth ran uncomfortably through my mind, but I pushed it aside. It was true no one had treated me that way.

But my words did nothing to soften Nik's expression. I frowned, doubt creeping in.

"You did hear everything, didn't you? You know why I have to help Grey."

"Help him? Is that what you were talking about when you said you were going somewhere?" His grip tightened, his eyes narrowing. "What hold does Grey have over you, Delphine? Have you found out what's causing the blight? If you're not a prisoner, why didn't you come back to me?"

His words still sounded harsh, angry, but I caught a trace of vulnerability behind the last question.

My heart softened as I realized he hadn't heard the whole story. He had been waiting all this time, confused and worried.

I smiled up at him. "Thank you for coming. I'm so happy to have a chance to see you again. And now you can take the full story back to the others."

"Delphine." There was a warning note in his voice. "Why do you keep talking about leaving?"

I grimaced. "We were wrong about Grey. I'm not saying he's a wonderful person, but he's not the cause of Tartora's problems. He's trying to fix them." I quickly explained how the islanders were behind both the blight and the storm and about Grey's plans to stop the war before it could launch.

Nik looked sufficiently concerned, but his face lacked the shock I expected. Instead his frown grew deeper and deeper.

"Grey told you this spiel, and so you decided you would leave us all without a word, get on his boat, and just sail away!" His voice rose slightly with each word, until the volume made me flinch.

I glanced over my shoulder, frowning into the lightening sky.

"Hush, not so loud. Of course I wasn't doing it without a word." I looked significantly at the tree beside us. "I thought you could hear everything."

Nik groaned. "Delphine! My ability has limits. And it certainly can't hear anything happening inside a closed house. I'm using root systems, remember?"

I winced. I had wondered about that, but then I'd forgotten again, caught up in the urgency of Grey's news.

"At least I came out here and sent you a message." I pointed at a nearby bush.

Nik laughed, looking as if the sound was reluctantly pulled out of him. "Is that why that was so loud and clear?"

I flushed. "I wanted to make sure you heard."

"Well you did a good job of tipping my worry into panic. I was already preparing to come when Phoenix showed up."

"Phoenix?" I peered into the surrounding trees, nearly bursting into tears when I saw the falcon perched on a nearby branch. "I thought he'd abandoned me!"

"I thought all kinds of terrible things when he showed up,"

Nik said grimly. "You have no idea how hard it was to wait until dark to start moving, or to wait for you to emerge once I arrived. I was about ready to start tearing apart tents looking for you."

Affection welled up inside me, and I put a hand on his cheek. He sucked in a breath in response to the touch, and I let my hand rest there for a second before dropping back to my side.

"I'm glad you didn't. That might have been a bit hard to explain." I chuckled.

"Thankfully I didn't need to. But other people are up and moving about now. We might need to stay hidden here until after the ship has left."

I nodded. "Yes, you should be safe enough here. And after we've left, you can move about freely."

"We?" He grabbed my arms again. "What are you talking about? You can't go with them!"

I shook my head. "Nik! Didn't you hear a word I said? I have to go. The whole of Tartora is in danger!"

"Delphine." He sounded dangerous, driven to the edge of desperation, although I couldn't understand why my words were having no impact on him. "I am not letting you get on that ship."

"Nik—" I tried again, but he cut me off.

"Think about what you're saying Delphine. Even if we assume that everything Grey said is true—that the islanders are the cause of all this and that he's the heir of their deposed leader—do you really think they're just going to bow the knee when he arrives unannounced on their shores?"

"It is true," I said, but my brow creased as I tried to remember the explanation for his question. I couldn't seem to think of a logical one, even though I *knew* they would accept Grey's leadership.

"*How* do you know?" Nik pressed on. "What evidence did Grey provide?"

I stared at him, unable to answer.

"I know healers can sense lies," Nik went on, "but you know Grey is a master at getting around that. He must have worded his story in a deceptive way. There are just too many holes in it for it to be true. If the islanders have been living on that island for a century, why are they suddenly attacking Tartora now? And if all Grey knows about his heritage are his mother's dying words, how, exactly, does he know so much about the islanders and what they're doing?" His voice tightened along with his hold until it grew so firm I winced. "And, most of all, why does he need you, especially? If Grey is going to overthrow the island's leadership peacefully, why does he need more than one powerful healer? If his story is true, you can stay right here with me, and Tartora will be saved, regardless."

"No." I shook my head. "Grey needs me to be able to save everyone. I'm essential."

"Delphine." Nik shook me slightly, his words hard-edged and his eyes terrified. "What has he done to you? Do you even hear yourself?"

"I..." I started, only to stop and frown. The roiling was back in my belly, but I still couldn't put words to any of it. "I'm sorry, Nik. I guess I'm not explaining it well. But please believe me. I'm certain about this."

Nik's desperate grip slowly relaxed, growing gentle. His hands ran down to my wrists and then back to my shoulders.

"I don't know what I mean to you, Delphine, but I'm begging you. Snap out of this madness. You cannot get on that ship."

"Nik." I looked at him, my eyes sad and pleading. "Think of Tartora."

"No!" The word was sharp, his eyes blazing now. "I'm thinking of *you*, Delphine. You cannot do this. I won't let you." His grip tightened again, and it flashed through my mind that he meant to hold me captive here until the ship had sailed.

But instead he pulled me closer and lowered his head, pressing his lips against mine. When I didn't resist, he pulled me closer again, one hand reaching up to cup the back of my head while the other wrapped around me.

Briefly his lips left mine, hovering half a breath away so he could whisper against them.

"Please, Delphine. I don't know what he's done to you, but please break free." He gave a growl. "I won't let him have you."

The last words seemed wrenched from him, and he immediately pressed his lips back to mine, more forcefully this time.

I sank into his arms, my roiling stomach a discordant note from the joy soaring through me at his embrace. Surrounded by Nik, breathing him in and kissing him back, it was hard to remember my earlier sense of urgency. What reason could there be to ever leave this moment?

"Delphine!" Nik pulled back again, his low, urgent voice not leaving me alone. "Please! Break free!"

I reached up to wind my fingers through his hair and pull his head back down to mine. He groaned as he came, his hold tightening as his lips once again crushed against mine.

Nik cared about me, that much was obvious. He claimed to care about me more than the entire kingdom. And standing here in his arms, I knew—down to my bones—that the same couldn't be said of Grey.

My certainty about Grey cracked, snakes of doubt slithering into the gaps. The spinning in my stomach surged, reaching up my throat. It had no place in this moment, and I reached for it with my power. No one belonged in this moment but Nik and me, and I would drive out the lingering whispers of Grey.

It had been months since I'd had need of my wall, but as soon as I decided to drive Grey out, it sprang back into being as easily as if I'd only dismantled it yesterday. It had been the first skill I perfected with my power, and the memory of it was strongly ingrained.

I let it push through me, driving the teeming discomfort with it, succeeding where my regular healing efforts had failed. In its wake, my mind and body felt light and free.

I stretched onto my tiptoes, leaning further into the kiss, finally able to focus on nothing more than the assurance of Nik's presence. But even as my feelings swelled, my mind sprang back to life. I pulled away, panting and staring at Nik.

It took him a moment to register my expression, his breathing ragged and eyes unfocused. But as soon as he absorbed my face, he snapped to attention.

"What?" he asked. "What is it?"

"I think it might all have been lies." I shook my head, confused. "Or some of it any way."

He fell back a step, running a hand through his hair and giving a strangled laugh.

"That's what I've been trying to tell you."

I shook my head. "No, you don't understand. I was *sure* it was the truth." I held his gaze, willing him to understand what I was saying. "I've never been so certain of anything in my life. I was uncomfortable about it the whole time, but every time I tried to think about the issue it was within the context of absolute unshakable certainty. I kept trying to think around my discomfort, but my thoughts couldn't reach a sensible conclusion when I was so sure Grey was the only one who could stop the islanders, and that he would do it without bloodshed—even that, for some reason he *needed* me there to succeed." My voice was trembling. "It's complete nonsense, but I couldn't see that."

Nik frowned, his demeanor growing serious as he tried to process my words. "So what changed?"

I flushed, thinking of his kiss, but it hadn't been the kiss alone. The kiss had only inspired me to...

"My wall!" I cried, realization hitting. "Back in Caltor, when Grey tried to use his healing power to attack me, I used my wall to push his power out of my body before it could harm me. I think I just did something similar. I couldn't shake that uncomfortable feeling, and I wanted to push it—and him —out of me, so I used my wall again. It's the first time I've used it here. I haven't even thought of it since I've never felt attacked."

An entirely different kind of discomfort welled inside me. Was that why Grey had been so unexpectedly pleasant ever since I arrived? The reason he let Miranda go without a murmur? He knew about my wall. Had he worried that it would protect me against—But my thinking stalled at that point. Protect me against what? What exactly had Grey done to me?

As a healer I could sense a lie—that was an innate part of my ability, one every healer possessed. So how had Grey fooled me so thoroughly? He hadn't just gotten away with a lie, he had utterly convinced me of a false truth. And not a single part of the whole business made sense.

"Did he actually lie to you directly?" Nik asked. "I've never heard of someone being able to fool a healer's ability to truth test unless they were using slippery words and evasive talk."

"I...I don't know." I frowned at the leaves, not really seeing them. "I can't explain how he did it. I just know how I felt before and how I feel now. Nik," I looked across at him, horror filling me. "I was just going to get on that ship!"

A muscle jumped in Nik's jaw. "I'm aware."

But now that the wheels were turning in my head, they wouldn't stop, racing forward too fast for me to follow. Everything that had happened in the last couple of days had been false, built on a mirage I still couldn't fathom. And if that was true for me, why wouldn't it be true for the others living in this strange oasis?

I thought of Ida, speaking fiercely of what she could endure for her new life, and of the boy who smashed the barrel, flipping immediately from brow-beaten to excited at the mention of our departure. Was everything they'd built their hopes on lies?

I tried to think it through, make sense of it. There had to be an island—that much had to be true. It was the only reason for Grey to be out here, building his ship. And someone other than Grey had unleashed a blight and a killer storm. I had examined every person in this camp, and even combined they didn't have the power to have done either one. The blight and storm were the work of plants and elements mages. They weren't here, so they had to be out there on the island. So perhaps what he'd promised his followers wasn't an illusion at all.

The next logical step took my breath away. I had come here utterly prejudiced against Grey—a man who had once stabbed me with a dagger. I had come here knowing he was clever and slippery and charming, and yet I had still been fooled by him. And not just fooled but utterly and completely taken in. Grey wasn't just charming. There was something far more insidious at play here, and Grey was about to take that strange ability of his to an island full of powerful and unsuspecting mages—an island he wanted to rule.

Icy cold trickled through me, starting at my crown and working its way down until I could no longer feel any warmth in the pre-dawn air. Grey wasn't going to the island to defeat the threat against Tartora, he was going to take control of it. If he sailed away, it would be to trap more people under his false sway, seeking power and his own little fiefdom.

We had to stop him. I had to stop him. I was at least partially responsible for this mess. I had walked into his trap like a fool. If I had reported back properly once I had answers, there would have been time for the king's forces to arrive and arrest Grey before his ship was completed. But there was no hope of them getting here now. There was barely even time for the two of us to...

The distant sound of activity had been growing louder, but

it took on a new tone as I tried to think what to do next. Loud shouts were echoing through the crevasse, and I caught several voices calling about tides as well as others that seemed to be calling my name.

Someone, perhaps Grey himself, had realized I was missing. But would they hold the launch for me and risk missing the tide?

If I charged out now and told them not to sail, no one would listen, and Grey would realize his hold on me had broken. I certainly had no way to physically sabotage the boat.

I looked at Nik, whose eyes were swiveling between the direction of the calls and my face, his eyes calculating and his face set. Nik could destroy a wooden boat. I had seen enough of his power to be confident of that. But how long would it take me to explain my thinking and convince him we needed to expose ourselves? Possibly more time than we had.

Because what happened if we succeeded? Our back up forces were a day's walk away, and we would be surrounded by a settlement of angry, disappointed people. There was every chance Nik would consider the risk too great. He had already said once this morning that he cared more about my safety than the kingdom. He would tell me it was too dangerous.

An even more unsettling thought crossed my mind. Even without the danger, would he want to stop Grey? Would King Marius? The king didn't know Ida and her past pain. He didn't know the horrible, slimy feeling of being duped and deluded and not even knowing it. What if he saw a threat—the islander mages—and a solution that required no risk from any of his own people?

Wasn't that the sort of bargain rulers made all the time? Trading the comfort of others for the comfort of their own people, and placing their kingdom's current security above the risk that they were creating a threat for the future?

All I saw was danger—the danger of handing Grey power large enough to destroy a kingdom. But it was possible King Marius would see something entirely different. What if he sent him on his way with his blessing?

"Delphine! Delphine! Where are you?" The cries were getting closer. I had to act now. There was no more time for thinking.

"Nik." I met his eyes, all my feelings for him bubbling up and filling my face.

He saw my expression and stilled, reaching to take my hands when I held them out.

"I'm sorry," I said, anguish creeping in.

He stiffened, but it was too late. The skin of his hands was warm against mine. I sent my power into him, and he collapsed into immediate, unnatural sleep.

He dropped in slow motion, crumpling downward. I only just managed to break his fall, preventing his head, at least, from hitting the ground. There was no time to place him in a more comfortable position, though. I had to get out of here before the searchers found us.

Blundering back through the greenery, I called loudly as I ran.

"I'm here! I'm here! Sorry!"

I stumbled straight into the arms of a small group of searchers, all of them looking tense and irritated.

"Sorry," I repeated, reaching for an excuse for my absence. I didn't find one, but it didn't matter. None of them cared enough to ask, all their focus on getting us aboard the boat.

I hiked my pack over my shoulder and let myself be swept up the gangplank and onto the deck of the ship. Most people were already aboard, but a few other searchers streamed on after us until at last the visible parts of the crevasse were still and silent.

Grey stood beside the wheel, annoyance on his face as he watched the final stragglers. I looked up at him with what I hoped was an appropriately apologetic expression, and he gave me a nod. Apparently I'd succeeded.

I was struggling to catch my breath, though, still swept up in the suddenness of my decision. I'd had no time to think it through and make a measured choice. I'd simply seen one way forward and acted on it. I still didn't even know for sure if I'd be able to stop Grey.

But my instincts told me that, for some unknown reason, I was essential to Grey's plan. His behavior had certainly seemed to suggest it. So if I was necessary for whatever he was planning, then it also followed that I was exactly the person who could most successfully sabotage it. I just needed to continue to play the part of a duped fool and wait for my opportunity.

A shiver ran through me. Alone. I had to wait alone.

All the way here, I'd always known that Nik was in the shadows protecting me. Even when I'd gone to Grey's camp, I'd been aware that he was nearby, tracking my movements. And I'd had Ember and Phoenix with me, as well.

My earlier panic after waking and finding Ember still gone hit me all over again. I had never intended to board this boat without my loyal companions. But neither could I regret leaving them to stand guard over Nik's unconscious body. I was alone, but at least I'd chosen it for myself. He'd been abandoned.

The boat lurched and groaned but didn't immediately move away from the shore. Several unhappy glances were sent my way as mutters passed back and forth about tricky passages and missing the opportune moment. But no-one spoke too loudly, and I caught a number of surreptitious glances sent toward Grey.

Strangely, their antagonism bolstered my spirits. It seemed I was right in assuming I was important—important enough to delay the launch and important enough that Grey's followers dared not criticize me too loudly.

Surely that meant I was important enough to destroy Grey's plan from within. I just needed to fool him long enough to do it.

TWENTY-TWO

There were fewer women than men among Grey's followers, and we were assigned a large cabin to share. It had bunks built along the walls, as well as hammocks hanging from the center of the room. By the time I found my way there, only one of the hammocks was left unclaimed.

I took it without complaining, already self-conscious about the ill feeling I had accidentally engendered. At least we had finally managed to get underway, and water was foaming around the prow of the ship as we sailed before an unnatural wind.

I would have liked to be on deck, but almost everyone else was there, and they apparently needed more time to forgive my early morning disappearance. Rather than stay where I wasn't welcome, I'd retreated to my cabin. But there I found two girls I'd barely spoken to previously. From the look they gave me, my presence wasn't wanted in the cabin either, so I fled again.

Without anywhere else to go, I ventured deeper into the ship, holding my skirt as I climbed awkwardly through an open trapdoor and down a rough ladder. Setting sail from the middle of the desert, we'd had no livestock to take other than a large collection of chickens. They were all housed on this deck, along with our supply of fresh water in barrels, and a collection of bags and crates.

I greeted the chickens, checking their health for something to do, although their companionship seemed lacking now that I'd become accustomed to Ember and Phoenix's constant presence. When the chickens could no longer hold my attention, I wandered the hold, exploring its nooks and crannies.

Both ends had a closed trapdoor, and I grew curious enough to pull one open. Another ladder led down into a second hold, this one apparently without portholes, given the darkness. I nearly gave up on the idea of further exploration, but two lanterns had been placed next to the trapdoor, inviting use.

After lighting one, I navigated the climb down the ladder one-handed, wondering what I was going to do with my time for the rest of the journey if I was already driven to this on the first day.

The deeper hold had even less of interest than the top one since it lacked the chickens. All I could see in the circle of my light were more bags and crates. But to my surprise, my power caught the presence of another person and two animals, deeper inside the cavernous space. What were they doing lurking down here without a light?

I held onto the edge of the ladder, not quite willing to let go of the sense of escape it provided, even as I held up the lantern and peered into the depths of the cavernous space.

"Is there someone there?" I called, although I already knew the answer. "Are you in trouble?" Perhaps they had somehow lost their light and were stuck here. Given the way we'd lurched through the first part of our passage, someone down here checking on the cargo might have fallen and been injured.

The faint sounds of movement reached my ears as my now-alert senses tracked the person moving closer to me. Why didn't he or she speak? My hold on the ladder tightened, until I noticed further details about the two animals. They weren't chickens escaped from the upper hold or other livestock either. In fact, they felt exactly like a fox and a bird of prey.

"Ember?" I gasped. "Phoenix?"

Orange fur entered the patch of lantern light, Ember trotting daintily forward to lean against my leg. I stared down at her, too astonished to move.

"What are you doing here?"

"I brought them," said a deep voice as a man stepped into the light, a falcon on his shoulder.

"Nik?" My mouth dropped open, and I left it that way, too stupefied to close it. "What are you doing here? *How* are you here?"

He gave me a stern, disapproving look. "Did you really think I was going to let you run off to try to stop Grey alone?"

I grimaced, too guilty to meet his eyes. "I'm sorry that I... There was no time, and I knew you would..."

"Yes, I would have," he said. "This is an inexcusably foolheaded endeavor, Delphine! What would happen if you got yourself into trouble with all your friends an ocean away? Luckily, your little trick wore off as soon as you ran away. It took me a few moments to regain my wits and work out what had happened, so I was too late to stop you, but in the chaos of the departure, I managed to swim out and climb aboard."

"So you've come along as a stowaway?" I asked, as incensed as him. "And that seems like a more sensible choice?"

He shrugged. "It was the only one you left me. I wasn't letting this ship sail away without me—not when you were on board."

"Nik!" I cried in a half-stifled shout, as the full ramifications hit me. "If you're here, who's going to tell the others what we discovered? They'll have no idea of the danger from the island!"

"We'll just have to find a way to get straight back there," Nik said implacably, showing no remorse.

"Ugh, you're impossible!" I muttered.

He stepped closer, but I noticed he remained just out of my reach. Guilt stirred. He had trusted me, and I had betrayed that trust.

"I really am sorry," I whispered. "I was making decisions under pressure, and....well, it wasn't my finest moment."

He stayed where he was, a silent statue in the flickering light, assessing my face with his eyes. I tried to look strong and trustworthy, while inside I remembered every time he had touched me—grabbing my wrist, cupping my cheek, taking my hand, touching his lips to mine. It had never struck me before just how much trust it showed to touch a healer, especially a new healer in training.

Had I just destroyed Nik's trust?

His face softened, and he stepped closer, coming fully into the circle of my lantern.

"You're right that you shouldn't have done it," he said. "But it's too late to worry about that. We're both here now, and what's more important is what we're going to do next."

I looked upward, into the hold above, an obvious fear hitting me.

"You've just stowed away on a ship with multiple healers!" I hissed, letting go of the ladder to grab his arm and push him further away from the trapdoor. "Someone is going to sense you down here!"

He shrugged, as if he'd already considered the risk and dismissed it as insubstantial.

"They aren't mage level strength which means they can't sense much of anything without physical touch. Their reach won't stretch this far."

"What about Grey?"

"Grey isn't the type to be climbing up and down ladders fetching supplies. He'll be on deck or in the captain's cabin, and from there he'll be feeling people all over the ship. There's no reason for him to take any particular note of someone being in the hold. You're the only one likely to discover me." A smile spread over his face. "And I was hoping you would—sooner rather than later, although you exceeded even my expectations on that one."

"Nik." I rolled my eyes, but I was also laughing.

He stalked closer, his eyes dropping to my lips. "I think we have some unfinished business from last time we talked."

"Nik," I protested again, putting my free hand up to fend him off even as he slipped an arm around my waist. "Be serious."

"I am serious. Down here in the pitch dark, wedged between a sack of potatoes and a barrel of flour, there's not a lot to keep my attention. So I've had plenty of opportunity to think about exactly where we left things." He leaned closer, only stopping when Phoenix ruffled his feathers disapprovingly.

Nik threw him a sideways look that was half amused, half irritated. "If you don't like it, there are plenty of other perches down here."

I put the lantern down so I could use both hands to push him firmly away.

"We need a plan. An actual plan. Not this." I gave him a fierce look, and he nodded meekly, his posture not matching his expression.

I rolled my eyes and crossed my arms. "We're here now—which I freely acknowledge is due to my own foolishness, at least where I'm concerned. I take no responsibility for you following me and compounding all our problems."

"Aren't you even a little glad to see me?" he asked.

I glared at him, hoping it covered my true emotions. Because I wasn't ready to confess to the enormous rush of relief I'd felt the moment I realized he was with me. And he'd even brought Ember and Phoenix. I'd thought I was alone, but I wasn't, and the feeling of lightness was incredible. But those were selfish emotions. I shouldn't want Nik to be here in this trouble with me, and I certainly didn't want Amara, Hayes, and the others to be left with no idea what had happened to us.

"How I feel is irrelevant," I said shortly. "What matters is what we're going to do next."

Nik looked disappointed at my words, and a pang shot through me. Did he really care so much? It was harder and harder to deny it to myself, but I had no idea what to do with his devotion or with my own messy, complicated return feelings. He was both an outcast and a royal prince, and neither of those identities made a future with him possible.

But before I could think of anything to say, Nik's expression hardened, his manner becoming businesslike.

"Clearly Grey found some way to influence your mind which shouldn't be possible. There's not much we can do while we're stuck on the ship in the middle of the ocean, but at least you can try to find out more information from Grey."

"Do you think he'll tell me?" I asked uncertainly, but even as I said the words, I suspected it wouldn't be as difficult as I was envisioning. Grey wanted to use me for something, and to do that, he was eventually going to have to explain what that something was.

"The fox will have to stay down here with me," Nik said. "Too many people saw you come aboard and know she wasn't with you. But you can take the falcon. He'll need a chance to stretch his wings, and he could easily have flown out to you before the ship sailed too far out."

He stepped closer again, but only to align his shoulder with mine so Phoenix could hop across to his favorite position. The falcon did so with alacrity, and I leaned my cheek against the softness of his feathered body. Feeling his weight on my shoulder again made everything else seem a little less frightening and uncertain.

It was still difficult to climb up the ladder, leaving Nik and

Ember in the dark, though. I'd hugged Ember close to my chest, whispering all the reasons she had to stay behind, but as always, it was impossible to know how much she understood. At least she accepted my departure silently, watching me go and standing close to Nik.

It felt a little better to know they had each other, but it was tempting to leave the lantern. Nik had refused, saying that a light in the deep hold might attract attention, but it was hard to believe he was really all right without one.

When the trapdoor banged closed, I told myself not to be fanciful and imagine there was any note of finality in the sound. I would be back as soon as I had something to report, and Nik would be fine in the meantime. The ship had been packed in enough of a rush that there were bags, boxes, crates, and barrels everywhere. I'd even seen a number of piles of planks that had no purpose I could fathom. Even if someone came down here for supplies, Nik could easily conceal the two of them among the chaos of jumbled cargo.

I didn't stop climbing until I'd made it all the way up to the main deck. Now that I had Phoenix with me, I couldn't be a coward and skulk inside the whole time.

The crowd had dispersed, although plenty of Grey's followers were scurrying around carrying out the various tasks of sailors.

I considered offering to assist but decided I would be more hindrance than help. I knew nothing about ships, having never been on one before.

Instead, I tucked myself against the railing where I would be out of the way and let my eyes roam over the horizon. The ocean went on and on, no matter what direction I looked, its enormity striking me all over again now that I was out in the middle of it.

The ship—which had seemed large and solid while anchored to Grey's simple dock—felt small and weak in the face of such a powerful force. A wave hit the prow, making me rock and grab for the rail. It didn't take much to imagine what it would be like to be out here in the middle of a storm.

I glanced up at the wheel, Grey still beside it, although he was leaving the actual steering to someone with an elements affinity. Had his claims about the storm been true? Had it really come from the island? It seemed logical, and if it had, it meant the islanders were ruthless and callous. We had to think of a way to stop not only Grey but the islanders as well.

I gripped the rail until my knuckles turned white, overwhelmed by the task ahead. My eyes stared blankly across the expanse of dark blue, the white tops of waves breaking up the monotony where the wind tugged at the water.

The flap of wings drew my eye as Phoenix glided back toward me, angling himself to land on the rail at my side.

"I see your friend followed you." Grey's voice came from behind me, and I barely stopped myself from stiffening. When had he come down from the quarterdeck?

I turned slowly. "Phoenix is very loyal."

Grey smiled, although the expression now sent a shiver down my back.

"It will take us several days to reach the island," he said. "And I want to put our time onboard to good use."

I raised my eyebrows. "What did you have in mind?"

"I'm hoping we can each teach the other a new skill." His voice was light, but the intensity in his eyes suggested this wasn't a minor matter to him.

"New skill?" It didn't take much acting to look confused. "I'm only an apprentice. What skill could I teach you?"

He leaned one hand against the rail, looking out over the ocean. I examined his profile, wondering if it could really be this easy. The ease of it all made me uneasy after the way things had turned out in the crevasse. What fresh deception was he preparing?

He abruptly turned his head, fixing me with his startling green eyes. "I've been fascinated with you ever since we met, Delphine. It's not often I meet someone with an ability that surprises me."

Unease filled me as I realized the obvious—Grey wanted to know about my wall. But I pretended ignorance.

"Me?" I kept my reply short, avoiding any comment that might have the taste of a lie.

"The first time we met, when I tried to test you, I couldn't reach you." He leaned forward, the eagerness in his voice and eyes betraying him. "And then again in the warehouse, when I sent my power into you, you pushed me out."

I drew back, letting one hand float to the place where he had stabbed me.

"The warehouse..." I put all my uncertainty into my voice.

Grey winced before quickly pasting his smile back in place. He took my other hand in both of his, fixing me with an earnest look that struck me as a lot less earnest than it had back on land.

"Let me apologize again for that. It was a terrible error in judgment and a shame that stays with me." He bowed his head in false contrition. "Of course, I never meant you any permanent harm since I knew you would be able to heal yourself."

I left my hand in his, blinking at his lowered head. I didn't feel any of the strange, unquestioning, unthinking certainty of before, just the normal sensations that came from my ability. Grey didn't need to use any special ability because he was telling the truth.

I sorted back through his words. He hadn't actually said he felt guilty. He'd called it an error in judgment and spoken of shame. Was he ashamed of having inflicted pain on another person, or was he ashamed with himself for letting his emotions lead him into a poor strategic decision?

Somehow I felt sure it was the latter. If nothing else, I was getting a firsthand lesson in how to manipulate words in order to avoid a healer's truth telling sense.

"Thank you," I said, thinking of the future value of the lesson in order to give my words the ring of truth.

When he looked back up, he was beaming. "I'm not surprised to find you so gracious."

He let the words stand as an apparent compliment, although I could guess the true meaning behind them. He still thought me in thrall to him, and that knowledge was far more welcome than any of his compliments could ever be.

"I don't know if I can teach someone else how to make a wall," I said. "I've never tried before."

Grey frowned. "Is it difficult?"

I tipped my head to the side, honestly considering his words. "Not for me. But I don't really understand how I do it. I created it almost as soon as I was activated, so at the time I was driven entirely by instinct." I had no desire to help Grey, but I also didn't want to make him suspicious. "Master Clay told me he tried to do it and couldn't."

I met Grey's face openly, keeping my features calm. He would sense the truth of my words, and hopefully they would help prepare him for his eventual failure. I didn't want him blaming me, but neither was I going to put effort into teaching him.

Giving false lessons to a healer turned out to be no easy task, however. There was only so much prevarication I could manage in answer to direct, detailed questions. And what I had thought might be an hour's lesson between Grey's other tasks turned out to be a marathon effort.

Grey might have taken the captain's cabin for himself, but he wasn't actually involved in sailing the ship. Given he was a healer, it made sense, but I had still expected him to be up on deck playing the part.

Instead, he shut us both in his cabin for the better part of two days as he tried again and again to recreate my wall. We didn't even break to eat with the others, instead taking brief breaks to eat the food that was delivered by one of his followers.

The cabin was almost as large as the one which housed all the females onboard, so there was plenty of room for us, but it contained few other luxuries. Apparently there had been barely time to make the basic furniture and no time for extra ornamentation. It made no difference to our efforts, although I soon grew bored of plain brown walls, plain brown floor, and plain brown roof.

We weren't alone, at least, since Grey brought in a steady stream of his followers, usually one at a time. All of them had a healing ability, and he had them attempt to make a wall as well as attempt to breach mine while he gripped my other arm, using his power to watch the interplay of our abilities.

Whether he tried to push his healing power into me himself or watched someone else attempt it, he couldn't find a way past my wall. And when we reversed roles, none of them could put up a wall to keep me out.

"Is this an ability unique to you?" Grey stared at me hungrily as the sun approached the ocean on the second day at sea. "How can no-one else do it? I understand the rest of them failing, given their weaker seeds, but even I can't..." He trailed off, his brow creased in a scowl.

As time had worn on without anyone making any progress, both my confidence and my curiosity had grown. Why were they all unable to replicate what seemed an easy feat to me? Faced with Grey's specific and repeated questions, I soon began to think about it in earnest. But even when I was trying to be helpful, I could think of no way to explain it.

"I had no idea it would be so difficult," I said. "I really don't know what's so different about me."

Grey stared at me, clearly frustrated, but unable to claim I was lying to him. He had failed, but he couldn't blame me. And from the way he was reining himself in, he wasn't ready to risk scaring me by unleashing his true anger and frustration. So far, I had been the only teacher, but he had spoken of both of us learning a new skill, so he still had other uses for me.

"What about my new skill?" I asked. "You said you were going to teach me something as well."

"Ah yes." Grey forced a smile. "It's clearly useless to continue our attempts at the wall for now, so it's time to switch focus." He glanced out the window at the setting sun. "However, it's getting late, and we're both tired. Let's come to it fresh in the morning."

I forced a smile and nodded, although I could barely contain my impatience. But as soon as I stepped out of his cabin, I realized what the early freedom meant. The night before, we had stopped our futile efforts so late that I hadn't had enough energy to do anything but fall into my hammock and snatch a few hours' sleep before starting over again. But now I had time.

I hurried for the open trapdoor that led to the upper hold, swerving away at the last minute when I saw two others approaching. I pretended an interest in the view out the nearest porthole until they had walked on, leaving the passage clear.

Half-tumbling down the ladder, I peered around in the dimness of evening. Was I alone down here?

A quick sweep with my power told me I was, so I hurried across to the closed trapdoor that led further down. Grabbing a lantern, my fingers trembled with my haste as I struggled to light it.

As soon as the flame blossomed, I pulled up the door and started down the ladder. By the time my feet reached the deck, Nik had appeared, Ember at his side.

"Delphine!" His voice was ragged, and he looked exhausted. He swept me into a tight embrace, speaking into my hair. "You're all right."

I let him hold me for a moment before pulling back. For a

second, he resisted my efforts before finally letting me go with a low groan.

"Do you know how close I was to sneaking out of here? I thought you would be back much earlier!"

"Are you all right?" I asked, sudden concern filling me. "Are you hungry? I never even thought of bringing you food! I thought—"

"That I was surrounded by stores of food?" He shook his head, impatient. "I don't need you to bring me anything—I just need to know you're safe."

"Oh. Sorry." But the more I thought about it, the deeper my frown grew. "You were thinking of coming out of hiding? Are you serious? You can't do that!"

He ran a hand through his hair, the lantern deepening the shadows on his face and making it look like he hadn't slept at all.

"There are no networks of roots here. I can't hear what's happening to you, and it's driving me to distraction."

I sighed. "You just have to trust me. I can look after myself."

He closed his eyes for a moment before opening them and grimacing. "I know. But there's not a lot down here to focus on instead."

I wrapped my hand around his arm. "I'll try to get down here more often. I promise. But I've spent the last two days locked in Grey's cabin, so I haven't had a chance to sneak away."

He stiffened immediately, his muscles leaping beneath my arm.

"He had you locked up?" From his growl he was ready to go find Grey right now.

"Not literally." I rolled my eyes. "But I'm trying not to raise his suspicions, remember? He's been trying to learn how to make a wall *this entire time*." I groaned dramatically in remembered exhaustion.

"You mean he can't do it?" The news distracted Nik from his dark emotions. "Is it so difficult?"

I shrugged helplessly. "It doesn't seem like it is to me, but apparently other people find it impossible. I have no idea why. But with his ability, I couldn't lie and give him bad instructions. By the end I was doing my truthful best, but we still got nowhere."

"Good," Nik said savagely. "The fewer weapons Grey has, the better."

I nodded my agreement, but I couldn't put the matter aside so easily. Why could I do this thing that no one else could do? It didn't make any sense.

"Did you learn anything else?" Nik asked. "Do you have any idea how Grey fooled you so completely?"

"Not yet. But I think I might get some answers tomorrow. We're due for another lesson in the morning, and this time Grey says he has something to teach me."

TWENTY-THREE

"I'm sorry, say that again?" I stared at Grey, too shocked to think about what emotion I should be pretending to display.

"Incredible, isn't it!" His eyes were shining, as if it had been difficult to hold in this secret, and it was a relief to finally talk about it. "It was the first thing my mother taught me after she activated me and taught me control."

His mother? The words pierced my shock, bringing confusion. But for once Grey wasn't guarding every word, and he didn't notice his slip or my reaction to it.

Grey had previously said his mother died just after they washed up on the mainland, but his current claim that she had been his activator had the ring of truth to it. When he'd told me about her death, it hadn't been my own ability that had perceived his words as truth but rather...

My thoughts tangled and stuttered, still struggling to take in Grey's revelation.

"How...how is that possible?" I asked. "You're telling me that anyone with a strong enough healing seed could learn a skill like that, and yet no one has discovered it except those mages out on the island?"

"They discovered it before the island," he said. "Sometimes new developments only spring from desperate necessity. I suppose this particular skill needed a disaster as large as the destruction of an entire kingdom to be discovered. How do you think my ancestors escaped the invaders a century ago—and without anyone knowing about it?"

I massaged my temples. "So, you're telling me that as a healer I can force someone to believe a lie? Any lie at all?"

"Not any lie." Grey sounded regretful. "The certainty will fade in the face of direct evidence to the contrary. For instance, if a traveler gets told they stayed in a red house in the last town they visited, they'll believe it for the rest of their life. But if you tell someone the house they currently live in is red, they'll shake off the mesmerization in a day because they can see with their own eyes that it isn't true."

I considered his words against the examples I'd seen. Miranda had become confused as soon as I showed up, starting to question everything and quickly agreeing to leave. Since Grey had mesmerized her into believing no one from her old life cared about her or wanted her back, that made sense. The simple fact of my arrival had provided evidence that broke the mesmerizing effect.

In my case, there had been no direct evidence available to me about the islanders or their intentions, so I'd had no way to shake off the false beliefs. I'd only managed it because Nik had made me doubt Grey himself strongly enough that I used my wall.

I shook my head at my own foolishness. I should have been using the wall since the moment of my arrival instead of being lulled into a false sense of security by Grey's manner. I had thought that if Grey made physical contact and tried to push his power into me, I would feel it and be able to take action, but it had been so subtly done, I'd missed it completely.

A new thought struck me. "Can you mesmerize someone without touching them, like with truth telling?"

"Unfortunately not. It's the greatest flaw to the skill."

I held in my look of disgust at his disappointment over the limitation. Instead, I tried to remember if Grey had touched me before telling me the story about his history. He must have, but I couldn't recall the exact details of our interaction.

"It's especially a pain if the mesmerization needs to be refreshed," he added.

"Refreshed? I thought it would last forever if it wasn't directly refuted by physical evidence to the contrary."

"You've studied with the law keepers, haven't you?" He sounded impatient. "There are shades of gray between no evidence at all and indisputable physical evidence. With enough circumstantial evidence, the mesmerization can start to fade. That's the mistake I made with the last batch of recruits." His eyes darkened. "I got arrogant and didn't refresh the initial mesmerization. I tried to gather too large a group before returning to the desert, and I lost control of the situation."

From the vitriol in his voice, Grey didn't like losing control.

Had he reinforced his mesmerization on me? I thought back over our interactions, remembering several occasions when he'd found a casual reason to touch me.

I suppressed a shudder, feeling a sudden desire to scrub every inch of my skin. How was I ever going to bring myself to let him touch me again?

"So this is what makes the islanders so dangerous," I said, remembering that I was supposed to be pretending they were my main worry, not Grey. But even as I said the words, they didn't make sense. "But so far they've attacked with a blight on our crops and a storm. Those must have been the work of plants and elements mages and doesn't have anything to do with mesmerizing."

"Doesn't it?" Grey looked amused. "I'll admit, the storm was the work of their elements mages, but are you so sure about the blight?"

"Healing power doesn't interact with plants," I said, still sure of that, even in the face of Grey's revelation.

He smiled slowly, the expression unsettling. "How do you know there ever was a blight?"

"Of course there was! I've seen the aftermath of it myself all across northern Tartora."

"You saw a field infected with blight?" He raised both eyebrows.

I shifted on my feet, impatient. "I saw the fields burned by the Guild mages. You said mesmerizing doesn't work if someone can see the truth with their own eyes, so there must have been blight. This ability doesn't allow you to control someone's actions and force them to burn a field."

Grey chuckled. "Do you really think you can't control someone through manipulation?" He shook his head at my apparent naïveté. "The islanders have a hundred years of practice, remember? Although even I had to salute the elegance of their approach in this instance."

I stared at him, and he instantly modified his expression. "A terrible thing, of course."

His words rang false in my mind. Grey didn't care about the lost crops or the ruined farmers. But I couldn't call him out on it. I wanted all the answers he could give me.

"Are you telling me they manipulated those farmers into burning their own crops?"

Grey frowned. "I think that would be beyond the power of mesmerization. As I said, elegant thinking was required in this case. I tracked them across the kingdom, and from what I've been able to piece together, it was a process of several steps. First, the islanders mesmerized the farmers into believing they'd seen blight and that they should contact the plants affinity at the Guild and stay away from the infected fields in the meantime. When the mages arrived, they found nothing, of course. But the islanders intercepted them on their return journey and mesmerized them into believing they'd not only seen blight but also burned the infected fields."

"But you said the farmers wouldn't have..." I trailed off as I realized the truth. "The islanders were the ones to burn the fields."

Grey nodded. "That is the conclusion I've come to. They burned the fields, and then convinced both the farmers and the Guild mages that the Guild were the ones to do it due to the blight. It's standard procedure in such a case, so it's easy to believe. And once the fields were burned, there was no evidence to break the illusion, so they'll go on thinking it forever."

"There was never any blight..." I shook my head as I fully absorbed the enormity of that.

There was no mysterious blight that couldn't be fixed by the Guild. For a moment I felt relief, but it didn't take long to realize that the effects on the kingdom were the same. There might not be a blight, but the unrest and food shortage were very real impacts of the deception.

It was hard to contain my emotions, but I had to try because Grey's initial lack of caution seemed to have worn off, his eyes tracking me more closely than before. He was worried this news was going to shake me enough to throw off his own mesmerizations.

"Teach me." I thrust out my arm, inviting his touch, although it went against every one of my instincts. "Teach me how to mesmerize."

Grey's eyes lit up, and I knew I'd made the right move. It was easy for him to believe this reaction because it aligned with his own. I was sure he'd been eager to try mesmerizing ever since he first heard of it.

Grey put his hand on my arm, his power snaking inside me. But it was a light, subtle touch that I almost missed since it made no attempt to connect with the various central systems of my body.

"Your tent back in the crevasse was such a beautiful blue," he said, almost casually, and I found myself nodding in agreement.

I could see the gorgeous, deep, peacock blue in my mind's eye. Grey dropped his hold of my arm, but I ignored him, distracted by thoughts of my old tent. But despite the harmless beauty of the image, something about it tickled at my mind, unsettling me.

I gasped as I remembered the feeling and where I'd felt it before. Instinctively I pulled up my wall, pushing Grey's power out of my body and purging the falsity from my mind. My tent had been ordinary canvas.

As soon as I was free of the grip of Grey's mesmerization, I remembered that I wasn't supposed to be able to free myself. I looked quickly up at Grey, but thankfully he'd released his hold before my instincts took over and had no idea what I'd done.

He smiled with satisfaction as he thrust a plain canvas bag into my hands. "This is the canvas we had access to back in camp," he said. "We used it to make a number of bags as well as all the tents. Your tent was never blue."

I stared down at the canvas in my hands, pretending to be struck by his words. After a carefully judged moment, I gaped up at him.

"I was expecting you to do it, and yet I still..."

He smiled broadly. "Powerful, isn't it? Just being on your guard isn't enough."

I shook my head as I remembered how it had felt. "I could remember the tent as blue! I could see it in my mind! How is that possible? How did you plant an image in my mind along with the words?"

Grey shook his head. "I didn't do that. You did."

"Me?"

"Our brains are incredibly clever—too clever for their own good, in this instance. Once you believe something implicitly, your brain cooperates and creates memories that match. That's where the power of mesmerization comes from. Once those false memories have taken root, it takes a lot to dislodge them."

"Incredible," I murmured, despite myself.

There was no denying how horrifying this ability was, but it was equally impossible to deny the curiosity coursing through me. I wanted to understand how it was done.

I didn't try to suppress the feeling, instead letting it show on my face and in my eyes. Grey smiled at my expression, convinced I felt the same way about this as he did. Sticking his head out the door of his cabin, he called for someone to join us.

At first I was just a silent observer, allowing my power to ride along with his as he convinced this new person that their tent back in the camp had been blue. And when he did it again to the next person, and then the next, I sensed the patterns of his power.

By the afternoon, I was doing it myself. The first time I succeeded, I let out an involuntary cheer, buoyed by the satisfaction of success. I couldn't deny the underlying thrill of power.

But one look at Grey's pleased smile brought me down hard. The slimy feeling I had felt when I first understood Grey's deception trickled through me again. I was playing games with people's minds, and while it was harmless deception on this occasion, no one should have that kind of power over someone else.

I couldn't refuse to cooperate, however. Too much lay in the balance for me to alert Grey to my true feelings. I would play along—at least until he asked me to deceive someone about something that actually mattered.

Even knowing the importance of fooling Grey, I was still exhausted by the end of the day. Doing it over and over again had made the slimy feeling fade, and somehow that was the worst feeling of all. I couldn't let myself become desensitized to using this new skill.

Once again Grey had simply handed me the answers I sought, and once again they had turned out to be a poisoned chalice.

Grey must have been pleased with my progress because he called everyone together to eat for the first time since we boarded the ship, his manner jovial and charming. He was delighted, making me conversely afraid. Clearly my mastering this ability was a crucial part of Grey's plan, and the thought made me feel as if ants were crawling all over me.

I managed to sit through the meal, but as soon as people dispersed to either their beds or night duties above deck, I hurried straight for the hold.

CHAPTER

TWENTY-FOUR

I almost fell down the ladder, landing in Nik's arms. He held me tightly, and I trembled, grateful he had been waiting for me. He was tense—I could feel it in his muscles—but he said nothing, allowing me to slowly calm at my own pace.

When I finally relaxed into him, his arms tightened even further.

"Do I need to go find Grey?" he asked, but he sounded like it was a joke. Mostly.

I nearly started shaking again but managed to hold it in.

"We should find a spot to sit away from the trapdoor." I glanced upward to where our light must have been leaking through to the hold above. "I don't think this will be a short conversation."

Nik led me through the maze of supplies, taking me to the small corner he had claimed for his own. He had placed the spare planks so that they formed a miniature makeshift cabin, using his power to fuse them together. It was enough to block him from casual view, at least, and inside he'd laid out several blankets into a makeshift bed. Best of all was the orange shape curled in the center of them.

Ember awoke at my arrival, trotting over to me eagerly and allowing me to scoop her up. I kept her in my arms as Nik helped me sit on the blankets. He sat next to me, his arm and leg pressed against mine, rather than facing me as I'd expected. But I couldn't bring myself to comment. I wanted him close as much as he obviously wanted to be there.

I told him everything Grey had revealed, detailing our practice session and my eventual success. He didn't bombard me with questions as I expected, listening in shocked silence instead.

"Show me," he said when I finally fell silent. His fingers wound through mine, holding my hand tightly and providing the contact I needed.

I took a moment to gather myself, not wanting to do it again, especially to Nik. But I understood why he needed to feel it for himself.

I stroked Ember's back as I cast around for an easily broken lie. My hand stilled as an idea came to me. It wasn't as harmless as the color of a tent, but it would be an effective demonstration of both the power and limits of this terrifying skill.

I took Ember out of my lap, putting her beside me on the opposite side to Nik and half covering her with blankets. She looked at me with bright eyes but accepted the arrangement, remaining still beneath my hand. I made no effort to disguise my movements, and Nik watched me with curiosity.

Once I was finished, and Ember was tucked out of his sight, I turned my head to face him. My power snuck gently into him through our still twined hands.

"Ember's dead," I said after a moment, letting my power implant the certainty of truth inside his mind. The ragged emotions of the day leaked out of my voice now that I was no longer trying to control them. "It was her heart. I tried to help her, but I was too late. Just like the eagle."

"Delphine! No!" Nik's eyes filled with horror as he stared

back at me, not once questioning my statement or pointing out he had just seen me place Ember out of his sight.

He twisted, pulling me into a hug even tighter than the one by the ladder.

"She was still young, wasn't she?" His voice sounded shaky. Was he crying?

Guilt clawed through me, and I pushed him back.

"No, no, she isn't dead. I didn't mean it."

But Nik shook his head, accepting my rejection of the hug but taking both my hands in his.

"I know it isn't easy to accept," he said, and I'd never heard his voice so gentle. "But denying the truth will only prolong the pain."

"No, she isn't dead." I said it with as much confidence and certainty as I could, but he merely continued looking at me with sad eyes.

Even I was shaken now, regretting my choice of example. This was different from the people standing in Grey's cabin, smiling at the memory of a rainbow of tents.

Ember scrambled out from under the blankets, letting out a sharp yip.

Nik shouted, almost tipping backward in his violent reaction to the shock. Looking from the fox to me, his face was pale even in the light of the lantern.

"She's...she's not dead," he said in a shaky voice.

My instinct was to apologize and comfort him, but I needed him to remember this—to understand the extent of it.

"That's the power of mesmerization," I said. "And that's it's limits."

For a long moment, we just stared at each other, both frozen in place, him still pulled partly back and me stiff and straight. I saw the emotions growing in his eyes, though, the shock replaced with horror and something even worse—fear.

"I'm sorry!" The words jumped out of me. "I should have

used a more innocent example. I just wanted you to see...But I shouldn't have done that to you."

More than earlier, I wished I could take it all back. I wanted to turn back time and never have Nik look at me like he was afraid of me.

The increasingly frantic tone of my voice propelled him back into movement. He wrapped me in his arms, murmuring against my hair.

"Shhh. It's all right. It's all right, Delphine."

When I calmed, we both pulled slightly apart so we could look at each other.

"I'm sorry," I said more calmly. "That was cruel."

"No." He shook his head. "I understand why you did it. I still can't believe I just...I didn't even question...But it was true. I felt it with such certainty."

I nodded, letting out a long shaky breath. "That's what it's like. I can't control you directly—if I tried to tell you to kill Ember yourself, you'd never do it. But just think of all the ways I could manipulate you."

Nik went still, his arms still partially around me, his face stricken. "They might not be able to tell me to kill Ember, but if Grey mesmerized me into believing you were dead, someone might die at my hands."

I stilled as well, frozen for a moment, before I pushed him away.

"Nik! How could you say that?" But one look at the dangerous expression on his face made me go quiet.

"I'm not saying I'm proud of it," he said hoarsely. "But I really don't know what I'd do if someone killed you, Delphine."

"Shh." This time it was my turn to comfort him, pulling him close. "No one's going to kill me. I'm a healer, remember?"

He put one arm around my back and tangled the other in my hair, pressing my head against his shoulder.

"They'd better not try."

I shook my head against him. "You should try to be a little less bloodthirsty, you know. No matter what happens to me, it isn't worth making yourself into a monster."

"Why would it matter?" The quiet volume of his words did nothing to disguise their bitterness. "Without you, I would have nothing."

I sat up straight. "That's not true!"

"It isn't?" He arched an eyebrow. "Enlighten me. What would be left to me in a world without you? I spent a year wandering the kingdom alone before I met you, so I know exactly what that life is like."

"But why do you have to be alone?" I asked, finally asking the question that had been burning in me for so long. "You have a family, and from what Amara and Hayes have said, they miss you. And you're a prince. I'm sure your old master would take you back and let you complete your apprenticeship like Serena is doing."

"My family were the ones to reject me," he said harshly. "They've made it clear there's no place for me at court."

"But how can that be?" I asked. "Are you sure—?"

"Of course I'm sure!" He laughed darkly. "The Triumvirate cut me out of the line of succession. It's not something that can be taken back. At least before, when Gia was crown princess, I had a purpose of sorts. I was the spare, in case anything ever happened to her. But now I'm nothing at all. My cousin, Evermund, will be king one day in my place, and there's nothing at all I can do about it."

I knew there had been a change in succession, but I had never understood why or the details of it.

"Your father just let them do that?" I asked, still unable to believe it. "Surely they can't just—"

"Actually they can," he said, cutting me off coldly. "My father can't rule without the Triumvirate, and he can't interfere in this law. It's an old one, from the beginning of both the throne and the Guild. The Triumvirate have always been against me from the beginning. Even when I tried to do everything they asked of me, they always had an excuse for why I'd done the wrong thing. Evermund will be king, and I will be nothing."

"Your parents must have been devastated," I whispered, trying to imagine how it would feel to have your children swept aside by forces outside your control.

Nik chuckled darkly. "That just shows you don't know my family at all."

My brows contracted. "Hayes says—"

"Hayes wants to believe the best of things. He has a positive nature." Nik's harsh tone derided such positivity. "He was always busy at the Guild. He knows nothing of my childhood."

"Tell me," I said, my voice soft. "I want to know about it."

Nik looked at me, unseeing for a moment before my expression registered and his arm tightened around me.

"Are you sure you want to know? It isn't a neat, pretty story."

"Of course I do!" I gave him a stern look. "It's a part of you, and I don't only want to know the pretty parts of you."

For a moment, he just looked at me, something reflected in his face that made my insides tremble. But then he tamped it down, hiding the depths of his feelings away as he usually did.

"From my earliest memories, I always knew it mattered that Gia was a few minutes older," he said, and it took me a moment to remember that Gia was his nickname for Princess Morgiana.

"But as small children we were always together, and everyone treated us the same. Sometimes I even forgot we were two separate people and thought of us as a single unit, two who would always be together."

I smiled, but before I could do more than picture the two of them as toddlers, he continued. "But then the rumors started."

"Rumors?"

"All the healers at the palace know not to privately test royal children until their official seed testing when they turn five. But people started to notice we were drawn to play in the gardens, and that after we'd been there, the flowers bloomed bigger and the grass grew lusher. Whispers began to flow around the palace about a plants seed."

"What's wrong with a plants seed?" I asked, indignant.

"Nothing, if you're a regular person." His eyes burned into the closest plank. "All three of the main affinities serve different functions, and all are essential to the well-being of the kingdom. Officially, none of the affinities rank above the others."

"But unofficially?"

He gave a sour laugh. "Elements is the affinity of warriors and kings. Elements controls tempests and tidal waves and brings down lightning bolts. Elements is the affinity of Tartora's royal family."

I was silent, remembering some of his conversations with Amara. This was why he had accused her of believing her affinity superior, although I'd never seen her show any evidence of such thinking.

"So Father brought our testing forward," Nik continued. "He told Mother it was to quiet the rumors and put the issue behind us. But even as I child, I sensed the truth. He was afraid."

"Afraid?"

"Afraid it was true." He swallowed. "I may have been young, but the memory of our testing is still crystal clear. I can recall my father's exact expression—the relief on his face when he discovered it was me, not Gia, who had the undesirable seed. That was the moment I knew."

"Knew what?" I asked, my heart sinking as tears welled in my eyes for Nik's childhood self.

"That Gia and I weren't the same at all. That we had never been one, and we never would be. We were always separate, never equal. I knew in that moment that I was the disappointment. But the worst thing of all?" His voice grew jagged, his volume dropping even lower. "Worst of all was that my being a disappointment didn't even matter."

"Oh Nik!" I threw my arms around him, squeezing his shoulders as tears slipped down my face. "I'm sure that's not true. I'm sure your parents love you too."

Nik leaned into my touch, as if he couldn't help himself, but he continued talking as if I hadn't spoken. "And the irony of it all? The irony is that Gia didn't even want the crown. When we got old enough for that to become clear, it was like constant salt being rubbed in my wound. Gia was the one who mattered, the one with a future, the one with the right seed—and she didn't even want any of it."

I put my head on his shoulder, unable to think of anything to say, and he rested his chin on top of my hair, breathing out deeply.

"My parents always thought she would come around to her duty—that it was just a phase, and she would get over it. But Gia was the one who got what she wanted in the end." His angry laugh sounded again, low in the confined space.

"For one brief moment, when they were forced to accept the truth, I thought they finally cared about what a disappointment I was. I thought maybe they would at last realize that if only they'd ever believed in me, I could have become what Gia never wanted to be. But it turns out there was always a better option than me."

"Evermund." The name fell heavily between us. "So your cousin will get the throne after your father's death. Do you...do you hate him for it?"

Nik ran a hand over his face, his smile bitter. "Sometimes I think it would be easier if I could. Just like I used to wish I could hate Gia. But Gia was always impossible to hate. And Evermund is...Evermund. He's everything Gia is not—focused, disciplined, controlled—and always dutiful. My older cousin has only ever wavered in his duty to the kingdom for one reason. And look how that turned out!"

"One reason?" He clearly expected me to know what he was talking about, but I had no idea.

"Airlie. The strongest elements mage to appear in Tartora in generations—and now sister to Calista's queen. She is the only person or thing Evermund has ever put before Tartora. And in return, he won her heart and secured her loyalty to our kingdom. Winning Airlie as our future queen was a coup I could never compete with—and Evermund wasn't even trying to be strategic. Even when he wavers, he ends up benefiting the kingdom." He shook his head. "Who wouldn't want him to be king?"

I drew a deep breath and let it out slowly, remaining silent because what was there to say? After a moment, Nik spoke again, trying for a lighter tone but failing.

"See? Even you can't bring yourself to say I'd be a better ruler."

I sat up straight, indignation filling me. I couldn't stop Nik from thinking about the other people in his life in any manner he chose, but I wasn't going to let him work me into his twisted narrative.

"Is being a ruler the only future that matters? Is everyone in the kingdom worthless except the best candidate for future king?"

My indignation ballooned inside me. It felt good to let my feelings out instead of having to bottle them inside as I'd been doing all day with Grey. I scrambled inelegantly to my feet and took two steps away before stopping and turning back, my emotions boiling over again.

"I have no interest in a life at court, or at the Guild, or even in the capital. I certainly have no interest in ruling anyone or anything. So I guess that makes me a worthless, useless person, unfit to be loved by anyone!"

"What? Delphine!" He jumped up, striding after me. When

he reached for me, I stepped back out of his grasp. "Of course I don't think about you like that!" He looked part concerned, part irritated.

I crossed my arms and glared at him. "Then why are you so determined to assume that everyone else thinks that way about you? You didn't lose something that should have been yours, Nik! You weren't born to rule—that was never your place. So why can't you let it go? Why can't you put your energy into finding what role you *are* supposed to fill?"

"Delphine, I—"

I waited, eyebrows raised, but he didn't finish, seeming at a complete loss in the face of my anger. Spinning around, I dashed out of the makeshift cabin toward the ladder.

"Wait!" he called after me, but I didn't stop. Climbing up to the upper hold, I checked carefully that I was alone before emerging fully and closing the trapdoor behind me with a bang.

If Nik was determined to be pig-headed, he could stew on his own. It had been a long day—a long three days—and I couldn't take any more emotional upheaval.

TWENTY-FIVE

I went to sleep with my harsh words running through my mind and woke up to hear them repeated again. But I couldn't bring myself to regret saying them. I had spent plenty of time thinking about how Nik's status as both an outcast and a prince stood between us, but it had never just been his position. His bitterness and anger were also a barrier, a well of darkness that I wasn't willing to be dragged into. If Nik couldn't confront his feelings about his past and move beyond them, then we could never have a future together.

Part of me wanted to run straight down to the hold, but I forced myself up on deck instead. I hadn't had the chance to spend time in the fresh air for days, and I needed it. It was also the move Grey would be expecting me to make. I didn't want him to start questioning why I spent so much time below deck.

He smiled when he saw me and waved from his position next to the wheel. As I neared my old spot by the rail, the ship juddered, swinging sharply left. I staggered and just managed to grab hold before I lost my balance.

I looked quickly up at the helm, but nothing in Grey's face, or the faces of the two men beside him, indicated there was a problem. When I peered over the edge, I saw a section of frothing water, sharp points of rock appearing occasionally among the white bubbles. It looked dangerously close to the edge of the boat and must have been the reason for our abrupt change of direction.

I sighed, wondering why I wasn't used to sudden movements of the boat by now. The whole journey had been a zigzag as we followed an unseen, narrow course, and I was long since glad I'd been forced into a hammock. Several of those in the bunks had been tossed out in their sleep when the team controlling our passage adjusted our direction in the water.

The stiff breeze that filled the sails was unnatural too, always blowing steadily and never from the wrong direction. I couldn't connect with it, but Amara's influence allowed me to recognize it had power laced through it.

I stared across the water, my eyes instinctively looking for landmarks of any kind and finding only the flat expanse of the ocean. I had always longed to see the ocean, but the more days I spent entirely surrounded by it, the less enthusiastic I became. All I wanted now was land beneath my feet again.

We turned a second time, but I felt the wind shift direction first and had the chance to ready myself, gripping the rail with all my strength. Once we settled into our new direction, I considered my last three days. At least in Grey's cabin, I had been too distracted to take much notice of the wild movements of the ship.

My mind skipped past the revelation about mesmerizing and back to the two days preceding it. Had we really worked so long and so hard only to get nowhere? Grey had never managed anything close to a wall, no matter how many times I told him to picture himself building it stone by stone.

But why?

The shock of Grey's lesson had driven the pressing question from my mind, but it floated back to the surface now. Why couldn't anyone else do what I had done as a new apprentice? I was reminded of how I had started out testing children's seeds without touching them when other healers always used contact. My ignorance kept driving me to do things other healers didn't even bother trying. But at least in the case of the testing, other healers of equal strength were able to replicate the feat if they wished to do so. What made the wall different?

"Maybe you need to be squeamish," I said out loud to the breeze, smiling a little at my own foolishness. "A lifetime of fainting and vomiting would be enough to..." My voice trailed into silence as I considered my own words.

What had Grey said about mesmerizing? It had taken a tragedy of epic proportions before someone stumbled on the skill. What if the same thing applied here? Not a large-scale tragedy but a small, intimate one.

My whole life used to feel like a tragedy—a joke I couldn't bring myself to laugh at. It wasn't just my squeamishness, although even Clay had said I had an extreme version of it. My father's teachings had also played a part. From almost my earliest memories I had wished my power away, longing for a different, weaker seed. Activation had been a frightening, impossible prospect, to be refused and avoided.

What if that was the necessity required to birth this skill? Grey was focused solely on the ability to block another healer's power, and that was what we had focused on in our attempts. But that had only been an incidental side effect of my original purpose. I had built my wall not to keep others out, but to block my own power. What if, before you could block away your ability, you had to really, truly want it gone?

Phoenix soared toward me, but I barely registered his presence, my thoughts racing and whirling. The more I thought about it, the more it made sense. I didn't want my power gone now, but I had already created my wall a thousand times. Bringing it up was instinctive and easy. But could I have done it the first time without that desperation to keep my own power at bay?

As I considered the possibility, I could finally believe that I might have been the only one to create a wall. Had there ever been another healer of my strength who had feared their own activation like I had? Given what could go wrong with healing power, there must have been some who came to resent it later, after a tragedy had unfolded. But by then they would have already been taught how to use their power, their minds set in the idea of what was and wasn't possible. Youths with seeds as strong as mine usually traveled to the capital well before activation and began learning the basics of their own affinity.

My wall had kept me safe until I didn't need it anymore, and then it had kept me safe again when Grey reached into my mind and overturned it. And there was a good chance I had only ever created my wall because of my father.

I didn't know what to do with that thought. My squeamishness had been the greatest weakness of my life, and yet it had turned into strength. Was it possible my history with my father could do the same thing? And if it did, did that mean I had to forgive him and let go of the ways he'd wronged me?

I wanted to hold onto my anger, but my words from the night before in the hold reappeared, unwanted, in my mind. I had berated Nik, chastising him for not letting go of his bitterness and anger. So why was I clinging onto mine so tightly?

I claimed I didn't want to be pulled into Nik's well of darkness, and yet, all the while, I was busily at work creating one of my own. My father had trapped himself in his anger and bitterness, and he had nearly trapped me in it with him. I had broken free, but had I seized my freedom only to make the same mistake and become mired in anger and bitterness of my own?

Phoenix gave his brief, chattering call and nipped at my ear.

"Oi!" I batted at him, coming close enough to unseating him that he had to spread his wings for balance.

"You think I should forgive my father, don't you, fine sir?" I ran a finger down his back while he regarded me steadily with one beady eye.

Even as I said the words, I felt a heaviness lift off me. The thought of going home still held little appeal, and I would never regain the closeness I had once shared with my father. But at least the thought of one day visiting the farm no longer filled me with revulsion and confusion.

"When was I reduced to this?" I muttered. "Receiving life wisdom from a bird." I couldn't help but smile, though. I had enough burdens to carry without lugging around an unnecessary one as well.

"If I'd realized all this three days ago, could I have taught Grey to make his own wall?" I mused to Phoenix. "Is understanding it enough to make a difference?"

I wouldn't know for sure without trying, and I had no intention of giving Grey any more tips. But I suspected no explanation from me would be enough. Grey wasn't the sort of person to ever wish away a single portion of his power. If sincerity was required, he would never be able to muster the necessary sentiment.

Someone approached me with a serving of bread and cheese and an apple. I accepted the lunch with a brief thanks and ate it on deck where I stood. As soon as I'd finished, however, I moved toward the door leading below deck.

Forgiving my father had softened my heart enough that I couldn't stay away from Nik any longer. I had at least had the wind and the sea and the sky to aid me in my reflections. He had nothing but darkness and the creaking of the ship's sides.

In my haste, I slid down the ladder into the upper hold, only to freeze at the sight of several people sorting through a section of bags and crates. Two of them looked up at my arrival, nodding a wary greeting.

I nodded back, my mouth suddenly dry. Picking a direction

at random, I hurried away from them, stopping at a pile of crates and pretending to examine them.

It seemed to take hours for them to finish their task, hauling away several of the bags. Creating a chain, they passed each of the bags up the ladder while I moved on to another pile of crates, pretending not to have found what I was looking for.

When they finally disappeared from view, I let out an explosive breath. I had gotten careless and was lucky none of them had questioned my presence in the hold. I would have to make sure that I came up with a good excuse for the next time I ran into someone.

Hurrying to the closed trapdoor, I climbed down, stopping awkwardly part way down to close it behind me.

Nik appeared, stepping into the light with a glance upward. "That's new."

"There were people up there when I came down. They've gone now, but I don't know if they'll be back."

He accepted my explanation without comment, and I looked around for Ember. But, of course, it was daytime, so she must have been sleeping back in their makeshift bed. Which left Nik and me to stand and silently regard each other.

I couldn't read his expression, blaming the flickering lantern light for giving him a foreboding look.

"I'm sorry," I blurted out at last. "I shouldn't have spoken so harshly to you when all the time I was carrying around the same bitterness toward my own father. I've known for a while now that he didn't deserve the intensity of my anger, but..."

"It's not so easy to let go of." Nik finished the sentence for me, his words calm and measured.

My eyes flew to his face. What conclusion had he come to down here alone in the depths of the ship?

"I decided to let it go," I said in a rush. "I won't ever go back to resume the life I imagined on the farm with my parents, but I want to be able to see them again one day. And I want to remember their love for me without it hurting."

"And you want me to do the same?" Again his voice was flat, giving away none of the emotion behind it.

I tipped my head to the side, considering his question. "It isn't about what I want. It's about what you want. Because I want you to be free, but that doesn't mean anything unless you want it too."

"I thought I already was free," he said. "When I left my old life to wander alone, I thought of it as freedom. And then I met you."

I shivered slightly at the way he spoke of our meeting, as if I was an axis that his life turned around. Before and after.

"I don't want the freedom to be alone anymore," he said. "And neither do I want to be chained to my past."

"You've forgiven your family?" I couldn't keep the eagerness out of my voice.

"Was there anything to forgive?" he asked in a strange tone.

I moved toward him, reaching for him without meaning to do so. He looked at my outstretched hands, his whole body trembling slightly, as if he was suppressing something that took enormous effort.

I lowered my arms again slowly, my eyes locked on his as I waited to hear what else he had to say.

"When you left last night—" The tremble was in his voice as well, and it took everything I had not to close the last of the distance between us and put my arms around him.

He swallowed. "When you left, and I didn't know if you were coming back, I—" He shook his head as if shaking off an unwelcome thought and glanced sideways.

I followed the direction of his gaze to see a mess of smashed wood and several broken objects I couldn't identify. Nik claimed it had been my departure that had sparked his wild emotions, but I knew it was more than that. I'd stirred up his problems with his family, and they were emotions he needed to face.

"When I came to my senses, I knew you were right," he said. "And so were they."

"Right about what?" I asked cautiously.

"Right that I was never suited to rule. I didn't get on this ship to protect the kingdom from Grey or the islanders. I came to protect you. In that moment, you were the only one I cared about, Delphine. And even now, I would walk away from the rest of them and never look back if you needed me to."

"But I don't—"

"I know you would never ask that of me," he said quickly. "But that isn't what matters. What matters is that I would do it. I thought the Triumvirate rejected me because they doubted my power. Even when they told me it was because I lacked the qualities of a ruler, I refused to hear it. I refused to see any deficiency in myself. But my father turned his back on his own son when the kingdom demanded it of him. And even I have to acknowledge that as far as Tartora is concerned, it was the right thing to do. A king puts his kingdom first—it's the most basic requirement for the role. And I don't think I've ever been selfless enough to do it."

He shook his head slowly. "I was fooling myself the whole time—telling myself I was doing things for the good of the kingdom when I was only ever thinking about myself. I was just like Grey—seeking power for its own sake not because I wanted to use it to help anyone else."

"We all lie to ourselves like that," I said softly. "We come up with admirable reasons for our actions to cover the selfishness or fear that is truly driving us. But this conversation right now is what separates you from Grey. Do you think he's ever peeled back the layers to look at himself as he truly is? Do you think he has any desire to do so?"

"Maybe there's hope for him yet," Nik said with a rough

laugh. "A year ago I was no different. And then I fell in love with you."

I froze, staring at him. He finally drew closer, standing a mere step away, although he kept his arms at his side.

"I love you, Delphine. More intensely than I thought I could love anyone or anything. So now I'm selfish in a different way. But at least you make me want to be better."

Unable to restrain myself any longer, I reached out and took his hands. "Maybe you're not made to be a ruler, but you're too harsh on yourself. You do care about the people of Tartora. I've seen it. You were tracking Grey before anyone else cared enough to notice what he was doing. You didn't turn your eyes away from the ones the rest of the kingdom preferred to forget."

"I know what it's like to be unwanted by your kingdom," he muttered.

"And you were out there in the middle of the storm in Eldrida," I continued relentlessly, "putting yourself at risk to rescue people. You didn't have to do that. No one would even have known if you hadn't."

He frowned but was apparently unable to come up with a suitable retort.

"There's more to you than just selfishness, Nik. And without the lure of a throne to lead you off track, you can finally work out what you were made to do. Remember what Amara said? We're all different, and that means we all show our love differently. You might not be well suited to making the strategic decisions that affect everyone, but that doesn't mean you can't make all the difference to some people." My voice lowered. "You've already made a difference to me."

Nik's fingers tightened around mine, his eyes latching onto my face with painful intensity.

"What sort of difference have I made to you, Delphine? I don't expect you to feel the same way I do right now, but do you think there's any chance that one day you might—"

I pulled my hands loose and grabbed two fistfuls of his shirt. For half a second, I stayed paused there, taking in his features. When I had first met him, I had found him simultaneously terrifying and attractive, and even now, the fire burning in his eyes scared me a little, although in a different way. I had no idea how someone like Nik could feel so intensely about me. But I had been fighting my own feelings for too long, and I didn't have the strength to resist any more.

Yanking him downward, I stretched up and smashed my lips to his. For a moment we were frozen there, his shock holding him immobile. Then his arms were around me, his lips were moving on mine, and he was whispering my name in a voice that sent a shiver all the way through me.

Giving up the fight completely, I lost myself in the kiss. But even as I did, an echo of fear lingered. This spark between us might lift us to new heights, or it might burn us to the ground. Even as the flames engulfed us both, I couldn't be sure which it would be.

TWENTY-SIX

It took all my self-control to fight my desire to spend the rest of the afternoon and all the next day at Nik's side. But I had to stay up on deck, visible to Grey in case he came looking for me. I couldn't risk his discovering Nik at this point.

If I found it hard to leave, Nik found it even harder to let me go. But even he acknowledged the danger.

"He's sure of me, ridiculously sure." I shook my head. "But I still can't take the risk."

"He underestimates you."

"He must." My words grew more heated. "But does he really think I'm so stupid that he can tell me about mesmerizing, and I won't question everything he's ever told me? I've even been using my wall constantly the last few days."

I knew Grey did still believe I was mesmerized, though, because he'd already refreshed his original lies several times since we'd come aboard. I'd become almost used to the horrible process. It didn't matter what he lied to me about. I recognized the feeling of having been mesmerized and knew how to drive his power out of my mind.

"We know where his confidence is coming from now." Nik sounded disgusted. "But I suppose it's working to our advantage in this instance. It must be hard to shake a lifetime of certainty that your words will be believed. After all, you're the first person he's ever told the truth to. But he isn't totally foolish. I notice he waited to tell you about mesmerizing until he had you in the middle of the ocean. From his perspective, if his plan goes awry, there's nowhere for you to run. He's probably trusting that if you show any signs of rebellion, he can find a way to mesmerize you again."

I shivered at the thought, even though I knew it was impossible. Now that I knew the feeling, he would never be able to fool me for long.

I still flinched when Grey called my name on the fourth day, however. But I managed to pin a smile in place before I turned around, and I made no protest about returning to his cabin yet again. I had grown to hate the wooden box, but I kept those emotions from my face and considered each word I uttered carefully.

"We'll arrive at the island not long past dawn tomorrow," he told me, successfully taking my mind off everything else.

"Already?" I didn't care how glad I sounded. Sailing wasn't for me.

He chuckled. "I'm rather anxious to arrive myself. But I need to prepare you before we go ashore."

"Do you expect trouble when we arrive?" I asked, afraid of how he might want me to get involved.

"No, no," he assured me with a forced air, although I could read the words were mostly truth. "I just need to give you a warning. It's different in my case because I'm family, but it might be dangerous if they learn you're also a powerful healing mage and know how to mesmerize. From what my mother reported, her family are obsessed with strength—to the extent that they don't even allow any cross-influencing on the island. But all that strength is carefully controlled. To keep you safe, I'm going to tell them you have an elements affinity. But, of course, you won't be able to use elements power, so it would be best to give them the impression you're weak."

I considered his words. "But aren't they healers themselves? How will you be able to lie about my affinity?"

His lips stretched, revealing his teeth. "Very carefully."

I wanted to protest, but there was nothing I could think of to say. He had framed his suggestion as keeping me safe, and there had been no hint of a lie about his words of caution. If being a healer would put me in danger from the islanders, then it was in my interest to fall in with Grey's plan. Especially since I couldn't let him know I was aware he had a bigger scheme underway.

I would just have to wait and see what request he made of me next.

"Make sure you sleep well tonight."

He still seemed overly pleased, which made me jumpy. But there was nothing I could do except agree and leave his presence as quickly as possible.

Given the tight confines of the cabin, Phoenix had been sleeping on deck, leaving me alone in my hammock. I wished desperately for his company or for Ember's warm, furry body curled at my side. Instead I had to make do with the sleeping sounds of women all around me as I lay and wondered what would happen to us all in the morning.

There was no time to sneak down to Nik after I rose. I could only trust his reassurances that he would find his own way off the ship. At least Phoenix was able to join me, taking up his usual perch on my shoulder.

Those of us not involved in guiding the ship gathered together on deck at first light. Already the island was looming before us, larger than I'd imagined and rising to a single, tree covered peak, the dark green a welcome relief from the blue all around us.

Our ship cut smoothly through the still waters, with no sign of rocks at this end of our journey. We approached not a sandy beach as I'd imagined, but a dock that reminded me of the one in Eldrida. A row of buildings lined the waterfront, although there would be no trade ships sailing in and out of this town.

From the look of the small vessels and fishing nets, there were plenty of fishermen, however, which had to explain the existence of the dock. Murmured conversations were taking place all around me, but no one attempted to include me in their exclamations and excited imaginings. Three days shut up with Grey in his cabin working on experiments the rest of them didn't understand had done nothing to soften the underlying antagonism from the beginning of the trip.

"It's more beautiful than I imagined," someone breathed beside me, and I turned gratefully to smile my agreement at Ida. It was nice to be included by someone.

"That tree covered mountain is like a feast for the eyes after nothing but ocean."

She laughed. "You didn't take to life onboard, then? Personally, I found the ocean peaceful." She lapsed into silence, as if remembering the past hurts that made the emptiness of the ocean so appealing in comparison.

I had no time to say anything supportive since various shouts were rising around us. Some came from among us as those with elements power worked together to maneuver the ship to the end of the long dock. But others came from ashore. Despite the early hour, some people were already up and about on the dock, and all of them had stopped to gape at our arrival.

One of the onlookers set off running, disappearing down a street that looked much like the ones I had seen in Ostaria, Caltor, and Eldrida. In fact, from what I could see, only the natural setting distinguished this island settlement from any city or large town in Tartora.

I glanced at Ida, wondering if she'd be disappointed by the familiarity, but her eyes were shining just as brightly as before. I cast another look toward the door that led below deck. Where was Nik right now? How was he preparing to disembark?

We made the lightest of contacts with the wooden dock, and several people sprang over the edge of the rail to receive the lengths of rope being thrown to them. Within no time they had the ship secured and the gangplank in place.

I had my personal pack over my shoulder, as we all did, but many people had a second bag as well. Clearly Grey's plan didn't include arriving empty-handed.

By the time we were ready to file off the deck and onto dry land, the fruit of the runner's efforts had arrived. A group of people—all of whom looked like they didn't usually spend their mornings on the dock—ran into view, coming to a stop just short of our landing place.

I examined the silk of their robes, and the winded expressions on their faces. These were people whose lives didn't usually require them to dash from place to place. I was surprised they were even awake.

We arranged ourselves loosely, me moving toward the back of the disembarkation line. But as Grey strode down from the helm to take the lead, he brushed past me, indicating for me to follow him. His movement had been subtle, but those around us had picked it up and reluctantly parted to allow me through.

I could have done without the honor, preferring to remain at the back away from the attention, but I had little choice but to obey. Grey ignored his followers, all his attention on what lay before us. He took in the dock and the buildings behind it in a single, comprehensive glance, his attention settling on the people waiting for us.

His usual air of confidence hung about him as he strode down the gangplank and onto the wooden dock. I followed eagerly, only to lurch slightly when I finally reached ground.

Why was the land moving beneath my feet? It felt just like the ship I had been so eager to leave behind.

I looked frantically back at the group gathered on deck, managing to catch Ida's eye. She appeared to be laughing at me.

Taking pity on the frantic look in my eyes, she waved me forward encouragingly, mouthing something I couldn't catch. But when I turned back to face forward again, I noticed there was something different about Grey's gait. He might not show it in his air, but he walked as if he felt lingering effects from being onboard. So perhaps this was normal after all.

I hurried to catch up with him, hoping the unnerving sensation would soon disappear.

A man, taller than the others, stepped forward to put himself at the front of the group. His clothes were the most elaborate, and now that he'd recovered his breath, his arrogant manner made it clear he was the highest-ranking person present.

I couldn't help immediately disliking him, but I wasn't sure if that was his manner or the fact he was likely a relative of Grey's. I hid the emotion, however, keeping myself a couple steps behind Grey. Hopefully all attention would be on him, and there would be none left over for me.

"This is a most unprecedented occasion," the man said, his tone far more conciliatory than I had expected. "You are the first visitors we have ever welcomed to our fair shores."

"It is not, however, my first time here," Grey said smoothly. "I have waited many years to return to my home."

Shock pierced the man's mask, the true emotion making it obvious how false his previous pleasant manner had been. His mind clearly worked quickly, however, as the jarring expression smoothed almost instantly into a smile.

"But surely...It cannot be that you are my missing cousin, Grey?"

"Indeed I am." Grey stepped forward to clasp his long-lost cousin's arm, the two of them slapping each other on the back in apparent delight at the reconciliation.

I tried to keep my eyes from widening perceptibly as I took in the odd scene before me. Anyone would think these two had been parted mere months ago instead of shortly after Grey's birth. I had assumed Grey's claim about being welcomed back with open arms as their leader had been an obvious falsehood —one he had only dared utter because he was mesmerizing me.

But this seemed just the sort of reception he had claimed was waiting for him. These people weren't just going to hand the island over to him, were they?

But no. A reminder of what these people were capable of was enough to eliminate that thought. They must be masters of manipulation, just as Grey himself was, and I should view all their interactions through that lens.

I examined the man again while he introduced himself as Ignatius Constantine, smiling and inquiring about the voyage as though he was genuinely glad to see us. But I suspected the only real emotions I had seen from him were the arrogance visible on his face in its natural, resting posture, and the momentary shock that had broken through following Grey's announcement.

"But what of my Aunt Chloe?" Ignatius asked. "She didn't accompany you?" Something in his expression looked off at this question, as though it carried far more importance than he wanted to reveal.

Grey bowed his head, his face dropping. "I'm afraid to say my mother has been dead for many years. Our crossing to the mainland took a terrible toll."

"A grave loss, indeed," Ignatius said in suitably solemn tones. "My father and Uncle Ambrose will be shocked to hear it. As will Grandmother, of course. She always believed her daughter was living happy and well in another place."

I twitched slightly, but thankfully neither of them noticed. Grey's mother was the one who'd been a member of this family? What about the story of his murdered father, the one who'd wanted to bring about change? Was that a complete fiction?

"It has always been my dream to return to her family and my first home," Grey said. "But it took me many years to gather those who also desired a new life and who could help me build a ship and travel here. I hope we will all find a welcome in this place."

"Of course." Ignatius raised his voice so that all those gathered behind us could hear. "All are welcome here! You have had a long and difficult journey, but I hope here you will find peace and a new beginning."

My lips twitched as I tried to make sense of this man who seemed a mass of strange contradictions. Nothing he had said had carried the feel of a lie, and yet I couldn't shake a profound feeling of distrust.

Ignatius stepped to the side slightly, placing himself directly in front of me. Inclining his upper half, he offered me his hand. For a moment I stared at it, trying to overcome the feeling that I was reaching for a hissing viper.

But Grey's presence loomed beside me, and his warning rang in my ears, so I hesitantly extended my own hand and allowed Ignatius to clasp it in his. He was murmuring empty words of welcome, but I could barely follow enough to nod and smile in the right places.

Most of my attention was focused on the tendril of power he was subtly sending into me through our hands. It took everything I had not to rip my hand from his or throw up my wall to drive him straight back out. But I knew I couldn't afford to reveal myself yet, so I stayed still, allowing him to plant a false truth inside my mind.

His words, which had previously only been a background noise, came into sharp and sudden focus. I wasn't sure why I had been so tense and worried when this family, the Constantines, were ready to welcome all of us into the life of peace they ruled over.

Ignatius let go of my hand promptly, moving to the next in line. Not that I blamed him. He clearly meant to greet us all individually—a truly gracious gesture—so he could spare only seconds for each person.

How delightful that there was no need for the scheming and deception I had expected. Peace and rest sounded perfect after the tension of the voyage. And Nik could stop skulking in the shadows as well. The Constantines wouldn't care that Grey didn't approve of him.

Of course, Grey himself might be a problem. I would need to tell Ignatius about his true nature as soon as I had the opportunity. Once he was taken care of, I would have no need to worry further. Clearly everything he'd said was lies—these people would never burn the crops of strangers across the sea or send storms to destroy them.

I relaxed, wishing only that the uncomfortable, twisted feeling in my stomach would go away. I was sick of niggling thoughts, and layers to everything. I was ready to—oh!

Pulling up my wall, I pushed it through me, driving out the unfamiliar power that was tainting my thoughts. Within seconds, my mind was clear again, a horribly familiar, slimy feeling taking the place of the peace I had felt moments before.

I recalled my thoughts of only seconds ago and shivered. I had been on the verge of telling this stranger about both Nik and Grey. It was unnerving the way the deception left my other thoughts and memories intact, and yet that one central truth reshaped everything else around it.

I looked behind me and saw Grey's followers had formed themselves into a line, eagerly holding out their hands for Ignatius's greeting. I glanced across at Grey, expecting to see him furious. He must know what his cousin was doing, that he was taking Grey's people and making them his own.

Grey's expression remained calm, however, only a note of speculation in his eyes. He must have been expecting something like this. I supposed it was the only way the Constantines would allow a foreign group to enter their island, so Grey couldn't prevent it.

I did, however, notice that Ignatius made no attempt to take Grey's hand. Even earlier, when they had first greeted each other, they had clasped arms and slapped backs, their hands carefully touching only sleeve and jacket. If Ignatius didn't know for certain, he was certainly aware of the possibility that Grey was a powerful healer who knew how to mesmerize. Apparently he wasn't willing to risk receiving what he so happily dispensed.

Had he not considered the possibility that one of the rest of us might have the same ability? Apparently he couldn't fathom that anyone—even the long-lost Grey—would have shared the skill outside their family line.

Was he checking for affinities, at least? Should I prepare myself for his already knowing I was a healer, and a powerful one at that?

On reflection, I thought he remained unaware. Surely he would have reacted in some way if he'd checked. I'd done mesmerizing myself, and it was a subtle, difficult skill that required concentration. And Ignatius was mesmerizing many people in quick succession, our numbers meaning he could afford only seconds for each person. My experience told me he would be highly focused, not having the time or capacity to check for anyone's seeds.

Not that it would have mattered that I was a powerful healer if I hadn't also been able to make a wall. I might know how to mesmerize, but ten minutes ago, I would have had no desire to use my power against any of the Constantines.

"Delphine." Grey placed a hand on my shoulder, the edge of one finger brushing against the exposed skin of my neck. He lowered his voice before continuing. "I hope you know you're my most trusted follower. If we're going to save Tartora, we'll need to stick close together and trust each other implicitly. The Constantines can't be trusted."

As soon as he finished the words, he stepped back. My eyes flicked straight to Ignatius, to find him looking our way, a frown on his face. It had been a brief interaction, and he was occupied most of the way down the line of new arrivals, but he must have been keeping an eye on Grey.

I wasn't surprised, though. He was a tricky man, and he must view everyone else with the same suspicion he knew he deserved. It was a wonder Grey had come from such an unpleasant family.

Something niggled at the back of my mind, and I jerked back in distaste, throwing up my wall again and purging my mind.

Breathing deeply to calm the disgusted shivers, I considered what I'd just learned. A mesmerization could be broken by hard evidence to the contrary, but it could also be overridden by a contradictory mesmerization.

I worried at the inside of my cheek. Grey had accepted that his followers were no longer his—at least for the moment—but he had taken the risk of reclaiming me immediately. I understood why, of course. I was both his most valuable follower and his greatest weakness. But in taking such immediate action, he had brought me to Ignatius's attention.

Even as the Constantine continued down the line, still clasping the last of the hands in ostensible welcome, I felt his eyes flicking several times back to me. He must have been wondering why I alone was the one Grey had touched.

Would he risk testing me? If his power was equal to Grey's, he had strength to do it. But would he take the risk of my sensing his probing? Testing an activated mage wasn't the same as checking the seed of a child. It could be done without physical touch, but I had always felt it in the past.

I felt no such intrusive probe now, so I could only assume he had decided to bide his time. Instead, he directed his companions to find beds for the new arrivals throughout the city.

"We can accommodate a few of you at the manor house," he told Grey, "but not all of you, unfortunately. Perhaps five or six of you can accompany me."

Grey nodded and gestured for five of us to come closer. I was unsurprised to be one of those selected but disappointed Ida was not. Instead Grey chose an eclectic mix, including some older and some younger. I hadn't seen him showing any particular interest in the other four previously, but they all came willingly enough. Given the way their eyes glowed as they looked at Ignatius, I suspected it was only a matter of time before Grey found a surreptitious way to renew his control over them.

Ignatius gave no visible sign he was aware of the danger, however, his false smile spread across us all equally. The others had started to disperse into the surrounding streets, walking in small groups, each led by a single local. Only our group had three locals at its head, since two of Ignatius's acolytes had remained at his side.

They led us up the largest street which ran in a straight line through the settlement. I would need a higher vantage point to see the settlement's full size, but it seemed to be a large town built at the base of the island's one mountain, cushioned between the slope and the sea.

Already the sensation of the ground rocking beneath me had faded, and I reveled in striding forward, free of the restrictions of one small deck. But I couldn't help glancing over my shoulder several times, straining to see some sign of a man and a fox disappearing from the dock.

I didn't catch so much as a glimpse of Nik, however, and it was hard not to imagine him trapped below decks. I would have given almost anything to have him walking beside me, my hand held firmly in his. But instead I had to keep my head high and walk down the street between two equally treacherous men, both of whom wanted to control me like a puppet.

The town itself was attractive—clean and orderly with houses in neat rows. Most of the structures had been built with dark gray stone, but a different, unfamiliar stone—deep black and glossy—had been used decoratively, giving the whole town an elegant air. Combined with the green mountain rising ahead of us, the lush blossoms that poked from unexpected places, and the hint of moisture in the air, it was easy to believe we were no longer in Tartora.

The central street led us all the way through the town, gently sloping upward until we reached the lush grounds surrounding a house far grander and more extensive than any other buildings I'd seen. It was built of the same stone as the other houses in town, but the similarity ended there. It wasn't a palace, like the one I'd heard tales of in Tarona, but it was clearly home to the leaders of the settlement.

Grey and my four companions looked around, exclaiming in delight at everything they saw. I did my best to mimic their behavior since I could feel the weight of Ignatius's eyes on me at frequent intervals. I was sure I was doing a poor job, however, given I felt far more dread than delight at the sight of the luxurious mansion.

But when we reached the front steps of the house, I realized the true source of my dread. Someone must have come ahead to give warning of our arrival because a formidable line of people were waiting to greet us. The Constantines.

Ignatius gave a loaded look to the people waiting for us. I half-expected them all to insist on shaking our hands themselves, but apparently there was some trust within the family, at least, because they settled for spoken greetings.

Grey stepped forward and bowed respectfully.

"Grandmother," he murmured to the formidable older woman who stood in the center of the group. Her hair was stark white, but it did nothing to make her look soft.

However a glint of something sentimental entered her eye as she nodded her head in response. "Young Grey. I never thought to see my fourth grandson a grown man."

Ignatius and a man who looked like an older version of him exchanged the briefest of glances, but I was sure I hadn't mistaken their discomfort with the matriarch's reaction. Did they see Grey as some kind of competition?

Seeing them all lined up, it was obvious why Ignatius hadn't questioned the family connection claimed by Grey. Not only had Grey known the route to the island, but he also possessed the same striking green eyes as five of the people arrayed before me.

"It gives me great pleasure to have finally made it here to

stand before you," Grey said. "And I must thank you for your acceptance of my people. They have come seeking nothing more than a safe harbor."

The white-haired woman nodded. "That much we can provide."

"Here with me are my strongest elements followers. They're the ones who brought our ship safely to your shores." He gestured at the five of us, and I suddenly realized why he had chosen the other four. On the ship he had said that his ruse about my affinity would have to be communicated carefully, and this was his strategy. It was true that the other four all had an elements affinity, so his words would ring true. And it would only be a natural assumption for me to be lumped in with the rest of them.

The matriarch nodded graciously at us all, and the people ranged on either side of her followed her lead. Only Ignatius remained still, and I hoped I was imagining that his eyes lingered on me.

A round of introductions followed, with a notable lack of physical touch from anyone, including between the Constantines themselves. Did that mean their mutual trust had limits?

From what I could gather, the matriarch—only ever referred to as Grandmother—had three children. From the order of their introduction, her oldest son was Augustine, the father of Ignatius. It made sense since Ignatius carried himself like the oldest son of an oldest son. Second was Ambrose, along with his wife Kendry, and their son Barnabas. And, of course, third was the missing Chloe.

Barnabas seemed an unprepossessing man next to Ignatius, and from the flash of fire in his eyes when he looked at his cousin, he was aware of it. But his mother seemed the most genuinely warm of the group, her weak blue eyes a reminder that she was the only one of them without actual Constantine blood.

No one mentioned Ignatius's missing mother, but a second younger man appeared, his late arrival rounding out their numbers to seven. He received mostly dismissive glances from his family, but someone hurriedly introduced him as Costas, another son of Augustine.

I gazed at the new arrival, wondering how Ignatius and his brother could have the exact same eyes and yet otherwise be so dissimilar. Not only was his coloring lighter, but everything about his bearing was as well. Even his expression displayed only interest and curiosity, without a trace of superiority.

I found myself wanting the chance to talk to him—preferably without the rest of his family around. But from the way he stooped to kiss his grandmother on the cheek, his smile affectionate, perhaps he was only a better actor than the rest. He certainly didn't seem to bear them any animosity, despite their attitude toward him.

After a few more pleasantries, we were invited inside for breakfast. It turned out to be a formal meal held in an enormous dining room with a long wooden table, polished until it shone. Seeing the tapestries on the walls and the fine carpet underfoot, I was glad I had sent Phoenix off to hunt instead of attempting to bring him inside.

To my disappointment, I was seated between Ignatius and Grey—the two people I would have liked to be furthest from. And as the meal progressed, I grew more and more certain I wasn't imagining the suspicion in Ignatius's eyes when they rested on me. Any time now, he was going to decide to test me. I had to find a way to placate his concern.

I racked my brain as his eyes bored into me.

"How did you find the passage?" he asked.

I almost admitted to disliking sailing until I remembered that anyone with a true elements affinity would feel at home on the sea. And it was true my cross-influence had made me comfortable on the waves, without fear of seasickness, but I had found the ship itself restrictive and unpleasant.

"The sea is magnificent, of course," I said carefully. "But I don't appreciate being surrounded by dead wood."

Ignatius smiled thinly. "I understand your sort prefer to be out in the elements directly. I suppose you would have rather swum."

"Not quite that, perhaps," I said with a forced smile, hoping my awkwardness wasn't as apparent to him as it was to me. Talking to him felt like picking my careful way through a nest of deadly scorpions.

Grey was watching our conversation, clearly alert and listening for every one of my words. His attention did nothing to calm my nerves, and I felt my heart rate increase.

Ignatius looked my way, his eyes narrowing, and I realized that as a healer, he would also be able to sense it. I sent my power toward my heart, ready to slow it back down to a normal rhythm only to stop myself at the last moment. If I acted too obviously I might tip my hand and reveal my affinity.

But I had to do something to distract his attention. I wished intensely for Nik's presence and assistance, and just the thought of him gave me my answer. Fear made my heart beat faster, but so did being in Nik's presence. Which meant I had to fake something I had no interest in faking.

Gritting my teeth and forcing a smile, I leaned slightly toward Grey, meeting his attentive eyes with as bashful a glance as I could manage. When he smiled back at me warmly, I tucked my hair behind my ear and smiled into my lap. Waiting one beat and then another, I snuck a sideways glance at him. He was still smiling at me, apparently having picked up on my intention.

By the time I looked back at Ignatius, he had one eyebrow slightly raised, a look of understanding on his face. Apparently my acting had been sufficient for the occasion, and it had even given an explanation for Grey's particular interest in me.

A serving girl appeared at my elbow, blocking my view of Grey, and I smiled at her more brightly than the service required. She was carrying a steaming pot of porridge, a cloth wrapped around its handle to guard her hands from the heat. She clearly intended to place it in the middle of the table, but between the placement of our chairs and the weight of the pot, it was a tricky maneuver.

A memory flashed through my mind of Grey telling me that the Constantines didn't allow cross-influencing on the island. In a flash of brilliance, I thought of a way to give Ignatius the final proof he needed.

Reaching for the metal pot, I wrapped my hands around its base, taking it from the serving girl with another smile. She gasped, but her smile returned when she saw I didn't shout from pain or pull my hands away. I placed the pot on the table in front of me, handing the cloth around its handle back to the girl.

If Grey was right about the islanders' lack of experience with cross-influencing, then they would associate a tolerance for burning temperatures solely with an elements seed. They might even be completely unaware that being cross elements conferred that particular protection.

When I finally risked another glance at Ignatius, he wasn't looking at me at all. Apparently, I had succeeded in shaking his interest. I smiled to myself, although my pleasure at my quick thinking dimmed when I saw the approval in Grey's eyes. But on this matter, if nothing else, our goals were temporarily aligned. Neither of us wanted the truth of my ability exposed to our new hosts.

Released from my worry over Ignatius, I finally paid attention to the rest of the table, only to find another pair of green eyes watching me. Costas sat across from me, and my display with the pot seemed to have roused rather than quenched his interest.

"I had hoped my new cousin might be elements like me," he said with a friendly smile. "But at least he has brought you with him."

I glanced at Grey who looked as surprised by the comment as me.

"You have an elements affinity?" Grey asked, leaning forward.

Costas chuckled. "It's uncanny how much like a Constantine you look right now. Astonished and mildly disgusted is exactly how they feel whenever they consider how they managed to produce a disgrace like me."

"Are you the only one with an elements affinity?" I asked.

His smile grew lopsided and self-deprecating. "In three generations, if you can believe it."

I raised both eyebrows. "But usually—"

"I don't know how it's done on the mainland," he said, "but here, Constantines only marry other healers. I didn't even know we had anyone in our lineage of a different affinity, so I was as astonished at my testing as everyone else."

"Everyone has to marry a healer?" I asked, my astonishment growing. It seems it wasn't only the regular people on the island who had their lives controlled by this family.

"Except for my rebellious Aunt Chloe, of course," he murmured, eyes on Grey. "How ironic that her son is the healer and not me."

His words should have carried a heavy dose of bitterness, but he said everything lightly, as if he had long since accepted his position as an outcast in his own family.

I wanted to question him further about Grey's mother, but I didn't dare do it with Grey sitting by my side. I wasn't sure if he even remembered that he had lied to me about her, or if he was merely trusting his mesmerization to hold regardless, but it didn't seem a good idea to display curiosity over the matter.

The Constantine matriarch abruptly stood, and everyone else put down their cutlery. It seemed the meal was over, whether we were finished eating or not.

I don't know what I expected to happen after breakfast, but the reality turned out to be an anticlimax. Ignatius and Barnabas both descended on Grey, sweeping him off with them for some sort of cousinly bonding or testing—I suspected they would claim the former while actually intending the latter.

The rest of us were shown to our rooms, where our packs were already waiting for us, and were then left to our own devices. I would have liked to explore the house, but I feared it would be frowned on. In desperation, I searched out Grey's four companions since their company would be preferable to sitting alone in my room for a full day.

I found them in the gardens in front of the house, and they welcomed me easily enough. Now that we were in such unfamiliar surroundings, they seemed to have forgotten the feelings they'd harbored on the boat.

"Are we really free to do whatever we want?" I asked, not quite able to believe it.

"I heard there's a market in the center square," one of them said. "Shall we see if we can find it?"

The others all seemed enthusiastic about the idea, so I trailed behind, watching them all in disbelief. I knew it wasn't fair of me—I had felt the power of mesmerization often enough to understand its effects. But it still seemed incredible that none of them felt the creeping sense of danger overlaying this strange place.

Their enthusiasm only increased when we reached the promised market, a bustling place that reminded me of all the markets I had visited in cities on the mainland. But as soon as I was standing among the stalls, I was forcibly reminded of the last occasion I had stood in a similar square. Looking around at the wooden stalls, all I could see was a different market, the stalls splintered and broken, the air full of driving rain and shouts of pain.

It took me a moment to shake off the memories, but it was long enough for me to lose my temporary companions. I spun in a circle, but they had completely disappeared into the crowd.

Instead of searching for them further, I wandered through the market alone. Seeing how established the town was, it was easy to believe a hundred years had passed. But in other ways it felt as if their separation from the mainland must have been recent. Even their style of dress echoed the current styles in Tartora.

A moment's consideration made me realize why. Some of the Constantines must have visited Tartora to enact their sabotage of the crops. They would have needed to blend in, and the new clothing they brought back must have started a trend here. It was easy to imagine that the mesmerized locals would follow their ruling family in everything, hurrying to copy their styles.

I wandered along the closest line of stalls, admiring the various wares while I watched the unfamiliar crowd. I was just leaning forward to examine a beautiful length of cloth when fingers twined into mine.

I jumped, whirling to stare in consternation at a familiar face.

"Nik!" I gasped, but he laughed and shushed me.

Pulling me away from the cloth, he tugged me into a quiet nook between stalls. He was gazing down at me with a happy expression, but I could only manage a horrified response.

"What are you doing walking around like this?"

He grinned at me. "And why shouldn't I walk around?"

"Why shouldn't you...?" I spluttered into silence, and he dropped a kiss on my nose.

I stared up at him in increased shock. I had never seen Nik in such a lighthearted mood.

"Don't worry so much," he said. "Surely you didn't think I would stay away from you?"

"But the risk! You'll be seen by so many people in a crowded place like this."

He shrugged. "And so what if they do see me? Locals will assume I'm one of the newcomers from the boat, and Grey's followers will assume I'm a local."

"What if one of them recognizes you?"

"They won't." He sounded supremely confident. "Those of Grey's followers who encountered me in Caltor are still in custody there. Only Grey himself has seen me before, and he's occupied up at the manor."

I stared at him. "How do you know that?"

He grinned again. "I have my ways."

I started to protest again, but he leaned in quickly and stole a kiss, silencing me with his lips on mine.

"I've been stuck in that hold for days," he said when he pulled back. "I'm going to enjoy being free. And I'm going to enjoy it at your side. For once, I'm free to walk through a market holding your hand, and there's nothing you can say to dissuade me. Please?"

He must have seen my expression soften because he smiled, his eyes flashing as he leaned closer to steal another kiss.

"You never know, you might even enjoy it."

TWENTY-EIGHT

I was too shocked by Nik's unexpected manner to keep protesting. But as we walked through the market side by side, I kept throwing him sideways glances. He caught me looking and flashed me a broad smile.

"Don't worry," he whispered, leaning close to speak into my ear, "I haven't been mesmerized into a different person. I can promise that no one on this island has made physical contact with me. I've been following Grey for over a year now—I have a lot of experience keeping myself safe from healers."

As he said the words, he lightly squeezed my hand where it was clasped in his, reminding me there was one healer he didn't protect himself from.

I shook my head at him, but inside I was smiling. I was used to brooding, intense, focused Nik, but I couldn't deny I liked lighthearted Nik as well. Was the change because we were no longer in Tartora with the shadow of his abandoned position hanging over him? Or was it because he had truly let go of the weight of bitterness he had carried for most of his life?

I still caught glimpses of the old intensity. When someone barreled past towing a hand cart and nearly knocked me down, only Nik's quick reflexes pulled me out of harm's way. And I recognized his look of ice-cold contempt when we overheard a stall keeper trying to cheat an unwary customer. But whenever he looked at me, the warmth I had previously only seen in veiled snatches shone from his face like a beacon.

When he murmured that a hundred similar days wouldn't be enough, it occurred to me that this was the first time we had ever spent time together without having either a focused purpose or Amara's presence with us. And I couldn't deny that it sent a thrill of pleasure up my spine whenever my eyes landed on him or when I thought about his warm, strong hand in mine. I had walked through a hundred markets, but it had never felt like this.

I couldn't entirely relax, however. Nik gave every appearance of having forgotten the danger hanging over us, but I couldn't put it out of my mind as easily.

Except as the morning progressed, I started to suspect he hadn't forgotten about it either. More than once I caught his eyes lingering on a local in a way that told me he saw the same thing I did.

"There's something strange about them, right?" I asked on the third occasion.

He frowned, not needing to ask what I meant or who I was referring to. Instead he tugged me over to the closest food stall and ordered two meat skewers. As they cooked, he tried to engage the stall keeper in the sort of polite, empty conversation Nik usually avoided.

"We're from the ship and just arrived today, so this is all new to us," he said, his openness about his origins making me twitch.

But when I looked around as surreptitiously as possible, I couldn't spot any of Grey's followers in our vicinity. Knowing Nik, he had probably been aware of that before he spoke.

"Aye, I figured as much," the stall keeper said before lapsing into silence again.

I frowned at him as Nik tried again.

"We came from the mainland with the missing Constantine grandson."

"That would explain it, then," the man said matter-of-factly, leaning over to add a pinch of spice to the cooking meat.

Nik exchanged a look with me before making a third attempt.

"We're looking forward to discovering the best food on the island."

The man immediately smiled broadly, his whole manner changing.

"You've come to the right place for that. You won't find anything better than my skewers. And if you want to wash them down with the freshest of beverages, I can recommend the stall across the way. The stall keeper is an excellent fellow who will give you a good deal, and I can assure you he grows the oranges himself, using only the freshest."

We glanced the direction he was pointing where a man of a similar age stood behind a pyramid of bright oranges. When he saw us looking, he gave a welcoming smile.

Nik accepted our cooked skewers while I murmured our thanks. After an exchange of glances, we crossed over to the other stall. The second stall keeper greeted us warmly, his focus on the sale. But once he began squeezing the juice, he fell silent.

"Oranges must grow well in this climate," Nik said conversationally. "Do you get a consistent crop?"

The man stared at him. "Our island has everything we could want and more."

"I'm sure it does," I said. "It's a beautiful place."

"But fruit especially must grow well," Nik said.

The man stared at him blankly.

"Because of the warmth," Nik finished slowly.

"We have all we need," he repeated in apparent confusion, as if he couldn't make sense of Nik's comments.

"What's your affinity?" I asked, trying to understand why the man found the simple conversation so difficult to follow.

"Plants." He held out our two cups, accepting Nik's coin in exchange.

We thanked him awkwardly and hurried away.

"That was odd," I muttered once we were far enough away not to be overheard. "Especially for someone with a plants affinity. It was like he didn't understand the connection between the weather and his crop's growth."

"That can't be true for someone with a plants affinity," Nik said. "Even if he wasn't taught it, his power should sense it naturally."

We fell into silence, drinking as we walked. The earlier light mood had disappeared completely, and I felt increasingly uncomfortable as I looked at the people milling around us.

"Do I want to know how you already have local coins?" I asked when we'd finished our drinks and returned the cups to the boy who came running after us to fetch them.

"I didn't steal it, if that's what's worrying you." Nik gave me a self-satisfied smile. "Unless liberating some supplies from the ship's hold counts as stealing. But since those belonged to Grey, I can't say I feel guilty."

I rolled my eyes but didn't have it in me to protest. My focus was now firmly on the people around us, and we attempted several more conversations with an equal lack of success.

"They all seem so...lifeless," I said after our last awkward attempt. "They aren't curious or interested in anything much. This is an incredibly closed-off community—how could the arrival of an entire ship not set everyone talking?"

Nik frowned, glancing along the closest row of stalls. "My first instinct is to assume they're holding back—that they know it's dangerous to talk about the Constantines, the ship, or anything related to them. But I don't think it's that. You can guard your tongue, but it's hard to keep curiosity from the eyes. And they don't seem afraid or even wary."

"Just genuinely uninterested," I finished for him. "I've never seen anything like it."

We continued wandering along, no longer touching. After seeing several of Grey's followers clustered around a leather worker's stall, I had refused to let Nik take my hand again. The other mainlanders hadn't appeared to notice us, but I could feel the lingering effect of their presence.

We finally reached the edge of the market, stopping at the final stall to buy several sweet buns. I hummed in pleasure as I polished off the first one. Whatever strangeness gripped these people, it hadn't affected their ability to cook.

Before I could take a bite of the second one, I noticed a pair of bright eyes fixed on us—or more specifically on the buns in our hands.

I smiled at the two young children who lingered just outside the edge of the market, as if they knew they would be chastised if they stepped inside. The older one drew back a little at the attention, but the younger one smiled more broadly.

I held out the bun, and he jumped up and down. Evading his older sister's grasp, he scampered forward and snatched it from my hand, as if afraid I would change my mind if he delayed.

"Fergus!" the girl snapped. "That's rude!"

"It's all right." I smiled at her and held out another bun. "We have plenty to share."

She hesitated. "Are you sure?"

"Of course." I waggled it encouragingly.

"See, Lumi," Fergus said around a large mouthful. "I told you they'd be nice."

"Us?" I asked in bemusement.

"Not specifickerly," Fergus said, still speaking with his mouthful. "Just the ship people."

I exchanged a glance with Nik.

"You were talking about those of us who came on the ship?" I asked.

"Of course." Lumi accepted the bun I was offering and took a daintier bite than her brother. "We've never had a ship arrive before. Even our ma says she's never heard of one coming. Not ever."

"And she's *old*," Fergus added.

Both children regarded us with wide eyes, expecting us to recognize the import of this news. I looked at Nik again. I doubted their mother was actually that old, but she was right that they'd never had newcomers before.

"It's natural to be curious," I said, picking my words carefully. "Is everyone talking about us, then?"

Maybe the islanders were better actors than we'd given them credit for, and their disinterest had been a show for the new arrivals.

But Lumi wrinkled her nose in an expression of disgust. "Of course not. The rest of them are never curious about *anything*."

"It's boring." Fergus gave a world-weary sigh that made me hide a laugh behind my hand.

"What about the other children?" Nik asked. "They must be curious at least?"

The nose wrinkle reappeared. "We don't play with them much," Lumi said. "They're just like their parents."

"Boring," Fergus spelled out, in case we were confused.

I considered this information, but it was hard to know what to make of it. What had happened to these people, and what made these two children different?

Fergus, who had finished his bun in record time, began clambering up a rough pile of stone that had been left against a wall in the mouth of a nearby alley.

"Careful!" Lumi called, her voice sounding more anxious than the danger warranted.

"Are the healers in town expensive?" I asked, curious as to the source of her excessive fear.

Lumi hesitated. "Not particularly. But there aren't many of them, and they're too weak to be of much use."

I frowned, exchanging yet another glance with Nik. Costas had told me that Constantines only married other strong healers. Did that mean they were hoarding the healer bloodlines?

"But in a town this size, there must be someone," I mused aloud. "Even if the Constantines are the only full healer family, there should be the odd one here and there—given the way affinities, and even strong seeds, can pop up seemingly out of nowhere."

Lumi stared at me as if she didn't know what I was talking about.

"I used to wonder the same thing," a new voice said, joining the conversation.

I jumped, startled by the new arrival, but the two children exclaimed in delight.

"Costas! Costas!"

Fergus jumped down from the pile of rocks to join his sister in swarming Costas. He smiled at them both, producing sweets from his pockets that distracted them enough that he was able to extricate himself.

"Delphine," he greeted me with a pleasant smile, his eyes traveling on to Nik with a questioning look.

"I'm Nik," the prince said shortly, looking at him with open speculation.

I tried to take a subtle step further away from Nik, remembering that Costas had witnessed my performance with Grey at the breakfast table.

"This is Costas," I said. "He's the second son of Augustine, who is the oldest Constantine son."

Costas cleared his throat awkwardly. "Actually, I'm Augustine's older son. I'm the same age as Barnabas, and Ignatius is the younger one. Thus the name."

I stared at him, and he seemed to misunderstand my confusion.

"I'm Costas now, but once upon a time I was Constantine Constantine." He shook his head. "No little boy needs to be saddled with a name like that."

"But...you're the oldest?"

"I know." He looked sheepish. "I'm well aware Ignatius is the one with *the look*."

"I'm not sure that's such a good thing in this case," I muttered, remembering my impression that Ignatius carried himself like the oldest son of the oldest son—an observation that was even less complimentary now I knew it wasn't actually his position.

"My Uncle Ambrose and Cousin Barnabas agree with you on that, I think," Costas said in an amused tone. "Since the oldest son's oldest son is such a disappointment and clearly cannot be heir, they think the torch should pass to Barnabas as the next oldest grandson."

I raised my eyebrows to hear him speaking so openly about the power dynamics in his family. Just in time I remembered I was supposed to be in thrall to the Constantines and rearranged my face accordingly.

"You seem sufficiently popular here." I gave him a sweet smile as I indicated the happy children.

He laughed. "With Fergus and Lumi, yes. As for the rest of them..." He looked across the market. "They like me well enough, I suppose. They're used to me, at least."

"That's because you actually come here," Lumi chipped in, surprising me with her awareness of the conversation. "Don't the others get bored never leaving their house?"

"Of course they leave the house sometimes, brat." Costas ruffled her hair affectionately. "You know that. They often go to one of the beaches or walk in the lower slopes of the mountain. And they come into the town on festival days."

She wrinkled her nose, an expression I was already becoming familiar with. "Not enough for us to know them like we know you."

"That's true," Costas conceded in a light tone, but something in his face gave me a different impression. I couldn't be sure whether he thought it was a good or bad thing that the townspeople weren't given the chance to get to know the rest of his family.

For the first time it occurred to me to wonder what sort of mesmerizations the Constantines used on their only non-healer son. Was he one of them, privy to all their secrets, or did his affinity make him another subject to be manipulated and controlled?

"I'm still curious about those missing healers," Nik said in a level voice that hinted at something more serious.

Costas turned to give him another interested look, while I glared at Nik from over his shoulder. Nik had done well at staying quiet so far. He should have kept it up. The last thing he needed was to catch the attention of a Constantine.

"The healers aren't missing exactly," Costas murmured, immediately understanding what Nik had meant. "Some of them have the very great honor of marrying into the Constantine family and helping to produce future healers of power."

His tone of voice suggested he considered it the opposite of an honor, and I wondered again about his absent mother.

"And the others?" Nik asked implacably.

Costas withdrew another couple of sweets from his pockets and gave them to the children, indicating they should perch themselves on a nearby planter box to eat them.

Once they were slightly removed, he lowered his voice. "It's a sad thing, but even a strong healing seed will do nothing to help you before activation. And there are so many potential accidents that can befall an adventurous child on an island like this—accidents that end in tragedy before a healer can be fetched." He paused thoughtfully. "Unadventurous children as well, apparently."

My mouth dropped open, and I was temporarily robbed of speech. Was he saying what I thought he was saying?

"That is…unfortunate," Nik said in a savage tone that gave the word a new meaning.

"Yes." Costas met his gaze steadily. "*Most* unfortunate."

I made no attempt to suppress the sick feeling swirling in my stomach. No wonder the Constantines kept to themselves. If their people had enough exposure to their rulers' true natures they would soon shake off their mesmerizations—as had happened with Serena and the rest of Grey's recruits in Caltor.

A sudden thought sent my eyes flashing to Costas. The Constantines were his family, and he lived with them on a daily basis. They might have mesmerized him a hundred times, but how long would those falsehoods ever stick? The evidence of their true nature would soon reverse the effect of their lies. No wonder he seemed different from both them and the regular islanders.

He looked back at me, his own face as full of curiosity as mine must have been.

"It must be difficult for the people to be without strong healers," I said, unable to keep the challenge from my voice, although I knew the situation wasn't of Costas's making. "Many must die needlessly."

"Not at all," he said. "Anyone needing healing—no matter how mild the ailment—will find an open door at the manor."

"Your family heals them all freely?" I asked skeptically, remembering Grey's lack of care for his followers. I looked at Fergus and Lumi, who were edging back toward us, their eyes moving between my leftover buns and Costas's bountiful pockets.

I handed over two buns, directing my question at Lumi.

"If Fergus had fallen and hurt himself on those stones, would you have taken him up to the manor?"

"Of course not! Ma won't let us go there. That's why he should be more careful." The last sentence was delivered with a glare for her younger brother.

"She won't let you..." I said slowly, processing that.

"She doesn't send us for the monthly checkups either," Lumi volunteered.

"Monthly checkups?" Nik asked, crouching down to her level. "What do you mean?"

"Don't you have those where you come from?" She regarded him with wide eyes. "Everyone else goes up to the manor for monthly health checks."

Nik rocked back on his heels, looking up at me.

"How...generous," I said with dismay, easily recognizing the true purpose of the *checks*. "When does everyone else start going for them? When they're children?"

Lumi shrugged, not overly interested in the topic. "When they're babies, I think."

"Babies?" I repeated slowly, trying to keep my horror from my voice.

No wonder the population of the island seemed so strange—lacking in curiosity and unable to follow a logical, sequential thought process. From the earliest age, their brains had been shaped and warped by mesmerization. How could you develop a normal level of rational thought when your thoughts and experiences had always been forced to bend unnaturally around unshakable truths—truths that needed no logical explanation or evidence to back them up, truths your mind wasn't capable of questioning? The central truths of their lives didn't come from reason, logic, observation, experience, or emotion, and every other strand of their thinking had been forced to twist around those central pillars.

"Is there anyone else who doesn't go for the checkups?" I asked Lumi. "Other than you and your ma?"

She considered the question for a moment. "There was Old Man Terrier."

For a confused moment I considered questioning the name but decided it was probably a title bestowed by the local children.

"He's a hermant," Fergus supplied, making all three of us stare at him.

"I think he means hermit," Costas said after a moment, clearly stifling a laugh.

Lumi rolled her eyes. "He's not a *hermit,* Fergus. He just has no patience for annoying children." Her accusatory look suggested she thought Fergus was the main problem and that she could understand how the old man felt.

"But I saw him at the manor just last week," Costas said.

Lumi shrugged. "He used to refuse to go, but then he got that fever."

"Fever?" I looked to Costas, who winced.

"It went through the town three winters ago. It was a new one, and my whole family had to come down from the manor and go house to house to stamp it out."

Lumi nodded. "Ma took us up the mountain at the first talk of a new sickness, so we escaped. But when we came back, Old Man Terrier was going to the manor for checkups like everyone else." She shrugged again.

I gulped, understanding what must have happened. After a lifetime of quiet resistance, a single illness had forced him into contact with the Constantines.

Without meaning to, my gaze met Costas's, and I read the same sadness in his eyes. Seized by a moment of recklessness, I spoke even more openly than I had so far.

"And your family is all right with Lumi and Fergus and their mother not going for these checkups?" I asked him.

He frowned. "Their mother lives a quiet, secluded life, keeping out of notice as much as possible. I'm not sure anyone in my family even knows they exist."

I stared at him, and he looked back, his gaze direct and open. There was no doubt Costas was different from the rest of his family, and his expression and words suggested he recognized there was something different about me, as well.

But being different on this island was dangerous. And I didn't know how far I could trust Costas. Was he just pretending sorrow over his family's actions in order to win our trust?

An insidious thought snaked into my mind. All it would take was a light touch, and I could make sure Costas saw me as safe and unthreatening. My power could override any suspicious word or action he might have observed.

Would it be such a terrible thing to tamper with a single morning's memories if it meant keeping Nik and me safe? If his family weren't above killing those who threatened their rule, then the danger was real.

But as I pictured myself doing it, every part of me rebelled. If I started down that path, where would it end? Just because I had the power to do it, it didn't give me the right to meddle with someone else's mind.

Instead, I would have to take a risk and choose to trust Costas.

Nik looked down at me with a question in his eyes, but I just shrugged, unable to explain myself. He might not agree with my decision—not when my safety was at risk—but that didn't matter. At the end of the day, this was my ability and that made the responsibility mine. I would not choose to mesmerize someone just to keep myself safe.

TWENTY-NINE

Costas offered to walk me back to the manor, and I put a quick restraining hand on Nik's arm before he could protest. I could see the storm in his eyes, but I glared at him until he sighed, his shoulders relaxing. Nik couldn't go anywhere near the manor.

"Thank you," I told Costas, who had watched the brief interchange with far too much curiosity.

He led me back through a maze of streets, bypassing the market square, and I caught enough glimpses of movement behind us to know Nik was shadowing us. He could do that all he liked as long as he stopped at the edge of the main town, not continuing on to the manor grounds.

But when we reached the edge of the manor gardens, Costas stopped as well, looking at me ruefully.

"You should probably go on ahead on your own from here. It won't do you any good to be seen with me."

I raised an eyebrow, and his self-deprecating smile grew. "They tolerate me because I'm family, but you won't win any points from association."

I wanted to protest and tell him I would rather be associated with him than any of the rest of his family, but I wasn't here for a social visit. Despite the guarded level of openness that had existed between us in the town, I had to remain wary.

So I merely nodded agreement and left him behind, glancing back over my shoulder only once. He was watching me go with the same curious expression he'd worn earlier.

Inside, I had to ask a young woman busy scrubbing the floor for directions to my room. She stopped her task and took me there herself, chattering the whole way about the plans that had been made in my absence. Apparently there was to be a party the next night in honor of Grey's return, and she was to serve at it.

"Wouldn't you rather attend than serve?" I asked.

"Me? Attend?" She threw her head back and laughed, a light, merry sound at odds with her words.

I considered pressing the matter or asking further questions, but after all my interactions in the market there seemed little point. Especially when her continued chatter revealed she had only been working at the manor for a month. Apparently all the staff changed regularly, a necessity if the Constantines wanted to keep the population at arm's length.

I half-expected lunch to be the same formal affair as breakfast, but instead I was served a meal on a tray in my room. I wasn't especially hungry after what I'd eaten at the market, and it wasn't long before I lapsed into severe boredom. I would have thought it impossible to feel so restless given the danger of the situation, but apparently an empty room and nothing to do produced the same effect regardless of any looming peril.

Eventually I escaped to the gardens, my boredom instantly lifting when Phoenix came speeding toward me. He must have been busy hunting or exploring our new surroundings when I left for the market, but he had clearly been on the watch for me since.

Calmed by his familiar weight on my shoulder, I wandered through the ordered, sculpted gardens which circled the manor.

When I reached a collection of rose bushes that were surrounded by a tall hedge, I paused and sat on a well-positioned bench. I obviously wasn't the only one to enjoy the artificial haven, but I couldn't deny it felt like a relief to be out of sight of the staring windows of the manor house.

I had barely begun to relax, however, when I heard a rustling in the hedge behind me. Whirling, I saw a bundle of orange and white fur pushing through the leaves.

"Ember!" I scooped her up and held her close. "What are you doing here? You're supposed to be with Nik!"

She looked up at me with her dark, liquid eyes, and my heart melted. But at the same time, I couldn't risk keeping her at the manor. Grey would definitely recognize her and question her presence.

Footsteps sounded on the gravel path, and I jumped to my feet, trying to hide Ember with my skirts. But only one person rounded the hedge, gazing in wonder at the profusion of roses.

"Ida," I exclaimed in relief. "What are you doing here?"

"We've been bringing supplies up from the ship, and someone said we're free to look around the gardens. They're so beautiful!"

She still bore the shining look of hope from earlier in the day, and I wondered what interactions she'd had with the locals.

"How are you finding it so far?" I asked cautiously.

"It's wonderful!" She sighed in deep satisfaction. "Everything is so beautiful and peaceful."

"Has anyone asked you any questions or shown any interest in you?" I asked.

"None whatsoever." She sounded delighted.

My heart squeezed. What had Ida experienced in the past that she found a complete lack of interest from anyone to be a delightful prospect?

But her words gave me an idea.

"Are you staying at the manor for the afternoon?"

She shook her head. "I'm about to head back to my host's house now that I've seen the gardens."

I stooped and picked up Ember, holding the fox out to the older woman. "Would you be willing to look after Ember for me?"

"Your fox?" Ida took her willingly enough, and to my relief Ember didn't protest either. "I didn't realize she was with you."

I nodded. "She came on the ship." I spoke the words matter-of-factly, as if there was nothing interesting about the situation.

Hopefully she wouldn't ask any questions—and neither would her hosts. With everyone so uninterested in the newcomers, I didn't think anyone would make a fuss about a single fox.

Ida wasn't a healer, but I'd had a feeling she would be good with animals, and it was clear I was right. From the way she was already fussing over Ember as she walked away, I should be worried Ember might never want to come back to me.

Phoenix pecked at my ear, and I scolded him loudly.

"Don't worry," I reassured him. "It's only for a little while. We'll get Ember back soon."

He settled slowly, ruffling his feathers, one of his eyes trained on Ida's disappearing figure.

"I didn't know you cared so much," I muttered, secretly delighted that the falcon had grown attached to Ember.

I just hoped I was right about being able to retrieve her soon. I didn't think I could keep up our complicated ruse for long.

The problem was that I had no idea what our next steps should be. How did we extricate ourselves from the situation safely without leaving Tartora open to constant attack?

I walked slowly back to the house, reaching the back porch just in time to see Ignatius and Augustine come striding outside, engaged in heated debate.

"Watch yourself, son," Augustine snapped, too absorbed in the conversation to notice me lingering among the ornamental fruit trees. "You're not the heir, and you won't be for many years to come. I intend to live a long life."

Ignatius, who was slightly taller than his father, looked down his nose at him. "I won't ever be the heir if Uncle Ambrose has his way. He'll push that weakling cousin of mine to the front if he can possibly manage it."

"Which is why I'm telling you that you need to moderate your behavior. You shouldn't have gone dashing off on your own this morning. My brother has been in your grandmother's ear about it all morning, saying you lacked proper respect for your elders and your place."

Ignatius's manner became even more haughty. "I received urgent word that a ship was already in the process of berthing. I could hardly delay to find someone more fitting. We can be glad I was there so quickly, or we might have been overrun before we knew what was happening."

His words sounded like the truth, but it was easy to read on his face that he had been more than happy to receive the message alone.

"Pretty words," his father snapped, clearly perceiving the same thing. "But no one knows better than the Constantines how useless those are."

"Guard your tongue, Father!" Ignatius said with heat, throwing a glance around the garden.

He caught sight of me at once, locking eyes with me before I had the chance to look away. I curtsied, mustering up a smile that must have looked far from relaxed. Ignatius's brows lowered, his eyes dwelling on me for too long.

When he finally looked away, it was to murmur a quiet word to his father, the two of them disappearing around the edge of the building.

"There's nothing to worry about," I murmured more to

myself than Phoenix. "He thinks I'm mesmerized, and nothing they just said could possibly have broken through that. Not from one conversation."

But I couldn't shake the feeling that I'd undone my efforts over breakfast, regaining Ignatius's suspicious interest.

I circled the building in the opposite direction to them, nearly colliding with Grey.

"There you are! I've been looking everywhere for you."

"For me?" I asked, relieved he hadn't found me earlier when I was with either Nik or Ember. "Did something happen?"

"No, but we have no time to waste." He smiled, looking far too pleased for my comfort. "The situation is even better than I imagined, but we shouldn't hesitate to get to work."

"What do you want me to do?" I asked with a sinking heart.

He was going to ask me to mesmerize someone, and the moment I refused, it would all be over. He would realize I'd found a way to break free from him, and I would instantly transform in his mind from his greatest tool to an adversary who needed to be eliminated. I would have to at least pretend I meant to comply while I worked out what to do instead.

"I need you to find Grandmother," he said. "She's been careful not to touch me, and the others have been equally careful never to leave me alone with her. She might be elderly, but she still rules this family. You, on the other hand, are just a young girl with an elements affinity. None of them will see you as a threat. Good work at breakfast, by the way."

I thought uneasily of Ignatius's suspicious eyes but said nothing.

"You want me to mesmerize your grandmother?" I asked, feeling sickened.

"Of course I only want to help my family," he said earnestly, as if only just remembering the line he was supposed to follow. "But I can't do that when they don't trust me. All I'm asking you to do is reinforce the emotions that Grandmother naturally feels. Just remind her how overjoyed she is at my return, and that she always loved my mother best. It's only natural she would want to have her daughter's son by her side, especially since I'm both her strongest and most trustworthy grandson."

I stared at him, barely restraining myself from rolling my eyes. Would my mesmerized self really have fallen for this line? Sadly I knew I had previously fallen for more outrageous lies.

And in truth, what he was asking wasn't entirely contrary to his grandmother's natural response. She really had seemed happy to see him again.

That thought allowed me to consider another one. Could I really do it? I had refused to mesmerize Costas, but that had been because I mistrusted the instinct that drove me to do it, driven as it was by my desire for self-protection. But this was different. I would merely be reinforcing an idea the grand-mother already had, and by playing along with Grey for the moment, I would ultimately be protecting her and her family from him, as well as all of Tartora from the lot of them. Working with Grey now would give me time to discover his full plan and work out how to undermine it.

"All right," I said. "I'll go find her now."

"Good girl." Grey's eyes glowed, and it was hard to keep my smile in place. I only managed it by thinking of how happy I was to be leaving his presence.

It took me a while to find the Constantine matriarch, sticking my head into room after room until I finally found her in a brightly lit sitting room presiding over a tea tray. She was pouring tea for her daughter-in-law when I arrived, and I saw a flash of something calculating and curious in her gaze before she quickly covered it with a false grandmotherly warmth.

"Welcome, child!" she called. "Would you like to join us for tea?"

I nodded, dropping a belated curtsy.

"I had been hoping one of the newcomers might join us."

She patted the sofa at her side invitingly. "I would so love to hear about life on the mainland."

Yes, I thought sourly. *Because you haven't had your curiosity and free thought sucked out of you by a lifetime of manipulation.*

On the outside, I smiled and accepted the offered seat. The elderly woman made no move to pour me a cup, however, instead reaching for my hand with both of hers. I braced myself.

After all my practice on the ship, I was confident in my ability to mesmerize. But this would be a challenge—both due to her strength and experience and because she would be trying to simultaneously mesmerize me.

My one hope lay in our deception. She had no reason to be suspicious, and unlike Ignatius on the docks, she wouldn't be in a hurry. Which meant I had a chance to get my mesmerization in first, before she began to confuse my mind. It would be a delicate matter, however, since I would need to watch my words. Ambrose's wife, Kendry, must be a healer as well, and she would sense any lie I uttered from the other side of the small table holding the tea set.

As soon as the grandmother's hands brushed my right one, gathering it up into a warm grasp, I sent my power slithering into her. I threw out only the tiniest tendril necessary, rushing into speech as I did.

"We're so grateful for your hospitality. Especially Grey. He has longed so much to be here with you all. And he's so strong." *The strongest!* my power echoed. "He clearly belongs here with his family." *You can trust him!* "I can only imagine how much you must miss his mother, your daughter, Chloe." *She was your favorite. How glad you are to have her son back.*

The grandmother's face instantly softened. "You're right, my dear. What a thoughtful young thing you are. But it is our pleasure to have Grey back where he belongs. I couldn't be happier to see him again."

Across the table, Kendry watched us with a slight crease

between her brows. But her focus wasn't on me or my words but on her mother-in-law. Was she worried about her attitude toward Grey? I had suspected from the beginning that the younger generations viewed him as a threat, and his aunt's expression seemed to confirm it. Her son, Barnabas, already had enough competition from his younger cousin.

I hoped Grey didn't expect me to mesmerize every member of the family, starting with his grandmother and working my way down. I had a sick feeling that might be his plan, however. If he didn't, they were going to turn on him sooner rather than later.

"But I hope you know you are also welcome," the grandmother continued, her words ringing in my mind with truth. "You can trust us to take care of you."

"Of course," I said, the agreement coming easily and naturally. "I feel fortunate to have made it to such an incredible place."

The grandmother smiled in satisfaction, dropping my hand and exchanging a lightning-fast look with her daughter-in-law that triggered a queasy feeling in my middle.

Responding to that feeling had become instinct at this point. I threw up my wall, driving the lingering effects of the woman's power from my mind.

As soon as it was gone, I could think clearly again. As soon as my mind was my own, exhaustion crashed over me. I couldn't stay in this room where I had to watch every word and expression.

I jumped to my feet. "Please don't call for an extra cup," I said in a rush. "I would be embarrassed to interrupt your afternoon ritual." I curtsied again to both women. "You've already done so much by welcoming me into your home." *So much damage,* I added silently.

"You really are a most considerate child," the grandmother said with a smile that showed more of her true calculating nature than her earlier expression had done. "I don't know what my third grandson can have been thinking. He's becoming fanciful in all the excitement."

I kept my expression neutral, pretending not to notice the hint of pleasure on Kendry's face at this criticism of Ignatius.

Curtsying again, I backed out of the room as if they were queens. As soon as I closed the door behind me, I fled down the hall, not stopping until I was back in my own room.

My heart raced, and I didn't even think about slowing it down. Had I really just done that? I had matched wits and power with a woman who had spent decades mesmerizing people, and I had come out on top. It was only because I had been the one with the element of surprise, equipped both to mesmerize and to protect myself against its effects, but I couldn't deny the feeling of power.

I took deep breaths, trying to calm myself. This reaction was what I feared most. I couldn't let myself become enamored with this new and dangerous ability.

I had regained some of my calm before the evening meal, but even so, it was a fraught event. Every look and word was measured—not just by me but by everyone else around me—until it felt less like conversation and more like the thrust and parry of a fencing match.

Costas seemed the most honest and open of the group, but far too often I felt his curious eyes on me. By the end of the evening I wanted to snap at him to stop looking at me—unless he was trying to put a sign around my neck for the rest of his family to see.

The pounding in my head became so bad that I couldn't help massaging it, reaching out with my power to ease it at the same time. My face relaxed as soon as the pain eased, but it tensed again when I looked up to see Costas watching me with an arrested expression, his eyes narrowing. I hurriedly turned to Kendry next to me and launched into speech, but I could still feel his eyes on me.

Even at the end of the interminable evening, Grey insisted on walking me back to my room. Ignatius's knowing look made my skin crawl, and Grey's pleased praise when we were alone had nearly as uncomfortable an effect.

By the time I closed my bedroom door and leaned against it, I never wanted to emerge again.

THIRTY

Thankfully, breakfast was delivered on a tray the next morning. According to the girl who delivered it, no one had time for a formal meal when they were busy preparing for the party.

I had opened my window the night before, letting Phoenix inside, and with the falcon to keep me company, I hid inside my room like a coward all day.

Eventually I had to emerge, however. I knew that if I didn't give Grey a chance to find me before the party began, he'd come barging into my room, and I couldn't bear to have him inside my one safe haven.

Sure enough, I'd barely stepped out of the house when he appeared. Grabbing my arm, he whisked me off to the rose garden.

"Everything is working perfectly," he said as soon as he was sure we were alone. "You might as well have released a hornet's nest in the manor house. They're all furious."

"And that's a good thing?" I couldn't quite keep the skepticism out of my voice.

Grey shot me a look, and I added, "Aren't you worried they're all going to team up and come after you?"

He relaxed at this suggestion that I was only concerned for him. I hoped he did mean to explain, however, since I was legitimately curious as to what he hoped to achieve by oversetting the Constantines' very fragile balance.

An unnerving smile spread over his face. "That's why we're going to direct their attention and anger elsewhere."

"We?" I asked, my voice squeaking.

"Don't worry, my dear." He patted my hand. "You've proven yourself more than capable. All my lessons have paid off."

Trickling cold started in my scalp and crept down. I wished I could block my ears and not hear whatever Grey was going to say next because I already knew I wasn't going to like it. I had convinced myself that it wouldn't do any great harm to play along with Grey for one mesmerization—that it was even serving the greater good. But in retrospect I could see my mistake. If the results of my efforts pleased Grey this much, then I had greatly underestimated their significance.

I had known it was the wrong thing to do to mesmerize anyone, but I had done it anyway. Now I was learning the lesson again—hopefully for the last time—but was it already too late?

"During the party, I'm going to lure Ignatius away," Grey said. "I'll find a way to keep him occupied just long enough. All we need is to have him out of sight."

"Wh...Why?" I managed to choke out.

"As soon as you see me disappear, you need to find Augustine. Mesmerize him into believing Ignatius is dead and Ambrose and Barnabas were the ones to kill him. That's all you have to do."

"Just...just that," I whispered weakly, and Grey nodded, apparently taking my words as understanding and agreement.

I could barely see him, though, my vision a haze as I finally realized what Grey was planning. He must have been assuming that, in my mesmerized state, I wouldn't understand his intentions. But he didn't know what Nik had said to me back on the ship after I mesmerized him into believing Ember was dead.

Back then, Nik had imagined a situation all too much like this one. He had said that you couldn't order someone to kill, but you could manipulate them into doing it of their own volition—for instance, by claiming someone they loved was dead. Grey intended for Augustine to retaliate against his brother and nephew, ripping the Constantine family apart in the most vicious and violent way, and ensuring that whoever was left at the end was easy pickings for Grey.

I wouldn't do it. However evil the Constantines were, there was no way I would be party to this.

But I couldn't say as much to Grey right now. That would be suicide. I had to at least pretend I meant to comply.

I went through the motions, glad Grey was too distracted by his plan to expect any particular input from me. If only I had come out of my room earlier. At this point, the party was almost ready to start, and I had far too little time to work out what to do.

I trailed behind Grey back to the manor house, racking my brains for a plan. But the harder I thought, the more any sensible ideas escaped me. Instead, my mind whirled in a circle, moving faster and faster and less and less productively.

One of Grey's female followers met me outside my room, gushing excitedly about the beautiful dresses we'd been loaned for the occasion. Her room was next to mine, and she was already wearing hers, a floating yellow concoction that reminded me of a dessert.

She wanted to accompany me inside to see mine, and I let her, my mind numbed by panic. The gown laid out on my bed was a deep forest green, and in normal circumstances, I would have been as excited about its elegant flowing lines as my companion. I had certainly never worn such a garment before.

As it was, however, I stepped into it mindlessly, letting the serving girl who arrived to assist me do up the endless row of buttons. She chattered away the entire time she buttoned, eventually breaking through my fog enough that I recognized her as the girl who had told me about the party the day before.

Her excitement hadn't dimmed in the intervening time, and she enthusiastically offered to arrange my hair. I agreed, glad I didn't have to think about it myself, and she somehow wrestled the tight curls into a complicated pattern of braids that criss-crossed my head.

Even through the confusion and panic, I recognized her skill, marveling at the face looking back at me from the mirror. I looked older, more confident, and more womanly. I just wished the appearance came with wisdom to match it. If only Amara was here to tell me what to do.

If I told the Constantines about Grey's plan, they would be more than a match for him with their numbers and combined strength. But where would that leave me and Tartora? If I did nothing, however, Grey would soon realize my betrayal and do something even more drastic—but this time I would be another name on the list of intended victims.

Far too soon, the serving girl was declaring me finished and ushering me out the door. Phoenix had already been banished outside, and I wished I had a beak and claws of my own so I could scratch and fight, struggling against the inexorable forces sweeping me forward.

But all I had was my words and my power, and I couldn't think what use either of them might be in the situation.

The room hosting the party was a large one I had yet to encounter, almost grand enough to be called a ballroom. The polished floorboards shone in the light of innumerable branches of candles, and a long table bent slightly under the weight of the food covering its surface.

Plants mages had filled the room with blossoms, their vines growing through the open windows and doors or twining upward from large pots placed around the edge of the room. They created a riot of color and scent, reminding me that we were far from home.

I had expected the party to be teeming with people, the room so crowded you could barely move. But while there was a small crowd, they were fewer in number than I had envisioned.

The Constantines themselves stood out, their clothes finer than anyone else's, the gold and silver threads sparkling in a way that suggested they were spun from the actual metals. But besides them, I could see only familiar faces from the ship.

I peered around the room, sure that I had to be wrong. But the more I looked, the more certain I became. When my eyes alighted on the same serving girl, now bearing a tray of drinks, I hurried over to her.

She beamed at me, her eyes shining as she looked around at the sumptuous room.

"Isn't it beautiful?" she breathed. "Even better than I imagined."

"But where are all the people?" I asked.

"What do you mean?" She surveyed the partygoers with a crease between her eyes. "I don't think anyone is missing."

"I mean, where are the locals?"

"The locals?" Her eyes traveled to a clump of Constantines standing close by. "You mean the Constantines? You can see Ambrose and Kendry over there, and just beyond them is—"

"No, no, I mean the regular people. From the town."

She burst out into the same peals of laughter as earlier, and I finally realized why she had found my original question so amusing. The idea of her attendance hadn't been laughable because she was low-ranking or poor within the town. It was because no one in the town had been invited to the party at all.

"Is anyone from the town ever invited here?" I asked. "As a guest, rather than a servant or patient, I mean."

Her laugh trailed off into giggles. "No, of course not. It's a very great honor that you've all been invited. You must be highly favored."

A sinking feeling made my legs tremble. I spun in a circle, taking in the scene again. The Constantines were now moving through the crowd, a handshake here, a light touch there, a pat on the shoulder. We weren't favored: we were new. All of this was designed to bind us tighter and tighter to this family and the strange life they lived on this island.

I caught sight of Ida's happy smile as she bowed her head over the grandmother's hand. I knew it must have been my imagination, especially at this distance, but I thought I could see her eyes growing more vacant and glassy. I shivered, stumbling my way through the crowd to seek the meager relief of the closest wall.

Strong arms steadied me, guiding me behind the closest large pot where the rest of the room was at least partially shielded from view.

I sucked in a deep breath and then another, the overwhelmed panic slowly fading, replaced with a sense of security. But as soon as my mind kicked back into proper motion, I looked up, the horrified feeling returning.

Nik had meant safety to me for so long that my body responded instinctively to his presence. But on this occasion it was betraying me.

"What are you doing here?" I hissed. "You can't be here!"

He smiled down at me like he had in the market, except I could see that this time the expression was masking his concern. He'd just seen the state I was in.

"Of course I had to come. How could I miss the chance to see you dressed like this? Delphine, you look stunning."

I brushed away his words, although some small part of my mind tucked them away to be brought out and treasured later.

"Never mind that. You really can't be here!"

"It was fine in the market," he said with his usual confidence. "And it'll be even easier here since it's more crowded. None of Grey's people will be surprised to see a local man dancing attendance on you—not when you look like that."

"No! Nik!" I grabbed his arm and looked up at him beseechingly. "You're not listening to me. They didn't invite any locals tonight! It's only people from the ship and the Constantines themselves."

I looked around frantically, trying to spot if anyone had already noticed him. At least we were tucked away, mostly out of sight.

"I'm not leaving." His voice was back to its usual steel. "Not when I haven't seen you since yesterday morning. And something has happened. I can see that clearly. I won't leave you. There is no risk I wouldn't take to keep you safe."

I moaned. Yet another reason why I shouldn't have hidden in my room all day.

"How is you being caught by Grey going to keep me safe?" I demanded.

"First tell me what happened," he said, unmoved by my pleading.

Shamefaced, I confessed what I had done at Grey's instigation and what his next step was. Nik shook his head slowly.

"That's extreme, even for Grey. This is his own family we're talking about."

"I don't think he sees them that way. From a few things he's let slip, I think he sees them only as the people who abandoned him and his mother. I'm not sure who he resents more for depriving him of the life of privilege he should have led—them or her."

"And now he wants revenge." Nik looked cold and unsympathetic.

"And even more than that, he wants to reclaim that life— but with no one at the top but him."

I looked through the leaves of a climbing vine and spotted

Grey across the room. At least he was talking with Barnabas, not Ignatius, so I still had a bit of time.

When I looked back at Nik, I found him watching me with a horrified, sick expression.

"What is it?" I asked, distracted.

"If he means to rule this island as the only Constantine, he'll be solely responsible for ensuring the family line continues. And as we now know, there are no other strong healers on this island for him to marry."

All the blood rushed from my face as I realized what Nik was saying. Grey may not have intended it from the beginning, but I had no doubt he would be willing to force me into the role of his bride through any means necessary.

"This ends tonight," Nik growled.

I grabbed his arm with both my hands. "Nik, wait, no! What are you thinking? We need an actual plan!"

Nik calmed slightly, giving me his attention. "You have a plan?"

I bit my lip. "No. But we need to come up with one. And I think…" I drew a deep breath. "I think we can trust Costas. I think we should include him in this."

"Costas? But he's one of them."

"By blood, yes, but not where it matters. He's not a healer, and it's clear that's all they care about. He's a complete outsider here."

Nik stilled, and I knew he was thinking of his own family. I only hoped he was seeing how much worse it could have been and remembering the good moments with his sister and parents—the moments I suspected Costas had never had.

"I think he was so open with us yesterday because he sensed there was something different about the two of us. I think he might be hoping for allies."

I peered through the leaves again, but I couldn't see Costas anywhere in the room.

"Where is he?" I whispered, frustrated. "We don't have time for any delays."

"I'll find him," Nik said. "If you leave, Grey might notice."

Reluctantly I accepted his reasoning. "Please hurry," I begged, and he nodded, already slipping away from me.

With a fortifying breath, I entered the crowd again, circulating toward the supper table, although I was sure I couldn't force any food into my leaden belly. All I needed was to be seen, to give Grey the reassurance he might need.

With every minute that passed, my tension rose, but there was nothing I could do to hurry Nik. All I could do was wait, and it seemed like the hardest task of all.

"Delphine!" Costas's cheerful voice nearly made me collapse with relief. Nik had found him.

I turned to greet him, his smile fading as he took in my wide-eyed expression. Grabbing his arm, I dragged him through a nearby full-length window and out onto the porch beyond. Tucking ourselves behind a tall, potted tree, I finally let his arm drop.

"Delphine? Is something wrong?"

I opened my mouth only to close it again when I realized I had no idea where to begin.

But Costas seemed to pick up on what was happening anyway. "Grey is making a move tonight? Even I can sense how unsettled everyone is."

I nodded. "He's planning to turn you all against each other."

"How is that possible? None of us will risk letting him touch our skin. My family are wrong-headed about a lot of things, but they aren't fools."

I took a deep breath. This was it. The moment where I was putting everything on the line.

"It's me. I don't really have an elements affinity. I'm a healer. A strong one. And Grey has taught me how to mesmerize."

Costas sucked in an audible breath, confirming my impression that to a Constantine it was unthinkable that the ability would be shared outside the family.

"I guessed there was something different about you," he said. "I even wondered if you were a healer. But this..."

"I'm so sorry, Costas, but I mesmerized your grandmother under Grey's instruction. I thought it was a small thing to do, just to ensure our place here. I didn't realize it would set off such a disastrous chain of circumstances."

"You've only been here two days. How could you know how deep the animosity goes between my father and my uncle, with the next generation following in their wake? Grandmother has been the only one keeping the peace for a while now, and when she greeted Grey so warmly, and then grew more and more pleased with him..." He sighed. "Even I didn't realize quite how delicate the balance of power had become in my family. But I suppose Grey is to blame for that, as well."

"What do you mean?" I asked. "How could he be to blame for the state of the Constantines before our arrival?"

"I suppose it's possible it might be someone else." Costas peered at me. "Does anyone else on the mainland know about our existence? I thought it was only Grey."

"As far as I know it is only him. Why?"

He hesitated. "Are you aware of some recent attacks on your homeland?"

"The false blight and the storms, you mean?"

"Yes. Ignatius is behind those. Not that he acted alone, of course. But there are plenty of strong plants and elements mages in the town, so he took some of them with him. He even took Barnabas as well to help with mesmerizing. But the two of them came back with very different ideas about what to do next."

"What do you mean? Are they planning further attacks on Tartora?"

"Barnabas thinks the retaliation was sufficient, and that we should go back to our established life as rulers here—with himself as heir, naturally. Ignatius has other ideas, though. He thinks Tartora is ripe for the plucking. He hasn't said it directly, but I think he has dreams of something greater than being the next lord of the manor. He wants a crown and a throne."

I gasped. "He wants to take Tartora by force?"

Costas waggled his fingers, his expression sad. "Not the normal kind of force."

I shivered. "He won't find it such an easy thing to keep an entire kingdom in thrall like he does with a single town."

"Would he really need to, though? Wouldn't it be enough to entrap key people at the capital?"

"Perhaps," I said slowly, unsure of the answer myself. But I was very sure I never wanted to see him try.

"But why is this all happening now?" I asked. "And why is Grey to blame?"

Costas's expression changed to one of surprise. "You don't know? Did he keep it secret even from his followers? He must have had some of them helping him, at least."

"I only came to Grey's camp days before we sailed," I said. "I know very little about his plans and actions before that."

"It's possible I'm wrong," Costas said, "but I don't think so. Someone attacked us first, and there's no one else it could have been but Grey. Of course, originally we had no idea Grey was still out there. We thought the mainlanders must have discovered our existence, so Ignatius convinced the elders to let him take a small boat to the mainland to retaliate. But on their return Barnabas claimed the Tartorans were as ignorant about our existence as ever. And when Ignatius was pushed, he had to agree. So now Uncle Ambrose and Barnabas blame me, saying I made a mistake."

"You? What does it have to do with you?"

"I'm the only one in the family with an elements seed—I'm

the strongest elements mage on the island, in fact, although my family doesn't value that. I was the one to tell them that the fire which took our crops wasn't started by lightning but by arson—though it couldn't have been anyone from the town, for obvious reasons. No one here could manage such a deception. And later, after their return, I was the one to warn them that the storm which sank one of our fishing boats wasn't natural. In fact, I was the one to turn the storm around and push it back the way it came from."

He grimaced. "Of course I found out later that Ignatius ordered a whole group of elements mages from the town to combine their power to make it larger and more potent. I had let it go by that point, so I didn't realize until much later when someone mentioned it in passing."

He gave me a shadowed look. "I suppose many lives were lost?"

"I'm afraid they were." I wished I could give him better news. "It hit a coastal city that had many ships out at sea."

He winced.

"But I'm not sure I'm following," I said. "You're saying that Grey came here first in a smaller boat—on a stealth mission—and burned your crops? And then he sent a storm after one of your ships? So everything your family did against Tartora was direct retaliation for what you thought were attacks from us?"

"That's right. Ignatius claims King Marius must know about us and be keeping the information quiet from the common citizens."

"He doesn't," I said. "I'm completely sure about that."

"As soon as Grey arrived, the answer seemed obvious," Costas agreed. "It all came from Grey. He was trying to destabilize the situation before his official arrival, and he succeeded more than he could have dreamed. He has several times referred to having been on the island before, but the others believe he means as a baby."

"How could they not suspect him?"

"Oh, they suspect him of wanting to take their place, but they're blinded in other ways. There are certain things they believe a Constantine would never do. After a century of absolute rule and control, they've bought into their own myth."

"Like teach someone outside the family how to mesmerize," I murmured.

He nodded, and I could read in his eyes why he hadn't fallen into the same trap. He wasn't a Constantine like the others, and he could imagine doing things they would never dream of.

"Even so, it seems impossible they wouldn't at least suspect him."

Costas shrugged. "Perhaps they do, privately. But Uncle Ambrose and Barnabas are set on pretending everything is normal and we can continue our regular lives, and Ignatius is just as set on insisting King Marius is to blame for everything. Nobody wants to admit that we were attacked, but not by the Tartorans."

"How come Ignatius and Barnabas didn't run into Grey at his camp when they came to the mainland?" I asked. "They seemed genuinely surprised he was still alive."

"They were. But that's because they took a different route."

"There's more than one?"

"Of course. There are at least three. The one you would have taken is the simplest and leads to the most attractive harbor on the desert side. But the people who live in the crevasse parted from our ancestors with ill will a century ago, refusing to take ship to the island with the majority. We would never use that route, although we should have realized Aunt Chloe would flee straight to them. She shared many of their ideals, so I suspect they welcomed her with open arms."

"Did you know her?" I asked, finally able to indulge my curiosity about the topic.

"Only as a very young child. But I have snatches of memory

of her still, and occasionally I've gotten Aunt Kendry to talk about her when no one else is around. She fell in love with a non-healer instead of the man assigned to be her husband. She defied the family and married her plants mage, and they wouldn't forgive her for it. She was merry and colorful and full of the sort of life that is missing from this island, and she wanted to change the way the family operated."

The story reminded me of Grey's original claims, although it was different in key respects. "So what happened?" I asked.

"Her husband died in an accident that was obviously not an accident."

"They had him killed!"

"My aunt snatched up her infant son and ran for her life. The only time she was truly happy on this island was during her brief marriage, so I don't think she was sorry to go."

"It's hard to sort out the truth from the fiction with Grey," I murmured. "But I think it's true that she arrived in the crevasse to find only a single elderly couple left. She would have been able to choose a house from the ones abandoned as their numbers dwindled, and the couple helped her get established and raise her son. She must have wanted a different life for him, but Grey doesn't seem to have taken after her. He heard her stories about life here and took a different message from the one she intended."

"Of course I did."

The cold voice sent shivers down my spine.

THIRTY-ONE

I turned slowly, not wanting to confirm what I already knew. Grey had found us.

"She stole me away from the life I should have lived," Grey continued. "A life of luxury where I ruled like a prince. And for what? So we could scratch out a living in the desert, with only two doddering old fools for company, surviving on the occasional trading trip to Eldrida? We could have moved to Eldrida, at least. No one would have known our true origins, and with her ability, we could have made a comfortable life there. But she could never let go of the island. These people murdered my father, but it was like she both loved and hated them at the same time."

Costas and I were both frozen and silent in the face of Grey's simmering resentment. I wished there was some way to show him the burning look in his eyes, and to make him realize that his mother wasn't the only one to carry an unnatural, unhelpful obsession with her past.

"But that isn't what's important now," he said, his eyes fixed on me and his silky voice promising pain and suffering. "It seems someone has learned how to deceive me."

"Grey." Costas stepped forward, as if to confront Grey, but I pulled him back. He had no idea what he was dealing with and no experience with combat.

"Where did you leave Nik?" I hissed at him.

"Nik?" Costas glanced back at me, clearly confused and speaking far too loudly.

I winced at the flash of recognition and fury on Grey's face when he caught Nik's name.

"Didn't he find you and send you to me?" I whispered urgently to Costas.

Costas started to shake his head, and I quickly hurried on.

"In that case he must still be out there looking for you. Go quickly and find him!"

Costas hesitated, and I shoved him away, angling him as far from Grey's reach as possible. Finally picking up on my urgency, he sprinted away, plunging back into the party. The bright lights and chattering voices were only feet away but seemed like a separate world.

"Our rogue prince is here, is he?" Grey asked in the same dangerously smooth voice. "I suppose he was a stowaway."

I tried not to show my fear. I hadn't been sure Grey realized Nik's identity after the battle in Caltor. But clearly he had.

"Nicely played, young spy," Grey said. "But you do know the fate of spies, don't you?"

Moving lightning fast, he lunged forward and dug his fingers into my braids. I screamed as he dragged me along, but the sound was covered by the sound of merriment inside.

I tried to dig my feet in and shake him off, but his grip was iron firm, and the pain propelled me forward.

Dragging me into the garden, he flung me onto the ground on a stretch of lawn some distance from the lights of the party. I tumbled down, only just catching my fall. As I rolled onto my back, I sent my power racing to soothe the pain in my scalp.

Grey stepped toward me, his green eyes flashing. Bending over, he grabbed me around the neck and pulled me upward.

"This time you're not going to have a thought left in your mind that's still your own," he growled.

Forgetting about subterfuge or my own power to mesmerize, I reacted on instinct, throwing up my wall. Grey's power tried to snake into me, but it got nowhere. He tried again, grunting in effort as he struggled to break past my wall.

But just like in our experiments on the ship, he got nowhere.

"That wall!" he spat out, his tone turning the word into a curse.

I glared back at him, putting all my defiance into my expression.

"Don't look at me like that," he snapped. "You've misplayed this time. If I can't control you, then you're no use to me."

His fingers around my throat tightened, cutting off my air supply.

My hands reacted on instinct, flying up to try to prize his fingers loose. But my physical efforts weren't the focus of my attention. Wielding my power like a battering ram, I shoved it into him through the connection of his hands.

He felt it coming, though, and jumped back at the first whisper of my touch, shoving me away with such force that I fell again.

"You dare...!" he sputtered, but I could see he was shaken.

For the first time he was realizing that when it came to our power, I outmatched him. He had taught me his trick, but he hadn't been able to learn mine.

The knowledge only made him more dangerous, however. He pulled his sword from its scabbard with a ringing noise that echoed in my head. I drew my own knife in response, but its length was tiny compared to the reach of his blade. I would have no way to stop his sword reaching me.

Once again he moved too quickly for me to flee, leaping toward me and slashing his blade across my throat. My hand jumped up to the warm liquid already spilling out of me, but my ability was even faster, closing the veins and sealing the skin before too much blood could be lost.

Grey growled in frustration, preparing to attack again, but a new voice made him freeze.

"She's a healer?"

We both turned to face Ignatius. He was standing tall, fury on his face and two brawny men at his back. Both of them were armed with swords, although I'd seen no sign of guards previously.

"What else have you been deceiving us about, *cousin?*" Ignatius asked, his eyes focused on Grey. "How many of your other followers are not what they appear?"

I tried to use his distraction to my advantage, edging slowly sideways in a bid to escape. But one of his guards moved to block me, his stance experienced and his blade menacing. I paused again, trying to decide if it was worth attempting to flee anyway.

I looked across at Grey and saw resignation in his eyes. He knew it was over.

I relaxed as well, an instinctive reaction, but it was the wrong response.

Once again catching me off-guard, Grey closed the distance between us. Grabbing me roughly, he threw me with all his strength toward Ignatius.

I stumbled forward, totally out of control, and collided with the tall healer. He shouted as if I was white hot and my touch burned him, thrusting me away. Both of his guards responded, converging on me, and in the darkness I caught a glimpse of Grey fleeing back toward the party.

"I don't want to fight you," I cried, but none of the three were listening.

"Get rid of her," Ignatius hissed, and one of the guards grunted in response.

A blade bit into me, searing pain spreading through my leg

as it severed a tendon. I threw my power at the injury, but it had no sooner healed than another burst of pain flared across my arm.

I stumbled backward, but the guards pursued me. Distracted by my healing, I didn't make it far before my foot caught on a root in the ground, and I went sprawling full length across the ground.

Both swords slashed at me at once, and I screamed, again throwing my power at the new wounds. I curled inward, throwing my arms up to protect my head and neck as I tried to keep the blades away from my most vulnerable regions.

My power was strong, and it could heal almost as quickly as they struck at me, but I could feel myself starting to weaken. My strength wouldn't last forever—I had experienced that firsthand.

But neither were my attackers going to stop. Not until I was dead.

My terrified, pain-dazed mind latched onto the thought. If I wanted it to stop, I had to die. Or appear dead, at least.

Another burst of pain, and another. I moved to block the pain and heal the worst of the injuries, but this time I left two surface wounds behind, leaking blood. Let them think I was already out of energy.

Another wound and then another. More wounds left on the surface.

But faking my death wasn't a simple task. My adversary was a healer, and a powerful one. He didn't want to risk touching me, but he didn't need physical contact to sense my heartbeat or the air scraping in and out of my lungs. Which meant I needed to stop them.

I let one more strike fall before sending what remained of my power to my lungs and heart, seizing them and holding them still. Almost immediately, my chest began to burn, but I found new depths of power and used them to soothe the sensation.

Another blow fell, but I remained limp, not responding to it at all. My eyes wanted to close, but I used my power to force the lids open, stilling their movement and dilating my pupils to their full size.

My vision went blurry, but I ignored it, holding absolutely still.

Only the use of my power allowed me to maintain the lack of movement. Already my body should have been spasming, forcing me to suck in air whether I wanted to or not. But I ruthlessly suppressed every sensation that would have forced that response.

"Stop," Ignatius called, finally bringing relief from the blows.

I waited another second and another. My thoughts were starting to grow fuzzy, my brain starved of air, and I felt strangely cold all over. But I had to hold on.

If I could maintain the ruse for long enough, then Ignatius would approach closer. The only way to be sure I was really dead was to touch me and see if he could reach me with his power. But the second he made contact, I would be ready.

A strange keening stabbed at my heart as a warm body threw itself at me. I had never heard Ember make that sound. A soft thud sounded as Phoenix landed beside her, his chattering call joining her distress.

I longed to sit up and reassure them, but I had to lie still.

I waited. And waited some more. Finally, I heard footsteps.

But instead of moving closer, they were moving away. The crunch of three sets of feet were returning to the party. He wasn't going to do a full check? Just how deeply ingrained was the Constantines' aversion to physical touch with another healer?

Another set of footsteps sounded, running toward me, and I

froze just as I was about to release my fatal hold on my body. Someone was returning after all.

But I couldn't hold back my heart and lungs any longer. I might be a healer, but I still had limits. If my brain ceased to function, I wouldn't be able to rescue myself. I had to act now, or—

"No!!" The heartrending cry was part grief, part horror, and part raging anger.

My blurry vision showed someone falling to his knees beside me. Hands reached out to touch my cold face, but they were familiar hands. I didn't need to attack the body they belonged to.

Instead I turned inward, sending a spark of power to restart my heart. As soon as it was beating again, I let my fire spread out through me.

The effort took my whole attention as I restarted every function of my body. But dimly, somewhere in the back of my mind, I registered that Nik had let me go, that he had stood and left.

Usually, his departure left me feeling cold, but this time I felt a flood of warmth as my blood circulated through my body again, my lungs contracting in painful spasms as they sucked in air.

Slowly the fog in my mind lifted as my brain received the air it needed again. My thoughts cleared, and the remnants of my power easily restored the rest of my body to wholeness.

I was still coated in blood, my gown torn in many places, but underneath it, I was whole and well. Ember barked, jumping in her excitement, and nearly knocking me back down. Phoenix took off, however, apparently needing to spread his wings and feel the air beneath him in order to express his joy.

"But where's Nik?" I asked Ember, my trembling hands stroking her fur. "I'm sure he was here. I heard him and saw him."

Slowly my mind recreated the last image I had seen of him —the image I had been too far gone to process at the time.

In it, his face was dark and twisted, the grief raw and overlaid with seething rage. And he had been turning away from my body, stalking back toward the party.

Slowly I went cold again. I tried to get to my feet, but all of me was trembling now, and I couldn't seem to find my balance.

Unwittingly, I had recreated Grey's plan. He had intended to fake a death tonight, and I had done exactly that. But I had never meant Nik to see me.

I managed to find my feet at last, but all I could hear in my mind were Nik's words from inside the ship's hold, repeated again and again. *I really don't know what I'd do if someone killed you, Delphine...Someone might die at my hands...*

I'd told him then that he should never become a monster, no matter what happened to me. But he'd retorted that without me, he had nothing to live for.

I wanted to believe his thinking had changed since then— he'd come a long way in processing his past, and his behavior in the market had showed how much lighter he felt. I wanted to believe he wouldn't recklessly throw his life away or do something he could never come back from.

But I couldn't shake off the glimpse I had seen of his burning eyes, stark in his pale face. There had been rage there, beyond anything I had ever felt. I wasn't even sure he was in his right mind.

I stumbled forward, my steps slow and halting at first but then picking up speed. The sounds of the party had disappeared, but I didn't want to think about what that meant. Surely everyone had just gone home—fleeing perhaps from the distant sounds of our fight. Or perhaps Grey had collected his people when he ran from Ignatius. I was sure he would have been reestablishing his own mesmerizations, even as the Constantines tried to implant theirs.

The garden stretched impossibly far, my feet taking too long to carry me to one of the open windows. As soon as I reached it, however, I wished the journey had been even longer.

When I had left, the room was alive with movement and voices. Now it was still and deserted. But not everyone had left.

Scattered across the floor were bodies. Bodies broken and bloodied, their eyes glassy and hearts no longer beating. Everywhere I looked were fallen stones and rent floorboards, all of them splashed with red.

Only one beating heart remained. I wanted to look away, to cover my eyes, but instead they were drawn inexorably to the one warm body left.

Nik. My Nik.

He knelt on one knee, his sword dripping red, and his other hand coated in it where it rested on Augustine's neck.

"Nik." It was a strangled whisper, a sound I hadn't meant to make, but it was enough to catch his attention.

He looked up, his eyes meeting mine. Instantly his terrible expression changed, shock holding him immobile, only to be replaced with a radiant joy and relief that was out of place in this room of horrors.

I swallowed and forced myself to look around at the destruction before looking back at him. He followed my gaze, his eyes skimming over the bodies, and I saw the moment his emotions changed.

His expression twisted, filling with horror as if he was seeing his surroundings for the first time. He stood, starting toward me. His hand reached out for me as he called my name, his voice somehow twisted and tender at the same time.

I stepped back, stumbling away from him, and he instantly froze, his face twisting further.

"Delphine," he said again, and the sound of his voice broke my heart.

But I didn't go to him. I couldn't.

Instead I did what Ignatius hadn't bothered to do. I forced myself to pick a path through the stones, approaching each body and checking they were really dead, although the effort seemed futile.

Ignatius and his two brutish guards were there, but so was Kendry, the pale eyes which marked her as an outsider closed for the last time. And so was Grey's grandmother, her body looking frail and old now that the vitality of life was gone, the spark of calculation forever extinguished from her eyes.

Ambrose lay beside Augustine, as if the two brothers had been united only in their final moment of life, and Barnabas lay on the other side of the room. He appeared to have been fleeing for the door, but he'd never made it.

All the Constantines were here except one. Somewhere, dimly, I had enough feeling left to be grateful Nik hadn't killed Costas in his blind, unthinking rage.

As if summoned by my thoughts, Costas's voice sounded from the garden, calling for us.

I moved woodenly toward the window where I had entered, stepping outside.

"Nik! Delphine! You're still here!" Costas slid to a halt at the sight of me. Leaning over his knees, he sucked in gasping breaths. "I thought you might be gone."

"Gone?" I asked, too dazed to try to make sense of his words.

"With Grey."

That got my attention.

"I found Nik and sent him after you, but he raced off too fast for me to follow. Before I caught up, Grey appeared, running like hounds were chasing him. He went straight into the party and collected all his people. My father and uncle would have stopped him, but Grandmother said to let him be. Knowing Nik would rescue you, I thought I should follow and see where they were going. I couldn't believe it when he walked them straight down to the harbor, loaded them onto the boat, and just set sail."

He regained his breath enough to walk toward us. "I thought you might have somehow gotten onboard as—" A sharp intake of breath cut off his words as he finally came close enough to see through the window into the room beyond.

His face paled, his eyes jumping from the horror in the room to my blood-stained gown and finally to Nik's bloodied hands and sword. After a long, awful moment, his eyes turned back to his grandmother.

"What..." He stumbled back a step. "What happened?"

He couldn't take his eyes off Nik, his face displaying the same emotions that were tearing me apart. Is that how I looked, with those haunted, terrified eyes?

No wonder Nik kept looking at me with that heartbroken expression.

"Did you...I...My family..." Costas couldn't seem to finish a sentence, his thoughts fragmenting before my eyes. "It's over," he finally mumbled. "It's all over."

What's all over? I wanted to ask, but even before I formed the words, I knew the answer. Everything. Everything was over. It had all been obliterated past hope of fixing.

Costas must have come to the same conclusion because he sent one last wide-eyed look at me before turning and fleeing the way he'd come.

"Costas!" I took several steps after him, but he had already far outstripped me. The direction of his flight told me he was heading back to the harbor. Was there another boat there? A small one, perhaps, able to be crewed by one—as long as that one had both the necessary power to direct his course and knowledge of the route. A person such as the only Constantine with an elements affinity.

Somehow there was room for fresh horror. Costas had said Grey had already sailed, which meant Costas was the only one left on the island who knew the passage through the rocks. Was he abandoning us alone here?

The enormity of it crashed over me. For an overwhelming moment, I wanted to flee as well. Not toward the harbor or a boat or anything logical—just away. I wanted to leave this shattered mess behind and escape.

But even as I thought it, Ida stepped through the gate, staring at the abandoned garden with confusion. Her eyes found me, and our gazes locked, her confusion deepening when she saw my state.

Not all of Grey's people had left. Not someone like Ida who had only ever wanted a fresh start and a new life. Her he had left behind. I thought of Lumi and Fergus in the marketplace with their bright curiosity so at odds with the adults around them.

I was the only remaining strong healer on an island full of people who might fall sick or injure themselves at any moment. People who had always been led by healers and didn't know how to think for themselves.

I couldn't run away. Amara had taught me I had a responsibility to use my power to help people, and there was no clearer need than this. In Eldrida I had promised to respect my own limits, but I had also promised myself that in exchange, I would never refuse to give when I did have something left.

I wanted to find a way back to the safety of Amara and Hayes and our friends, but someone had to help these people rebuild from this destruction. And I was the only someone left.

"Delphine," Nik's tortured voice hit my already shredded heart, shattering it even further.

He stepped outside, coming closer, reaching for me. I stumbled backward, shaking my head.

"I'm sorry, Nik, I can't. Don't..." I shook my head, wishing I could turn off my emotions and feel nothing at all, if only for a moment.

But I couldn't afford to be weak in a moment that called for strength. I forced myself to plant my feet and stand strong, to meet his eyes without flinching.

The truth hurt—unbearably badly—but I could see everything clearly now. I had wondered if the spark between us would lift us up or burn us both to the ground, and now I had my answer.

I couldn't turn my face from it, though. I had too many witnesses filling my head, echoes of too many past Idas showing me the way.

Serena, telling me she would return to her old master, despite how she was now viewed in Tarin, so she could finish her apprenticeship and rejoin society.

The courage in the eyes of the couple who said they were selling their farm and leaving their whole life behind to give their injured daughter hope of a future.

The people of Eldrida, laboring through the violent storm to save their neighbors, and then coming out the next day to face the destruction and begin rebuilding.

"You're wrong about love, Nik," I whispered. My voice was quiet, but I knew he heard because I saw the words land, like blows across his face. "This isn't love. I know that you would burn everything and anything for my sake. But that isn't what I want. Love doesn't want to burn the world down. Love is willing to kneel in the ashes and build the world back up."

"Delphine," he tried again, but he couldn't seem to form a full thought.

I wanted to weaken, to run to him. But people were counting on me, and I couldn't give in to an impulse that was so clearly destructive.

"That's what I'm going to do here, for these people, as best I can," I said. "So if you can't help, stay out of my way, Nik. We're over."

I had to turn away from the look on his face, still afraid of myself and the love I couldn't help but feel despite everything. But my eyes landed on Ida who had stopped to pick up Ember and was now walking slowly toward me. And at the same time, a weight landed on my shoulder as Phoenix swooped in to land.

Slowly courage began to fill me. I might not have the strength for the task ahead, but I wasn't alone. Together we would find a way to do what felt impossible alone. Together we would free these people from the lies and find a way back to the mainland before Grey wreaked more destruction there.

I would see Amara again, and this time, when I did, I wouldn't have to be ashamed of my actions.

My heart thumped painfully, and I pressed a hand to it. Later there would be pain enough for all my past mistakes, but right now I couldn't give in to it. Right now, I had to think of the future.

I nodded at Ida and took Ember from her outstretched arms.

"Prepare yourself," I said. "It's going to be a long night."

NOTE FROM THE AUTHOR

Read the conclusion to Delphine, Nik, and Amara's story in book three, Tempests of Truth.

Or go back and read about the restoration of the fallen kingdom and Nik's history in A Mage's Influence series, starting with Seeds of Glory and Ruin.

To be informed of future releases, as well as A Mage's Apprentice bonus shorts, please sign up to my mailing list at www.melaniecellier.com.

And if you enjoyed Storms of Allegiance, please spread the word and help other readers find it! You could start by leaving a review on Amazon or Goodreads or Facebook or any other social media site. Your review would be very much appreciated and would make a big difference!

ACKNOWLEDGMENTS

Somehow this middle book became the longest book I've written yet, despite being written during burnout recovery, and I'm so grateful to everyone who assisted in its creation and polishing—as well as all those who kept me sane in the process! No matter the length of the book or the timeframe required, my wonderful team never lets me down.

So, Rachel, Greg, Priya, Ber, Katie, Mary, Dad, James, Karri, Rebecca, Marina, Cheri, Shari, Brittany, Kitty, Aya, Lyra, and Marc—thank you from the bottom of my heart.

And thank you to God who helps us keep going when we think we have nothing left to give.

ABOUT THE AUTHOR

Melanie Cellier grew up on a staple diet of books, books and more books. And although she got older, she never stopped loving children's and young adult novels.

She always wanted to write one herself, but it took three careers and three different continents before she actually managed it.

She now feels incredibly fortunate to spend her time writing from her home in Adelaide, Australia where she keeps an eye out for koalas in her backyard. Her staple diet hasn't changed much, although she's added choc mint Rooibos tea and Chicken Crimpies to the list.

She writes young adult fantasy including books in her *Spoken Mage* world, her *Mage's Influence* world, and her various *Four Kingdoms* and *Kingdoms of Legacy* series that are made up of linked stand-alone stories that retell classic fairy tales.